Industrial Revolution

★ ★ ★

R T Cutforth

For Kate

"Time: That which man is always trying to kill, but which ends in killing him."

– HERBERT SPENCER, ENGLISH PHILOSOPHER

One

"Good morning, Seth," the doctor said. "Are you going to cooperate with me today?"

I laid still with my eyes closed. I had been asleep for a while, I thought, but it was hard to tell. My face was hot and my stomach ached with hunger. My tongue felt thick, sandy and foreign in my mouth and a sick, pulsating pain surged through the length of my body.

"I… I don't know anything."

"Convince me."

I slowly opened my left eye, the right still swollen shut. The immense room with its black granite floors greeted me, the same as it did every day. Candles and oil burning lamps surrounded the dirty hospital bed I was lying on, bathing the room in a flickering orange light.

The sheet that covered me, once crisp and tucked tightly, was now loose, wrinkled and bloodstained. Thick leather straps held my arms and legs fast to the bed. I'd stopped trying to wiggle free during the doctor's absences; there wasn't any point. The more I struggled, the tighter they cinched.

Several glass jars of multicoloured liquid were lined up on a metal table close by. Long, thin plastic tubes ran from the jars into me, pumping liquid in and drawing it out. The candlelight cast strange, disjointed shadows on the bed, table and jars. The room was thick with the smell of burning wax and kerosene.

The doctor stood over me, tall, pale and gaunt. His skin was creased and pockmarked, hanging loosely from sharp cheekbones. Round, gold spectacles were perched halfway down his nose. In the lenses the candlelight reflected, hiding his eyes. His face was framed by long, black, razor-straight hair streaked with white.

"Water." My voice was unrecognisable to me.

"After you tell me what I want to know." His voice calm and still. He didn't sound like a man who'd spent days beating a man half to death.

I'd been over this a thousand times. I wasn't sure exactly how long I'd been lying in this bed; but it had been at least a week. I felt as if my world had never been anything but the doctor and his fists.

"I told you," I started, my voice barely above a whisper. "I don't know where I am. I don't know where I'm from. I don't know who I am." Speaking was painful, I had to choose my words carefully. I had to get this man to stop hurting me.

"The only reason I know my name is Seth is because that's what you told me it was."

The doctor's finger shot out toward my face, finding purchase in the swollen mass above my right eye. He sliced into it with his fingernail and I felt it burst.

I cried out and shook my head back and forth violently, clamping my eyes shut tight until I felt his thumb retract. Warm liquid flowed down my cheek and across the bridge of my nose into my good eye.

The sheet was yanked off my body.

"Open your eyes," the doctor said. "Take a look at yourself".

A thick, chalky warmth moved from my eye across my face. I was going to throw up again. "I can't!" I screamed. Again, I jerked violently in the restraints, the bed rattled and shook, but held tight as if welded to the floor. The world was dark and everything was pain.

"Oh, for god's sake," the doctor said.

A heavy, stinking towel landed on my face. He rubbed the liquid off and out of my eyes roughly, splaying the wound apart. I screamed again, but it was muffled by the towel. I tried to move my face away from his grip, but his long fingers tightened through the cloth like a vice.

The towel was removed and his frigid hand slapped down on my face. He pried the lid of my good eye open, forcing me to see what he wanted me to see.

"Now, look!"

Through the blur of tears I saw my battered body. Heavy bruises reached across my arms and legs and spattered my stomach. The fresher ones were black, the older ones had gone a sickening green and yellow. I was terribly thin. My appendages mere twigs and my ribs were visible through the stretched skin of my chest. The warm liquid flowed again from the wound above my bad eye. I shook my head free from the doctor's grasp and clamped my eyes shut again, plunging my world back into darkness.

"Please," I tried to scream out, but there was no sound.

The doctor's hand returned, this time clamped around my jaw. He turned my face sharply to the side and his breath was on my cheek. "If you don't want to see, I'll make it so you can't see."

I opened my good eye again just in time to see his fist coming down.

Two

"Large pizza, please."

"Alright, mate," Bill said.

Bill was a fat man who wore a white hat, white trousers and a white apron. He was the only man around who was overweight and the only one who wore anything white.

If someone had seen the two of us speaking to each other, they would have assumed we had come from different worlds. Emaciated and filthy with matted hair, shredded denim jeans and 'I love Manchester' t-shirt, I was barely the same species as the full faced, glowing man who stood in front of me. By Manchester standards, he was a rich man. He had a functioning shop, gardens bursting with vegetables and a hunting rifle with which to protect them both. Practically everything I owned was contained in the old, black leather backpack swung over my shoulder.

Bill's shop in the Northern Quarter was similar to most buildings in the city; the ones that were still standing. Chipped, redbrick walls rose up high above our heads to meet large wooden beams at the ceiling. The floor was also redbrick with cracked pieces of industrial tile spotted here and there. A large chimney stack stood behind him with a large hole punched into it at shoulder height that acted as a makeshift pizza oven. Orange and black embers in the hole were visible through the wobbly heat haze. Two long, wooden tables stood in front of him. They were mismatched and split, but had been carefully refinished in oil and polished to a shine. On the tables were arranged four equally spaced, spotless, stainless steel containers filled with red sauce, rocket leaves, eggs and pickled courgettes. Balls of mozzarella floated in water in a large cast iron pot.

A number of shiny metal trays were stacked high on the end of the table closest to me.

Bill was a friendly man who laughed loudly and bragged about knowing the names of all his customers despite being 'the only pizza place in the whole of Manchester'. I was taking a grave risk being in here at all, the doctor warned me of the dangers of speaking with locals. The need for comfort and some sort of life, they had begun to re-accept each other, to identify their own needs and realise that surviving in a world alone was a difficult thing to do. How they would respond to a foreigner remained to be seen and if I had any sense at all, I would do my best to steer clear of other people.

For weeks, I'd kept to myself and spoke to no one, but the threat of starvation had forced my hand.

★ ★ ★

It was summer in Manchester when Bill had first found me. In the dead city in which I found myself, I survived only on things that could be scrounged or stolen. A jar of pickled broccoli when the seller's back was turned, an ancient tin of beans under the rubble of an ancient newsagents. There were rats everywhere to eat, but they were difficult to catch and I wasn't entirely sure what to do with one even if I managed to catch it.

By the time Bill had found me, I was little more than knees, ribs and elbows. The wild garlic that sprouted through the cracks in the pavement in front of my apartment block was the first food I had seen in a week and I was shoving it into my mouth by the handful.

"Oi, don't eat that! I need that for the pizzas!" Bill shouted.

Before I had a chance to move, his hand was on my shoulder. I turned and tried to get away, but he held me in place. He leant down toward me and I put my hands up over my head.

"Give over, will ya? I'm not going to hit you. Here!" he said and plopped a pizza on my lap, the steel tray warm against my legs.

"Get that into you."

Despite his bulky waddle, I hadn't heard Bill come up from behind and wasn't sure that what I had just witnessed was real. For weeks I'd survived on terrible, miniscule bits of food, and then in an instant, I'd been presented with more food than I had ever known.

The smell hit me and my mouth was wet. A small stream of drool escaped my bottom lip.

"Well? What are you waiting for?" he asked. "Pickled peppers and hawthorne leaves, mate. Beautiful."

I looked up at the man. Was it a trick? A mirage?

"Don't worry, mate, I got plenty more. Lord knows I could do with a few fewer of the beggars." He laughed and rubbed his round belly. "Come by 'shop tomorrow and I'll sort you out with some more."

The top of the pizza was hot. It was real. I pinched the melted cheese with my fingers and brought it to my mouth. The cheese was soft and the salt triggered a heavy yearning from deep within.

"You know where my shop is, don't you?"

Of course I did. Not a day went by that I hadn't dreamed of going in.

"Right, see you tomorrow," he said before turning away.

"And stay out of my bleeding garlic patch!"

For the briefest of moments, I considered saving the pizza, stretching it out, but the smell didn't allow it. I ripped the pizza up by the handful and stuffed the hot dough and sauce into my mouth. I chewed as fast as I could to make room for the next handful, but it wasn't fast enough. Hunks of pizza slopped out and onto my shirt. I scooped them up and shoved them back in. My stomach lurched with the sudden onslaught of food, threatening to throw it back up but I managed to keep it down through sheer force of will. Fistful after fistful I stuffed, stretching my cheeks and stomach to capacity. To beyond capacity.

Even as I stood before the man now, I could not recall what the pizzas tasted like despite devouring every crumb and licking the tray clean.

★ ★ ★

"Oi, wakey wakey!" Bill was snapping his fingers in front of my face. "I said, is it only one pizza today?"

I nodded.

He reached under one of the tables into a large white pail and retracted a handful of flour. The flour landed with a puff of white as he tossed it down roughly onto the tabletop and spread it out with both hands.

"I'd love to know what goes on in that head of yours, my friend," he said.

He spoke in a clipped and conscious way that seemed to be measured and somehow completely natural at the same time. His mouth barely moved as he spoke. Even his hard c's and t's were formed in the back of his throat, without much use of his tongue or lips at all. Perhaps he saved them for tasting.

I smiled; it seemed like the correct thing to do. "Not a lot."

He stopped spreading and knelt down to grasp a metal ring in the floor, groaning as he pulled open a large, wooden door to the cellar. He stepped around the open door, and clumped down the stone steps, breathing heavily as he descended. I shivered as the cool air flowed out of the hole across my bare ankles.

This was the place that saved my life. The pizzas were gorgeous, but it wasn't just the food that caused me to return time after time. The short escape from the painful loneliness and depravity that existed outside the shop's walls was the only pleasure in my life. It was the only place that made me even a little bit happy. I suppose 'happy' was pushing it, perhaps, 'made me feel less like killing myself' was more accurate.

Bill's head bobbed up and down as he plodded back up the cellar steps. He was wheezing hard, carrying a small ball of white dough, wrapped tightly in cellophane. Where he got that cellophane I could only guess. He reached the top step, placed his hand on the open door and let it drop back into place with a loud *ker-clunk*.

"I would give me left bollock for a working refrigerator, I tell thee."

I smiled again for his benefit.

Bill unwrapped the dough and placed the square of neatly flattened cellophane carefully to one side. He then tossed the dough onto the table and punched at it with his meaty fists, taking great joy in the action. After a few great wallops, he stretched and kneaded the dough several times, before raising it onto his fists and tossing it expertly into the air, once, twice, three times letting it drop on the fourth toss onto the oak table with a hard slap.

I was his only customer on that day, which was not an uncommon thing. Even a shop as popular as Bill's rarely catered to more than one person at a time.

"I don't suppose you've found me anything of value this time, have you?" Bill asked.

I shook my head.

"You know where the list is," he said spooning and spreading red sauce onto the soft disk of dough.

I walked to the end of the table and grabbed the clipboard hanging on the wall. The list was scrawled on a ripped piece of cardboard in black ink.

ITEMS

1. *Dried or cured meat of all kinds.*
2. *One stainless steel, industrial kitchen container. SEE ME.*
3. *Salad veg, tomatoes especially. ASK FIRST.*
4. *Soap and/or cleaning supplies, the stronger the better, 'Mr Muscle' Oven cleaner RICHLY REWARDED.*
5. *PROPER booze, for DRINKING. NO chemist shit!*

CHORES

1. *Dishwashing 1 evening*
2. *Garden weeding 3 hours*
3. *Hauling water 4 trips*

Will barter other services with PROFESSIONALS or SKILLED TRADES ONLY (Bricklayers especially).

Lists were beautiful things. In the chaos of this city, structure of any kind was a treasured thing, but I think it went deeper than that with me. Lists just made sense. Whenever I looked at one of Bill's lists, things seemed to somehow slot into place in my mind. Direction is what I needed in this place and it was precisely what Bill gave me from our first meeting. Do this, don't do that, get me this, be here at this time. Perhaps fear of the doctor's wrath was not the only reason I continued to do what he told me. Maybe it was the fear of freedom; fear of a lacking sense of purpose that kept me in my assigned flat, in my assigned city.

Even though I could not remember my old world, it was easily apparent that Manchester used to be a city of structure. The hospitals, the old Town Hall, the police stations. I had no evidence that whatever city it is that I came from had a similar structure, but I knew it to be true. Structure. It was what made the buildings soar and kept the streets clean. It eased minds and kept families together. The blast may have initiated the city's destruction, but it was a lack of structure that finished her off, of that I was certain.

I looked up from the list. Bill was sprinkling shredded pork and pickled courgettes onto the pizza. He drew a ball of mozzarella out of the water and sliced it up thickly, dealing the slices out around the edges, his hands a blur.

"How many pizzas does the weeding get me?"

"One. THIS one," he said. He cracked an egg into the pizza's centre, lifted it carefully with both hands and tossed it into the oven.

"Make it two and you've got a deal."

"Two pizzas? Ha! For that, I want a day."

I shook my head. "One afternoon, four and a half hours".

"Deal."

We shook hands on it.

"Fine, scratch that one off. You can have the other pizza after the weeding is finished."

I pulled the pen out from under the clamp on the clipboard, and scratched *Garden weeding* off the list.

"I'm glad you chose that one if I'm honest," he said. "You may want to scavenge yourself up a pair o' gloves. Thistles taller than you. Thicker as well."

What the big man didn't know was that I actually enjoyed weeding. Plunging my hands into the soil, grasping a plant at its base, pulling slowly, consistently until the roots pop, pop, popped under the ground releasing their grip one at a time. To clear a plot of land; to make something clean and perfect in a world of such decay helped to keep a person's mind sound. It wasn't as good as standing here watching Bill assemble a pizza, but it was a nice distraction from scavenging, from worrying about every little thing.

Bill slid a large wooden pole into the oven and hooked the pizza onto a steel tray in one smooth movement. He sprinkled the rocket onto the bubbling cheese, and passed the pizza to me, tray and all.

"See you Saturday."

I nodded my thanks at him, turned and opened the door to leave.

"And bring me back that tray!"

The city outside was empty as usual. I looked up and down the street twice to make sure no one was watching. I had allowed Bill into my life, first out of desperation, then companionship, but there was no guarantee other locals would be as welcoming. The bruising on my wrists was faded now, but the pain was still there in places. A reminder of what the locals could be capable of.

I could never let them take me back to that room. In my backpack lived a large, rusting, knife I found in a drawer somewhere. When I packed my bag in the mornings, the knife was placed so I could feel its hard edge against my back through the leather. In front of Bill's pizzeria on that muggy, summer's evening, I could feel it and its comforting presence settled my heart rate and spurred me on. With that knife, I would not die without a fight. Seventy days the doctor had given me to recover my memory. Fifty-four days from today. If they were to come for me before then, they would not take me alive.

Satisfied of the Oldham Street's emptiness, I stepped out of the pizza shop and moved quickly toward the centre of the city. A strange pink twilight fell on the wrecked streets, making a nice change from the usual grey. The derelict and crumbling buildings on both sides of the street were there as always. The old tattoo parlour with its windows blown out, its rusted and mangled venetian blinds rattled through the open windows softly. Inside, the walls blackened with mould and fire.

Next door stood the remains of a trendy coffee shop; another windowless redbrick building. Rusted metal stools with ripped upholstery, deadened coffee machines and sharp pieces of shattered crockery were strewn about the place. Bricks, tiles and rubbish filled every corner. The ceiling on the second floor was caved in and the pink light streamed in from above.

Every morning, when I awoke, I had the same thought: that this world was a bad dream. If I spun around three times and blinked twice, everything would return to normal. Whatever normal was.

What little I could see of the asphalt was broken and spotted with deep holes and rancid pools of water. The city centre was buried under a thick layer of broken brick, glass and twisted metal. Rusted, burned out and overturned cars lined the streets and pavements, their wheels jutted out at odd angles and steel shards poked out from the rotting rubber tires. Large, thorny weeds and bushes pushed up through large cracks in the asphalt and clung thick and leafy to the sides of the buildings, their roots clawing the redbrick like skeletons fingers. There were many of those as well; cracked and flaking human bones littered every square inch of tarmac and dirt.

On one particularly grim scavenging trip, I discovered a makeshift graveyard at the edge of the city centre with bodies stacked in graves so high, the top of the pile couldn't be reached by earth thrown from a shovel.

There must have been thousands of people in this city once. Millions. But, once the dead had outnumbered the living, the chore of burying people in graveyards must have become overwhelming and pointless. The smell of the decaying corpses made the city centre uninhabitable for years. The doctor said I was lucky to have showed up now and not ten years ago. I didn't feel lucky.

Up ahead, the end of the street opened up into an enormous square. A large, empty fountain lay dormant behind a stone statue of a headless Queen Victoria. Three and four storey buildings in redbrick, white stone and black slate lined the square on all four sides. All in similar states of decay. Roofs caved in, chunks missing, windows smashed. Anything of value looted long ago by scavengers. This was where I lived.

The smell of the pizza was again becoming too much to take. I tip-toed across the square avoiding the glass and rusted metal. Hunger clawed at me, but I didn't want to eat just yet. Evenings like this, with neither wind nor sheets of rain were rare; I wanted to enjoy it.

I had made this trip many trips before and had remembered every stray nail and shard of glass. Evenings spent pulling things out of my feet had been plentiful, but fruitful. I had become adept at avoiding hidden hazards in the junk piles. Being crippled in this place would be one's death. Bill was my only source of food and he didn't deliver.

I moved quickly, almost skipping, across the destroyed square into a large, darkened department store and past vast, empty shelves. The ceiling tiles were long gone, exposing large, broken pipes and vents. The escalator stood frozen in the darkness. I launched myself onto it, dancing around the sharp, twisted metal cleats that extended from the escalator steps.

The first level was empty. Most of the floor had burned away with only the steel joists remaining. I left the escalator and walked toward the large open window at the front of the building facing the square and the setting sun. Across an exposed beam I moved, one hand held the pizza aloft, the other extended sideways for balance. As I moved toward the edge, I could see the square come sharply into focus through the huge, gaping holes where the glass windows used to be. I didn't look down through the missing floor, my gaze was fixed on the buildings in the square. At the window, I sat down with my legs dangling over the edge.

From this height, the scale of the destruction was deathly apparent. I always felt a strange, almost sick sort of fascination with this sight. Like I was only a visitor here. One day a helicopter would swoop down and take me away from this place, take me back to America. 'I hope you learned your lesson,' a man in an orange jumpsuit would say.

'Oh yes, sir, I sure have. I will never take my life for granted again!' And then I would be whisked back to my old life somewhere to be greeted by a family waiting at an airport in my hometown. In America.

If only.

There would never be any whisking. This was where I lived. This was where I would always live. This was where I would die.

The only thing that kept me going was the two memories I'd recovered since my days with the doctor and the euphoric thoughts of remembering the ones that had been lost.

I was an American, whatever that meant. It was the reason I sounded different from Bill and why little of what I saw around me made sense. I was a stranger not just to this apocalypse, but to the country itself. The other memory was one of gears and levers. Of buttons, switches and digital readouts. Of monitors and of wires and plastic pipes. A machine. Inside my backpack was an old piece of cardboard with a list of my own, a list that contained exactly those two things.

I didn't get many evenings like this. The square spread out before me, a wide, endless, sea of broken stone, brick and twisted metal. The last of the sun's pink light reflected back off the jagged, cracked glass of the city's few modern skyscrapers and down through the large cavities of the old Victorian banks and the cathedral.

I tore a strip off my pizza and began eating. Pizza in a wrecked department store was far from fine dining, but it was slightly more civilised than scrounging for wild garlic. I scanned the nooks and crannies of the busted buildings for people, but could see no one. In the few, brief hours between day and night, the city was mine. It wasn't long the dark would make me retreat to my home, but for now I was safe.

Often, a teenager wandered these rubbled streets always with an armload or two of garbage. His clothing was strange, a long purple cape and hat with an elongated brim and pigeon's feathers stuck to the side. His eyes were always down, scanning the ground before him as he moved. He was the only person I ever saw around the town centre at night and I was always careful to keep my distance. But even he seemed to have taken a night off. On that night there was no movement, no sound at all; not even a breeze. The stray plastic shopping bags that often brushed past like urban tumbleweeds lied dormant and unfettered in the muck and stagnant water of the streets.

The only thing to be heard was the sound of my own chewing.

After finishing the last piece, I zipped the tray into my backpack, stretched out along the beam and closed my eyes.

What did my mother look like? Did I have a girlfriend somewhere? A wife? Did I have an embarrassing middle name? How did I make my way from America? I would have taken anything my mind was willing to give me, any crumb of a clue as to who I was or what the hell I was doing in such a desolate and desperate place. But my mind didn't cooperate; it never did. Smeared faces, muffled speech were all I was ever given. The answers seemed painfully close. I wanted to reach out and touch those weak visions, to throttle them into focus, but they were always just out of reach. I scrunched my eyes together tightly, trying to will the faces forward.

A cool evening breeze grew up from the ground and flowed over me, fluttering my hair. My body took advantage of what little rest it would get, for it wouldn't be long before the terrible dreams would come. It was the same every night; always the pain, always the torture, always the doctor.

Three

The last thing I remembered before passing out was the doctor again leaning over me. He was holding a small pocketknife; the blade dripping with my blood. His spectacles were perched on the tip of his long, crooked nose and his lab coat was spattered with small dots of red.

Even in the rare times when the doctor was gone and I was able to open my eyes, I couldn't see much. Many of the candles and lamps had burned out. What was once an enormous room was nothing more than a ring of dim light barely big enough to encompass the bed. The sound of my laboured breathing was all I could hear. The doctor could still be in the room for all I knew. Watching me from the darkness.

I tried moving my mouth to produce saliva, but it only brought more pain to my swollen and split lips.

The doctor was relentless with his questions. 'Who are you?', 'What are you doing here?', 'Where did you come from?'

I didn't have answers and I told him as much in between screams. Before long, I started inventing answers, anything to stop him from hurting me. He didn't believe anything.

The pain was everywhere. I tried to shift my hips slightly to ease the pressure on my spine, but found that I couldn't. Even slight movements were excruciating.

The quiet times in the torture chamber were confusing ones. When the doctor wasn't asking me questions, I asked them of myself: How long had I been in that bed? How long had it been since the doctor had left? Had I been sleeping? Those times could be almost as bad as the time spent with the doctor. The inbetween times. Every minute of inbetween time that ticked by was a minute closer to him starting on me again.

I often imagined him sitting behind some two-way mirror, watching me while impatiently checking his watch. Drinking coffee and counting the minutes; looking forward to starting where he left off and being annoyed by the waiting.

"Just kill me," I said. A whisper all I could manage. "Please, please, just kill me".

The room was silent. Had I spoken out loud or had I just said it in my head?

"Kill you? Is that what you said?" the doctor asked. He didn't even sound out of breath.

I heard a small click and the splash of something being dropped into a bowl of water. Followed by a loud bang of wood meeting metal table. The mallet.

"That may happen eventually, Seth, but not for a while." He spit my name out like saying it burned his tongue. "Not for a long while, indeed."

The doctor took in a deep breath and again forced open one of my swollen eyelids with his fingers. It was useless to squirm. It was useless to fight him, to resist. With his other hand, he held the mallet high above my body.

Good. He was going to finally end it. I relaxed and waited for it to come.

"That's enough." It was a man standing behind my head.

The doctor looked past my bed toward the voice and released my bruised eyelid returning me to the dark. "Are you sure?" he asked, his words bouncing off the walls of the empty room. It was barely a question.

The man behind my bed spoke again, his voice deeper, but just as detached as the doctor's. "There is nothing more we can do for him now. Clean him up and prepare him for dispatch."

The sound of the mallet hitting the metal table again and skittering across the floor. I could feel the heavy restraints loosening around my right wrist and then my left. The straps clunked against the aluminium bed frame as they dropped down. The blood flowed into my hands. I squeezed my fingers into fists to quell the pins and needles. The straps on my ankles were released. The last time I had seen my wrists and ankles, they were red raw under the straps, I didn't want to think what colour they were now.

"Can you move?" the doctor asked me without sympathy.

I tried lifting my head off the pillow, pain shot through the length of my spine. I heard myself moan before resting back down.

"I'll take that as a 'no'."

His heels clicked as he circled the bed.

"You'll be happy to know I haven't fractured anything. I was very careful," the doctor said. "Had it been one of those other Neanderthals, you never would have walked again."

★ ★ ★

I woke to find the doctor examining me. I didn't know how long I had been asleep, but I was able to open my eyes a crack. I was still in the torture room, the candles had been replaced and relit. The walls were pale and the paint chipped and cracked to show the breezeblocks underneath.

The doctor tapped his fingers around a bruise on my thigh and wiped blood from a cut just above my knee. He moved across my body and around it, methodically and gently prodding each bruise and assessing each wound. I didn't respond to his touch; I couldn't respond. As ever, I was at the man's mercy.

"Say Ahhh," the Doctor said. He lifted my head back and opened my mouth with both hands and peered inside. "Yup, all there."

He turned my right arm over so the palm faced up. Two large needles grew out of my forearm. Long thin tubes led from my arm to the jars of liquid on the steel table.

He pressed down on my arm where the needles were buried and slowly pulled them from my veins, they came out long and wet with blood. He daubed the holes in my arms with a rag and tossed the needles into a bowl of water on the table. He held the rag down hard and flipped it over, held it down again several times until the blood stopped flowing. He then rubbed a small amount of some black, sticky substance into the hole left by the needles.

I felt nothing.

"It's official, you're not dead," he said, a hissing chuckle escaping his lips. *Esh-esh-esh-esh*, like someone releasing air from a tyre, pinching the valve stem in quick intervals.

He stood up, turned away from me and removed his bloodied lab coat, tossing it on the table. He set to work wiping the blood off the needles and the pocketknife. Without his jacket my torturer looked desperately thin, his shoulders narrow and hunched. If I'd seen this man in the street, I'd have felt sorry for him.

I tried one last time to move my head; I wanted to see the man who stopped the doctor from killing me. I lurched my head back twisting around to look behind the bed toward where the voice had been. Pain surged through my neck and behind my temples. My head felt as if it were separating from my shoulders, but I had to see. I forced my bruised eye open further causing tears to come out in streams.

There was no one there. Only more chipped breezeblock and the shadows of the bed and the table flickering in the yellow candlelight. Perhaps I'd conjured the voice.

The bed was moving, the wheels squeaked and creaked.

We moved toward a flat, grey light emanating from a doorway in the far corner of the room. Behind my head, the doctor was pushing the bed, pushing me away from the yellow orb of light created by the candles. I hoped never to be there again.

"It's painful now, I don't doubt, but you'll be as good as new in a few weeks."

The bed jarred as it rolled over something on the floor. He laughed again and I felt his lips brush my ear as he whispered.

"Give or take."

Four

I was lying on a mattress damp with sweat. Girly, looping brass rails decorated the head and foot. Everything was pink; the sheets, curtains, wallpaper, everything. The room was pink everywhere except where it was grey. Flat, grey light hovered in the room, dulling everything it touched. A cold breeze followed the grey light in through the smashed window, billowing out the tattered curtains.

The dictaphone.

I reached down beside the bed and fumbled around looking for it, but it wasn't there. I leaned over the side of the bed and looked under. The black, plastic dictaphone had settled into a crack in the floor. Thank God.

I snatched at it and pushed the play button. "Good morning Lucy," I said. Lucy began singing along to a pop song.

I relaxed onto the bed and held the recorder close to my chest, scanning the room a second time to make sure what I was seeing was real. Lucy's faded pink sheets and two filthy pink pillows lay scrunched at the end of the grimy mattress and her chipped, pink desk of drawers sat across the room. The mornings were always the worst.

I closed my eyes and breathed in deeply, absorbing the little girl's song. It calmed me in the mornings, after the nightmares. It wouldn't be long until I had to put it away—before the thoughts of what happened to this girl would force me to turn it off—but at that moment, it was bliss to hear someone sing so clearly and so free from worry or doubt.

Lucy probably borrowed her father's dictaphone when he wasn't looking. Her father was a writer who used it to catalogue his thoughts, or perhaps a policeman who used it to record witness statements. Someday Lucy's voice might be interrupted by her father describing a scene from his next play or that of a panicked victim giving a statement. I didn't want that day to come; I wanted the song to last forever.

There were many discarded music players lying around, but they all had internal batteries that needed a mains socket to recharge. Useless in a place without electricity. Lucy's dictaphone used batteries, good old fashioned double A's. The small cache of batteries in a buried Chemists brought her back to life, but she wouldn't be around forever. Six packs. The thought of life without her was terrifying.

I kissed the player, turned it off and shoved it back under the bed. "See you tomorrow morning, Lucy."

I sat up on the bed and rubbed my eyes. The stack of misshapen, pink teddies were still piled in the corner. Their fur matted and their button eyeballs dangled from loose threads or missing. The bear I held when I went to sleep last night had made its way to the floor. I picked it up and examined it, running my thumb along one of the seams where the stuffing was coming out. The bruises on my arms and face were almost gone, but the scars on my hands and arms were still visible. I placed the bear back onto the bed. I would need it again tonight.

I stood up, stretched and walked toward the window, scratching my backside under my shorts. My underwear was barely there, fraying and as grey as the sky, speckled with holes. It would be nice to find a crisp white pair at some point.

My fourth story window looked out over the canal and hundreds of other apartment buildings. I pulled my shorts down and hung my penis out the window, careful not to cut myself on the jagged glass at the edges. I pissed down the side of the building, the cool breeze raised goose bumps up on my naked stomach and legs.

The apartment blocks outside were in the same state as the department stores and shops in the middle of town. Crushed bricks, peeling paint, burned-out windows. Trees and bushes poked out of the windows and grew off the sides of the buildings at odd angles. At some point, the canal outside my window must have held clear water but not anymore. What water that was still there was black, stagnant and filled to the overflowing with rusted cars, twisted shopping trolleys and mountains of ripped plastic and busted refrigerators. As I watched the canal, a rat crawled over the algae-covered hunks of metal and splashed into the muck.

I shook out the last few drops, drew my shorts back up and pulled on the same pair of dirty, denim jeans and grey 'I love Manchester' t-shirt that I wore every day. The clothes and the backpack were gifts from the doctor. He'd hissed with laughter as he handed me the shirt; his idea of a joke.

I yawned, scratched again and walked into the bathroom.

I thought about cleaning the bathroom each morning when I entered, but it would be impossible. Nothing short of a chisel and hammer was required to remove the black stains from the bath, and the toilet was little more than a pile of smashed porcelain. Before I knocked the wall out that separated the bathroom and my bedroom, the windowless bathroom was always dark. There was slightly more light now, in fact, on a sunny day there was almost enough light in there to shave by, but Manchester's skies were rarely accommodating. Most mornings there was barely enough light to see my own face in the mirror, which if I was honest, was not entirely a bad thing.

What I could see in the mirror, I barely recognised. It was the same gaunt stranger that greeted me every morning. Red splotches at the corners of both eyes were all that was left from the doctor's torture and they grew smaller by the day. I rubbed my hand over my long stubble and smiled widely. As the doctor said, my teeth were indeed all there and were, frankly, the only part of me that looked ok. I pushed my nose back and looked into my nostrils hoping there was something in there that would jog my memory. I stuck my tongue out and moved it from side to side. I closed my mouth, pursed my cracked lips and opened my eyes wide with my fingers. Nothing.

I needed a shave, but the experience would not be pleasant. Cold water, bad light and long stubble made for less than ideal shaving conditions. Had I shaved the day before when my stubble was shorter, I may have gotten away with it, but the thick black hair currently sprouting from my face would not go without a fight. No, it was best to wait for a sunny day when I had more time to heat some water over the fire. It didn't really matter anyway, I was only going to be spending the best part of the day waist deep in mud. It wasn't like I was on my way to the President's dinner or something. I didn't see many men around town, but the ones I did see all seemed to be clean shaven. Bill's face was an advertisement to hygiene, the man even *smelled* good. The sight of clean shaven men wandering through mountains of junk felt odd; I put it down to the glut of toiletries scattered across floors of empty houses and under broken tables and couches. You couldn't stick a spade into the random muck without coming up with razor blades and toothbrushes. I had collected a stockpile of both and piled them in what was left of my bath.

I picked up the pail of water beside the sink and splashed water onto my hairy face. It was cold and it felt good. I tilted the pail back and drank from it, emptying it. I held the last gulp in my puffed out cheeks. I picked my toothbrush off the sink, placed a strip of toothpaste on it, spat the water on the brush and started brushing. Once finished, I spat the toothpaste into the sink and looked around the room for more water to rinse my mouth out, forgetting I'd just emptied the pail.

"Shit"

I wiped my mouth with my arm, smearing it with used toothpaste.

There were other pails on top of the building set out to catch the rain. If there was one advantage to living in this terrible city, it was the almost endless supply of water.

The second bedroom was down the hall. That one was more suited to a man of my age, with its adult furnishings, but for reasons I couldn't even explain to myself, I was more comfortable in Lucy's room. I had no choice but to live in this apartment, it was one of the conditions of my freedom. The doctor marched me blindfolded to the front door of the apartment building from the detention centre after my days in the torture room. If I concentrated hard enough, I could probably retrace my steps but there was no reason to do so. The detention centre was the last place on earth I ever wanted to see again.

My kitchen was dark. In the time it took me to walk from the bathroom to the kitchen, it seemed to have darkened outside. The doors hanging off of the empty cupboards and crooked drawers were just visible in the ashen gloom. The exposed brick walls and brushed steel appliances disclosed the kitchen's trendy beginnings. Rich people used to live here.

I opened the refrigerator door and retrieved the rest of last night's pizza. The fridge didn't work and the door stood ajar, the seal long since eaten away. Even if I had the electricity to power it, the flapping door would have let the cool out. It didn't stop me from putting food in there.

The knowledge that a cold pizza's place was in a refrigerator lay embedded as solid and unarguable in my brain as the fact that breathing air was inherent to survival, whilst more important things—like my own mother's face—hovered warm and blurred in the stratosphere that surrounded my skull.

I scoffed two pieces of the pizza. It was cold and the cheese was hard, but it was still delicious. I placed the other two pieces into a filthy plastic container and snapped the lid shut. Plastic containers were another thing there was no shortage of.

The living room was lighter; the grey light passed through the large, glassless patio doors and spilled on to the wooden floorboards and ragged furniture. The patio itself was long gone. A shiver ran through me as I walked across the cold floor in my bare feet.

It would be dark early this evening despite it being the middle of summer. Once those clouds moved in, they stayed all day. I should've put the boards over the windows last night, I was lucky it hadn't rained. The couch and chairs were in tough shape, a little water could hardly make them worse, but splashing through morning puddles in the floor wasn't pleasant.

My backpack sat atop the upright piano. I couldn't play a tune, but some nights it was nice to sit down and plonk away at the keys. Anything to break the unending silence. I tossed the pizza container into my backpack and shouldered it. I pulled on a pair of mismatched socks that were hanging off the back of the chair and shoved my feet into my beat-up work boots.

After lacing up my boots, I walked to the front door and opened it, the light from my apartment invaded the darkened hallway causing wild, squeaking shapes to scatter, retreating from the light.

The boards, you idiot!

I moved back into the apartment and slid the large pieces of plywood over the patio doors. With the boards up, the apartment was dark but for a few cracks of grey light peeking in through the sides.

The hallway was illuminated by the small, grey rectangular beams of light peeking out from under the doors of the other apartments. A sudden urge to lock the door gripped me, just like it did every day, but I didn't have a key. I was one of only a handful of people who lived in the city centre and besides, what could anyone possibly want to steal?

I walked along the hallway and down the stairs, feeling my way down the walls with my hands. More squeaking shadows scurried around me as

I descended. A heavy mass brushed my boot and I kicked at it. It tumbled down the steps, screeching with each bump on the way down.

There was a long day of scavenging ahead of me and I had to get to it. There were forty-three days before the doctor made his first visit. I needed to remember everything before then.

Five

The rusted rails of the abandoned train line pointed me toward my destination.

My shovel rested on one shoulder and my backpack over the other. I could feel the reassuring edge of the knife through the leather. The sun threatened at times, but it was still very much Mancunian grey.

Large, twisted branches grew in wild thickets on either side of the tracks, the tops of which reached high above my head. Small birds flitted amongst the thorny brambles and fat bumblebees lumbered from flower to flower so bloated with nectar as to be barely capable of flight.

The tracks themselves were clear. A skinny path had been stomped into the vegetation by people who made their way to and from the city centre. My own feet had been responsible for much of the stomping. Dry cowpats and wheelbarrow tracks gave away the railway line's main purpose as a trade route. Locals brought food and livestock into town to barter with other locals like Bill. For the first few miles out of the city centre, I could follow the boot prints I laid yesterday and the day before, but they were gone now. I was further down the line than I had ever been. In unknown territory. Again.

The tracks were a good place to be if you didn't want to be noticed. Unlike the spaghetti-like roads of Manchester, the railway line was long and straight. This was important if you wanted to see people approaching. I could see locals coming toward me from miles away and could easily melt into the weeds until they passed. On the streets, you never knew what lie in wait for you around each corner. I had nothing to trade; the only thing I offered these people was fear. The doctor's warning was heavy in my ears: *No one likes foreigners here.*

★ ★ ★

The weeks recovering in the detention cell after the weeks of being tortured were strange ones. The man who had almost killed me was now the one nursing me back to health. The doctor seemed to take as much pleasure in this part of his job as he did in the torture itself. It was impossible to tell which of his two personalities was the true one— the happy torturer or the happy healer? They couldn't both be real. One of them had to be an act, no sane mind could make the switch between the two so quickly and mean it. My money was on the happy torturer.

The healing room was similar to the torture room; Frigid, clinical, massive. Endless walls of chipped breezeblock. The grey paint peeled off in great chunks revealing the even greyer blocks beneath. Shiny steel tables and instruments, white cupboards, floor of black granite. For days after the torture, I remained on the hospital bed, only now the straps were gone and the doctor changed the sheets twice a day. The tubes had been removed and I was eating solid food—If you could call it that—porridge, green salad and boiled potatoes. Dirty plates remained on the table beside the bed for no more than a few minutes before the doctor would clear them away. It was in this room in those strange days after my torture that the first memories of the machine began to make themselves known. Strange robotic arms inside a glass dome, swishing and swaying to and fro, building something up from the ground. I briefly considered telling the doctor of it before quickly grasping the fact that divulging a memory that was only partially formed could put me back into the torture room. I decided to wait and consider myself lucky the memory of it chose the healing room to make itself known rather than the torture room. It may still come in handy as a bargaining chip.

He fed me pills by the handful that he said were penicillin, but they could've been anything. When I was able to stand and walk on my own, he immediately put me through various stretching exercises and painful physiotherapy. Lunges, squats, even dumbbells. "Getting fit was the quickest ticket out of this place," he said. I had no reason to believe he'd ever let me go but what was the alternative? I wanted anything to be out of the man's company, so I worked hard. Lifting weights was difficult, my atrophied muscles strained and pulled in an almost chronic state of spasm.

Each lift was a necessary agony. The doctor encouraged me to take it easy, but fuck him. I lifted the weights in the morning, in the afternoon and at night even when he wasn't around.

The doctor had plenty of things to say in those days. 'We didn't hurt you for the fun of it, we did it for our own protection, the protection of our citizens' *The protection of our citizens*. What possible harm could I have caused? Most of the locals I'd seen were as insane as he was and armed to the teeth! Bill was the only one who seemed to have even a modicum of humility or sense.

I was a lamb out here in this broken world, the doctor told me as much himself. He reminded me of it constantly.

"Don't worry, Seth, we believe you now. We believe you have temporary amnesia. Hopefully we'll come to the same conclusion sooner next time we see you. Avoid all this mess."

Next time. The words hung in my ears and I felt sick. He wasn't kidding when he said 'we' either. There were others in the building; I could hear their footsteps at night, their muffled murmerings. Any thought I had of overpowering him and escaping had long since evaporated. I did what I was told.

"You really don't remember anything of the blast?" the doctor asked. I shook my head.

"Remarkable. I know your memories are muddled, but how could someone possibly forget that?" he said and ripped a blood-crusted rag off my leg relieving it of hair and hunks of scab in the process.

"Jesus!" No matter how many times the doctor did that, it never hurt any less.

He dipped two fingers into a large metal tin of black goo and rubbed it into the wound. It smelled of rotting things, but it cooled the pain and stopping the bleeding. He applied a clean rag to it, allowing the goo to hold the rag in place.

"There. That should do it." he said, standing. He walked over to a wash basin in the corner, dunked his goo-covered hands into it and scrubbed hard, splashing the water around violently.

There were small, rectangular windows up high near the ceiling, too high to be able to look out of. The flat, grey light invaded and landed on the sheets and tables, making the already clinical, lifeless room look even more clinical and lifeless.

"What do you mean, 'The Blast'?" I asked. "Do you mean a bomb or something?"

He stopped scrubbing and lifted an eyebrow at me. His skin took on the colour of robin's eggs in this light, the creases in his face more pronounced. He lifted a soapy finger and waved it at me. "I'm afraid you are going to have to give us something first. You'd do well to start remembering."

★ ★ ★

I kicked a stone off of one of the rails, sending it skittering down the track.

The doctor never did tell me about the 'blast'. What it was or why it happened, why the world was gone. After a while I stopped asking, it was clear he was not going to tell me until I was able to remember something worth trading.

Without stopping, I unshouldered my backpack, unzipped it and reached inside for my cardboard list, scanning it as I walked.

> Things I know
>
> 1. *I am an American.*
> 2. *There is a machine in this world that I must find*
> 3. *The date is August 7th, 2062.*
> 4. *The world was destroyed by some sort of "blast"*

I stopped walking and gave the fourth point a moment's thought before pulling out an old pencil and erasing it with the worn pink nub on the end. I brushed the eraser bits away, turned the cardboard over and started a new list.

> Things the Doctor has told me
>
> 1. *The world was destroyed by some sort of "blast"*

Two sparrows leapt into air from their hiding place amongst the thick greenery to my left. I watched them as they flew away from me down the railway track, crisscrossing over the other's path in figures of eight, flapping their delicate wings madly in both escape and in play as sparrows do.

I tapped the pencil on my bottom lip, felt the roughness of the worn eraser with my tongue before adding a second point to the list.

Things the Doctor has told me
1. *The world was destroyed by some sort of "blast"*
2. *My name is Seth*

I placed the list back into the backpack, reshouldered it and continued down the track. The only bit of information that was of any use to the doctor was my dreams of the machine and until I remembered what it was or what it had to do with me, I couldn't tell him about it. Answering any follow up questions with "I don't know" was not an option.

He'd given me only a few bits of information while I was his prisoner, but I could hardly take his word for anything. The name 'Seth' could be true, I supposed, but if he did indeed know my name, why would he keep asking me who I was? A quick look at Bill's makeshift calendar had confirmed the date but finding out what the doctor's 'blast' referred would not be so easy. Bill didn't know the details of how the city had been destroyed, or if he did, he wasn't interested in telling me about it.

Broad throwaway statements about riots and poverty were all I ever got from him. He didn't seem scared to talk about the end of civilisation; it just didn't seem to interest him at all. He preferred to talk about pizza and gardening. Why the streets were lined with shredded pieces of former human beings was a non-issue, not worth talking about; a waste of breath. He preferred to hone in on the beautiful things in his life and ignore the terrible. I would push him for more information as the seventy day deadline loomed, but for now I didn't want to risk offending him and losing my one source of food.

The suburbs were part of my more immediate plans. The city centre was long since stripped of anything of value, so the suburbs were home to most of Manchester's residents. Living out there would have made for an easier life for me as well—it would certainly be closer to the scavenging sites—but the doctor insisted I stayed in town.

'For your protection as much as theirs,' he said, referring to the locals. Until I lost my accent or found something worth trading in the market, I needed to keep my interactions with them to the barest of minimums. Bill was a sound man, but I'd be stupid to think everyone would be like him. Naivety was a luxury I could ill afford.

Living in the city centre meant a 10 mile walk to and from the apartment every day to do my scavenging, but I couldn't risk the doctor's (or the locals) wrath by living elsewhere.

The doctor gave me an identity in case anyone ever questioned me. I was born on a farm in Derbyshire shortly after the explosion, my parents were farmers and I'd learned my survival skills from them. Most locals didn't venture more than a couple miles outside their front door, he said, so they wouldn't be able to tell a Derbyshire accent from an American one. Even an idiot like me knew it was a flimsy story, but it was nice to have something prepared to say if cornered. Being from Derbyshire was as believable as anything my own mind could come up with.

A life of solitude was the price one must pay as a foreigner living in England. It was a miserable existence; my only company a pizza man (who didn't seem to care if I was from Derbyshire or Timbuktu) and the hollow voice of a little girl long dead. It would have been nice to've been able to talk to other people. The nights in the apartment were devastatingly dull. Without electricity, music was out of the question unless Lucy decided to sing me a song and the few books I had managed to find were wrecked. Plonking the piano keys and listening to Lucy sing took up most of my spare time. It wasn't a life, and yet, it *must've* been better than the world I left in America, why else would I have made such a long and perilous journey?

Being an American was the only thing on my list that I knew for sure. Even more so than the machine. Not just because the doctor told me I was American, or because I recognised my own accent as American. It was more than that. I *felt* like an American.

The Americans did worse in the so-called "darkening" that followed the blast, so said the doctor. The country had fallen into war; war that he believed was still raging. This was the reason they were so keen to jog my memory. They needed an update on the situation over there and they were especially curious about how I wound up face down washed up on a Liverpool beach with no ship to speak of.

I wished I knew.

The third train platform was coming toward me. Like the first two I passed, they were abandoned and overgrown. A crooked sign poking up through the weeds the only indication that this was a station at all. *Urmston* read the sign, the letters chipped and blue and peppered with rust.

"Urmston, last stop!" I said out loud to no one.

I placed both hands on the concrete platform and hauled myself up onto it. Hopefully, I would have better luck here than with the other two stops.

The windows of the station house itself were smashed and the insides empty and black. Spider's webs heavy with dust and as thick as velvet stretched across the open windowsills.

I walked past the station and up a flight of stone steps onto Urmston High Street.

It was a small, unremarkable town centre, very much like the first two suburbs on the train line I'd already searched. A butcher's shop, a super-market, a travel agents, a coffee shop, a couple of newsagents and several shops advertising houses for sale. The most interesting thing about the town was the lorry sticking out of the local KFC.

Several, yellowed advertisements hung loosely in the glassless window of a estate agents.

Three bed semi-detached on a charming street.

The original prices of £230,000 had been crossed out and replaced with £150,000 which was also crossed out and replaced a couple more times settling on £12,000 before someone had given up trying to sell it completely.

An overturned drinks machine lied smashed and looted in the street; the rusted soda cans that spilled from it, twisted and empty like dead sol-diers. Checking for full ones would be a waste of time.

The butcher shop was next. The once proud candy-striped canopy over the window now hung in tatters over a flimsy metal frame. Steel trays and containers rested crookedly inside the smashed window display. Shattered glass, tiny animal bones and hunks of petrified flesh lined the bottoms of the containers.

I reached in and withdrew one of the metal bins. I was getting good at reaching into broken windows without cutting myself on the shards of glass.

I tipped the bones out into the street and examined the shiny metal bin closely, scratching at a rusted bit at the corner. It was not good enough for Bill. I tossed it into the street, it clanked as it tumbled over the cracked asphalt. I grabbed another, checked it, tossed it, checked another and tossed it as well. None of these would meet Bill's exacting standards. Too much rust, too many dents.

The travel agents next door was even more useless. The only thing it offered was a yellowed poster advertising a trip to America. My home country.

Get the fuck out while you can scrawled across it in black spray paint.

Various, faded photos of smiling people on beaches and in cities with grand skylines. Drinking coloured cocktails and riding roller coasters with their eyes closed.

The Americans did worse than anyone. War rages even now.

The other shops on the street looked the same as the ones in the city, crumbling, smashed, burnt and empty. At the end of the town, the shops gave way to large two and three storey redbrick terraced houses. The houses were in fairly good nick, some even with windows in tact. I'd looked through many houses like these before in the city and in the other towns on the railway line, but they had been picked clean by other scavengers. The problem with the good houses was not what they didn't contain, but what they did. Walking into a house full of unsuspecting locals was the last thing I wanted to do.

A large, house-sized hole ruined the long, perfect straightness of the line of terraces. A pile of broken redbrick, dirt and smashed plaster was stacked high in the empty space; the blackened half-walls and burnt timber all that was left to identify it as a former house. Some of the brick walls loomed high over my head teetering as though they would fall at the slightest push. Many houses in the suburbs were blown completely apart like this. It was strange. You never saw an entire street's worth of houses razed to the ground, no, it was always in ones and twos. A large blast would have destroyed them all; it was another reason to doubt the doctor's theory.

The mounds of former houses were the best bet for finding things of value. In my first days of scavenging, I had wandered from house to house, apartment to apartment searching for things to eat, things to trade, to no avail. The rubble made for a good barrier against people and the elements. At the bottom of these piles, even canned goods were still possible. Finding anything of value was always a thrill, but in the piles, you were finding things other people had *missed*. There was nothing better than that.

I looked down the street in one direction and back down again the way I came. There was not a soul around. That day I was the mayor of Urmston, its head honcho, its CEO, its king.

The pile of rubble in front of me was covered with a thick layer of earth and vegetation, the result of dozens of seasons passing over top. I dug my work boot into the pile, pushed myself up and kicked my other foot over top, creating makeshift steps as I climbed. I repeated this movement one foot over the other until I reached the top, tossing jagged bits of metal and chunks of roof tile out of the way on the way up.

The pile was only about fifteen steps high. I looked over to the house next door and estimated that I must have been standing on top of the first floor. Hopefully, only the top floors had collapsed leaving the ground floor and cellar in some kind of useful order.

There was no time to waste. I unshouldered my pack, dropped to my knees and began pulling out large chunks of grass, earth and spiky greenery with my bare hands. I'd only been in this place a couple weeks, but my hands had already started hardening. My first forays into the piles were painful ones, I'd spent many an evening with my hands soaking in water and wrapped in old towels, my fingers and palms cut to ribbons on thorns and nails. I had workers hands now, with thick callouses and deep lines cut into my thickened fingers as if etched by tiny rivers.

Once I'd cleared a large square into the top of the pile, I picked the spade up and buried the blade into the dirt. I dug quickly shifting great hunks of earth out of the hole with each throw.

Once most of the dirt out of the way, I tossed the shovel aside and hoofed the rest of the debris out with my hands; Bricks, pieces of breeze-block, chunks of bed frame and wardrobe, cracked bones. I hated finding bones, especially ones with hardened flesh still hanging off of them like those ones. Skulls were the worst, I could only hope the worms had picked it clean before I came across it.

Once I dug down so that my shoulders were at the top of the hole, I grabbed the shovel again and punched the blade through the rotten hardwood of the first level, tossing aside the cables, pipes and sodden pieces of wood. The rusted pipes and rotten wood gave little resistance, but the heavy timber beams were solid in place. I smashed the wooden slats with my boots, holding myself up by the beams.

I had been hoping that once I cleared the floor away, it would be a quick drop down into the ground floor, but it wouldn't be that easy. The ground floor was dark and full of rubbish. The chance of finding anything for Bill in this mess was slim, but it was too late in the day to start on a new pile. I had to carry on.

The one saving grace was the lack of earth in the ground floor. The rubble here was looser and could be tossed out of the hole by hand. Again using the next door's house as a guide, I estimated that I was moving down into the kitchen. Through the broken timber and smashed plaster I kicked and crawled, tossing large pieces of house out of the hole as quickly as I could.

Down through the rubbish I descended, stopping only for a splash of water from my plastic bottle or a bite of cold pizza. When the thick heat inside the hole became too oppressive, I removed my sweaty t-shirt and tossed it into the backpack. You could hardly call it a shirt anymore, it was so filthy and full of holes. Perhaps the house would offer up a replacement.

As I descended into the house further, the room opened up. There was little brick and breezeblock at that level, the walls seemed to be mostly in tact. Down through the bits of smashed crockery, snapped plastic, twisted metal and crisscrossing hunks of wood, I could just see pieces of floor tiling at the bottom. The sight of the floor spurred me on and I continued down and down, climbing into the open spaces when they were big enough to allow it and bashing through anything that blocked my way with the shovel.

I stomped the shovel down hard on a large cabinet, smashing the rotten wood to cinders and tossed the pieces aside, revealing a large hood fan underneath. The hood fan wasn't burned which was a good sign, however, this was an odd place for the oven to be. If this house had a similar layout to the one next door, I should have been digging down toward the kitchen sink. I had to assume the hood fan shifted in the collapse of the house. I picked it up and shoved it into an empty space beside me and moved more bricks and pipes out with renewed vigour. I needed to reach the sink today; I was all out of favours with Bill.

What little light I had on that grey day was fading fast as afternoon became evening. If I didn't find something soon, I was going to have to call it a day if I was going to get back home before dark.

I snapped a large piece of timber in two with the shovel and picked the pieces up to reveal a large granite slab. A pang of excitement surged through my chest. I pushed an old kettle out of the way and followed the slab along until it led to a stainless steel sink.

Underneath the sink I could see the door that would lead to the cleaning supplies. And in front of it was a space for me to shimmy down into. I stopped again and took a breath. Dust swirled around my face. I coughed and looked for a clean spot on my arm with which to rub my eyes but there wasn't one. Every part of me was covered in smeared dirt and muck. I blinked the dirt out of my eyes. I listened. The evening's stillness interrupted only by the soft songs of the curious housemartins above. I covered my eyes with the backs of my hands and allowed myself a split second of hope—a fleeting vision in my mind's eye of a cabinet packed tightly with all manner of bleach, polish and cream cleanser—before dashing it away.

I dropped down in front of the cabinet under the sink and opened the door.

There was nothing.

No glass cleaner, no powder, no dishsoap and no oven cleaner.

Fuck.

Bill's kindness had its limits. I was to go hungry tomorrow. I stood up and kicked the cabinet door, smashing it into four pieces.

What kind of animals lived here? Not even a bloody sponge. I turned around and looked up at the sky, the clouds were blackening and I could feel the cooling air making its way down the hole. I didn't have time to feel sorry for myself; I needed to get home. Walking in the dark was never a good idea.

I looked up through the web of timber and pipes, up through the zig-zagging path I had created and started climbing back up toward the light.

I reached up to grab an outstretched pipe and heard a sickening crack below my feet. I stopped moving and listened. The house scraped and moaned again, this time from all around me. Something metallic snapped on my left, and the floor below cracked hard again giving me the briefest of warnings before disappearing beneath my feet. I jumped, but it was too late. I got a glimpse of sky before the world thundered past me.

I fell through the floor and dropped into the darkness below.

Six

The disfigured mess that emerged from the machine was a surprise, even to me. That's not to say that there weren't subjects more grotesque than 2B156, but this was the first to be worse than the one that had come before.

The reconstruction room was bright, white and pristine. The buzzing white fluorescents emphasised every deformity in the subject, not a hint of shadow to hide the monster. The hit of adrenaline that had pulsed through me when I turned the machine on was replaced with nausea, heavy and thick. Sweat gathered on my forehead and underarms. It was important not to panic.

2B156 was a setback.

In the months prior, I had made distinct improvements. Eyes had found homes in their sockets, organs had been built more or less in the correct positions, even the skin seemed to have taken hold properly and dried into the right colour (give or take). I was making progress.

It was apparent almost from the beginning that there was something very wrong with 2B156.

The skin wasn't right as soon as the first few layers of were printed. The robotic arms swished around precisely in the loops and lines that they had done hundreds of times before; depositing drops of tissue, muscle, cartilage and bone with each swipe. Normally, the skin was smooth and flawless, but on 2B156 there were seams. There hadn't been seams in a subject's skin for a long time. Years.

In addition to the visible seams, the skin also wasn't setting properly. In many places, it looked to be melting like a clay model that had spent too much time in the sun. It seemed solid enough to be built upon, but it wasn't pretty.

The skin was the least of my—or should I say her—worries.

Bone, muscle and tendon were building up nicely, but the legs were far too thin causing the knees to bulge. As the nozzles started building up toward the hips, the steel supports shot out from the back wall and snapped into place around the legs just above the ankles and knees. In the last few models, the supports hadn't been necessary, but I was thankful for them this time as the legs were unable to stand on their own. The mess was going to be difficult enough to clean up as it was, if it had collapsed, I would be there all night.

I thought about stopping the reintegration at that point, but I needed to know what had gone wrong in order to make improvements in the next model. A full investigation would be necessary. 2B156 was going to set me back months.

The upper legs were too thin as well and the hips balanced precariously on top of them. Again, a third set of supports snapped out and attached a steel codpiece tight around the groin, but not before I could see that its genitals were missing. Had the system been hacked? How could it have gone so wrong? The calculations were perfect and the raw materials had been checked and re-checked.

Up and up 2B156 rose from the ground, the robotic arms of the bio-printer whizzed across its abdomen, laying down lines of organic tissue, stopping only to discharge a blockage or to have its nozzles brushed clean.

2B156's bellybutton was the last part that looked remotely human.

Above the waist, organs were building up at the correct x's and y's, but they were most certainly not at the correct z's. The gut formed too far forward, the pink intestinal walls and stomach appeared on the outside of the abdomen. Its pink gallbladder, liver and lungs followed. Later I would discover that the ribcage was in the correct place, but the displaced organs were bisected by and fused into the curved bones.

The machine could see what I saw. On the monitor warning prompts flashed over an image of the former Miss Brooks. The machine knew something was amiss, but showed no signs of stopping. The robotic arms continued with their work, methodically laying down further lines of blighted tissue; its great silver brain programmed to proceed at all costs. Only I had the power to stop it and I had no intention of doing so;

I would watch it right to the end.

Seven

When I awoke, it was dark and clear. The full moon shone down on my motionless body. I was covered in busted bricks, dirt and chunks of wood from the floor above.

My head ached and for a few panicked moments I didn't know where I was; my mind still swirling with visions of mutilated body and the machine.

The sight of two heavy joists stretched across a hole in the ceiling brought my situation back into focus. I was still in the house and I had fallen. Bent nails jutted from the joists at odd angles and chunks of wood and ripped cloth hung down in tatters. Beyond the joists lay only the darkened sky pinpricked by bright stars. How long had I been out?

The nightmare produced by my brain couldn't be true, couldn't possibly be the machine that invaded my mind in the recovery room under the doctor's care. But it was so vivid. I could smell the body and feel the disappointment of a failed experiment.

2B156 was a setback.

I filed the visions of the machine away to be processed later. I had more pressing matters at the moment; I was trapped in the bottom of a house on the verge of collapse and I was in pain.

Chunks of plaster and dirt slid down my front as I sat up and rubbed my head. I brushed the dust out of my hair and pushed the bricks and rubbish off of myself. Thick dust coated my chest and arms; white like chalk in the moonlight. My hands seemed ok, they weren't even cut. I stretched my fingers open wide and squeezed them tight twice to make sure. I kicked chunks of timber off my legs and wiggled my toes; nothing seemed to be broken.

I needed to be more careful. Had I fractured a leg or found myself pinned under the rubble, the room would have served as my tomb.

I stood up slowly and rubbed a twinge in my lower back under my jeans. It was tender and most definitely bruised, but again, not broken.

Moonlight streamed in through the circular hole in the ceiling, illuminating my body and the pile of debris I was standing on. Most of the ceiling was still in place, only a circle, a shovel's length in diameter, was missing where I had fallen through.

I brushed the dirt out of my hair and felt another small, wet wound on the back of my head. It was sore to the touch, but the blood had already started congealing. Dust particles puffed and swirled in the light emphasising further the empty blackness of the room beyond the circle of moonlight.

The floor above was low; I could just about reach the joist above my head standing on tiptoes. The thought of escape at that moment was tempting, but hunger was starting to set in. There was no harm in having a look while I was there.

I walked out of the light into the darkened corner of the cellar with my hands out. Blue-black shapes around me made themselves known as my eyes adjusted to the dark. Boxes of old books, stacked chairs, a lawn mower.

A hallway in front of me led further away from the moonlit pile of debris. Down the hallway I walked feeling my way along the walls with my hands. They passed over a light switch, a couple of hooks, a picture frame and an old mop. A mop, eh? So this guy actually did clean up after himself. I fiddled around at the base of the mop, hoping for some cleaning products but came up short again.

The walls were old brick and the paint chipped off on my hands as they slid across. The moonlight was still there behind me, as bright as before, but ahead was a blackened void. A tiny glint of light reflected off the dials of what I guessed was an old washing machine at the end of the hall. Everything else was black.

I moved toward the washing machine. My hands stopped at a large impression in the brick wall. After about a hand's width inside the impression, my fingers touched timber. I knocked on the wood, but it made little sound, the old wood soft and spongy to the touch.

I slid my fingers up to the top where wood once again met brick and then down the front. The wood reached down to the floor and up about a foot over my head. I slid both hands across the middle of the door, guessing at the doorknob's location. After a few moments of feeling for it, I found it on the far right, slightly lower than I'd expected. The door was small, only slightly wider than my shoulders.

A surge of adrenalin pulsed through my chest with the thought of what terrible things could be beyond the door. I wanted to cut my losses and get out of there. It seemed pointless to keep going; the darker it got outside, the more dangerous it was for me. Messing around in the cellar under the destroyed house was risky; I should really have been trying to find a way out of this place. The basement would still be there tomorrow, the search would be easier in the daylight. Even a Manchester daylight.

The moonlit pile of rubbish beckoned. It would be a long walk home, the longer I pushed it off, the more likely I'd be discovered.

Digging all day just so to come back tomorrow to find some other local emptying the cellar of cans of industrial strength oven cleaner and freeze dried pot noodles? No, that would kill me. This was a cellar; there could be wine behind the door. My stomach growled loudly in the dark.

I grasped the door handle tightly and turned it. The plastic knob snapped off in my hand.

I tossed the knob onto the ground. It shattered into a million small plastic pieces.

Missing cleaning products in his kitchen and cheap, plastic door handles on his doors. I truly hated the person who'd lived here.

I pushed the moist wood of the door to test it and felt it give under my hands. If the owner skimped on door handles, logic would dictate his thriftiness would apply to his selection of doors. It was just asking to be kicked in.

I obliged by raising my booted foot and thrusting it forward, catching the door perfectly at half extension. The wood smashed into pieces and the hinges snapped off and skittered satisfyingly across the concrete floor.

The stench of decay and mould wafted out of the room, hitting me like a blast wave. It stung the back of my throat and filled my lungs, making me gag. The smell of death was getting easier to take, but the funk coming from that room was worse than usual. There was *dead* in this city, and then there was *freshly dead*. I covered my mouth and nose with my hand, kicked what was left of the door out of the way and walked into the room.

It was windowless and pitch black. Freshly dead may be bad on the nostrils, but it was like gold dust to a scavenger. Freshly dead meant it had been shielded from the elements. How shielded that room was couldn't be known, but last time I smelled a freshly dead room, I came away with actual food. Actual food from *before*. Tinned tomatoes and tuna. I coughed, the sound flat and echoless. Again the adrenalin coursed, this time out of excitement more than fear.

I squeezed my fist tightly to steady myself. I didn't want to get too excited, there was still every chance I would leave this house with nothing but bruises. The owner of the house didn't even own cleaning supplies. The chance of food or anything else of value being stored down here was remote.

I stepped forward and kicked something soft; it gave with a sickening squish. I fell forward, shot out my other foot to stop myself from falling and promptly buried it into the soft thing with a pop. I waved my arms around trying to regain my balance. I jumped backward and could feel something sharp scrape against my boot as I retracted it from the soft thing. My arm came down on a shelf, smashing it. My butt hit the floor right on the sore spot and my elbow slapped against the concrete. The tinkling of small, metallic things hitting the floor rang out from the darkness.

Burning pain radiated from my elbow down my arm and into my fingers. My back throbbed and the smell coming from the dead thing was terrible. I coughed hard and laid still trying hard to keep my pizza down. I squeezed my elbow tight and rubbed it until the pain became bearable. I truly hoped this dead thing was the owner of the house.

Everything in my mind and body was telling me not to continue into this room, but I had to. It was personal now. I no longer cared if I came away with nothing more than an old dog's bowl and a fistful of wingnuts. I was going to finish my search.

I sat up again and slid away from the soft thing in the centre of the room and located the wall once again. The shelf I smashed in my fall was attached to the wall and parts of it still remained. On it I felt some old rags, some large pieces of plastic and the odd nail. Nothing of use. Just before I reached the end of the room, my foot hit again ran into something. Something solid.

I bent down and moved my hands over it. It was a smooth metal case of some kind and it was huge. It was also a very strange shape, round on the ends and square at the top. A seam ran around the outside of it where the two halves of the case met. Large, metal clasps dotted the case's circumference at regular intervals, holding it tightly shut. It was at least half as high as the wall and twice as long as it was high. The clasps popped off easily and the inside of the case was covered in a hard foam. A cushion of some kind? Whatever was in here, it was being protected.

Inside I felt long, smooth metal tubes and wires. The tubes were connected to a chain and metal wheels with teeth. And pedals.

My breath caught in my throat. I'd found many bicycles in the piles and in the streets, but none of them had been rideable. Chains rusted solid and snapped, tyres eaten away. This bike was different. The bars were smooth, the chain was tight, even the leather seat was intact. I pushed my hands out along the tubes toward the wheels. The spokes felt strong and the tread on the tyres was heavy and thick. A shiver rippled through me and I realised I was holding my breath. The only sound was the blood pumping in my ears. I wanted desperately to run out of the room with the bike in my hands to see it in the light, but I resisted. It could be a glorious find, the greatest, but I had to be very careful.

I breathed out slowly and lifted the bike from its case. It was light in my hands, it urged itself into the air, stretching as if from a long slumber. I stood up with it and carried it toward the door. As I left the room, the moonlight caught the metal bits and the machine revealed itself to me. Even in the dim moonlight, it was obvious just how good the bike was. Rugged, with thick tubes with strong welds and heavy duty suspension, yet it could be lifted with two fingers. The frame was not steel or even aluminium; it was titanium.

I recognised the bicycle; I recognised the quality of it. The materials, the design, it was built by someone who took their time. Machines didn't put the bicycle together; it was handcrafted, sculpted. Other than being flat, the beefy tyres looked in good shape, as did the titanium handlebars and crank set, even the cassette cogs were sound.

I made a few more trips back into the blackened room, my eyes saw more with each trip. There were tools in the bottom of the case, two small bottles, two fist-sized boxes and a can. My fingers rolled over a small straw taped to the can's side. Pay dirt. It must be WD40; Bill loved this stuff.

Back in the light, I took stock. Spanners, a bike pump, two boxes of inner tubes, a patch kit, a bottle of oil and, yes, a can of WD40 that was at least half full. There were a few surface cracks in the spare inner tubes, but even they looked usable. The owner of this house may have been a slob, but he knew how to take care of a bike.

I unscrewed the top of the pump, attached it to the valve on the front tyre and pumped it slowly, careful not to overstress the inner tube. Every time I pumped, I listened for escaping air and heard nothing. The limp piece of rubber tightened slowly until it was a solid mass. I did the same with the rear tyre, only to find that it too held the air. I popped the top off of the oil bottle and squirted some into my hand, feeling the thick sticky liquid with my fingers. I squirted a big glob into my palm, squeezed my fist around the chain and rolled the pedals around. The chain moved through my oily hand, orange and rusty going in, dark and smooth coming out. I squirted more oil into my hand, ran the chain through a second time and then a third until the whole thing was coated.

I leaned the bike against the wall and searched for a set of stairs. It wasn't long before I found them in a far corner. They were collapsed and covered in earth and debris from above. The only way out was the same way I came in.

I returned to moonlit hole in the ceiling and looked up. Most of the crisscrossing pipes and beams had collapsed or shifted out of view in the fall, giving me an almost clear view of the sky. The weakened floor combined with the missing pipes, beams and other climbing handholds would make my escape from the kitchen above all the more difficult. But that was a problem for the future. I had to get out of the cellar first.

I lifted the bike up front wheel first toward one of the two exposed joists above my head. With one hand on the frame and one on the back wheel, I pushed it up and hooked the front tyre around the joist. As the bike hung suspended, I picked up the spanners, the tubes, bottles and the WD40 and tucked them into my pockets and waistband of my jeans.

I jumped up to grab the second joist, but my hands slipped off the bottom lip and I fell back down in a hail of white dust. I jumped again and missed a second time, bringing down more dust. The third time, I jumped higher and grabbed the joist tight with both hands. Straining, I swung a leg up and hooked a heel over the top. I then pulled a second leg up and swung it around so I was clinging onto the bottom of the beam with both hands and feet. The spanners and cans leapt from my pockets and waistband, reacquainting themselves with the floor below.

I hung there for a few moments with my arms shaking contemplating my next move.

How was I supposed to get on top of the beam from that position? I looked past the beam into the starry night for the answer and received only silence. There was no way to get on top of the beam from there so I unhooked my legs and dropped back down.

Again I scoured the room and found a stack of dusty plastic chairs. I picked up the stack, moved it under the hole, twisting the chair stack until I created a flat spot in the rubbish. I re-gathered the spanners and WD40, shoved them back in my trousers and slowly stood up on top of the chair stack. It teetered, but I managed to stand up. I could now reach the bottom lip of the I-beam and could probably grab the top lip at a jump. I needed to get both hands onto one side of the beam and pull myself up and I needed to do it on the first try. I'd fallen onto the cellar floor enough times for one night, thank you very much.

I focused on my target and visualised the jump in my mind. I bent my legs slowly, coiling, careful not to tip the stack of chairs over. I raised my arms to head level, bending them to match my bent knees.

I inhaled deeply and leapt.

I was in the air with my arms and legs at full extension, the chairs tumbled away beneath me. Both hands grasped onto the top of the beam and I held onto it firmly. As I pulled my face above the bar, I slapped my arms down flat on top of the beam. My arms were burning and my shoulders felt like they were separating, but I continued pulling until I was able to swing my legs up and lie flat on top.

The bike was still hanging on the other joist. I took another breath and pushed my legs underneath myself and rose to a standing position with my arms out at my sides to balance. The joists were barely thick enough for me to stand on with both feet side by side.

I took a quick survey of the area. Luckily for me, very little of the kitchen was disturbed in the fall. The oven, dishwasher and most of the cabinetry were where I had left them. Had they come tumbling down through the hole, I wouldn't have ever woken up. Unluckily, the pipes and beams that had acted as my ladder down into the kitchen were now collapsed and scattered around the hole. Two lonely pipes were all that was left stretching across the ceiling, taunting me with their distance. They could be in orbit for all the use they were to me.

I kicked a foot out and planted it onto the other beam. I leaned down and lifted the bike up by the front tyre gently, careful not to scrape the tyres on anything sharp. As the bike made its way up, I grabbed the frame and pulled until the bike was above the beam before lifting it onto my shoulder. The bike was virtually weightless, moving easily as if the very air was where it was most at home.

Again I scanned the room for an escape route. The windows were caved in and full of earth and bricks, it would take me days to dig my way out that way especially without my shovel or a sturdy place to stand.

With the bike on my shoulder, I walked across the joist, balancing with my arms outstretched, kicking pieces of debris off the beam as I walked.

In the corner of the ancient kitchen, a door had been uncovered as the rubbish had shifted and fell through the floor. On the other side of the door would be only earth; more digging would be required.

Once I'd reached the edge I tested out what was left of the floor by stepping on and pushing down. The floor gave slightly, but held. Carefully, I transferred more of my weight onto the ledge until I was standing on it with both feet. One step at a time I walked toward the door, testing each footfall before committing. With each step the bike got heavier and by the time I reached the door, wet trails of sweat dripped down my dusty arms.

The door had no handle, only a hole where the door handle used to be.

I pushed on it as I had done with the door in the cellar; as I do with all doors before opening. It flipped open with a crack and smacked into my shoulder, knocking me reeling. A blink of silence was punctured by the sound of six smooth stones squeezing out of the earth and tumbling past my feet on the tile floor. It was the only warning I got before the earthfall of debris roared in through the open door. I jumped out of the way as the landslide of dirt and old bricks rolled past me down the hole to the cellar. Tumbling debris struck my back and shoulder, pinging off the bike as it thundered past. I shimmied to the end of the floor and collapsed to my knees, turning away with my hands over my head, gripping the bike on my shoulder tightly. The rubble continued to crash past me, large stones and pieces of brick bounced off the door and walls.

As quickly as it started, it stopped. With my eyes closed, I slowly felt my shoulder for the bike. It was still there.

I opened my eyes to see more moonlit dust coming up from the now sizeable pile through the hole in the floor. Through the door, a makeshift rubble staircase was left and at the top of it, nothing but stars and sky.

With the bike over my shoulder, I burst through the doorway, sprinted up the pile and out into the night, leaving a trail of falling debris in my wake.

On the street I stood with the bike–with my bike–looking it up and down. It was even more beautiful on the road than it was in the cellar. I felt a weight at the bottom of my trouser leg, I shook it to see the dented can of WD40 come tumbling out. The spanners and oil bottles were gone, which was a shame, but I wasn't going back in. Not into that house, not any time soon. I had bigger, more immediate plans. Under this sky and that moon, through those battered streets, I would ride.

I pushed down on the handlebars to test the suspension. The shocks wheezed, but they bounced back.

The full moon was close and huge, the bike was fierce in the moonlight. I stood, admiring my find for a moment. What I had in front of me wasn't just a toy, what I had was the ability to move, to cover large distances. What I had was freedom, in short, the most valuable thing in the world.

I straddled the bike and pulled on the brakes. The levers flapped limply, giving no resistance. Between my legs the snapped brake cables hung loosely from the frame. A minor inconvenience, I had no intention of using them anyway.

Inhaling the cool night air deeply, I raised myself on to the saddle and pushed down on the pedals. The chain squeaked and rattled, but it was moving.

I pushed the bike forward, watching the houses and shops begin to slide past.

I sliced through the empty street in front of me, weaving around the holes and cracks in the asphalt and around the bushes poking through. Nature would eventually reclaim these streets, but not on that night. On that night, the streets were mine.

Past the shops and the train station over the bumps and around the rusted cars I pedalled, gathering speed. The wind rumbled past my ears and the dirt blew off my arms in wispy streaks. The cool night air rolled over my body, raising goose bumps on my chest and arms.

It was the first time I'd dared the streets. There was no reason to hide anymore. Who could catch me? I was the fastest thing in all of creation. I swerved down one street and up another, left, left, right, left. I didn't care where I was going or who saw me. I pedaled on with abandon, my problems, the scarceness of things, the hunger, the doctor's threats, the murderous locals, everything melted away behind me in so much dust.

I pedalled harder, pushing the bicycle further and faster. Derelict pubs, giant ash trees and long grass whistled past. The houses whipped past in a blur, firelight in the odd window disclosing its human occupants. I flew by a park, scaring a large flock of starlings out of the trees and into the night sky, their huge numbers silhouetted against the enormous white moon as they dived and ducked in unison creating swirling shapes.

I screamed after the fleeing birds. A long, primordial scream. Cracked and carnal, the wild sound pierced the air. My eyes were wide and my lips stretched wide across my face as I laughed. The weeks of fear and despair were cast from my body as I ploughed through the night.

I turned left onto a four-lane expressway, the bike groaned as I leaned into the turn. The road looked as though it was built to transport great hulks back and forth to the city centre. I pushed my boots into the pavement and brought the bike to a stop.

This must have been the main road into and out of Manchester. The city centre was at one end of this road, at the other end was the rest of the world. Darkened, twisted streetlamps poked out at the night at odd angles. Strings of ripped paper flapped from enormous advertising hoardings in the burgeoning breeze.

The machine was down that road, the machine that made human beings. In the still air of that moment, I allowed myself a peek at the vision I had tucked away whilst climbing out of the cellar. The terrible torso built up by the machine. The dislocated shoulders and exposed collarbone, the deflated, nippleless breasts. I told myself I would watch it to the end, but I stopped the machine just south of the chin. I could not look my monster in the face.

It never would have had a chance to sing, to make babies, to know love.

A rat with a mouthful of something I wanted to know nothing of plopped itself down through the open front window of a burned out car.

Perhaps I'd done 2B156 a favour.

The machine was my ticket out of England; I couldn't explain why or how, but I knew that finding it would change everything. The doctor lied to me about my early beginnings in this place, I did not wash up on a Liverpool beach, I came to this place, to this England pre-apocalypse; in the beforetime. I would eventually remember the machine's location and when I did, I would take this road in the opposite direction, but for now I would go home.

I pointed the bike back at the city centre and began pedalling.

The bike was enjoying its newfound freedom as well as I was and it urged me on. The wind rushed at me, stinging my eyes. Faster and faster, I flew past old chippies, vacant car dealerships and a football stadium that towered far above the buildings that surrounded it like the great Roman Coliseum.

I swerved around the huge empty metal husks of cars and busses and around the young trees punching through the pavement. Ancient, blackened traffic lights passed over my head as I pushed further toward the city centre. Children's toys and discarded furniture littered the ground and endless, jutting, advertising hoardings littered the air. Large billboards, small ones, strewn across the motorway, perched at the side. The advertisements were on buildings and busses, on cars, painted onto the street and plastered to the sides of bridges. Their messages now faded and empty.

The road opened up further as four lanes became six, the dead cars now came at me thick and scattered. I weaved through the automobile gauntlet like a skiier swishing down a mountain slope. A rusted sideview mirror bounced off the back of my hand and clattered onto the asphalt. My hand was cut, but I felt nothing. I was drunk on abandon, I was invincible.

I soared down the curving exit off motorway and back onto the bendy city streets. Over the cobbles past the once swanky bars, I cycled. The bars little more than piles of brick, ripped velvet and speckled chrome. I whizzed past the imposing white stone buildings of the old financial district and into the northern part of the city where Bill's pizza was located. Somewhere in the darkened building, Bill slept. Soon, the

WD40 in my waistband would be putting a big smile on his big face; his days of squeaky hinges were behind him. And I would eat for a week.

I saw twelve people on that ride, *twelve*. A small family sitting down to a meal in a window, a man alone on his front step playing a guitar. There was no one in the city centre except me and my friend in the purple cape and hat. Trudging through the muck with his eyes fixed on the ground, his arms full of their usual broken pieces of plastic. I cycled close enough to see the frayed ends of his cape and yet still he did not look up. Not even a wild, shirtless man on a bicycle could distract him from his garbage collecting. He was a odd even by the standards of this broken city, but I supposed that was to be expected.

Feral dogs rummaged through rubbish, stopping only to turn and bark at me as I blitzed past. Cats and foxes scurried across roads, mice hanging from their jaws. I'd seen more in one night than I had in the three months since I woke up in the doctor's clutches.

I felt lighter than air, the bike was almost floating now, leading me toward my apartment and my bed.

My apartment building was now in sight and as I approached the front door, I could something that was not there that morning when I'd left. It was three pieces of paper nailed to the front of it, flapping in the wind. I rode up to the door and skidded to a stop.

The first piece of paper was a note. It simply read:

This is what the people of this place are capable of.

It wasn't signed, but it was obviously from the doctor. Underneath the paper were two faded black and white images. One depicting a teen-aged boy standing over a man, beating him to death with a metal pipe and the second showed a young Bill. He was thinner and his eyes were wild as he held a woman by her hair, dragging a carving knife across her throat.

Eight

The following morning I laid in bed staring at the mouldy ceiling. The rain tapped the open windowsill as Lucy's tiny dictaphone voice pretended to interview a friend for a talent show.

The sight of Bill murdering that woman kept me awake for most of the night. It couldn't have been the happy old Bill I knew, the Bill with the wide smile and round belly. But it was. His face was thinner, his hair thicker and darker, but it was most certainly him. If a man as soft and as kind as Bill could take a person's life in such a way, what chance did I have with one of the not-so-nice locals? I thought of jumping on the bike and riding straight out of town, away from the doctor, the murderous locals and most of all, the destruction. I couldn't remember exactly what the countryside looked like, but the image my mind elicited was a beautiful one full of trees and long grasses. Of squirrels and songbirds.

But there was no food in the country. No shelter.

My stomach was empty and aching; grumbling every time I shifted position. Lying still seemed the best thing to do. It had been a full day since I'd eaten anything. The dirty yellow pail of water beside the bed kept the hunger pangs at bay, but it wouldn't be long until I wouldn't be able to ignore them. Something soon was going to have to be done. Escape would have to wait.

Where did food come from? How did one make it? My mind truly was an terrific void. I watched Bill make dozens of pizzas, I could tell you how to assemble one, but how did one source the components? I understood that the meat on the pizzas came from the animals I'd seen on the trade routes, but what of cheese, what of tomatoes? How did one find such things? It must be the most elementary bit of knowledge for the locals. Finding tomatoes and cheeses must be as natural to the average person as breathing. My mind was more concerned with bicycle parts than with food. Desolate was the wrong word to describe my brain, no; my mind was broken.

As if confirming that thought, my bike taunted from across the room. I could tell you every little thing about the machine down to the last detail. Which parts were titanium, which were aluminium and which were carbon fibre. I could do it with my eyes closed. The ceramic disk brakes on that bike were top of the range. The derailleur was Japanese. Derailleur was a French word; I could even spell it properly. If I was someone viewing myself from above, some sort of puppeteer or God, I would laugh at the sorry sight beneath me, the simple wretch who could replace a snapped spoke one-handed, but who was entirely incapable of feeding himself.

The WD40 stared at me from atop Lucy's pink chest of drawers, reminding me how easy it was to get food. My stomach growled again, a long steady rumble like distant thunder.

Yesterday was a wake up call. The blown up houses were dangerous places. Finding little pieces of worthless junk would feel more like work and less like adventure with every shovel full, especially now that my food supply was cut off. The tiny daily victories will quickly lose their appeal and I would find little joy in my work.

What was the point of doing it now that I no longer had Bill to trade with?

It wasn't just the food I was losing by abandoning Bill; it was his company. I still owed him a couple days of farm work. That WD40 was meant to pay off my debt and get me enough food to sustain me until I found the next tradeable thing.

I could steal food from Bill when he was asleep. There was a store of vegetables and cheese under his feet. If I got desperate enough, perhaps I would risk it, but not yet. I knew what the man was capable of. I'd probably have a better chance at staying alive by facing him with the can. Stealing from one of the carts that rolled into town was also an option, but the women who pushed them looked fiercer than Bill.

I had another day and a bit on the water before the hunger would be too much to bear. I would see what this day was to bring first and decide later.

Lucy and her friend were now arguing over something. I closed my eyes and listened to her voice, trying again to remember. Images of unrecognisable places that felt familiar formed on the backs of my eyelids like always. A blue carpet on a living room floor, paintings on the wallpapered walls, black tiles, faceless men in suits and ties. It was impossible to know if the images my mind assembled were real memories or simply teasing falsities manufactured by my brain to torture me. The doctor invaded my thoughts with his hammers and knives.

I opened my eyes again. The ceiling was still there, but the rain had stopped. Lucy was now singing to herself with no accompaniment. Would my memory ever come back? And if it did, would I be able to separate memory and imagination? Memory and dream were one in this world; coalescent and indistinguishable as separate entities. The not remembering was maddening, but the knowledge of the punishment I'd receive from the doctor for *not* remembering was much worse. Sometimes I wished the doctor would just show up and put me out of my misery.

My days with Lucy were coming to an end as well. I had been greedy, listening for longer than I should have. I stopped the tape and the room was again silent but for my groaning stomach.

I rubbed my face and looked down at my naked body. I was desperately thin, my face had grown long and my beard and hair were thick, the grey wisps sprouting from my temples were a further reminder of my mortality. My face was the only thing I had from my previous life and it was changing before my very eyes. Pretty soon, I'd have nothing at all.

Except the machine.

I got up from the bed and walked into the living room. Rainwater had collected in small pools on the floor.

My backpack was on top of the piano; inside it, my knife was stashed waiting, almost begging to be used. I opened the bag and withdrew the knife, its sharpened blade cold to the touch.

I walked back into the bathroom and looked at myself in the mirror. I tossed Lucy into the sink, she clinked off the sides and settled at the bottom.

My bloodshot eyes stared back at me.

'Tell me about my machine,' I said. My voice was a croak. How long had it been since I had spoken?

I slapped myself hard across the face and looked straight back into the mirror. My cheek immediately pinkened and went warm.

'Think for fuck sake!' I said, slapping myself a second time, harder.

And again.

Nothing. Not only did nothing come forward, but it felt like I was pushing things back.

My ribs were showing through my skin. I grasped the blade of the knife by the blade and squeezed the sharpened side into my palm.

The blade drew blood and searing pain momentarily replaced everything else. I welcomed the pain and felt hope for a moment that the machine's location would reveal itself to me. I squeezed my eyes tightly closed until tears gathered at the edges. But my mind did not cooperate.

I screamed at my reflection, dropped the knife into the sink and punched the mirror. It cracked, cutting my knuckles open. I punched it again. This time the glass shattered and large chunks rained into the sink. Blood trickled from my fist where the glass had embedded itself.

I planted my bloody fist into the hand I cut open with the knife and twisted the pointed glass into my palm, grinding it into the flesh like an auger. The pain was immense and I screamed out. I clenched my teeth together and forced myself to take the pain. Tears dribbled down my cheeks and disappeared into my beard.

Still nothing.

I pulled my fist away, leaving a pool of crimson in my palm. In the large piece of mirrored glass still attached to the wall, I could see blood trickling from my mouth from where I had bitten my lip.

My brain wasn't even bothering to conjure images this time, choosing instead to present me with a blank nothingness deep enough to drive a bus into.

Defeated, I pulled the pail up from under the sink and poured water over my bloodied hands. I squeezed out a couple pieces of glass from my fingers and flipped my lip over to inspect the cut there.

There was something in my mouth.

I spat blood into the sink and opened my mouth, leaning in close to the shard of mirror. There was a small black dot on the inside of my bottom lip.

I flicked through the pointed pieces of mirror in the sink, pulled out a large piece and held it close to my face. I walked into the bedroom, grabbed my shirt from the back of the bed and wiped away more of the blood from my lip. I stood by the open window to where the light was best and flipped my lip down again with my fingers. It wasn't a dot at all. It was a number, a small, black number '6'. How many times had I looked at this face in the mirror and not seen that?

I pulled my lip down further; there was more. It was an entire line of numbers tattooed in black ink, separated by full stops:

64.22.66.50

I released my lip and stared at my greying face in the shard of mirror, searching the lines and bits of grime for a clue, but the eyes and mouth of my reflection only returned my questions unanswered.

What did it mean? Was it a date, a code? Coordinates of some kind?

I flipped my bottom lip over a second time and there the numbers remained. Sharp and black against the pink.

The doctor could've put them there simply to brand me as a foreigner, but why wouldn't he have told me? Refusing to show me yet another example of his control over me was not his style. He would've loved showing me the tattoo; I could almost hear his hissing laughter.

It couldn't have been the doctor; the numbers were too perfect. Too straight, too symmetrical. The repeating sixes and twos were exactly the same as their twins that came before. Too precise to have been applied with a heated needle. The numbers weren't drawn, they were *plotted*. Numbers like these needed a machine to get right. A *machine*.

I dressed, drank down half the pail of water and left the apartment, my backpack bouncing as I ran down the steps. My bike over my shoulder raised high, the can of WD40 on the dresser remained.

★ ★ ★

I was back in Urmston, digging through another pile with renewed vigour. The rain had stopped, but the red dirt was thick and heavy with water and it wasn't long before I was again covered in muck. This pile wasn't as high or unstable as yesterday's, there were no teetering walls or soggy floors here. Only a mound covered in mud remained where a library once stood.

I was looking for a map. Roads, place names, anything that may look familiar, anything that could point me toward the machine. It was a long shot in the extreme, but I didn't know what else to do. I should have been searching for food, my stomach was in a twist, but this was more important. The urge to leave Manchester was becoming too strong to ignore. A library was as likely to find food as any other pile anyway. Killing two birds with one stone. The meaning of my lip numbers, the machine, the meaning of life could be brought up with the next shovelfull.

Besides, I had the WD40 as a last resort.

I dug quickly and with purpose, unearthing books, old CDs and broken pieces of computers. *Learn to play the Guitar, Living with Bipolar Disease, How to Be a Better Lover.* I tossed them aside, moving quickly down toward what I hoped would be either a staff kitchen or the Geography section.

How to be a better lover. I could've done with a fuck, now that no one mentioned it. With anyone.

In my mind, two of the crusty old cart-pushers I saw walking the tracks a couple weeks ago removed their shirts. The two of them started kissing me, kissing each other. I took a slug of water from my plastic container and flipped through the pages of *How to Be a Better Lover*, hoping for photographs. There were none, only a few water stained drawings of embracing couples. I placed the book in my backpack for closer inspection later.

Did I have a wife somewhere, or even a girlfriend? A child? Children?

I certainly didn't feel like a father. I hadn't a single fatherly inclination that I could think of. My jeans and tshirt were hanging off me, my hair and beard were long, my face filthy. The idea that I could be responsible for a child was ludicrous. Fathers knew they were fathers didn't they? Forgetting your own children couldn't be possible.

I wasn't fatherly at all. I could barely be classed as an adult wandering the streets, struggling to feed and clothe myself. I was like a blind orphan stumbling through a black forest with my arms out. A person could forget a lot of things, but no matter what, he could never forget his children. Surely that's something buried too deep in one's soul; Too ingrained in the blood and balls.

The hole deepened, earth and books gave way to more earth and more books, none of which were even remotely useful. I was mucked up and sweaty and I was starving. A couple more fruitless scoops and I would have to declare defeat and face the murderer with the can.

I picked up the shovel and shoved the blade in with my boot. It clanged sharply, reverberating in my closed fists.

I dropped to my knees and scooped the sodden earth away with my hands. Large, curved oak planks strapped with heavy iron clasps emerged from the mud. Every scavenging mission had brought me something new, but what I was looking at now was different from anything I had found before. The thing at my feet did not belong buried amongst the remains of a destroyed library in the middle of a suburban town centre, it belonged under the sands of a desert island or on the deck of a pirate ship. It was. Well. Well, it was something so bizarre, it needed saying out loud.

"It's a treasure chest."

Excited, I pushed the earth away from the centre until I located the edges. I struck the spade into the earth in front of the chest, and removed a few shovel fulls of earth and debris. Once I made my way down the front, I could see that it was indeed a treasure chest, complete with heavy, iron lock hanging down at the front. It could only have looked more like pirate gold if the lock had been fashioned into the shape of a human skull.

I dug a small trench around the lock to make some room to hit it with the spade. I held the spade aloft, pointing the sharpened end directly at the lock, where shackle met body and brought it down hard.

The rusted lock snapped in two.

I dropped the shovel, removed the lock and pulled up hard on the lid; as hard as I could, but the lid remained as if welded in place. I wedged the spade underneath the lip of the lid and pushed down on the handle, straining against its weight.

The lid creaked open a crack, but the hinges were seized tight. Once I had wedged a big enough space with the shovel, I slipped both hands in and pulled up on the lid stomping down on the bottom lip with my muddy boot. Slowly, the hinges crackled and the lid opened.

Bones.

Useless, disgusting, bones. Ripped clothing and stretched, blackening flesh clung to the folded skeletal body. Thankfully, it was face down.

I had wasted half a day on this chore, half a day I could ill afford. The skeleton didn't climb in himself, judging by the awkward angles at which his legs were bent. The former man before me had been stuffed into the chest. I felt like climbing in myself.

"Ooh, nice bike you have here!"

Hot breath caught in my throat. I looked down at the skeleton hoping the voice had come from him. It hadn't. The voice was big, behind me and very much alive. The lid slipped from my fingers and slammed shut.

"I said, 'nice bike!'" the man shouted a second time.

I turned around slowly, face first with my body following suit. At the bottom of the pile stood a very large, very black, man. He must have been 6'5 and almost as broad as he was tall. A large pink polo shirt stretched tight over his chest. Hard, black arms rippled with muscle erupted from short sleeves and tree trunk-like legs thrust forth from a pair of dusty green combat shorts; the fabric fraying at the edges where they struggled to contain his massive legs. His enormous black head was topped by an even more enormous black afro peppered with grey. In his hands was my bike, my beautiful bike, the one possession I had; my only transportation to the machine. How could I have been so careless?

My backpack was on my back where it was supposed to be, but it felt too light all of a sudden. I ran my hand down the outside feeling for the hard edge. It wasn't there. A cold realisation. The knife was still in the sink.

Outrunning the man was not an option. He looked entirely capable of scaling the pile in one step. He also happened to be holding onto a working bicycle.

As if reading my thoughts, the big man put the bike down and climbed the pile toward me. He didn't climb it in one as I had guessed, but it wasn't far off. Three steps to my six or seven. I staggered back around the oak chest, putting the large box between the man and me.

"I'm Henry," he said, extending his huge hand out to me over the chest.

His lips spread wide over an enormous smile, the wrinkles at his eyes and mouth deepened to make deep trenches in his face. It was a face that had seen too many things and like everyone else in this place, had spent too much time outside.

My eyes were transfixed on the heavy claw he shoved at me. His fingers looked thicker than my wrists.

"Now, what you do is say 'Hi Henry, my name is so and so. I'm pleased to meet you. This is how conversation works."

He could've ripped my arm out at the shoulder if he wanted to, but I had no choice. I extended my hand.

"Seth."

My tiny hand disappeared into his. His hand was hard and calloused, but the grip was soft. He was used to shaking hands with lesser men.

"Seth, eh? Ooh, I've never met a Jew before. What's yer surname? Goldstein or summing?"

He spoke differently to Bill. Where Bill clipped his vowels short, Henry lengthened them and drove the words heavily through his nostrils. I shrugged and retracted my hand. What had the doctor done? If he didn't want me to be known to be foreign, why had he given me such a name? I had no idea what a Jew was but I hoped to hell this big man liked Jews.

"What have you got there?" Henry asked, pointing at the chest.

I shrugged again.

"Lemme guess, dead body?" He grasped the lid in one hand and flipped it open. The muscles in his forearm flexed through his skin smoothly as if powered by hydraulics. They weren't arms, they were steel girders covered in muscle.

"Bingo!"

How had he known about the body? The box looked nothing like a coffin. Could Henry be the man who'd stuffed him in?

"Uh, yeah," I said shuffling around the chest creating maximum distance between us.

"Wayhey, she speaks!" Henry laughed. His laugh was friendly and surprisingly high-pitched for a man of his size and age. "Find 'em all the time, mate, stuffed in all kinds of places. I found one the other day smooshed into a beer keg. A flipping beer keg, can you believe that? I reckon he climbed in himself. Not a bad way to go if you ask me. Better than being eaten, eh?"

Eaten. I backed slowly out of the hole.

"You forgot the bloody wedding ring, ya dick!" Henry said pointing into the hole. "You're not very good at this scavenging lark are you?"

He reached in with both hands and snatched the ribcage, spine and pelvis out of the wooden box in one. The bones crunched and snapped like dry twigs. The skull plonked into the bottom and rolled over. Half of the face was there, the eyeballs and lips, black, rotten and dry. He tossed the spine aside and thrust his hand back in, this time pulling out an arm. Leathered skin stretched across the thick knuckles of the hand hanging limp off the end of the arm. A large gold ring dangled off the deflated third finger, threatening to drop.

"Fuh-lipping eck, it's got a bloody diamond in it!" Henry said, holding the stinking hand, arm and all, close to his face. He laughed again.

His laugh really was like a little girl's; it could have been Lucy laughing. It was infectious. For a moment I forgot myself and had to stop myself from grinning.

His smile disappeared and the danger snapped sharply back into focus as Henry cracked the bony finger in two and pulled it clear of the hand, the dried flesh giving little resistance.

The ring slid off the now severed finger into Henry's waiting palm. He tossed the arm away and slipped the ring onto his own pinky finger, it came to an abrupt halt at the first knuckle.

"Oh he-eLO!, lager shandy please!" he said bending his wrist daintily and wiggling his fingers. "What kind of softie has a diamond in his wedding ring? No wonder he was stuffed into a trunk."

Henry bent over and rummaged through the trunk. My bike was behind him, perhaps I could just get around–

He popped back up holding the skeleton's leg, foot and all. "Man, he was a fat bastard. His knees are a mess!" Thick, blackened flesh and pieces of black cloth hung off the leg. His skeletal knee looked the same as the hundreds of other skeletal knees I had seen scattered about. Henry's expertise on the human body did little to calm my nerves.

"Diamond wedding ring, pin-striped suit, fat arse. He's a solicitor. Defo a solicitor! Puts a smile on your face to see 'im rotting in a trunk, don't it?"

He was looking for an answer from me. I had no idea what to say, but I needed to say something.

"'He' you said? How can you tell it it's a man?" I was stammering.

"Easy, mate, his cock is right there at the bottom".

I looked after his pointing finger into the trunk.

Henry fell over onto his back clutching his stomach, laughing hard, in loud childish *HEE HEE HEE's*. I felt my cheeks flush.

"Oh mate, that was good." Henry said, wiping his eyes and standing. "Here," He tossed the ring to me. "You want to hold on to that one."

I caught the ring.

"What good is this?" I asked.

Henry laughed again, "Fuh-lipping heck, mate, how have you survived this long? No wonder your skinny arse looks a shit and a half away from St Peter's gate." He shot an arm toward me, it landed around my shoulders before I had a chance to move.

"Come on, mate, I'll let you buy me a drink."

Henry's grasp was friendly and welcoming. His arm weighed heavy and warm on my shoulders. I knew there was a very good chance I was walking to my death, but fuck it. If there was one thing I needed, it was a drink.

Nine

Henry led me back into town; he walked while I pushed my bike. The sky was brightening and clouds strafed swiftly across the sky. The sun poked through the clouds at intervals throwing rolling shadows over the buildings and trees. We walked for hours. We walked the main road out of Urmston, down the large freeway and through town, Henry gabbing the whole way. He talked in a steady stream which suited me just fine; the more he talked, the less I'd have to. The afternoon air was still cool from the morning's showers and the wind blew softly, drying my clothes. I brushed the worst of the mud off my arms and shirt as I walked and Henry talked.

My lips were dry and hunger clawed at my insides, but I stayed with the man. I took another pull on the water in a feeble attempt at fooling my stomach into thinking it was full. Henry helped himself to it without asking, replacing the bottle into my hand with only a few drops at the bottom; the air empty of his voice for only as long as it took for him to stop drinking. Bill's place was open for a few more hours yet, judging by the sun in the sky; I would see how the day would play out with Henry. The image of Bill slicing the woman's throat imposed itself on my thoughts. I was in no hurry to see him; I would see where Henry was taking me. As long as it didn't take much longer.

Henry played tour guide as we walked, pointing out the small wheat fields he'd planted in front of two large brick office towers. Growing wheat was easy in the city centre. It was always hotter in the centre than in the outlying hills; the huge buildings held the heat and broke up the wind. He'd set up an irrigation system pulling water from the eaves of the buildings. The topsoil wasn't brilliant, as much of it had been buried under asphalt and cobbles for centuries, but it was manageable. "The key is knowing that the wheat *wants* to grow," Henry said.

Other people tended crops and even livestock in the city centre as well. Henry showed me a private garden hidden behind an old art gallery that housed pigs and chickens. He pointed up to the greenery growing from the rooftops of the four and five story shops. When I'd first seen them in the days after my interrogation, I'd assumed they had grown naturally. On closer inspection, I could now see that the leaves were different from the plants on the ground and many plants were strapped to willow branches and bamboo poles. 'Allotments' Henry called them. The word itself had no meaning, but listening to Henry, I understood it to mean places to grow food. There were dozens of people in town I could see now. A flash of a hand behind a window, A shovel arcing through the air on top of an old record store. The people weren't exactly hiding, but they weren't advertising their presence either. I couldn't believe I hadn't seen any of them before.

We walked through the city centre and down a long, straight road past huge Gothic buildings and square modern apartment blocks of the former university. Like every other building, these were in various states of decay. Smashed windows with fire-blackened sills.

A small fir tree was growing out of the middle of the street, the asphalt peeled back from its base. Henry had no idea how the trees had made their way under the asphalt; he assumed some 'nobhead' was planting them. Trees were not Henry's thing, no; the big man was into cars. He had names for all the wrecked cars on the road: Renault Megane, Peugeot 307, Ford Transit; it didn't matter how burned or rusted out they were he knew every single make and model. "Limited slip diff. Only available on the '14 model, that's how you can tell," he'd say proudly or "those alloys are aftermarket. Why would someone do that? Tacky, that is."

He grabbed me by the arm and pointed at a pile of rusted metal down an alleyway, "You see that one?"

I nodded.

"Bugatti Veyron. Fastest production car ever built. Only 200 of 'em and no one round 'ere owned one. What's it doing there? No one knows. Beautiful car that was, I've got the badge at home, I—"

"Zero to sixty in two point four seconds," I said. So much for keeping quiet.

"Top speed two hundred and fifty three point eight miles per hour. Eight litre, Sixteen cylinder, quad turbochargers, single overhead cam." The words tumbled out of my mouth like rocks off a cliff.

Henry laughed his girlish laugh and patted me on the shoulder, almost snapping it in two. "You see, I just knew we'd get on!"

Turbochargers and overhead cams I was good at. Children, family and lip tattoos? Basic human survival techniques? My expertise in the top speed of a German supercar was so terribly, so monstrously pointless.

Henry tugged my arm again and pointed at a burned out double decker bus. "That's the 15 there. Would've taken you up to your dead Urmston mate with the fruity ring. That one ran long into the Darkening. Many of the drivers kept going despite the collapse of the bus companies, didn't know what else to do but drive the buses I guess".

Henry used the term "Darkening" just like the doctor did.

"What?" he asked. I was staring at him.

"You said the 'Darkening'"

Henry stopped walking. "Yeah?"

"Oh, I just. It's just that I heard someone else use that term the other day."

Henry laughed again. "Did you hit yourself on the head with that shovel? Everybody calls it that."

I forced a laugh. "Oh, yeah. Sorry I didn't realise."

"Mate, you're a funny one," he said and started walking again. And talking.

It wasn't just cars, bus routes and wheat fields that took Henry's fancy. Henry knew *everything*, or at least he seemed to. "That's the studio where Corrie was shot", "That building housed a first edition of Origin of the Species", "That place did a lovely chip butty". His voice had a sweet, complex bassoon-like tone. It pitched smoothly up and down like an ocean liner on a wavy sea. It was hypnotising. He could be saying, "And now, I'm going to slowly slide this shiv into your ribcage," and you would just grin and nod. Oh, go on, then. His smile and humour coupled with his disarming laugh made it impossible not to like him. Besides, if the big man was going to hurt me, there was little I could do about it.

Henry would know things I needed to know as well. He would know what the world outside the city was like, the origins of the Darkening. And he enjoyed talking. All things that made him a good person to know;

a useful person. I would spend the rest of our walk lining my questions in a tidy row, ready to be asked in the right order. The road ahead seemed to be coming to an end, our destination could not be far. Tonight, I would have some answers to my questions from this man, or I would be killed. Either way, things would be better than they were at that moment.

The university buildings gave way to more blackened, smashed shop fronts, large redbrick museums and overgrown parks. The grass and weeds were shoulder high and wild late summer flowers interrupted the green of the grass with splashes of reds and blues.

"They used to call that bit *The Curry Mile*," Henry said and pointed down the street toward a line of what used to be free standing buildings but were now little more than piles of snapped timber and ever more brick. Shattered glass, twisted iron and endless rows of smashed neon signs was all that was left. Most buildings had been razed to the ground. "Raj keeps his pub open here out of spite," Henry said, "to respect his *Indian ancestors*," he mimed camply, like he had told me whom or what 'Raj' referred to. Which he hadn't.

"Bloody stubborn bastard, there are much better buildings; much more *convenient* buildings in the centre of town. He's a right pain in the arse if you ask me. Whoops, watch out!"

Henry reached down and picked up a large, rusted wheel axle in my path. It was enormous, one from a bus or a semi trailer. "You see what I mean?" he said holding up the twisted piece of metal. "That could've taken your foot off. Why would any bugger choose to operate down here? Bloody Curry Mile, it'd be easier walking through hot coals."

A winding, makeshift path had been carved through the oxidised metal hulks and busted building material. Henry tossed the axle into the rubble, his huge neck and back muscles flexing through his polo shirt. "You may want to leave the bike here, you'll get a puncture wheeling it any further."

I picked the bike up, hooked the frame over my shoulder and kept walking.

"Mate, if I was going to nick it, I'd have punched your head off and taken it when I first saw ya," he said, smiling.

"I'd just rather not leave it out if that's ok. It's not heavy."

"D'you know how many people come down here? Fuh-lippin none, that's how many." Henry scratched at the back of his afro and shook his head, "You're as bad as Raj, you are."

We followed the path as it snaked through the debris, Henry tossing more rusted hunks of metal and plastic off the path back onto the piles of rubbish.

The place was a disaster zone. I couldn't believe we'd find a standing structure at all, let alone one trading as a pub.

The path turned right onto the pavement and ended at another massive heap of rubble. Henry looked at me and shook his head a second time before reaching toward a white, painted door seemingly attached directly to the pile of junk. The door stuck at first, but the big man rattled it until it popped open with a crack and a loud wheeze from the hinges. "The man is half mule, I tell thee."

He held the door open and motioned me to go in first.

I hesitated. I had known while we were walking that the moment would come when I would have to walk through a door on his command. If my empty life was going to become more bearable, if I was going to fill in some of the gaps in my brain, in this world, I knew I would have to trust him. But now that we'd reached our destination, now that I was staring the decision in the face, I wasn't so sure I wanted to know anymore.

"Will you get in there for criminey's sake? Fuh-lippin eck."

Henry's hand was on my back before I could protest and he shuffled me inside bike and all.

Henry closed the door mumbling something to himself. I turned back, toward him and he made a frustrated flicking movement with his hand, directing me forward. There was no turning back now.

The inside of the pub was nothing like the outside. Huge candles in long, wrought iron holders rose up from the floor to cast warm light on dark walls of grained wood. The windows were boarded up and mismatched tables were scattered about the room surrounded by antique wooden chairs, metal bar stools and plastic lawn chairs. Intricately woven grass tablecloths trimmed in red silk were placed precisely on the tables and screwed up pieces of paper were stuffed underneath many of the table legs to keep them level. The room was perfumed with smells of burning beeswax, fried onion, and herbs.

"No bicycles in here!" A small, brown man waved his arms at me from behind a large bar. His wavy white hair with bushy white eyebrows and moustache made for a striking contrast with his dark skin. He looked elderly but without weakness. He was wearing a white, collared shirt rolled up to his elbows exposing deep brown arms, the skin sagging and loose in places, streaked with wisps of white hair. Gold rings adorned all ten of his arthritic fingers and several gold bangles wrapped both wrists, clinking as he clamoured.

"Leave it out, Raj, he's with me," Henry said.

Raj shook his head and tutted, "No, no no my friend. I'm trying to run a respectable pub here. Does this look like some ruddy bike shop?"

"Mate, have you seen this place? It's a bad day in Chernobyl on the other side of that door. What difference is a flipping bike going to make?"

"That may be the case, but in here, No. Bikes. Would you like it if I came over to your house and had a uh… a *dump* in your sock drawer?"

Henry rolled his eyes and grabbed my elbow, turning me back toward the door. "Fine, we'll go then. C'mon Seth." There was a kitchen in that place somewhere and the smell coming from it was intoxicating. Something in that place was being *cooked*. Something wonderful. I couldn't leave that place.

Before I could stop Henry, Raj came skittering out from behind the bar and grabbed us both by our shirts, "Fine, fine, bikes allowed for today only."

And to Henry, "You are a right pain in the arse, you know that?"

"Yeah, I know," said Henry, winking.

Raj led us past the tables toward the bar. He really was small, his head only came up past my waist. There must be a box on the other side for him to stand on.

The restaurant was empty except for a young man sitting in the corner stuffing his face with a plate full of perfumed food. His large purple hat was on the table and his cape hung loosely around his body.

The man from the town centre.

The cape was frayed and torn at the tips and the velvet was worn away in patches. An old shoelace held the cape to his neck, tied in a bow. Under his cape, he was wearing a skin-tight purple shirt, tatty purple tights and large black boots with shiny buckles. Wild wisps of blonde hair puffed out over his ears and matted across the top of his bald head. The balding head and the windburned face attempted to camouflage a youthfulness, but his soft eyes and lips gave him away as a teenager. He chomped away loudly. Rice was everywhere; on the table, on his face, he'd even let some drop onto the floor. How could he be so frivolous? As usual, he ignored me as we passed, pausing only to push a pair of thick, taped–up spectacles up his nose between mouthfuls. Licking the floor where the rice had fallen seemed like a perfectly reasonable thing to do.

"Hey, who is that man?" I asked Henry.

Henry shook his head. "Dunno. He's said maybe three words to me in the whole time I've known him. I don't even know his name."

"What were the three words?"

"Eh?"

"The three words. What were the three words he said to you?"

"I don't know, do I? It's just an expression innit." He then leaned in close and whispered. "I think he's a bit 'special'."

I looked back at the boy again. He was tipping the plate up now and dumping the food into his mouth. And onto his lap. If he'd heard Henry's insult, he didn't show any sign of it. My stomach twisted painfully at the sight of the boy eating and saliva bubbled up to my lips. I could not leave this place without eating.

Henry again pushed me toward the bar and to Raj. I leaned the bike up against a table and took one of the stools, keeping one eye on the eating boy. Henry sat down and began drumming the bar top with his beefy hands.

He leaned in close while Raj circled the bar. "Raj took over this place during the Darkening," he whispered. "Many people died trying to take it from him. Don't let his diminutive size fool you, he is no one to mess with."

God, who wasn't?

Henry leaned back and stretched. "Before Raj, this used to be a proper muslim place. No booze, no pork. In't that right, Raj?"

"How the hell should I know?" Raj replied.

Henry continued. "Raj relaxed the rules somewhat after the Darkening. In fact, this is one of only two or three places you can get a proper beer in Manchester. That's irony, that is."

"It's not irony at all," Raj answered. "I am not Muslim, you thick black bastard. How many times do I have to tell you this?"

Henry batted a hand at him.

The red trim on the tablemats was echoed in red painted wood trim on the bar, skirting boards and cornices. The bar was even bigger up close, extending across the entire width of the room. It was ornately carved and well oiled. Raj started wiping the top in slow circles. All manner of bottle and coloured liquid lined the wall behind him. The bottles reminded me of the bottles in the torture room. I placed my hands in my lap; they were shaking with hunger. I needed to find a way to get this man to give me some food and I needed to do it quickly.

"Oi. That beer isn't going to pour itself, chop chop!" Henry shouted.

"Account's overdue," Raj said, shrugging at Henry and continuing to wipe the top of the bar.

Henry wiggled his ring finger at me and nodded toward Raj.

I pulled the ring out of my pocket and held it out to the little man.

Raj stopped wiping, took the ring from my outstretched palm and held it up to a lit candle behind the bar. After a moment of examination, he held it back to me. "Worthless," he said.

Henry scoffed. "Who do you think you're talking to? That diamond is the biggest thing this side of Nagasaki and don't think I didn't see the '999' engraved into the band."

Raj sneered and pulled a small magnifying glass out of his back pocket. He looked at the ring again through the glass, turning it over once.

"Four dinners, six beers."

Four meals? *and beer?* All those gold trinkets I'd tossed aside in my digging! Bracelets, necklaces, earrings, I had found them all. The nights of eating anything I could scrounge, the bitter nuts off trees and berries off hedgerows. A fruitless day's search finished by a night of being sick or lying awake so hungry thinking I would die.

Four full, cooked meals. I could scarcely imagine such a thing.

"No chance mate!" Henry said. "That ring makes the other ones on your fingers look like children's toys."

I grabbed Henry's arm to stop him from ruining things. The big man flicked a hand at me off like I was a wasp going for his beer.

"I've seen plenty of rings like this!" Raj snapped. "I've got a drawer full of them at home. Better than this one! They're ten a penny these days. Fifty a penny!"

Henry folded his massive arms and raised his eyebrows at Raj. Raj looked at the ring through the magnifying glass again.

"Ok, because you're a good customer, six dinners, six beers."

Six dinners? A *week's* worth of food. More. Depending on how big the plates were, it could be possible to stretch that out for a month.

"I think—"

Henry shushed me and looked back at Raj. "Now you listen to me, my little Muslim friend. I've brought jewellery in 'ere for flipping years and that is the finest ring I've ever seen."

Raj raised a finger to protest. Henry carried on speaking, louder.

"Which means it is the finest ring *you* have ever seen. Twenty-four karat. Even I know what that means. Pure gold, that is. One hundred percent."

"Big deal!" Raj said, bunching his face up and folding his arms.

"You will give my Jewish friend here eight curries and twelve beers, you'll give me five and five and you'll forgive my current outstandings."

Henry winked at me. "Call it my commission."

He could have all of it if he wanted! At that point, I would have been happy with licking the bar for whatever dropped from his plate. I didn't care if the curry was made from roasted rat with a side of cat's heads. The spicy, earthy smell in the room was murder. I didn't speak, I didn't hardly breathe. A few moments passed before I realised my mouth was gaping open. I closed it with a snap and swallowed.

"Ha! You've been drinking pond water, black man and it's gone straight to your head. No, it's worse than that. You have finally gone completely batshit."

Henry snatched the ring back from Raj. "Fine, we'll go somewhere else. I'm sure Dotty will love this, she'll give us enough veg to make hundreds of our own curries. Or Bill. I think I'm more in the mood for pizza anyway, isn't that right Seth?"

Yes, that was just what I needed; a confrontation with a man mountain and a murderer. "Actually—"

"Of course you would. Let's go." He bullied me out of my seat by my shoulder. I moved to speak, but Henry would have none of it, instead turning me toward the door like I was made of paper.

"Alright! seven and ten for him and four and four for you," Raj said.

"And my bill?"

"You're dreaming, mate! You are already into me for a couple suppers."

"Okay then," he said turning away again.

"My holy god, you're a horrible black bastard! Fine! Give me the bloody thing."

Henry smiled wide and shook Raj's hand, placing the ring in his small palm as he shook. "Pleasure as always, Rajinder."

"Go fuck yourself," Raj said, scowling. He placed the ring over his thumb and twiddled it, trying unsuccessfully to stifle a smile.

Henry spoke again. "I believe I'll have one of my curries right now, and this skinny beggar needs two, I reckon."

Raj stuck his head into a doorway behind the bar and shouted, "Oi Dave! three curries. And spit in one of them!"

He hopped back up on the box, pumped the wooden tap up and down filling two glass mugs with foaming gold-green liquid and placed them in front of me and Henry.

What had just transpired? Was I actually going to eat for weeks and drink *beer*? An actual proper beer? I felt like crying.

The mug vanished into Henry's hand as he held it up. "It's not going to drink itself," he said.

I picked up my glass and cheersed him, tapping my glass against the thick fingers surrounding his mug. He tipped his back and emptied it in one. I was not going to do that, I was going to savour it. I brought the glass to my lips and took a gulp. The bubbly liquid trickled down my throat. It was fizzy, very strong and had more than a little hint of something leafy to it. It triggered something feral deep within my gut. I poured the contents down my throat despite myself allowing it to overflow and run down my cheeks. I closed my eyes to block out all distraction. My stomach welcomed the bubbly liquid warmly. The beer was beautiful and I could feel it immediately start work on my head. I didn't know what hidden agendas these two men were hiding, but I no longer cared.

The locals don't like foreigners.

They could kill me as long as it was after I finished my beer and food; I would even show them where to stick the knife. Talking to them could leave me open to being tricked or hurt, but I was so tired of having only my own cracked thoughts for company. If this was to be my last night on earth, I was going to enjoy it.

Henry, as if reading my mind a second time, plonked his empty mug back onto the bar. "Right, so who are you then?"

I choked on my beer, coughing a good glug of it back into the glass. So they weren't going to let me finish eating first.

Henry patted me on the back, "Ooh, sounds like a good story."

"Not really," I lied. I caught my breath and placed my glass back on the bar. "It's as boring as yours I imagine."

"Oh yeah?" Henry said. "We'll see about that."

I tipped the rest of the beer down my throat and placed my glass on the bar.

"Well, go on then," Henry said.

"My family and I had a farm in Derbyshire," I said, remembering the story the doctor had given me. "Cattle, chickens, that sort of thing."

Henry smiled and grabbed my wrists, turning them both over to expose my palms and fingertips. "Mate, if you're a farmer, I'm Margaret Thatcher."

I didn't say anything. I couldn't say anything.

"You've got prettier hands than Raj's missus. And those are some pretty hands, I tell thee."

Raj rolled his eyes and started wiping down the bottles behind the bar with an old rag.

Henry released one wrist and dragged his fingers across the top of my other hand. His fingers were like cold stone; like volcanic rock. "What d'you... keep these in cotton wool or summing?"

I had thought my hands had toughened up, I'd been working that shovel for weeks. I'd spent many a night soaking the cuts in water and peeling off blisters. But Henry was right, compared to his, mine looked brand new, fresh out of their wrappers. Even compared with little Raj's ragged paws they looked puny and soft. I pulled my hands away, scrambling for an answer. "We had machinery that took care of most of the hard work, my hands–"

I was interrupted by Henry's laughter.

"Fuh-lipping machinery?!" Henry bellowed. "What kind of *machinery* did you have?"

"You know, tractors. Combine–"

Henry laughed again, "A combine flipping harvester?"

His mouth snapped open overwide like it was hinged. And he howled. His stuttering girlish laugh morphed into deep wheezy barks. The big man squirmed on his stool penduluming back and forth, holding his stomach like it would burst.

The lie sounded ridiculous even to me. Why did the doctor think that would work? The answer was obvious. He didn't think it would work, he never did. He wanted me to be killed by the locals. The foreign name, the ridiculous Derbyshire farm story. This must have been his plan the whole time, let the locals do his dirty work.

The door was a good fifty feet away, if I jumped on my bike and ped-alled for it, I could just make it. I stood up off the stool.

"Oh, mate," Henry collected himself, his laugh petering off, "That was good. Hey, where are you going? you haven't had your food yet!" Was his tone getting darker? I had to get out of there.

"Maybe I'll collect my curries tomorrow. I should really–"

"Nonsense!" Henry said. "Mate, if you don't want to tell us, you don't have to."

I looked at the two men for a moment, weighing my options.

"Oh mate, give over! I couldn't give a toss anyway, just making con-versation. Sit down, willya?"

I looked at the door again.

"We've only just started drinking for god's sake!"

Raj had a green bottle in his hand, screwing a rag around the top and blowing off the non-existent dust.

After a few moments, he put down the bottle, re-filled my mug and plonked it down in front of me.

"You see?" Henry said. "Even crusty old Raj wants you to stay."

Outside that door was my cold and lonely apartment. The yellow glow from the candles coupled with Henry's huge grin gave the impression of a great warmth in the room. My stomach was empty, my life was empty. Even if my memories somehow magically returned, what then? Was the doctor going to reward my sharing of my life story or of a machine that was probably destroyed with keys to some untouched Kingdom? At best, he'd give me a one way ticket back to America. At worst, well I didn't want to think about that. No matter how things turned out, there was one universal truth to face: I could not go on alone.

I sat back down. "That one counts as half," I said pointing at my mug. "There was still beer in it."

Raj scowled again.

Henry laughed and slapped me on the shoulder. "Ha! Now we're talking!"

We drank long into the night. I wolfed down both of my curries, a spicy one with chicken and a mild spinach and potato. They probably weren't my first curries, but if I could remember the other curries I'd eaten, those two would not have been as special. As far as I knew, the food Raj served was the finest thing that had ever passed my lips. There were advantages to starting from scratch. That night, I revelled in my own ignorance. Everything I touched and tasted in this world was new. My memories were still missing, but so were my past transgressions. I had nothing to compare this life with and took some comfort in that. I hadn't a chance to reflect on it before now; I'd been too busy surviving. Now that the surviving was taken care of, at least for a little while, I could relax a bit. Not too much, of course, but a little.

I certainly had no intention of telling them everything, so when I heard the words coming out of my own mouth, I was surprised. I didn't have to tell these men anything. Henry had already let me off the hook. I could've sat there and quietly drank my beer, wrapped myself in the warm intoxication the liquid brought and lost myself in the smells of Raj's place and the sound of Henry's voice. But I didn't. I told them everything. I told them about my first meeting with Bill and how the pizza man had saved my life, the isolation and terrible loneliness of not being able to speak to anyone, the dreams of a woman's touch. I told them of the doctor's torture and the demented visions of a machine that made human beings. Henry sat wide-eyed, listening. It must have been the longest the big man had ever sat still and quiet. Raj stood stone-faced as well, filling my glass every time I'd emptied it. That wasn't to say it was the drink that had me talking, no, I told them everything simply for the sake of telling them everything. For the sake of sharing private things with other people. For the sake of hearing my own voice out loud. As I spoke, a great weight lifted, an apparition, a transparent poison escaped out through the top of my head leaving behind a shiny new man as pure as the day I was born; unshackled and unburdened. I laid everything out for them; I even showed them the tattooed numbers on my lip. The room grew ever more comfortable and soft, its heavy warmth soaked into my cheeks and fingertips.

And when I finished laying my soul bare to these two scary locals, these two *survivors*, I half-expected to be killed. All it took was some food and a couple beers and they'd gotten everything they wanted from me. Everything and more.

But they didn't kill me. They didn't hit me with hammers or slice my skin like the doctor did. They didn't hurt me at all and they didn't probe me for more information. They believed me. You could see it in their faces. They knew I had told them everything and that everything I had told them was true. They didn't doubt a word of it. Who could make up such a thing? They both simply stared, silently, mouths agape, trying to process what they'd just been told.

Henry rewarded my honesty with a story of his own. The story of his last day before the Darkening visited him.

Ten

Henry sat in front of the television in his parents living room. The lights were dimmed, his hands were outstretched and his pudgy fists were clenched and rotating around and over each other as if he was holding an unseen steering wheel. His chair swerved back and forth smoothly in tune with the movements of his hands, the hydraulic cylinders under the chair pumped up and down, sloshing him around like an overfull water balloon. Hard techno intermingled with automatic gunfire pumped out of the enormous speakers dotted around the room and from the chair itself. Flashing white light reflected in the pair of 3D goggles that were strapped to his bloated face, hiding his eyes. Green numbers arose from the console displaying his heart rate and breathing on holographic digital readouts.

A navy Yankees cap was perched on top of his head pushing the dark black curls of an afro out the sides and back of his head. Greasy black spots bulleted his swollen cheeks and his t-shirt clung tightly to his marshmallow body, emphasising the rolls of his stomach and tits. Swollen blobs of stretch-marked flesh flowed out over the top of a pair of black trackies. His legs splayed out across the chair like a turkey ready to be dressed.

While turning the floating steering wheel, he flicked his fingers twice as if pulling a pair of gun triggers. The room filled with the sounds of laser pulses, explosions and assorted splattering.

"Yes! Fucking take that you alien faggot!" he shouted.

He lifted an arm like he was opening a cockpit door and stood up. *Psssht click*. His trackies hung low exposing a pair of striped boxers and the tops of two bulbous mounds that were his arse cheeks.

He reached down to his side, clenched his fist, lifted his arm to his chest level and gave his wrist a flick. *Pssssht vwoom.* A green beam of light emerged from his hands.

"Fucking come on!"

He stepped forward, lifted the light sword above his head and brought it down quickly and with great force. *Vwoo Wooom kraack!* A wild inhuman scream followed by a sickening *splat-thud* engulfed the room.

"The empire is mine!" Henry shouted.

He jumped up and swung his arms around madly, spinning, shouting and kicking the air. "Fuck yes!" *crack!* "Eat this!" *krak-squish!* "Alien wanker!" *Vwoom vwoom splat thud!*

He swung the light sword up over his head, twirled it, and hammered it down again into an alien corpse that existed only in his goggles. His t-shirt climbed up over his jiggling belly as he moved.

Jumping and spinning in the air, he barrelled the light sword around his back. "Ha!" *splat!* falling back to earth with a bang and rolling around on the ground. A roar filled the room and Henry jumped back to his feet arcing the light sword up. In his glasses, a three-armed alien was sliced in two. "Yeeeeeeees!"

As he stood celebrating his battle win, his trackies fell to the floor exposing himself.

The light sword disappeared and the lights in the room brightened.

"Game stopped due to unsafe heart rate," A female voice said sharply.

"What?!" Henry shouted, his trackies still around his ankles.

He wrenched off the goggles and threw them at the console. They connected with a crack. He stepped toward the console, tripped on his trousers and tumbled to the floor with a clatter.

Winded, he rolled onto his back clutching his groin and gasping for air. "Stupid... Fucking..."

Slowly, he collected himself; first sitting up, then standing, wheezing and holding his crotch with both hands.

He pulled his trousers up and kicked the console. Stupid fucking thing. It was only a plain GForce, all his mates at school had the GForceX. The GForceX could be modded to circumvent the heart monitor. It was embarrassing.

The boys at school weren't actually his mates, Henry knew this. How could they be? They were beneath him. Jealousy was an ugly thing. He had everything; the fastest bike, the hottest clothes and of course, the coolest trainers; he was the first and still the only one in school with a pair of Apollo thunders. High tops. Old school design with modern flair. Bespoke, one of a kind; the shoe people took moulds of his feet! The four days of waiting he had to endure while they constructed his shoes were torture for him but the looks on the other kids' faces when he walked into class with them on was worth it. They all wished they were Henry then, which made his parent's refusal to buy him a new GForceX all the more insulting.

"Let's see what Father Christmas brings you," his mother had said.

By the time Christmas would come around, there would be something new and the GForceX would be completely pointless. Women did not understand technology.

Henry walked to the sink in the kitchen, ran cold water over a dishrag, walked back into the living room and tossed the rag over the console's heart rate motion sensor. He snapped the goggles back onto his head and kicked the reset button.

A booming voice filled the room. "Get ready, soldier!"

★ ★ ★

"What do you mean, you're grounded?" Henry said into the tiny microphone attached to his goggles. On the other end of the line was his best mate, Trev.

"Mate, you are the biggest pouf I've ever known."

He was back in the chair, this time laying back and watching two young asian women moaning and kissing each other. He moved his hand into his pants and began massaging his crotch.

"So, just sneak out then. How is she going to know? She's a thick scally cunt like you."

The girls turned toward Henry and began unbuttoning the fly of his virtual jeans.

"Holy fuck, have you seen this new Japanese 3D porn thing? It's fucking brilliant. Oh no, of course you haven't, you haven't got a GForce have you? Maybe I'll let you watch it over here one time... not."

The girls pulled down his virtual jeans and began rubbing the mound that stretched the tiny pair of briefs to capacity. Their eyes widened and they both smiled.

"It's so big," the prettier one said.

"Mate, I'm not doing this on me own, am I? C'mon, it'll be ace!"

The prettier girl moved toward the mound, reaching into the underwear. Henry poked the air again, pausing the video.

"Right. I'm coming over. If you're not outside waiting for me in exactly 20 minutes, I'll kick your arse myself."

Henry touched the side of his goggles causing the microphone to retract. He pulled them off his head and tossed them aside.

"I'll see you girls when I get back." He blew a kiss at the screen.

★ ★ ★

Trev was hiding behind a hedge in front of his house when Henry arrived. He was wearing a hoodie that was two sizes too big and a pair of black trackies despite the thirty degree heat; both of which stained and torn. In his hands was a rusty old BMX, with missing spokes and a tyre-less rear wheel. Henry wheeled up on his bike, a Kasasuki Raptor. It sparkled in red, gold and chrome in the sun. Dragonskin tires and grips, stunt pegs, and mag wheels. It could only have looked less like Trev's bike if it were a horse.

"Ah, look who has decided to grow a pair of bollocks," Henry said. Sweat poured off his forehead and down his back, gathering in his armpits, crotch and back of his knees. Every crevice where bloated flesh touched bloated flesh was saturated. He was used to it.

"Keep it down willya? Mum's in, int she?" Trev said, pointing at the house behind him.

"Oh, so I shouldn't shout then!"

"Shhh! Fucking ell mate, you'll get me killed."

"Alright, alright," Henry said lowering his voice. "You are such a little bitch."

The two boys pedalled away from the house down the street. The rim of Trev's back wheel rattled against the asphalt.

"Mate, that bike is a disgrace," Henry said.

Henry put Trev through this every time. If it wasn't his bike, it was his clothes or his house. He knew Trev had to take it, the little scrot had no other friends.

"Maybe I'll give you this one when my Dad buys me a new raptor. This one is old now anyway, I'm almost embarrassed to ride it."

Trev looked up at him, "Really?".

Henry laughed. "Get serious, will you? Do you know how much this bike is worth? Give it to you? On this estate? It'd get nicked before you could say 'teenaged pregnancy'. I'd be better off tossing it in the canal."

Trev's street was rough. He only lived one neighbourhood down from Henry, but the difference couldn't be more pronounced. Blocks of dilapidated flats arranged in quadrangles, intersected and connected to each other by long, potholed streets. Plastic bags and flattened beer tins rolled across the spotty grass and cancerous hedges. Discarded drug needles lie scattered amongst the rusted shopping trolleys and cars in varying states of disrepair. Not even that day's blazing sunlight could improve it, in fact, it made it all the worse. At least when the weather was miserable, the drizzle could be blamed. It was the nicest day of the year and the estate still looked like hell.

"I would rather die than live here, mate," Henry said. "I don't know how you do it. I mean, surely your mum could get back on the game and make a few extra..."

"Shut up, willya!"

Henry laughed. He would have felt guilty for saying that about Trev's mum, but it was true. She was living on the dole. If she had gone back on the game they would have more money. He was simply stating a fact.

"Here, just a sec. Check this." Henry stopped pedalling and reached into his coat. When he pulled his hand back out, he held a revolver. It was heavy, shiny and black.

Trev's eyes widened, "Whoa, where'd you get that?"

"Sources, mate. You don't want to know."

It was his father's gun. Henry had made a habit of going through his father's things, his parents were almost never home. To his father's credit, the gun was locked away in a metal box, he just hadn't realised he had a son capable of picking locks.

"What are you going to do with it?" Trev asked, a mixture of fear and excitement in his voice.

"I'm going to shoot it, dummy, what do you think? Come on."

Henry put the gun back in his coat and pedalled ahead of Trev, bunnyhopping onto the pavement. Trev followed as closely as his bike would allow.

Henry led them through the streets before cycling down a grassy hill toward the outdoor patios of Castlefield. Trev's bike slid sideways down the hill, his legs outstretched, braking with his feet.

The trendy bars were empty and the doors looked locked. Usually on a sunny day like that, the outdoor patios would be heaving with Manchester's beautiful people, laughing and drinking cocktails.

They followed the path down the canal past more posh apartment flats that had been converted from the old factories and mills of the Industrial Revolution. As they cycled down the canal path away from the town centre, the buildings disappeared behind them, replaced by the vacant lots and iron bridges.

Under the third bridge, Henry skidded to a stop. Trev rolled close behind, dragging his feet along the ground. Henry looked at Trev and put a finger of one hand to his lips and pointed at the water with the other. Two large swans floated quietly.

"Here," Henry whispered, handing Trev his smartphone.

"What's this for?"

"Filming, dummy. Just push that button when I tell ya."

"You're not going to shoot them birds are ya?" Trev asked.

"Of course I am. I have a public to entertain don't I? How do you think I got fifty-six thousand followers?"

Trev looked at Henry and back at the swans. The birds floated toward the two boys.

"Look at the stupid things," Henry said. "They're coming toward us!"

Trev looked around nervously. "What if someone sees us?"

"No one will see us. Didn't you see? The pubs are shut. There's no one around for miles. It's almost as if..."

Henry held the gun at his hip and looked around. He was right, the immediate area was bereft of human life. The sun was high in the cloudless sky and the world was completely still. Beer tins, fast food wrappers and leaves floated unmoving in the dark canal water. The canal bisected an industrial area, a factory that made cereal and biscuits loomed high on one side and a collection of storage warehouses were stacked together on the other. All of which should have been buzzing. There was no smoke rising from the tall chimneys, no beeping of reversing forklifts and no shouty cackling from usually ever-present builders. Even the dependable hum of the Chester road traffic had gone AWOL. It was as if they were standing in a vaccuum.

"...As if we were meant to shoot them."

Trev looked down at his shoes and fidgeted, moving from one foot to the other. Henry pulled the gun out of his jacket and pointed it at the approaching birds. The swans were now only a couple arms lengths away.

Trev lowered the smartphone. "Why don't we just go shoot some cans or summing?"

Henry looked back at him, "Oi, keep that camera up. Push the button and quit being such a pussy!"

The swan was at the edge, lifting its beak toward Henry, looking for some attention or a scrap of bread. The swan poked curiously at the gun's barrel as Henry held out straight with both hands.

"Look at the stupid thing. It *wants* me to shoot it."

Trev sniffled, "Mate, don't do it. It's not hurting anything."

Henry ignored him, staring down the barrel of the gun. "What do you think will happen if I–"

The gun went off and kicked backward out of his hands. The swan's head exploded, spraying Henry's face and hands with its blood. Henry fell backward and the gun fell into the grass.

"No!" Trev shouted.

The swans neck flopped back into the water, blood spouting from its neck in a lazy arc.

"Fuck!" Henry shouted, getting back to his feet. He was already wiping the swan's blood from his face. "Stupid fucking bird! You wrecked my shirt!"

The second swan flapped furiously across the water, in an attempt to escape the same fate. Henry picked the gun back up, pointed it and shot several times, the barrel popping and bucking in his hands with each shot. Two spots of red appeared on the bird's wing and it fell out of the air, back into the water as he clicked the gun empty.

Trev screamed and tears streamed down his cheeks. He dropped the phone into the grass, got back onto his bike and pedalled away as fast as he could.

Henry dropped the gun and started wiping the blood off his face. "Fuck sake!"

The second swan twitched and rolled in the reddening canal. Blood bubbled from its mouth as it squawked and flapped, struggling to keep its head above water.

Henry thought about chasing Trev down, but changed his mind when he saw his phone on the ground.

He ran over and inspected the phone as the second swan gurgled as it drowned. The first swan had flipped over onto its back and was now lying limp, its bright orange feet standing straight up in the air.

Henry ignored the dead and dying swans, turning his attention to his phone, brushing off the dust and grass. A long scratch stretched across the back. Fucking Trev. Henry would deal with him later. On the screen was the frozen image of the second bird, its white feathers stained red. He wiped his bloody fingers on his shirt and swished the screen to start the video.

It was brilliant.

Trev had held the camera steady the whole time. He'd even managed to get the second bird as it tried to escape. Henry watched it a couple more times, slowing down the first swan's head as it disintegrated, playing it over and over again.

That evening he would go home, replace the bullets in his father's gun and upload the video; tomorrow he would be an internet God.

As for his bloody clothes, he would simply dump them and tell his parents that scallies in Trev's neighbourhood stole them. He could probably scrub his Apollo Thunders clean, but why bother? They were looking a bit scruffy anyway. He wouldn't be allowed to see Trev anymore, but what did he need the little chav for anyway? By the end of tomorrow, he would have all the friends he would ever need online. If he played it right, perhaps manufacture a tear or two, he would get that GForceX as well. Henry's parents would be horrified when told about the clothing robbery and they would do whatever it took to make their poor son happy.

Unfortunately for Henry, they would never get that chance. Henry would never see his parents again.

Eleven

The broken mirror puked my image back at me.

My hair was long, my beard was filling quickly, what else was new? Red spots and streaks at the edges of my eyes confessed a heavy, sickening awakeness that confessed the slow, empty hours of pacing in front of the living room window looking out into the night hoping for my mind to return and the sun to rise. The wind howled through the tall buildings, over the empty canals and through the corroded iron bridges. I watched the night and let its darkness flow over me. The night wind carried no foul smells like it usually did. On that night it smelled strangely of the sea.

The sky was lightening in the east, the woollen clouds revealed themselves, hanging thick and unmoving across the sky.

A week of digging fruitlessly had passed since my first night with Henry and Raj. Visions of the machine had stopped and I was no closer to discovering the secrets of my lip tattoo.

The ashen light began to illuminate the latest cardboard list on my lap.

Things I know
1. *I am an American living in Manchester*
2. *The year is 2062*
3. *Gold buys food from Raj, cleaning supplies buy pizza from Bill*
4. *Somewhere in England there is a machine that builds humans that I must find before the doctor visits*
5. *The top speed of a Bugatti Veyron is two hundred and fifty three point eight miles an hour*

Things the doctor has told me
1. *The world was destroyed by some sort of "blast"*
2. *My name is Seth*
3. *Bill is a murderer*

With a cracked pencil, I scratched out a third category with a single entry:

Things Henry has told me
1. *The true cause of the end of the world is not known.*

I rolled the list over and over in my head several times trying to squeeze out other pieces of information I may have missed. Was there something else in Henry's story or in the piles of dirt that I'd forgotten?

The items on my list were few and stagnating.

Henry said he hadn't told that story to anyone in years, and it was obvious it was not one he enjoyed telling. The words were difficult for him in parts, especially when he spoke about Trev. The big man spit the words out as if he were still the little, spoiled, fat boy to illustrate his own hatred for his former self. His former world.

When Henry spoke of shooting the swans, I felt nothing. No sympathy for the birds or for Trev and certainly no sympathy for Henry himself. Once it became obvious we were reaching the end of his story and he hadn't told me anything of the Darkening itself, I found myself growing impatient. An impatience that grew even stronger as I sat there in my ratty living room chair, looking at my list.

The thought of again sloshing around the soggy hole over the collapsed library was a depressing one. My muscles ached with the previous day's digging and my head ached with the previous night's drinking. My mouth felt like it was covered in a thick fur.

I found the pail under the bathroom sink and drank long and deep. My tongue soaked in the liquid and expanded like a sponge. After taking in several large glugs, I placed the pail back under the sink and buried my fingers into my temples to keep the pounding blood at bay. My eyes scraped dryly in their sockets and my cold knees cracked as I stepped around the apartment.

In the following evenings spent at Raj's pub, I got little more information about the Darkening from either of them. Riots, protests, some racially motivated, some political.

"Riots because there were no jobs, no food then everyone started getting sick. 's bout it really."

When I asked Henry what had made the people sick, he simply shrugged his shoulders. Raj ignored the question altogether.

I briefly thought about going back to bed, but I was quickly getting through my curries and the day of the doctor's visit was fast approaching. My muscles would get no rest today, today was another day for digging. More bloody digging.

I threw my clothes and boots on and left the apartment.

Outside, the sun burst briefly through the clouds just to pierce my aching brain with its brilliance. I put a hand over my eyes and a second over my mouth and stood still trying not to throw up. A week of drinking Raj's poison was catching up with me.

After a few moments of standing still, swallowing the encroaching bile and breathing in the outside air made me confident enough to remove my hand from my mouth. Clouds closed over the small bit of blue, choking out the sun.

I shook the cobwebs out of my drink-muddled head and surveyed the street in front of my apartment. It was the same horrible street it was every day.

I'd left my bike upstairs.

Christ, maybe it was a day to stay in bed.

"What time do you call this?" Henry asked.

I turned my head to face the voice. Henry was sitting on a bent, steel parking bollard.

I blinked twice and looked again. It was not a hallucination. Big man, massive afro, polo shirt, combat shorts.

"I erm don't know," It was understatement in the extreme. Had I ever known what time it was? I slept when I was tired and woke up when I was finished sleeping. Or in the case of last night, I didn't sleep at all. Time had nothing to do with anything.

"It's bleeding 10.30 or thereabouts. I've put a day's work in already."

Well, good for bloody him.

"I've been waiting here for going on half an hour."

I massaged my temples again and attempted to make sense of what he was saying. Was I supposed to meet him today? Had I even told him where I lived?

"What're you doing here?" I asked. My head was hammering and it felt as though things were crawling around the inside of my stomach. Politeness was going to be hard to muster.

Henry stood up off the bollard and approached me shaking his head, tutting.

"Charming"

His beefy arm dropped around my shoulders like an anchor and he gave my arm a good squeeze like we had been friends for years.

"Let's go find you that map, eh?"

The map. The thing I was digging for over the last week. The thing I was looking for today. I had told him about the machine and about my memory loss and the hope that a map of the city or of the country would help me remember where the machine was or perhaps shine a light on the meaning of my lip tattoo. I remember telling him all these things. What I didn't remember was inviting him.

Before I could speak, Henry shuffled me forward toward the town centre. The train tracks to Urmston were in the opposite direction.

"Urmston's the other—"

"Bollocks to that," he interrupted. "It's Market Day innit?"

On the doctor's advice, I had never dared the market but I had seen the people as they made their way to town along the railway tracks; pushing wheeled carts in front of them and pulling farmyard animals on leashes behind. I watched them pass from my crouched position amongst the weeds.

The locals don't like foreigners.

I had big Henry with me, but I couldn't ignore the fact that he was one of them, one of the locals, despite his big smile and huge embracing arm. And I was well aware of his haggling ability from the interaction at Raj's place. Perhaps "skinned Jew" was worth a pizza or two in trade. Or worse, a Jew sex doll.

Henry's smile lingered on his face and his arm remained latched to my shoulders the entire walk to the town centre. Despite the chill in the air, Henry's arm and his body felt as if they were connected to a furnace. It wasn't long before I was sweating with the heat, but I didn't say anything. The warmth of his body seemed to be curing my hangover and if he wasn't bothered by the smell that was coming off me as a result, then neither was I.

As we walked, he again played tour guide, naming ever more cars and pointing out hidden garden plots within the buildings. An ancient record shop was now an enormous greenhouse and a boarded-up ex-shoe store doubled as an underground music venue. "Bloody hippie music though. First thing I do when the electricity comes back is find an electric guitar."

The market itself was held in a small square of land near the old mall, one of the few places in the city free of rubbish and bones. Henry removed his arm from my shoulders as we approached; and I stumbled as my knees discovered that he'd been holding me up.

The 'market' was comprised of three makeshift, wheeled stalls. On the stalls themselves and spread across tables with folding legs, a mishmash of random items were displayed. Pies with latticed tops, round loaves of bread with dark crusts, old toys, books, jewelry and of course, toothpaste and toiletries. Behind the stalls stood three crusty old women with dour faces, their eyes focussed directly on me.

Bill's place was only a few streets away.

This is what the people of this place are capable of.

Fear pricked me in the back of the neck and my muscles seized. The map was not going to work. I was going to be stuck here in this terrible city with these terrible people forever. Maybe I should be looking forward to the doctor's visit. I took a few steps backward in the direction of my bed, the women eyed my retreat with suspicion.

Henry swivelled on his heel and pulled me forward by the front of my shirt. "Come on, willya? Jesus, you're worse than a woman!"

I grabbed his hand with both of mine and tried to pull away. He released my shirt and allowed his smile to break open his face. "What's the matter with you? You're embarrassing me here." He leaned in close. "You think these women will hurt you?"

I looked over his shoulder at them again. Their eyes were still on me, their expressions unchanged.

"Dot is like a hundred and eighty two years old for flip's sake."

He dropped his arm across my shoulders again and pushed me forward to the stalls toward the cheerless women.

"What pies you got, Dotty?" he asked.

Dotty sat on stool with her arms crossed. She wore a stained tracksuit, striped in red and black and a matching scarf. Long, thinning, white hair was tied back in a ponytail exposing long, looping gold earrings hanging from oversized old-lady ears. Her face was deeply wrinkled and her eyebrows grew long and bushy. Spikes of hard grey whiskers poked out of her chin and ears and enormous breasts flowed over her crossed arms like spreading lava. A small crest was embroidered into her tracksuit jacket and pants, a gold shield with a red devil holding a trident. Two words circled the crest: "Manchester United". She really did look a hundred and eighty two.

She looked up in thought for a moment before dropping her gaze on Henry. Her yellowing eyes moved so slowly you could almost hear them creak.

"Blackberry, Blackberry apple, Apple mint and Apple."

Henry looked the pies over and gave them a sniff.

"Blackberry Apple please love."

Without moving, Dot spoke again.

"Stale or Posh?"

"Depends. What does half a wheatsheaf get me?"

Dot creaked her eyes toward the sky a second time and brought them down.

"Am I getting some actual wheatgrain, or is it going to be all chaff like last time?"

Henry twisted his face up in mock disgust.

"I beg your pardon! You got the best stuff, the wheat closest to the drainpipe ya cheeky cow."

Dot stood unfazed by the insult.

"Coulda built me a straw hut with all that chaff," she said.

"It'd be a darn sight better than that council flat you live in now," Henry said punching me in the elbow and laughing at his own joke.

Dotty's eyebrows furrowed and her horrible eyes were on me. "What are you laughing at?" she asked.

I was standing amongst four locals who had survived an apocalypse. I didn't know who I was or where my family was and I was less than a stone's throw away from a serial murdering pizza maker. If there was one thing I wasn't doing, it was laughing.

"Nothing. I wasn't laughing," I heard myself mutter.

"Leave 'im alone, willya?" Henry said. "You keep talking and maybe you'll get the wheat growing on the east side. Cold shade and rusty drippings is all it ever gets."

Dot left her eyes on me. It was a fierce look that said 'If Henry wasn't here, mate, your ragged flesh would be feeding my ragged cat'. She drew a hand across her face, making a crackling sound as her hand rolled across her hardened whiskers. I looked at Henry again for guidance, but he only stood smiling. Her eyes creaked over my body before resting again on Henry and she breathed a deep sigh before standing. Her tracksuit bottoms matched the tops. Without her arms to prop them up, her breasts fell to waist level and a sleeve climbed up her arm to reveal a patch of purple veins.

"Posh, I guess."

She picked up the best looking pie of the bunch and handed it to Henry.

"Two weeks," she said. "That's five sheafs you owe me now."

"Yeah, yeah," Henry said taking the pie.

Henry gave me a look of surprise like he'd forgotten I was there.

"Oh yeah. You got any maps?"

Dot sat back down and re-crossed her arms. Her eyes squinted and she shrugged.

"You know, a map? Place names, roads, points of interest?"

"Who's it for?" she asked flicking her eyes at me.

"Will you behave yourself? Jesus. It's for me, alright?"

She sat unmoving. Her arms remained crossed.

"You got one or not?"

Dot rolled her eyes skyward a third time, presumably to index the lists of items in her brain. After a few long, wordless moments, her eyes rolled back down.

"Get you one by next Tuesday," she said.

"You may as well get that to us next century for all the good it'll do us. I'll ask Marge instead."

Dot sniffed. "Marge? You'll be lucky to get a half full tin of beans and old penny from that one."

"I heard that!" said the second lady in the stall opposite. That was presumably Marge.

"Good!" shouted Dotty.

Marge was younger and thinner than Dotty, but looked equally as mean. Large, dark eyes punctuated a long, olive-skinned face. Her lips were cracked, but full, and her straight, mouse-coloured hair fell on broad shoulders. Her grey sweatshirt fell heavy and loose, disguising any hint of a breast and the muscled arms that punched out from where the sleeves had been ripped off only further detracted from her femininity. Despite the mannish exterior and the sharpened scowl she was currently showing to me, one would almost describe her as 'pretty'. Certainly by Manchester standards anyway.

I flicked through a pile of books on the table in front of Marge in order to avoid her gaze. Books by Stephen King, Ernest Hemingway and a Japanese name I couldn't pronounce. Murako something.

"This ain't no library, sir," Marge said putting heavy emphasis on the 'sir' and revealing a missing front tooth.

I snapped my hand back. Forget the map, I just wanted to get out of there.

"Hiya Marge," Henry said.

Marge turned to Henry, unfurrowed her brow and slightly relaxed the tenseness in her face. It was probably as close to a smile as Marge got.

"Morning," she said.

"How much for them books?" Henry asked pointing at the books I had touched.

Marge answered with an almost playful shrug.

Henry picked up three of the books in his hand, placed them under his armpit and nodded toward the back of the stall. "And them girly magazines back there," he said.

Marge picked up three magazines and fanned them out. They were beat up and barely legible. What little wasn't torn or worn away was a joy to behold. Women with naked thighs and breasts. Maybe Marge's stall wasn't so bad.

"The middle one," Henry said and Marge held it up. "Yeah, Razzle. Them're the good ones."

She passed the magazine to Henry. "Put it on your tab, shall I?"

Henry turned away without a word. "Let's go," he said to me and began losing himself in the girly magazine.

We were not making our way to the third stall. We appeared to be leaving the market and I realised I would never be coming back here. Certainly not without Henry.

"Shouldn't we ask Marge about a map?" I asked.

"Nah, she ain't got one."

I looked over Henry's shoulder at the third stall. The woman standing there was motioning us over. "What about that other one?" I asked.

Henry continued flicking the pages as he walked. "Who, Jill? Nah. She never has anything good. Besides it would pee Marge and Dot off if I went to her."

Jill was now motioning with both hands pointing to her table madly. I stopped walking.

"She looks like she might have something."

Henry snapped the magazine shut and grabbed me by the arm. "You crazy, mate? Marge'll kill me". He turned me away from the stalls and pushed me out the same way we came in.

"What does Marge care?"

"She hasn't a map ok? Believe me." Henry rolled his eyes and bunched his face up. "Besides, Marge is kinda my girlfriend."

Together we walked down the streets of town toward my apartment. When we hit a large intersection, Henry opened the girly mag back up and began walking away from me toward Raj's. The morning's activities had rejuvenated me. I wasn't exactly looking forward to going back to Urmston, but I felt like I could manage it.

"Do you want to go to Urmston with me to try to find a map?" I asked.

Henry looked up from the mag like I had said the dumbest thing on earth. "What for? You heard Dot. She'll get you one Tuesday."

"Besides, I've got shit to do today," he said holding up the magazine and smiling.

"Oh yeah," he said and walked back to me. He pulled the books out of his armpit and thrust them into my arms almost knocking me over in the process. One book by Stephen King, one by Hemingway and one by a Japanese guy. Murako something.

"Merry Christmas," he said and again buried himself in the mag. "I'll lend you this one when I'm done with it."

"But, I don't have anything to give you for them," I said to the big man.

He ignored me and walked away.

I decided to go to spend the day searching Urmston anyway but, as usual, Henry was right. It was a complete a waste of time.

Twelve

The next morning, a dirty atlas greeted me at my front door, a full four days early. I added one more thing to my list of 'things I knew for sure' along with the machine, the fact that I was American and that I was an idiot. I knew Henry was my friend.

The atlas was perched on the corner of the bathroom sink, opened to a faded map of the Northern England. The pages were puffed up, wavy and water-stained, the spine little more than a hunk of cardboard.

The dictaphone was perched on the corner of the sink opposite the atlas. Lucy was speaking, a tiny voice speaking to me from the past. A voice that had been dormant for decades. She was pretending to accept an award for "Best Singer In The World". A friend was interviewing her, asking her what it was like to win such a prestigious award. The pair giggling in between questions.

I poured over the map looking at the towns surrounding Manchester. There were literally thousands. Bolton, Preston, Stockport, Radcliffe, Farnworth, Heywood, Hyde. I started at Manchester's centre and spiralled my finger outward passing over each town and city in turn, rolling the names over in my head to try to twig a memory into being. It didn't even need to be about the machine anymore, I would take anything. A city that did nice beer, a museum I had patronised, a famous restaurant, an ancient battleground, a familiar landmark of any kind.

I flipped the page over to a blown up view of Manchester city proper. I scanned downward over the street names and subdivisions.

Nothing came to mind. The placenames were as blank and foreign as I was myself. I had told myself that this city would be where I would spend the rest of my days, but I hadn't actually believed it. There was something about the machine that compelled me on. I had been sure the map would point me in the right direction. I'd been wrong.

Before I could spend too much time feeling sorry for myself, Lucy and her friend vanished from the dictaphone. A young woman was speaking.

"Hello Daddy."

My leg jerked, pushing my chair and me clattering into the floor.

"Please if you get this, I had to leave the apartment. I'm sorry, but things are getting too crazy in town. I hope you get this, I am staying with Jo at her parents place until things cool down, they live on Forty-three Spath road…"

I scrambled into the living room, dictaphone in hand, looking for paper and something to write with.

"… it's in West Dids, I think you know where it is. Sorry, what's that?" Another girl's muffled voice in the background, giving directions.

The living room was a mess. I bashed my toe on the coffee table sending screwdrivers and other scavenged junk clattering to the floor.

"Shit!" I took my throbbing toe into my hand and scrunched it tightly in my hand trying to quell the pain.

More muffling as the two women talked about something away from the microphone.

I hopped around the living room on one foot, the other still in my hand.

An old black felt pen sat scattered amongst the rusted tools and bits of metal on the floor, its lid settling in another location. I dived for the pen, crunching an elbow on the coffee table on the way down. I shouted again and punched the floor. This table was going out the fucking window once I was finished with the pen.

The woman's voice was back again.

"… Yeah, ok. It's on the corner of Spath Road and Victoria just past Barlow Moor Road—"

I dragged the pen across the floorboards, the black trail of ink I had expected failed to materialise.

"Goddammit!"

"—you know Daddy by that horrible chippy with the, hm actually you probably don't know it, I'm not sure it was there when you were around."

I shook the pen twice. The batteries would die and the pen won't work. The address will be lost forever! I dragged the pen across the floor again. A small, beautiful, black line squelched onto the hardwood.

I wrote quickly.

43, corner of Spath and Victoria, West Dids, Barlow Moor road, shit chippy.

"God, I don't know why I'm leaving this, you've been gone so long. If you get this, come and find me. I love you Daddy. I'm sorry I had to leave. See you soon."

The Dictaphone went silent.

The older voice was Lucy, I was sure of it. Her voice had gained some age, but it was still one of innocence; one that believed in better times ahead. A pre-Darkening voice. New Lucy must have been at least twenty, Young Lucy, Lucy the child would've been six or seven. In an instant, fifteen years had vapourised. I looked at the black piece of plastic in my hand. "I love you too, baby."

I didn't know this girl; this young woman. It was certainly not my daughter, but I had to see if she was alive. I laid on the floor for a few moments. How would I know where these streets were? I barely knew my own name.

The answer came to me before I could finish the thought. I got up off the floor and clamoured back into the bathroom. I scooped the atlas up off the floor and scoured the streets a second time.

The atlas's main purpose was guiding its reader in between towns and cities; traversing the cities themselves was subordinate to this main function and as a result, the map of Manchester was tiny, taking up only a small corner of the page. If this West Dids place was too small, it wouldn't be shown.

Again, I drew lines across from left to right with my finger one line underneath the other, scanning down.

Swinton, Eccles, Salford, Trafford… Urmston! So that's where I'd been digging. Stretford, Chorlton cum Hardy, Didsbury, Withington…

My dry throat clicked as I swallowed hard.

Didsbury.

That's it, West Didsbury. It was so close to where I'd been digging. While Henry was educating me on the finer points of Manchester's monetary system over the body of a dead lawyer, she could've been just over the way. Talking to her friend. She would be much older now, in fact, she must be close to Raj's age. What was she doing at that moment? Could it be possible that she was still alive? I didn't dare allow my mind to entertain that thought for long.

The residential roads were too small to be listed on my tiny map, I would just have to move West through Didsbury and search it street by street.

I ripped the page out of the atlas, ran back into the bedroom, threw my feet into my boots and wheeled the bike into the hallway and down the stairs.

Outside, the air was flat and dirty but the roads were dry.

I dragged a leg over the bike and pedaled forward one rotation before stopping dead.

A man was watching me from across the street.

His purple hat was perched on his head at an angle and his cape draped over his shoulders as usual but he wasn't shuffling along picking up garbage like he usually did. He was standing, razor straight and unmoving beside a brick building across the street his eyes locked onto me through his spectacles.

My breath caught in my lungs and my legs refused to move, seized like rusted pistons. For a few long moments there was no sound or movement, just the two of us watching each other, neither of which completely sure of what to do. His face didn't disclose any sign of malice, in fact, he looked to be playing with the frayed ends of his cape.

Before I could say anything, he turned and ran away, his cape flapping behind him as he ran.

Into the suburbs I pedaled. Toward Didsbury, pumping my legs hard, wheeling around the potholes and rusted cars and junk, following the map and what street signs I could find to my goal; to my Lucy. What would I say to her? 'Hi, I'm Seth, I found your message to your father. I can't tell you anything because I don't know anything, but hey your little girl tea parties helped me through some tough times?' She would think I was clinically insane. And she'd probably be right.

The man in the purple hat knew where I lived. Scattered about my apartment were things I had gathered and that could be stolen, I supposed, but my three most valuable things were in my pocket, on my back and under my feet. It was unlikely Lucy herself would be at the end of the mission, but I had to know for sure. I was running out of time with the doctor and I needed some sort of stimulation to reignite my deadened mind. If the purple-hatted man wanted to help himself to some old books, rusty screwdrivers or plastic pails, he was welcome to them.

Out of the city centre I cycled, past the unending strips of redbrick terraces and shredded never-ending advertising hoardings, shops and apartment blocks. So many bending streets, so many identical houses of redbrick. How could a man have ever found his own home in the days before the Darkening? People must have started at one end of their street and tried their keys in all the doors making their way along until they found one that fit their key. My task was not going to be as easy as I'd hoped.

Many of the road signs were gone and the ones that were left were faded to the point of being illegible. The street I was on now was called "Princess Road". It looked bigger than Barlow Moor in the atlas, so I hoped I could just keep riding in a straight line until the two roads intersected.

The ruined houses and shops on either side of the road gave way to enormous oak trees and tall, wild hedges spilling into the ancient pavements. Before long, a large intersection was laid out in front of me. Four roads with six lanes each, coming together in a single point. There were no trees in the middle of the intersection, just high grass on all four corners, poking through the cracks in the asphalt. I could see down the road in all four directions, but nothing to mark it as Barlow Moor. The atlas suggested this might be the right road, but how could I've known for sure? The map was too small to be of much help. I took a chance and pedaled down the new road, hoping for the best. If it was the wrong way I could always come back.

I pumped my legs and the bike responded, just like it always did. A cemetery and more houses whizzed past. A road sign was just viewable through a thatch of weeds. I cycled up and pushed the weeds out of the way to reveal enough letters to just make out two words: "Palantine Road". I checked the map, running my finger down Barlow Moor Road until it hit Palantine. I wouldn't need to make my way back to the intersection, I was on the road into West Didsbury.

I tucked the map back into my pocket and soared down Palantine. I wouldn't need it anymore, the roads were too small to be marked. From then on, I could do nothing but cycle down the curved roads, checking street signs on the houses and fences and crossing my fingers.

I passed a number of streets following what signs were still there and retracing my path when I'd gone wrong. Once I was sure a section was covered, I cycled back to the starting point and tried another, checking streets, looking through windows and opening doors. Didsbury town centre, like all the others, was smashed, decrepit and empty.

My stomach was rumbling again.

My scavenging mind wanted to check these houses for more than just Lucy, but there wouldn't be enough time in the day to do both.

I stopped the bike in front of an old hairdressers, pulled the plastic water bottle out of my backpack and drank deeply. A young tree was growing up out of the pavement and through what was left of a skeleton's abdomen. His legs and arms were missing, his neck cricked awkwardly and his deep, questioning eyeholes looked straight up. Chewed flesh hung off the bones and skull in shredded pieces and his leather mouth stretched into a frown exposing rotten teeth. What few of them were left in his head.

Sorry pal, no water for you.

I twisted the lid back onto the bottle and zipped it into my backpack.

The sky was at full greyness, I guessed it was close to midday. I would be able to search another couple sections of Didsbury before the sun went down if I hurried. I pushed my feet down on the pedals and turned down another road identical to the other thousand or so roads I had already searched.

Near the end of road, perched between two houses, sat a building with a small, blue sign swinging from an outstretched iron rod. As I cycled up to it, I could see an image of a smiling, cartoon fish. Beside the fish in scratched blue letters was the name: "Kaptain Kod". It looked horrible enough.

A short, brick wall curled around a small parking lot in front of the building. I rode along the fence looking for a road sign, pushing the weeds away where they grew too thick. In the middle of the fence, a sign appeared behind the weeds near the bottom, half-buried in earth. With my hands, I dug down, again. Digging with my hands had become a daily ritual, I was good at it now. Like some demented badger. The sign made itself known, rusted right through in places, but just enough letters in tact to be readable.

Victoria Road.

I had found it. Lucy's sanctuary was only a few streets away. The *real* Lucy. I rubbed my stubbled chin and let my hand fall down to my chest. In my haste I'd forgotten to put on a shirt.

Oh, what difference did it make? She wasn't not going to be there anyway. What were the odds? How many empty houses had I seen on this ride? How many had I seen in the weeks of scavenging?

Bloody thousands.

Thousands and thousands of houses. And how many people? A couple dozen maybe? I could have cycled here in nothing but my pants and an eyepatch and it wouldn't have mattered. I could have cycled here ball-assed naked.

But there was no harm in looking. After a morning of searching, counting a few more streets wouldn't kill me. Three in total. I pushed the bike forward, moving slowly. Counting.

I didn't need to count the third street because Lucy's friend's house was visible from street two. It was on the corner, and it was immaculate. The copper number 43 was still on the door, green and flaking with age.

On this street of perfect houses, hers was the most striking. All the windows were whole, the wooden trim was painted, even the mortar in between the bricks had been patched up in places. The bushes were trimmed and neat and the grass in the front garden was *mowed*. My skin was electric, my chest and stomach a farm of gooseflesh.

Smoke was rising from the chimney.

I rode up the front drive slowly allowing the thrill of the moment to course through my body. I leaned my bike up against the hedge and tried the door.

It opened with a creak. Surprising, considering it looked brand new.

"Lucy?" I called into the house.

No answer.

The inside of the house was even more orderly than the outside. The floorboards had been recently stained, waxed and covered in colourful rugs. The carpet on the stairs was like new and there was even wallpaper on the walls.

A feeling of dread came over me. Something deep inside pulled at me, urging me to get back on my bike and start pedalling, to get as far away from this place as I could. I could feel a presence in the house and I had no idea what that presence was.

I had to know.

The doorway to my right led to the living room, it couldn't have been more different to my own in town. Matching furniture, heaving bookshelves, even art on the walls. Paintings. An earthen mug sat on top of a dark, unchipped coffee table. Steam was rising from it. A book was stretched open beside the mug. On the cover it read "A Love Long Lost."

"Hold it." A woman's voice demanded from behind, heavy and breathy. A sharp, cold pressure in my side. A knife.

I stopped moving and raised my hands.

"Who are you?" she demanded.

"Seth," I said without hesitation.

There was no sound in the room. I stood without moving and held my breath. I'd made a terrible mistake coming in to the house, I knew better.

After a pause she said, "The American who doesn't speak to anyone."

How did she know that? I turned my head and moved to ask her that very question.

"Shut up," she interrupted and dug the knife into my ribs. I didn't think the blade had cut into my skin, but I couldn't be sure.

I shut up.

"What do you want? Can't you see this house is taken?"

The woman's voice was much deeper than the teenaged Lucy. That could be possible, she would be older now.

"I was looking for someone. I was told a woman named Lucy lived here."

"There's no one here by that name."

There was a chance she was lying to protect herself.

There was a pause for a few awkward moments while we both decided what we wanted from the situation. Had the knife gone slightly slack? I couldn't feel it digging in as much. Either she had let it slip while she assessed the situation or my body was simply getting used to its presence. I could feel my knife in my backpack, tempting me. It would be stupid to go for it, even if this was Lucy, it wouldn't be the Lucy from the dictaphone, it would be Lucy who survived the Darkening. A local. She'd have me skinned and chopped into tiny pieces before I had a chance to turn. In fact, killing me was probably looking like the cleanest solution to her at this point. If not now, it would be soon. I needed to say something.

"Are you sure you don't know her? Perhaps there were photos when you moved in?" I lowered my hand toward my jeans pocket, "I have this recorder—"

"Don't move!" she demanded, re-applying pressure on the knife.

She reached around with her free hand and thrust it into my front pocket. She moved like lightening. I gasped, it had been ages since a woman had been that close to me. That close to *it*.

She retracted the dictaphone from my pocket and clicked the play button.

Lucy's little girl voice flooded the room. Lucy, the teenager had returned to Lucy, the little girl. She and her friend were singing again.

"What is this? You some kind of paedo or something?"

"No, no. I found that. That's Lucy. That's who I came to find."

My brain was fighting a battle with my tongue. Of course she was thinking I was crazy, why wouldn't she? A dirty man who likes little girls who let himself into her house. A man with no shirt! Goddammit!

"I just wanted to see if she was ok," I said.

The room went silent again as she snapped the dictaphone to a stop. "Dunno, seems pretty weird to me."

It was becoming an effort to keep my hands up. I was sweating now, I could feel the drips materialising from my armpits and sliding down my ribcage. I wasn't smelling too keen either. So far, I had not given this woman a single excuse to let me live and I couldn't think of one. I shifted my weight from one foot to the other.

With a finger of her free hand, she drew short curved lines on my sweat soaked back. She then grabbed my right arm and twisted it behind my back, dragging her finger along it as well.

"Where'd you get them cuts?" she asked.

The lines she had drawn with her finger were not random. They were in examination of the scars given to me by the doctor. I'd never seen the ones on my back, but judging by the lengths of the lines her inspecting finger had drawn, the scars weren't exactly small.

"I was tortured." Quick, to the point and honest was all that would work with this woman. Of that, I was certain.

"Huh," she said.

After a long pause and a deep sigh, she released my arm and withdrew the knife. "I suppose I should offer you something to drink."

I put my hands down and turned around. Her heavy voice had disguised a rather small form. She was taller than Raj, but not by much. Her razor-straight black hair was cut into a bob, framing a tanned and freckled face. Piercing blue eyes set slightly apart with weather-beaten wrinkles at the edges. She looked as though she was in her early forties, but it was impossible to tell with people in this place. Hell, I couldn't tell how old I was.

"You should knock before you enter someone's house, y'know?" she said pointing the knife at me as if scolding a child. Despite looking nothing like him, she spoke in the same way as Henry. Long, nasal vowels, soft r's and t's. She skipped the 't' in 'enter' entirely.

"I'm sorry, I–" I started.

"Ordinary or Nettle? Have a seat."

Was that a question? I didn't know how to answer it so I sat down on the couch.

"Tea, dummy. Ordinary or Nettle," she repeated. Nettle pronounced Neh-o.

I understood the words that time but had no idea what they meant.

I shrugged.

"Well you're getting nettle then. Bags of ordinary are getting harder to find these days."

She turned away and walked down the hall. I peeked around the corner to watch her walk. A faded cowboy shirt was fitted at her small waist and flowed over her round backside. Her denim jeans hugged her curvy legs and were rolled up at the bottom. She didn't walk so much as she pounded the ground with her feet. She was only small, but you wouldn't know it by the sound she made when she walked. If you only had your ears to warn of her approach, you'd almost have mistaken her for Henry. How had she snuck up on me so easily?

Henry's hips didn't sway like hers did, however.

I unshouldered my pack, sat back down on the couch and placed the bag in between my feet. My knife was in there. The woman was tiny, but I needed to remember the doctor's words. Henry and Raj were friendly enough, but that didn't mean everyone would be. I needed to be vigilant.

I was filthy. My jeans were stained black with grease from the bike and the red muck of the dirt piles. I slid forward on the couch cushion as far as I could until I was perching on the very tip. Limiting my contact with the unblemished cloth of the sofa was important. I moved my hand across the soft cloth on instinct before I realised that my hand was filthier than my jeans. When was the last time I had a proper wash? Even the boys in the pub were cleaner than me. In my mind's eye I pictured their clothes. They were old and tatty, but they weren't dirty. Even the messy kid in the velvet cape slopping rice into his mouth like an old sow looked better than me. Before I could stop it, my hand sought comfort on the beautiful knitted afghan folded neatly and draped over the armrest. I snapped my hand back, tucked my elbows in and folded my hands in my lap.

"I'm Zara!" Zara shouted from the kitchen.

I decided then to believe that she wasn't Lucy. She didn't sound like Lucy at all; even an older version. Her voice was gruff, almost raspy. She hadn't flinched at the sound of little Lucy's voice. Surely, she would have gasped, or shuddered, given me some sort of sign had she recognised her own childhood voice.

What are you, some kind of paedo?

"I'm Seth," I repeated.

Her laugh was sharp and wheezy. It was not a young woman's laugh.

"So you said. Milk and sugar?"

Again I was at a loss. "Yes please?"

She brought the tea into the living room and handed it to me. No milk, no sugar. "Haven't got any milk or sugar," she said. She plonked herself into the couch opposite, picked up her mug and drank with a loud slurp. "Bloody hell, now mine's cold!"

The tea in my cup was green and smelled of rotten vegetables.

She crossed her legs, placed her mug in her lap and turned toward me. The denim swished as her legs scissored. The freckles on her face peppered her neck and down into the bit of her chest exposed by a couple undone buttons. I wondered if the freckles went further down. Down onto her heaving breasts. She was wearing a bra.

"I've heard quite a bit about you, actually."

I was staring at her heaving breasts. I blinked twice, forced my gaze to the floor and sipped my tea. It tasted as bad as it smelled. It tasted as if she had soaked her feet in it. If my face had accidentally divulged my disgust, she ignored it.

"Oi! I've heard a lot about you, I said. You deaf as well as stupid?"

I shook my head and had another gulp of the terrible tea. It was vile, but it was warm and I didn't want to be impolite.

She sat back into the couch and looked at the ceiling, fingering the handle on her mug and grinning as she spoke. "I hear you like pizza quite a lot, you ride around on your bike like a lunatic and you don't talk to anyone. Suz in town says you hide in the bushes when people pass. She thinks you're well weird."

So much for keeping a low profile.

"Oh really," I said. "What do you think?"

"Dunno, haven't made up me mind," she said. "You could do with a good scrub, that much's for certain."

I shifted in my seat. A quick look down revealed the small grease stain I was leaving on the couch. I moved my leg over top of it and hoped she didn't see it.

"You hungry?"

"Always," I said without hesitation. It didn't feel right to admit that to a woman somehow, but it was the truth. I was more than hungry, I was starving. As usual. In my haste to find Lucy, I didn't think to collect a curry from Raj's beforehand. Was this a result of the amnesia? It must be; who forgets to eat? Perhaps I wasn't suffering from amnesia at all, maybe I was just a hapless moron who barely knew day from night. Maybe I always had been.

She stood and walked into the kitchen and beckoned me to follow. She didn't say much, chit-chat was not something people around here were good at. Henry seemed to be the only one with any kind of proficiency in it. Raj, Zara and (to a great extreme) the doctor got straight to the point. No messing about with pleasantries. Who are you? What's your deal? What are you doing here? Their questions punctuated by bouts of silence. People didn't seem to mind long silences here. I was growing tired of them; the silences. I was going out of my mind with them.

She moved about the kitchen with a clinical efficiency. Blackened pots and pans foamed and sizzled over a redbrick barbecue on the other side of the open window. She disappeared into the cellar, returning seconds later with food of all kinds. Potatoes, french beans, parsley and a fat fish. An overturned spoon was a blur in her hands, the fish's scales pinged and popped away from the silver skin like snow. She reached across the sink and tossed the fish through the window onto the barbecue and plopped four small potatoes into the bubbling pot.

"Can you put some more wood on that fire," she said. It was only half a question.

My eyes were transfixed on the barbecue.

She grabbed my arm and prodded me toward the door in the corner. "Just go around the outside, the wood is stacked under the tarp. Three pieces should do."

How had I found myself in this situation? I was looking for a young girl on a dictaphone and now I was being given orders by some woman I'd never met.

The door led from the kitchen to an enormous back garden. The gardens of her former neighbours were now her gardens. Pieces of fence marking out where the old boundaries used to be still stood in places, but for the most part she had taken over. Each confiscated garden had been long and skinny, twenty feet wide by at least a couple hundred feet long. Zara's adjustments had made her garden at least three hundred foot square. There were growing things everywhere.

Flowers of all shapes poked up from pots and hung down overflowing from baskets. Tiny flowers dotted bushes in their thousands and strong stemmed flowers thrust skyward in clusters from manicured beds. Pinks, purples, reds, yellows and blues. Large leafy plants spread out wide across the ground and tall thin ones rose above my head attached to bamboo poles. Lettuces, peas and all kinds of other fat vegetables were bursting through the soil and drooping down from long stalks.

"Mate, that fire ain't going to stoke itself!" Her hand gesticulated through the window, pointing madly at the wood pile.

The barbecue was simple enough, just bricks (of course) stacked up in a cylindrical sort of tower, wide at the bottom, tapering as it ascended. The blue tarp was beside the barbecue, stretched over a neatly stacked pile of wood. Each piece of wood was cut to the exact same length and breadth. Her grand stack of perfectly chopped wood stood in stark contrast to the pathetic array of broken cabinetry and sticks currently chucked next to my fireplace. It was embarrassing.

I lifted the tarp and slid three chunks of wood into the fiery hole at the bottom of the barbecue. As I stuffed the last log in, a burning log dropped down and seared my hand. I snapped my hand back out, banging the back of my thumb on the brick. I swore and sucked my fingers.

Zara passed me a wooden spoon through the window. "Stir those potatoes while you're out there. And flip that fish over."

I stirred and flipped as I was told. Her hand cleaved the air again, depositing a handful of chopped greenery on the fish. She plucked a steaming new potato out of the boiling water and squeezed it in her fingers. The soft, yellowy flesh burst through the pale skin. She tossed the potato back into the pot and took the pot off the barbecue back into the kitchen.

"Is that fish done?" she asked through the window.

She may as well have asked for the circumference of the sun. The fish looked like a fish.

"Christ," she said. "Squeeze it with your fingers."

I squeezed it. It felt like a fish.

"Oh, just give it to me."

I grasped the handle of the pan. It was scorching.

"Yow!" I screeched and pulled my hand back.

She gave me a look through the window like I'd just hurt myself petting a kitten. She reached out and brought the pan back in through the window. She pinched the fish and shook her head at me in disgust.

"Come on, then."

In the time it took me to walk back into the kitchen, she'd dumped the steaming potatoes into a blue glass bowl, arranged the fish on an oval serving plate and produced a green salad.

She picked up the fishplate with one hand, the salad with the other. "Grab that will you?"

I picked up the bowl of potatoes up and followed her into the dining room. Seven wooden chairs surrounded a large wooden table. The chairs looked too perfect to sit in. A blue, oval tablecloth stretched across the table and three white, knitted place mats were lined up neatly across the centre. She placed the plate of fish on the large place mat in the middle and the salad on a smaller one beside. She pointed at the other place mat and sat down at the far end.

Forks and knives, plates and glasses full of water. Something inside me recognised this. I couldn't figure out why this made sense, but it did.

I placed the bowl of potatoes on the third place mat and sat down.

The smell was lovely.

She sliced through the fish lengthwise with a knife, peeled the flesh away from the spine and plopped half of it onto my plate. Steam rose up and warmed my face. I picked at the soft, white flesh with my fingers and shoved a large chunk into my mouth.

The texture was unlike anything I had ever eaten. Soft and salty, like eating sea foam. The soft flesh and crunchy skin set something off in my mind. The fish, the herbs, the forks and knives, even Zara herself touched something that sent sparks to my fingers and toes. I couldn't explain why, but something about this felt right, something about this moment felt *real*.

I grabbed another handful of the fish and a small potato from the bowl and shoved them into my mouth, snorting as I scoffed.

She shook her head at me again. "Good grief, you weren't kidding".

"I'm sorry," was what I tried to say. What I actually said was "Mime thoy".

I chewed it and swallowed.

"It's been a while since I had any manners," I didn't know what I meant by that.

She stabbed at a piece of fish with her fork. "You are weird."

What could I have said to that? She was right, of course. I was weird. Shirtless, covered in muck and oil, plopped into this tiny paradise as if I'd fallen from the sky. I couldn't have looked more out of place if I'd been a chimp who'd escaped the zoo. I didn't care, the food was too good.

I shoved another mound of fish, potato and salad in my mouth and chewed. She took tiny bites with her fork and sipped her water.

"Who was this Lucy then?" she asked.

I swallowed again and wiped my mouth with a greasy hand. Lucy.

The question took me by surprise, I'd forgotten all about her. *Was* she said. Not *is*.

"I don't know actually. A little girl, well, I guess she's not really a girl, more like a teenager. Actually she'd be older even than that now I guess."

"You two are really close then?" she said, teasing.

We were very close, thank you very much.

Lucy was more than a little girl on a recorder; she was my connection to another place, another time, to my own sanity. I was sitting in the last house she had ever lived in and I was never going to talk to her again.

It was foolish to think Lucy could still be alive somewhere. Everyone else was dead, what made her so special? I wiped my mouth and hands with a cloth napkin. The house itself could be Lucy's final resting place, her body was probably rotting in a chest in the attic or under the house somewhere. And here I was, a pig of a man. Eating. Eating. While Lucy lingered somewhere, a dead and dusty pile of bone amongst the other dusty bone piles in the gutters of an even deader city.

Who was this woman sitting across from me and why was she feeding me? Why did I stay? My stomach tightened with the thought of Lucy's death, but I ate anyway, swirling chunks of fish and potato together and shovelling them in. In Manchester, only a fool refused to eat.

Zara finished chewing and pointed at my hand with her empty fork. "So, who gave you them scars then?"

I scooped the last bit of food off my plate, chewed quickly and swallowed it down.

"Don't remember," I lied, wiping my mouth with the napkin. The comfort and welcome I felt when I first sat down was slithering away leaving behind cold, prickly doubt. This woman was very quick to accept me into her home. She'd given me food and not asked for anything in return. Behind her, burning logs crackled and snapped in a cast iron fireplace. Practically everything on the table was made of glass or crockery and it was flawless. A Chaise Longue, with wooden feet to mimic lion's paws and upholstered in fur relaxed in a corner of the room. Unlike Raj's grass tablecloths, the one on the table was cotton and intricately weaved. This was the house of a rich person, a person proficient in bartering. It was not the house of a person inclined to handing out free lunches.

"You don't remember?" she said with a smirk. "You sure about that?"

The knife she threatened me with was nowhere to be seen. There were knives on the table, but they didn't look capable of piercing flesh. The table hid her bottom half and potentially the other knife. My backpack with my knife inside was in the living room opposite.

"I don't remember much of anything if I'm honest." Not a lie.

She drank water from her glass and cut the rest of the fish on her plate into small pieces.

"So I've heard"

I didn't know what she meant by that and I didn't want to know. I pushed my chair back and began to stand.

"You're wondering why I'm feeding you. You're thinking I have plans for you? Nasty plans?"

She stood up from the table. She was at least six inches shorter than me and unarmed.

I moved to speak; she lifted a finger to silence me, unbuttoned the cuff of her cowboy shirt and rolled back the sleeve of her left arm.

"You're right to be wary, I don't feed just anyone. Survival of the fittest out here, mate. But–"

She held her arm out. Three, straight, inch-long scars criss-crossed her arm near the elbow, on either side. They were much older than the ones on my arm, but they were the same length and in the exact same positions as mine. The doctor was nothing if not consistent.

I rolled my fingers over the scars on my arm and across the two on the back of my hand.

Zara held her tiny, unblemished hand in the air and twiddled her fingers.

"I must have cracked before you did," she said. "I ain't got those ones on my back like you either. You must have held out a long time."

She was right. The doctor had started with my forearms and moved to my hands, feet and torso in order. I rubbed the scars on my hand and shoved them into my pockets.

She rolled her sleeve back down, rebuttoned and picked up my empty plate.

"Dessert?" she asked. Neither of us mentioned the man himself, the man in the white coat; his handiwork spoke for him. We ate brownies and chatted about nothing much. Vegetable plots, bicycles and rainy days. We had nothing in common except for our time with the doctor and the city itself and neither of us had any interest in speaking about either.

Thirteen

My apartment was a cave. The warmth and civility of Zara's place made mine feel all the more cold and savage. The tatty couch in which I was sat, the mouldy walls and floorboards, the empty cupboards all existed in antipathy of her house. The pale, flat sky peeking in around the windowboards further emphasised the apartment's grimness. Outside, I heard the rain clawing against the rotten window frame, rotting it ever further with each drop. Loneliness, fear and hunger, was that what life was to be?

Across from me in answer to my question, the doctor perched on the piano stool. He looked exactly as he had done last time I'd seen him with his glasses, lab coat and thin, lipless smile; the only addition, a small canvas bag strapped around his shoulder. Beside him stood a large man in camouflage trousers. A dented, military helmet was strapped tightly around his sagging neck and a green tank top stretched over a round belly. Dark sunglasses sat askew on his round, middle-aged face and in his hands he held a large black machine gun, pointed at me. Behind me a second, shorter soldier of equal dress and girth rifled through my backpack.

They were at least a full month early. I rubbed my throbbing mouth where the soldier in front of me had buried his fist when I walked in the front door. A confounded squeak was all I could manage before the two soldiers had me contained, disarmed and sat on this couch.

"Sorry about that," the doctor said, pointing at my mouth. It felt like years since I'd heard the doctor's voice. It was as blank in my apartment as it was in the cavernous torture room; as unfeeling and square as a brick.

The fire burned hot in my fireplace and reflected in his round spectacles just as it did in the torture room.

He neither acknowledged the machine gun pointed at me nor did he apologise for it. I didn't have any new information for this man and I was going to be punished for it. If not with wooden mallets and knives, it would be with fists and bullets.

"Nuffink in 'ere but a knife and an old list," said the soldier behind me. He stepped around the couch and deposited both into the doctor's waiting hands. The doctor dropped the knife onto the floor with clunk, held the list up to his eyes and read quietly for a few long seconds before putting it in his chest pocket.

"Well, that's disappointing," he said.

I needed a plan, an idea, anything. I needed to get out of there.

The second soldier took his place beside the other, crossing his arms, waiting for the next order.

"Do you ever wonder why the death of this city doesn't bother you?" the doctor asked. The question was directed at me.

I sat staring at the holes in my jeans wondering if speaking was a good idea. I decided against it.

"You know, the other people in this city couldn't take it. The death, I mean," he began, pointing at the boarded up window. "Most of the deaths were suicides."

The doctor stood up and walked toward the fireplace, leaned down and threw two pieces of chopped wood from a large pile that wasn't mine onto the fire.

"You can keep those, by the way," he said flicking a finger to the pile of wood.

He continued pacing, swirling his long, heavily knuckled fingers in an oval. His long hair motionless as he moved.

"You are not put off by it at all," he said, pacing. "After the bodies started piling up, people could no longer bring themselves to the city centre. Only a few, the ones you see around now ever got used to it. And it took them a long, long time to adjust."

He stopped pacing and looked me in the eyes through his spectacles.

"Not you," he said pulling the piano stool closer to me and taking a seat. "On your first day in this place; On Day One, you trudged along the bones and skulls as if they were mere cobbles. Don't you find that strange?"

The soldier holding the gun shifted his position, but stood firm. The second stood watching me waiting with the doctor for an answer. I didn't have one for them.

"I see on your list that you don't believe my story about that blast. You were right not to, it was a lie."

His lipless smile reappeared. "It shows progress. Perhaps not as much as we would've liked, but progress nonetheless."

Without warning, he bent down and put his hands on my knees and leaned in close to my face. I turned away and closed my eyes tight, unable to look the terrible man in the eyes. Two treasonous tears leaked down my cheeks.

"Tell me about the machine," he whispered. His breath hot and reeking of rotten things.

Somewhere in a dark hollow in the base of my brain, a voice spoke of "*dying with dignity.* Words from the past spoken by a man I didn't recognise in a black hat and clothing. His face like old leather and his eyes squinted against a sunny sky.

Easy for him to say.

If there was one thing the bespectacled grey man on the other side of my closed eyelids had taught me in that moment, it was that I did not want to die. I wanted to leave this apartment and go out scavenging. I wanted to ride my bicycle again. I wanted to drink with my friends.

The pressure of the doctor's hands on my knees lifted and I felt his face retract from mine. "Take your hands down, please."

I lowered them to see the doctor holding my list with an outstretched arm. Behind him, smiles rippled across the faces of both soldiers. They were taking pleasure in this. Beside me on the couch, my backpack lay open and empty.

The smaller soldier who'd been searching my backpack now twirled the sharp end of my knife into the fingertip of his left hand. The bigger one with his crooked sunglasses appeared to be looking off into space, but the machine gun pointing between my eyes suggested otherwise.

The doctor flipped my list around so the text faced me. He tapped a long, crooked finger below the second item in my list marked *Things I know.*

"I ask you again. Tell me about the machine."

It had been weeks since I'd had the vision of the woman being built up in layers; her skin first melting, then hardening in drips like candle wax. 2B156 was a setback.

"I had a dream about a machine," I said. "A machine that makes human beings."

The soldiers stole a quick glance at each other, but the doctor didn't twitch.

"I don't know what it means. It's probably nothing."

The doctor turned toward the soldiers and nodded toward the door.

Without argument, the first soldier shouldered his rifle and shoved his way past the couch toward the door. The second gave the knife in his hand four more twirls before handing it to the doctor. The doctor took the knife and slid it into his belt.

"We'll be just outside," he said as much to me as the doctor.

He walked past the couch with his eyes on me as he passed. Behind me his heavy footfalls clomped across my kitchen floor and out the door, pulling it shut, but not closed.

"You're lucky," the doctor said. "Had you given us nothing, you would have been killed."

He leaned back, smiled wide and laughed in his hissing laugh exposing a mouthful of rotten teeth. "You ruined poor Dempsey's day. He'd been looking forward to killing you for weeks." Dempsey was the knife-twirler, I'd have bet my life on it.

The fireplace popped and an orange ember shot from it, landing on a floorboard near a bit of ancient carpet. The doctor stood, walked toward the ember and calmly stepped on it; it crunched and smoked under his twisting boot.

"The machine is not nothing," he said. "It is very much real and it is the only reason you are still breathing."

He unzipped the canvas bag and pulled out a long, white wire.

"Hold out the the index finger of your right hand, please."

My hands were clamped together in my lap. I squeezed them tighter. "Why?"

"Because," he said, opening his hand to reveal a big toe sized metal clasp. "We need to be sure you're telling the truth."

He squeezed the clasp open and closed twice before letting it snap shut the third time.

"One question, Seth. That's it. You give the right answer and I am out the door."

I unlatched my hands and held it out to him. My extended finger trembled, vibrating the air between us.

He hands flashed toward me and the clasp snapped tight around my finger so quickly, it made me jump. The rusty clamp clicked as it struggled to keep hold of my trembling finger. The doctor paid it no notice, his eyes and his mind were focussed on the job at hand.

"Where is the machine?" he asked.

Four small words that would most likely be the last I'd ever hear. A hollow panic ran through my insides like a cold bolt of lightning. Down from my head, into my throat before finding purchase in my chest. Blood pounded in my ears and sweat gathered in my armpits and at my temples. The last time I'd said 'I don't know' to this man, I was beaten and cut almost to death. The polygraph hadn't helped me then, why would it make any difference now?

Under his lab coat, my knife lingered in a belt loop. If I was lucky, a couple quick slashes at the doctor would be all I'd get before my body was pumped full of bullets, or worse. Two beads of sweat cut new tracks in my cheeks, parallel to the ones left by tears before leaping from my chin and falling heavy and wet into my lap.

"Answer the question, please."

The doctor's back was to the fire, his face in shadow. The orange glow was a corona around his head, his long hair was like a hood; the edges of his gold glasses touched by firelight. I rattled through the town names in my atlas, Rusholme, Reddish, West Didsbury, Preston. I could tell him a town and hope for the best. Who's to say the machine isn't in one of those towns? At the very least, it could buy me some time. Anything was better than the three words the doctor hated; the three words that were in fact the truth.

"I don't know," I said.

The doctor gazed into the bag, holding the zipper open with a thumb and forefinger. Inside the bag was no bleeps, no flashing lights, no movement or sound at all. The room was silent except for the crackling of the fire and soft murmurs of the men in the hall.

The wood in the fire popped again, a second, larger ember arced from the fire and landing on a scrap of carpet and rolling across it. The doctor ignored it this time, his eyes remaining fixed on the insides of his case. The orange orb pulsed and hissed, sending a thin trail of smoke barrelling into the air.

And yet the doctor waited. Waited for the thing, the tiny machine to finish its work.

My finger had gone crimson under the pressure of the squeezing clasp. I sat as still as possible and tried to quell the shaking in my hand. The ancient polygraph was not a reliable piece of equipment, I needed to stay as still as possible. I had told the truth and I needed the machine to display that.

Behind the couch a black circle has started to form in the bit of carpet under the smoking ember. A tiny flame puffed up as I watched and began eating at the carpet around the orb. And still the doctor sat unmoving, unbreathing; statuesque and stone silent.

The flame split and moved slowly across the carpet in three directions, growing as they consumed the fuel the carpet provided. I tensed my arm and brought a knee under my elbow, willing it to stop shaking. The shaking slowed and the clasp stopped clicking, but small tremors continued. If only there was some sign that the polygraph was running, a whirr, a buzz, anything. But there was nothing.

The flames in the carpet spread and spread further and further away from the ember, gaining strength as they moved. It moved closer to the couch, to where the fabric hung down in threads.

The doctor's hunched back rose and fell as he took in a large breath.

"That's fine," he said and snatched the clasp from my finger. He coiled the wire into an efficient ball, dropped it into the case and zipped it up.

"Not so difficult, now was it?"

I rubbed the pain out of my finger and set my eyes on the floor. If 'that's fine' was doctor-ese for 'You're of no more use to us', I did not want to know.

He stood up and looked at his watch. "By the way, the seventy days is still in effect," he said. "Thirty days from today".

He reached across the darkness with long bony fingers, pinching my right cheek with one hand, pointing at my face with a finger on his other hand. When he spoke, his voice was not his usual dead monotone; it was dripping with venom.

"Remember where the fucking machine is before then."

He released my face and gave me a hard slap that rattled my teeth leaving his eyes on me for a long moment before turning and heading toward the door.

As he grasped the handle, he turned back to me, his body almost invisible now in the dark.

"Here," he said and the knife whizzed past my face and smacked into the windowboard with a hollow thunk.

"You'll need that with the company you keep."

And then he and the soldiers were gone.

When I was sure they had left the building, I stomped the flames out of my carpet and coiled myself into a ball on Lucy's bed, staring awake at my bicycle all night and thanking Christ I hadn't yet added the discovery of a lip tattoo to my list.

Fourteen

The following day I packed the atlas, a day old curry and my knife in my backpack and cycled for the edge of the city. On the other side of my door, almost predictably, the doctor had left me a couple more photos.

One of a teen-aged Henry snapping a man's neck, and one of little Raj relieving a woman of her head with a double-barreled shotgun. Like the photo of Bill, they were black and white and taken long ago.

Henry's furious teenaged face was unlike anything I'd seen on the adult version. Bared teeth, thick veins popping from his neck and arms, clenched fists; it was the look of murder. The body in his hands was twisted into odd angles, his eyes and mouth frozen in a scream. Like the photo of Bill, it was taken from above, the force of Henry's attack apparent even in the still photograph. Raj's was even more obvious, the tiny man standing with the gun at eye level and the woman in front of him whose head was little more than a smear of black. Her hands stretched out in front of her and both feet off the ground. High heeled shoes and bulges of breasts through her shirt the only thing to identify her as a woman.

Raj I could imagine being capable of such a thing; there was a hardness to him bubbling underneath loose, old man skin and quaff of white. His eyes and the manner in which he moved about the bar disclosed a business-like precision. Raj didn't look at you with soft eyes; he studied you. When he wiped the tables or polished bottles, there was always one ear on your words and one eye on your actions. He was friendly enough in the pub, but when Henry whispered his warning to me, I knew they were not loose words, they were words to take seriously.

Many people died trying to take his pub from him. Don't let his diminutive size fool you, he is no one to mess with.

What I couldn't believe is that the man who had an arm and smile for everyone could be the same man that could take a life in such a violent way. The man with the twittering laugh, the fields of wheat and the obsession with old vehicles.

In a way, Henry's photo was worse. There could be dissociation involved with shooting a person, or even stabbing someone. You could blame the gun; It wasn't me! The gun went off! It was an accident! Henry killed a man with his hands. The same hands that enveloped tiny beer mugs at the pub, the same hands that he held over his eyes as he lurched on his bar stool, riotous with laughter.

When I arrived at my destination that day, it wasn't the edge of the city where I found myself. It was Zara's house.

Zara had survived the doctor. She had survived the end of the world. She would know how to survive the outlands as well and she would tell me how to do it; at least I hoped she would. I stayed at her house that day, I went back the very next day, the day after that and the day after that. Each evening, I returned to my apartment despite the risk it posed. The doctor could return at any time, one morning I could wake to see him standing over me with his knives and hammers, but it was a risk I had to take. Living in a different house against the doctor's wishes was not an option. He had seen me talking to Bill, to Henry and Raj. It was only a matter of time before a photo of Zara found its way to my front door. There were only two options for me: stay in the apartment or leave the city. Leaving was going to be my only option soon, but I needed to know how to live first.

Zara didn't seem to mind my presence at all, in fact, she seemed more than happy to have me around. Our relationship grew more comfortable by the day. The initial sexual attraction seemed to slowly dissolve, not least because she didn't seem to fancy me at all. The feelings of lust weren't gone completely, of course, and never would.

It was a bit of a con job, what I was doing. Using our shared torture at the doctor's hands to guilt her into showing me how to collect food and scavenge for useful things, but that didn't mean our relationship couldn't go further. She didn't know I would be gone soon. Sex was something people needed. You could have all the glass plates and barbecues in the world, and it wouldn't mean anything without companionship.

And it wasn't like there were men lined up to her front door either.

If only I had remembered to put on a shirt on that first day. She would never forgive me for showing up to her house in such a state. In her eyes, I would always be the grubby, awkward idiot who stained her couch. No amount of scrubbing now would change that, although that didn't stop me from trying. Almost before I knew I was doing it in the mornings, I found myself shaved, trimmed and deoderised.

Either she hadn't noticed my new appearance and smell (or lack of therewith) or she didn't feel it necessary to comment on. Disclosing my memory loss to her was a mistake, she has treated me like a little boy ever since. A slow little boy. There was nothing sexy about that.

Our days together were more than tuition in life skills. It was simply nice to be around her; to be around a woman. There was something about a woman's way and voice that made the pain of existence easier to take. It wasn't simply the pitch or timbre; the beauty of a woman's voice was unquantifiable.

Especially Zara's voice.

You couldn't help but feel comfortable in her presence. Her calmness, her ease, the way she breezed through this terrible life was contagious. Comfort was something you could not put a high enough value on in a place like this. The absence of worry even for just a short while was worth more than a hundred buried trunks of gold rings.

Well, maybe not a hundred.

Being around Zara was good for my scarred brain as well. Although memory of the machine seemed as distant as ever, I was happy to find out that the things I was learning from her were sticking. Potatoes were ready for picking when the flowers died, onions could be planted over winter, Fish heads made good soup. Somehow, I plugged the dam of outgoing thoughts; found places for each one, hanging them in parts of my mind like oil paintings.

I didn't really have access to other women, especially now that Lucy was gone. I'd only been introduced to the adult Lucy before she was taken away from me. There would never be any more batteries to bring her back to life; of this I was certain. If only I had realised earlier what a fragile thing a battery was. I have found hundreds of them with Zara, but all had been rusted and burst. Zara's stunned look brought this fact sharply into focus when she found I'd wasted working batteries. When I told her I had used them to power a dictaphone for weeks, the stunned look turned to one of loathing.

"A dictaphone? You used the batteries to power a bleeding dictaphone?"

She had stared at me, speechless, mouth agog, fantasizing about all the little appliances should could've powered with a dozen double A's. I daren't tell her of the nights I fell asleep with the dictaphone on, waking the next morning only to find I had completely drained a fresh pair.

Wasting batteries was just one more reason for her not to sleep with me.

Zara's home was addictive. She was addictive. I wasn't entirely sure why she endured my almost constant presence, it certainly wasn't a love thing. At first, I thought it was respect for surviving the doctor, but the more I am with her, the more I feel like a pet project. She was definitely the type of person who was easily bored and now that her house seemed in order, she needed a new project to keep her going. Or maybe a new pet.

I didn't care. I didn't even mind being treated like an idiot, but I needed to try harder to hide my mental shortcomings. I couldn't risk her getting bored with me. With Zara's help I was getting stronger, more capable by the day, but I was still a fair way from self-sufficiency.

The cool air and early evenings signalled the start of my very first autumn. In the quiet moments, my mind teased me with fleeting glimpses of what autumn was. The changing leaves seemed perfectly natural, but the ripening fruit hanging from trees felt quite peculiar.

"You really can't remember apples?" Zara asked with a *tsk*.

Of course I could remember apples, I just didn't realise they grew on trees.

It was the beginning of October and Zara was giving me a crash course in 'proper autumn scavenging'. Rooting through bushes and hedgerows, gathering what was left of raspberries, blackberries and rosehips for tea. Stinging nettles burned my hands and arms as I attempted to clear a path to a blackberry bush, but Zara pulled them from the ground in bunches without wincing. Squishing rotten berries in my hands seemed to alleviate the stinging somewhat and I was careful to limit the rubbing and scratching at my wrists to when Zara's back was turned.

After we filled our baskets with fruit, she led me to another neighbourhood near her house that had been only given a passing glance by the other scavengers. "This was a rough area," she said. "We'll be lucky to find anything other than a stash of faded porno mags and the odd crushed beer tin, but it's on the way home anyway."

"How old are you?" I asked her.

She stopped walking and sneered at me.

"What kind of a question is that? How old do you think I am?"

I looked at my basket and gave the question some honest thought.

The wrinkles and the thin lips suggested advanced years but she a face that aged well, slightly round at the cheeks with flawless skin.

"Forty-six."

She dropped her basket and assigned both hands to her hips. Two green apples plopped out of her basket as it hit the ground.

"Cheeky bastard! You think I'm forty-six?"

Had I guessed too high?

"Even if you thought I was forty-six, you wouldn't actually say it. Forty bleeding six!"

She bent over, shuffled the apples back into her basket and picked it up in a huff.

"How old are *you*, then smart-arse?" she said pointing at me.

I wasn't actually sure. Some mornings when I looked at my face, I thought I was in my thirties, despite the healing scars and bruises. I didn't have the heavy creases at my eyes and mouth like the others, but the greying hair at my temples made it difficult to gauge. The longer I lived in this place, the faster I seemed to age, a result of long days outside and malnutrition. Some mornings, I could look fifty.

"You don't even know, do you?" she asked.

I shrugged and shook my head. She turned away and angrily stomped away, mumbling to herself.

"Forty-six. Retard doesn't even know how old he is."

I'd definitely guessed too high. I scrambled after her, jogging to keep up as she hurled more abuse at me.

Henry and Raj had both been around before the Darkening, I knew that much for sure. Henry was a child during the Darkening and he was at *least* forty-six. Raj was pushing sixty if my guesses were anything to go by. Which, if Zara was to believed, they were not.

Maybe the reason Zara managed to live so well these days was because she had nothing to compare her present life with; she simply didn't know how good life used to be. Perhaps cars had always been heaps of rust for her and glass windows had always been luxuries. Perhaps she was an aftertimer.

Perhaps I was born after the Darkening. My knowledge of bicycles and cars acquired after the fact through books or stories of the past told to me by a father or an uncle. My childhood could have been spent knocking about broken American streets, playing in burnt out cars, imagining what life must used to have been like before the Darkening. It must have been like that! Henry was older than me and he was a child when the Darkening had happened, how had that not occurred to me before? I was sure I had built the machine, but how could that be true? How could I have built 2B156 in a world without electricity? Either electricity still exists in England, or the machine itself is somewhere else. Or it truly is a figment of my imagination.

The doctor and my short-circuited brain were the only sources of validation for the machine's existence and neither of them have proved to be reliable.

"Oi! Keep up, willya?" Zara was shouting at me from far away. I had stopped walking and was standing in the middle of the street.

But I had nothing but the machine to believe in. Without it, all I had was a few murderous friends and a few short weeks to live.

I did as I was told and ran to catch up.

We didn't find much in the empty houses of the rough area. As she had predicted, the houses hadn't been touched, the dust was thick and unsettled on the couches and chairs. The odd gold plated necklace here, a cupboard full of moth-eaten towels there. It was easier searching the houses rather than digging through the dirt piles in Urmston, but it wasn't as rewarding. Exploring dusty bureaus and chipped cabinets was scavenging, almost stealing. Digging through the piles was treasure hunting.

We were about to finish for the day when Zara came across an old wooden box beneath a smashed television set. A tiny lock hung limply from it. She pushed the TV off the box, ignoring the flying glass as it crashed into the ground.

She gave the lock a sharp tug. It snapped in her hand. "Bullseye."

In the box were six bottles. "These people must've died early on in the Darkening," she said pulling one of the dusty bottles from the box.

"Why do you say that?" I asked.

She wiped the dirt off the bottle's peeling label and held it up triumphantly. *Aristocrat Vodka.* "If they'd lived on into the Darkening, these wouldn't be here."

She replaced the bottle, closed the lid and smiled.

"C'mon Sethie, let's get pissed."

★ ★ ★

Get pissed, we did.

Back in her kitchen, Zara plonked her basket on the kitchen counter top and instructed me to do the same with my basket and the box of booze.

"Glasses are up there. Grab two and fill them up. I'll be in the garden."

I did as I was told.

Soon, I'd be drinking; and not Raj's herbal beer either. Proper booze from the old days. With any luck the vodka would trigger a memory, remind me of times past. Perhaps I had some sort of special attachment to Aristocrat Vodka. Maybe I drunk it at my wedding or my son's graduation, or perhaps I drank it just for the sake of drinking. Yes, with any luck I was an alcoholic in my former life. A smile crept across my face; A joke. Was it my first one?

The kitchen was growing dim in the grey evening half-light. There had always been a weird feeling whenever I was in Zara's kitchen, like something was a bit off, but it wasn't until that moment that I realised what it was.

There was no stove and no refrigerator.

Not only were the large appliances missing, but the slots in the cabinetry that would have housed them were missing as well, like they had never existed. On closer inspection, I could make out the join where the fridge and stove had been removed and where the new cabinets had been built in, but it was barely noticeable. I ran my finger along the seam to the floor. She'd even put new cabinet doors in! Above, where the hood fan would've been was filled in as well with cupboards.

The woman was obsessed with perfection. Squares and symmetry. You could see it in the house everywhere you looked. The bookshelves on either side of the fireplace, the chairs spaced evenly around the dining room table. The wood pile, the perfect cone shape of the barbecue, the tools hung up in her cellar with felt pen drawn around them. Even in the garden, the flowerbeds on either side squared off and identical. Not a bush, not a flower out of place. Maybe I wasn't the only sick one.

That was two jokes I had made. Quick succession as well.

There were several large candles on the counter top. There wasn't any matches; Zara had gone one better. In a drawer was a collection of stones and metal files used to light them. Zara had showed me how to do it, but was insistent I didn't use them until I got better at it.

The candles were of uniform shape and colour; a creamy, butter-like yellow. Even the ridges were identical, the lot of them made from the same mould. They were homemade!

I could never let Zara see my place.

The glasses were in the cupboard as she'd directed, organised neatly into different categories. Tall thin ones, short fat ones, mugs with handles and glasses with bowls at the top, connected to flat, glass bases by long stems. Those ones looked the nicest and they felt the nicest too. The bowl sat perfectly in the crater my index finger made when I balled my hand into a fist and the stem dripped down in through my clenched fingers to meet the base at the bottom. The stemmed glasses were just as likely as any of the others to be vodka-drinking glasses. I took a bottle of Aristocrat from the box and filled both glasses to the top. The vodka had a strange smell that hit me in the back of the throat. I recognised it but couldn't fully grasp from where. It wasn't entirely offensive, like something rotten, but it didn't smell like something one would actually want to drink. It certainly didn't look as nice as Raj's beer. But Zara didn't seem concerned, so neither did I.

With short, smooth steps I walked into the back garden, the glasses of vodka in both hands, being careful not to spill. It wasn't every day that I had vodka to drink.

Zara was on her hands and knees, her face to the ground in front of a fire pit, blowing into a glowing stack of old paper and twigs. After three hard blows, flames flickered up from the middle of the stack. Satisfied the fire was taking hold, she stood up and tossed some larger pieces of cut wood and a chunk of a broken furniture on top. The flames welcomed the bone-dry wood, snapping and crackling their thanks, sending tiny sparks popping out into the grass. Zara didn't look concerned about the glowing orbs sitting in the grass, so neither did I.

"Now, that's what I call a drink!" she said. There was her laugh again. It was a dirty laugh, the laugh of a naughty old woman who'd just been caught doing something she should be embarrassed about, but isn't. She grasped the glass by the stem and gave it a quick once over before shaking her head. "You really are bonkers aintcha?" she said. "Cheers!" She clinked her glass against mine and took a long, hard glug from the glass.

She closed her eyes tightly and sucked in air through pursed lips. "Oh mate, that's good. It's no Grey Goose, but it'll do. It'll do nicely indeed."

I brought the glass to my lips and attempted a small sip. Zara grabbed the base of my glass and tipped it. The liquid poured into me, burning all the way down. I coughed and spluttered and pinched my nose hard in an attempt to stem the pain. My stomach was on fire. Tears gathered at the edges of my eyes and more of Zara's wicked laughter was in my ears.

After a few clenched moments, the burning subsided, replaced by a heavy warmth in my gut. When I was sure it was safe to start breathing again, I wiped my eyes and released my nose.

★ ★ ★

"Do you believe in God?" Zara asked as we sat drinking beside the fire she had built.

I was sitting on an old sofa in front of the fire, wrapped in a duvet Zara had deemed acceptable for outdoor use. The fire reached high toward the night sky where invisible clouds hung thick and warm, protecting us from the stars and the endlessness of space like a second duvet. The vodka had yet to revive a memory, but it was certainly doing a good job in getting me drunk. I thought about her question. I had no idea how to answer it.

She answered for me. "I didn't think so. Only rich people can afford to be atheists."

"What, like you?"

She laughed at me again, and put a hand to her mouth so as not to spit vodka. The orange firelight flickered on her face.

"I'm rich, am I?" she said after swallowing. "Look around you mate, I live in the bleeding third world."

I shrugged. "You're doing better than me."

"Jesus, who wouldn't? You're thick as pigshit," she said with a grunt.

I would've taken offence had it not been true.

"What I mean is, in a destroyed world, a person who has what you've got would be considered rich. In fact, I'd say that you are the richest person I've ever known. Tea and Vodka are worth more than silver and gold in this place."

She raised an eyebrow at me. "Getting a bit philosophical in our ine-briated state are we?"

Yes, I supposed I was.

"Well, Einstein, answer me this," She leaned toward me on the arm of her reclining chair. "How do you know the whole world has been destroyed?"

It was a good question. The doctor seemed quite sure of it and so did Henry come to think of it. It hadn't even occurred to me that a place still existed that wasn't dead bodies and smashed brick.

I stared at the flames for a moment. Zara stood up with difficulty, teetering over the wood pile at the side of the fire pit. The fire pit's wood pile was a mini version of the towering stack by the barbecue. Neat and tidy. She picked two large logs off the top and tossed them on the fire, just stopping herself at the last moment from following them into the flames. She staggered back to the chair and slumped into it. Booze splashed out of her glass and onto fingers she was now licking.

The warmth of the fire on my face complemented the tickling warmth in my vodkaed belly. The fire burned hotter with the new logs and I had to shield my eyes with my cooling hands until it was again bearable. Wrapped in the duvet in front of the fire, drunk with heavy eyes, I felt like a great hibernating bear wrapped up with her cubs. Zara sat with legs out, her duvet crumpled at her feet. My duvet was much heavier than hers. She'd given it to me saying that I would need it more than her. I believe the word she used was 'pansy'. I can be a pansy for one night if it meant feeling like I felt right now. I took another sip of the vodka. I would pay for this tomorrow, but for the moment, I was warm and Zara was talking about the Darkening. If I was very lucky, I could probably avoid going home all night.

"Now China," Zara started. "If there was a country to come out of the Darkening scot-free, it's them yellow bastards. No mamby pamby pseudo-socialist bollocks like us." She filled her glass back up with cop-per liquid from a second bottle, folded her legs underneath herself and handed the bottle to me. I emptied what was left in my glass and filled it with the new liquor.

"No health and safety, no safety nets. Communists they were. Government first, people second. Sacrifice the few to save the many." She took another swig. She swayed back and forth as she spoke and her accent seemed to change.

"No, before we lost contact with everything, those boys went in with tanks. Sorted everyone out right quick. Not us. We weren't supposedly barbarous enough to shoot at our own people." She took another swig. "At least, not at first."

I couldn't tell if what she was saying was true or if it was just the booze talking, but I didn't want to stop her. Knowing more about the Darkening was important if I was to find the machine.

"People were fed up of living like slaves. Of being lied to," she said. "We knew the end was coming for years and years, you couldn't turn the telly on without some greenie going on about it. Riots was hardly a new thing in this country, but many didn't seem to even know what they were rioting about."

She cleared her throat and sat unmoving, entranced by the flames.

"You can only rape the land and shit in the air for so long before it blows up in your face I guess. We got too comfortable papering over the cracks. If the cod disappears, catch mackerel, when the mackerel runs out, catch turbot, when the fish are gone, eat more beef. When everyone starts getting sick, make more drugs. Snow in July? put on a coat, thirty degrees in December? take it off."

She turned her eyes from the fire and looked in mine.

"When lightning strikes in a pine forest and ignites a year's worth of dropped needles, the fire it creates burns so fast and hot that you barely see it. Poof! The trees, the brush, the deer, the birds—everything— is burned black in an instant."

"But," she said, raising a stiffened finger.

"But. When the fire goes out, new shoots begin to appear and crea-tures emerge from burrows dug deep into the ground as soon as the fire is out. The surviving squirrels and woodpeckers may be singed and they may have even lost their children, but the next year, the forest comes back stronger and more vibrant than ever. More food, less competition, balance is restored."

She took a long pull from her glass and spit into the fire. The alcohol ignited into liquid orange as it splashed against the coals.

"When the fires are not allowed to burn, when they are *controlled*, the animals grow fat and overabundant. Food sources dwindle and fights that were once just to prove who was strongest were now fights for survival; fights to the death. And all the while, year on year, the needles tumble from the trees piling on the floor, unnoticed by the warring animals below. When the fire comes this time, when it can no longer be controlled, it comes as an inferno. It burns hot. And slow. Everything dies."

I watched her for a moment as the fire crackled. Her eyes threatening to close.

"You made it out alive," I said.

She laughed.

"Of course I did. When the fire burns all your food, you have to find food in places that you wouldn't ordinarily look. Unholy places."

I didn't have to ask to know she was talking about cannibalism.

"Don't look at me like that, sunshine," she said. "You know the taste of human flesh as well as I do. Just because you don't remember it don't mean it isn't so."

The fire was dying down. I smiled at her but I didn't want to delve into it further, even if she was kidding. It was clear I wasn't going to hear anything else of use about the Darkening that night. If there were memories of eating people buried deep within my mind, they were ones I'd just as soon not remember. As much to change the subject as anything else, I asked her about her time with the doctor.

"What d'you mean?" she asked, the bottle in hand.

I pointed at her arm. Under the heavy sweater she was wearing, deep scars criss crossed near the elbow. The scars that matched mine.

She brought the bottle to her lips, tipped it and swallowed three times before slowing tipping it back level, her lips releasing the rim with a hollow pop. She wiped the dripping booze from her lips with her wrist.

"You don't get to ask me that, yet."

She turned away from me and closed her eyes, pulling her duvet tight over her scrunched body. Before long, she was snoring.

The question was reckless; I knew it before I'd even asked it, but she was the one who offered the scars to me at our first meeting. I wouldn't make the mistake again, not until I'd remembered everything.

The flames rolled slow and small over the last few hunks of blackened wood. Somewhere far away a dog howled.

The embers flickered and the smoke swirled. My eyelids felt heavy and thick like wet towels. I pulled the duvet up around my neck as the night's cool air descended with the fire's retreat.

Fifteen

Sixteen days until the doctor returned.

I was awakened by the howling wind and pouring rain. I got out of bed and nailed the boards over the windows, but not before large puddles had collected on the floors of all the rooms.

Streams of water leaked in through spots in the ceiling and down the walls. The candle wicks were soaked, but I managed to use one of Zara's files and a firestone to start a fire with a couple of damp table legs and some paper. The apartment was dark with the boards up, but there was enough light from the fire to see the shapes of the furniture.

It was colder now and I huddled under the heavy, waxed jacket I had found in an old shop and sat in front of the fire until I was warm enough to encourage my feet into action.

I had only a few pieces of wood by the fireplace. There was some food in the busted refrigerator, but nothing that would set my taste buds alight. It was mostly potatoes from Zara's garden and a couple armloads of apples. I grabbed an old pot from the cupboard, poured water into it from the pail and placed it onto a metal barbecue grate over the fire. The wood hissed as the water made its escape from within the burning chunks. No matter how small I cut the potatoes, there wasn't going to be enough wood to cook them through. In my first few days, crunchy potatoes and apples would've been a gourmet meal, but now it sounded about as appealing as a snot pancake.

I was getting better at scavenging food, but most of what I gathered remained at Zara's as payment for her tutelage.

There would be more wood in the other apartments but I couldn't face them. With the weather as it was outside, the hallway would be as black as ink and the other flats were even more depressing than my own. Many of them were unsafe, the floors damp and eaten away. No, I'd be happy with crunchy potatoes today. Hopefully the rain would be finished tomorrow and I could go out looking for wood then. Or I could leave the city altogether.

It was clear that I was never going to discover the machine's location. My brain was indeed doing well at remembering the things that had happened to me since I awoke in the doctor's clutches, but the early glimpses I was getting of a life before the doctor has vapourised.

Somewhere close by, Bill, Henry and Raj sheltered themselves from the rain. Bill had never come to collect the two days gardening I owed him and if Henry and Raj hadn't been to my place looking for further companionship. It was almost as if they knew about the photos the doctor had given me and somehow felt too guilty to show their faces or perhaps pissed off that the doctor had thwarted some of their devious plans for me.

But none of them had shown me anything but kindness. A kindness that I feel I should have treated with suspicion, but didn't. If they did intend to carve me up like their victims in the photos, they were the best actors in the world.

The broken windows and mouldy walls, the dwindling supplies and friendships, everything was pointing me toward leaving the city, or at least the apartment for good. But there was more to this apartment than just the doctor's threats, there was a familiarity and a strange comfort of home. Putting up the weatherboards and gathering water, I could have done them with my eyes closed. The fire was pathetic and the smell of damp terrible, but it was mine. Only a fool would live here knowing the doctor could show up at any second, but if there was one thing I could add to a Things I Know For Sure list, it was that I was a fool. In a sick way, I wanted the doctor to come calling again.

On Day One, you trudged along the bones and skulls as if they were mere cobbles. Don't you find that strange?

I walked to the fridge, felt around the darkened shelves for Zara's potatoes. I found them on the second shelf where I had left them a few days ago. They felt spongy and had eyes sprouting from them, but I pulled them out anyway, flicking the sprouting bits off with my fingernails and chopping them into small, chunks with my knife, the white flesh marbled with black.

I grabbed the potato pieces, walked them to the fire and dropped them into the pot. The water was completely still. I tested it with a finger; it was stone cold. I tossed what was left of my wood onto the fire; two jagged pieces of chipboard and a few sticks. My boots were by the door. Outside it was pouring, but the idea of remaining in the too small, too dark apartment all day was more than I could bear. The fire was as small and cold as I was. As it stood, there would not be enough heat to even warm the potatoes through. Perhaps, Zara still had more to teach me.

I walked over to my boots and slipped them on. My toes were now showing through holes in the top and the grips on the bottoms flopped loosely when I walked.

★ ★ ★

The other flats were in much worse shape than mine. The floors below me were completely burnt out. Only the concrete walls, metal floor joists and bits of brick and piles of charred wood remained. The floors above were untouched by fire, the building must have been one of the lucky ones to catch fire while there was still a fire brigade. Or more likely, the endless rain put it out. It didn't matter; the rooms in the upper floors may have escaped the flames, but they did not escape scavengers and vandals. Everything had been removed so I knew not to waste any time looking for anything of value. I would just grab some of pieces of old wooden furniture for the fire and return to the apartment.

I moved from door to door on the sixth floor and gathered as much broken pieces of broken timber flooring as I could. The rain poured in through the open windows and most of the wood was soaked through. In the bedroom of the last flat along the hall, I managed to find a few drawers in an old dressing table. The fronts of the drawers and the top of the dresser were wet through, but when the drawers were pulled out, the insides were dry. I hauled the six drawers out of the room, two at a time and stacked them up by the stairs. The chipboard drawers would easily break into pieces so there was no problem fitting them into the fireplace, but they would burn very quickly. Without a fire, it would be a cold night in the apartment. Too cold.

I thought again of cycling back to Zara's. She would have a fire on and some hot food. Cycling in the pissing rain would be manageable, but I wouldn't be able to take the pitying look on her face. Thunder cracked again and the rain bucketed in to the empty apartment through the open window. I promised myself not to waste the next sunny day.

After dumping the drawers by the stairs, I made my way up to the roof. I still had a half full pail of water in the apartment, but there was no harm in grabbing another one.

At the top of the stairs, I leaned into the heavy metal door with my shoulder and pushed. It popped open and I was greeted by the full force of the wind. Even though it was still morning, the sky was black. A flash of lightning rippled across a piece of sky far away, followed closely by another rumble of thunder. From that spot, I could see the rooftops of the urban wasteland that was Manchester. A sea of collapsed roofs, exposed, blackened beams and crooked and crumbling chimneys. In the middle of it all stood four skyscrapers, three smaller ones surrounding a large green one in the middle. One of the smaller skyscrapers was sliced in half from top to bottom, like a bolt of lightning had cut through its centre splitting the building in two. Looked at it for too long made it feel as if it were swaying. If I stared at it long enough, the floor beneath my feet would begin to shift. Sometimes when I gazed out at it, I would have to grab at the doorjamb to stop myself from falling over. The rain slapped my face like tiny needles and it was only moments before my hair was soaked again. My jacket deflected the rain, but my boots were another story. I was getting quite used to having wet feet.

Usually, when I looked out across the roof, I would see at least twenty pails lined up together all overflowing with water, but at that moment, there were only five or six to be seen. And those five or six were tipped over and rolling across the gravel rooftop in the wind. I always placed them near the door for fear of soft spots in the roof. To save the pails now would mean risking a fall, but if I left them, they would be blown off.

I zipped my coat up to my chin and walked outside onto the roof.

I stepped gingerly, testing each step before giving it my full weight. The old roofing felt squelched under my feet through the gravel. The closest pail was a dozen steps away, rattling against an air conditioner in the wind. One foot in front of the other I moved. On my third step, my foot punched straight through the felt up to my ankle, the rotten boards underneath giving no resistance at all. I pulled my foot back up and stepped back.

The pails were lost. One wrong step and I would fall through. Lightning flashed again, this time closer, and the rain lashed down harder.

I walked back into the black stairwell, the door slammed shut behind me.

I rubbed my temples and laughed at myself in the blackened stairwell; the sound thumping dead into the walls like it had been sucked in by the masonry itself.

Tomorrow I would leave the apartment for good, the doctor could do what he wanted. I would get on my bike, make stops at Raj's and Bill's, get as many curries and pizzas as the WD40 and few pieces of gold would buy me and if they allowed me to live, I would leave this terrible city forever.

I would ride out to the other towns and into the country and find another town without doctors and dead things or an old farmhouse in the middle of nowhere in which to spend the rest of my days, however many more of those I might have.

Would the doctor bother pursuing me? Thunder crashed on the other side of the door and a pail could be heard skipping across the gravel top. If the doctor wanted to chase me, he was welcome.

I opened my jacket and felt inside, my chest was perfectly dry.

I shoved two of the drawers under my arms, took two more in my hands and descended the stairs to my apartment, barely touching the steps as I took them two and three at a time.

My body floated and I was dizzy with thoughts of cycling and eating wonderful things.

The fire had died down and the living room was almost completely dark. I walked toward the glowing embers and with renewed vigour, smashed them into small pieces with my bootheel, stacking the broken pieces and smashing them into smaller ones over my knee. Wood chips rained down with each blow, covering my feet with dust. I gathered the wood up and slid two large chunks into the fireplace under the pot. The flames took hold of the chipboard immediately. Back in business.

I pulled a full set of cutlery, two plates and a couple bags of tea in a rusty can. Zara had inspired me to make a better life for myself; I was now gathering things I used to throw away. There were also Henry's books.

Reading, eating off plates and sleeping in front of the fire was how I would spend my last night, dreaming of what I would find and do in the towns I saw in the atlas. Bolton, Preston, Stockport, Radcliffe, Farnworth, Heywood, Hyde. I could go further than any of those places, I could ride until there was nothing, I could ride to the coast! This time tomorrow I would be in a whole new place without the doctor and without Manchester. If in the morning, I decided push the embers onto the couch and leave the whole thing burning, it would be no less than was my right.

Fuck Manchester, let the whole city burn for all I cared.

I reached into the fridge and pulled one of the books out that Henry had given me. It was the book by the Japanese writer, Murako something. This book had once occupied the space under Henry's arm where a man had once lost his life. Probably more than one.

"Erm, you're Seth right?" the voice was behind me.

Terror gripped me by the back of the neck. I spun around and looked into my living room. The rising flames illuminated a human shape standing in the far corner. I fumbled over the kitchen surface looking for my knife, knocking the book and other things onto the floor.

"I... I'm not going to hurt you," the shape said.

The man struck a match under his chin bathing his face in orange light. The small flame caught in thick glasses perched on his nose, fastened with duct tape. I couldn't see the colour of the hat and cape in the matchlight, but I knew they were purple.

I searched the floor for something to defend myself with. The knife was at my feet. I picked it up and pointed it at the man. "Who are you?!"

He staggered backward and raised his hands, the match still lit. "My name is R-Roosevelt." The match burned down into his fingers. He hissed in pain and dropped the match, plunging the room into near darkness again.

I charged the darkened space where the boy had been standing and tackled him. He cried out as we both crashed into the floor. I wrestled him underneath me, sat on his chest and held the knife to his throat. He didn't put up a fight, choosing instead to hold his hands over his face.

He coughed and moaned underneath me.

"I'm f-from the bar?" he said.

I knew who he was; I had seen him many times in town, gathering garbage. At Raj's place stuffing his face. The eyes behind thick glasses peering at me from around the building opposite my front door. I had thought about following him that day, perhaps I should have.

"What do you want?"

"Can you please get off? You're hurting me."

I dug my knee further into his chest. He moaned again.

He made no attempt to throw me off. His stretchy clothing squeaked as he moved his arms over his face. His body was very thin, I felt as if I could break him in two with the smallest twist of my hips.

"I'll let you up, but if you come for me, I will kill you. Do you understand?"

"Yes!" he shouted.

I stood up slowly keeping my knife pointed at his face. Roosevelt exhaled deeply as I released him. The fire was burning bright now and most of the room was visible.

He turned over onto his side, reached for his hat and pulled it close to his bespectacled face. He plucked a few pigeons feathers that had fallen from his hat and tried in vain to stick them back on. After a few pained attempts, he tucked the feathers into the waistband of his trousers and put the hat back on his head.

I had not seen his face up close before. Greasy pimples on his cheeks and chin glistened in the firelight and his eyeballs were swollen and grotesque, amplified and twitchy behind his thick glasses. He looked like a man who was not made for this world. He didn't look like he was meant to survive the Darkening, in fact, he looked as if he'd spent the Darkening hiding under his bed. He stood up slowly and pushed his glasses up his nose. A long crack now bisected one of the lenses. I followed him with the knife as he stood up.

"If you are going to kill me, please do it quickly," he said.

His eye twitched as he stared at his boots. I repeated my question.

"What do you want?"

He shrugged his shoulders like a little boy. "J-Just the password. I was hoping you'd tell me the password," He kicked his boot into the floor and fidgeted with his cape. "But you don't have to if you don't want to."

When I had seen him around town, I had wondered at his sanity with his arms full of garbage. Always with his head down, impervious to distraction. In the bar, he didn't even look up as Big Henry and I passed by his table. Unbothered as rice spilled from his mouth onto his lap and the floor. At the time I thought a person so frivolous with food must be one who lived without fear. Even big Henry, a man who *really* had nothing to fear finished every grain of rice on his plate, he licked his plate clean.

But as I stood there now looking at Roosevelt with his stupid, over-sized hat and tatty cape, I experienced a new feeling. A feeling that I hadn't experienced for anyone but myself; Pity. I lived in the worst apartment in the whole of Manchester, surrounded by murderers and their skeletal victims, was about to leave on a journey that would most likely end in death and yet the only thing I could think of at that moment was how bad I felt for cracking his glasses.

I lowered the knife, walked back into the kitchen and picked up my book and tin of tea up off the floor.

He peeked up from his boots and hurried past me toward the door. He grasped the handle and opened it.

"What password?" I asked him.

He stopped moving. He looked into the hallway, pondering the question. He dropped his gaze to his feet and again fidgeted with his cape, pulling it around him for comfort. His glasses slid down his nose again. He pushed them back up and spoke to me still with his eyes on his boots.

"Your website. The p-password."

Not a single word in that sentence made sense. I rubbed my eyes with both hands.

"The n-numbers. You know, on your lip?"

So he had been listening to us in the bar after all. How could this timid little garbage collector possibly know what my numbers meant?

"The conversation in the bar. Raj's bar?"

"Yeah, I know what you're talking about. You were listening in?"

His eyebrow flicked and he choked back a tiny smile.

"I'm always listening," he said as he picked at a peeling bit of paint on the doorjamb, his eyes still unable to meet mine.

I moved to the fire and stuck a finger into the pot. The water was lukewarm. I popped a piece of potato in my mouth and chewed. It was as hard as chalk.

When I looked up at Roosevelt, he was still flicking at a piece of his cape. His face suggested a boy in his late teens or even early twenties, but his crazy get-up and fidgeting made him look a lost little boy.

I looked at the ceiling and breathed a heavy sigh.

"So what about this password then?"

The tiny smile reappeared on his face and grew across both cheeks.

He walked through the door into the hallway, motioning me to follow him.

I could never have stabbed him, that much I knew for sure. I knew it the second I had my knife at his throat. I didn't have what it took to do it, to kill a man. I doubted I could even kill the doctor when the time came.

It was a distressing thought.

There was probably little chance he knew anything about my numbers, but what the hell; I was certainly out of ideas and tomorrow I would be gone anyway. Spending my last night in Manchester with the little creep was not what I had planned, but what the hell. There would be many a lonely night to catch up on my reading in my future. At least I knew Roosevelt was a man I had no real need to fear, his twig-thin legs looked barely up to the challenge of keeping him upright. I picked up the pail and dumped some water on the flames. The wood hissed and smoked and the apartment slid back into darkness.

I grabbed my backpack and followed the strange man through the door.

Sixteen

The rain was still lashing down outside, thunder pounded the skies and lightning flashed. My jacket kept my chest dry, but my jeans were soaked and water poured into the cracks in my boots. The rain looked to be soaking through Roosevelt's velvet cape and into his tights, but he didn't seem remotely bothered by it.

It was impossible to tell what time it was. With all that had happened that day, it felt as if I had been awake for ages, but it had probably only been a couple of hours. It might still have been morning.

Roosevelt walked in front of me at a brisk pace, scanning the ground as usual. I followed him through the streets. He didn't look back once.

"Where are we going?" I asked.

He pointed without stopping.

He was pointing at the green skyscraper in the middle of the city. What's more, he was pointing at the top.

"You don't mean that tower?"

He didn't say anything, he just continued walking, quickening his pace.

The skyscraper looked even more unstable from close up. The lightning flashes illuminated the deep green windows caked with grey muck. Shredded curtains puffed out of large black rectangles at random intervals where the windows were smashed or missing completely. A bed frame teetered through an open window on one of the upper floors.

The megastructure rose higher as we approached. Lightning flashed again. An entire floor's worth of windows were missing a third of the way up. Through the smashed windows, the wind howled, wolf-like, urging all who approached to turn and go back the way they came.

Unfazed, Roosevelt advanced on the tower. He swung one arm back and forth and held his hat on against the wind with the other. He coasted across the shattered pavements and streets, zig-zagging around the piles of rubbish with ease. He never wasted a step and never looked up. Every now and then I was forced into a run just to keep up.

We turned a corner and the bottom of the skyscraper spread out before us. Smashed beds and television sets ringed the building. Crushed glass was everywhere, piled over my head in some places glittering like emerald sand dunes. It crunched under our feet as we approached like dead insects. I'd seen the tower many times, but was always careful to give it a wide berth.

There were bodies everywhere. I had gotten used to seeing dead people in the streets, but not on this scale. In some places they were stacked three or four deep. Most of them little more than stretched and twisted lengths of blackened skin and cracked bones. Thick pieces of dried flesh were strewn about amongst the smashed glass and furniture. A body lied supine over the top of a car. His arms were detached and lay rotting on either side of the car; his mouth stretched wide into a frozen scream. Rats that had been feasting on its face scattered into dark corners as we approached. Blackflies swarmed over the putrefying guts spilled over the bonnet. The man was not a victim of the Darkening. The body was too fresh. I swallowed the bile that rose into my throat.

This was insane.

"I'm not going in there," I said.

Roosevelt ignored me and kept moving toward the entrance.

I stopped and said it again.

He stopped and turned back toward me.

"What's the matter?" he asked.

"What do you mean, 'what's the matter'? Look around."

He shot me a questioning look. A look that suggested walking over mountains of smashed glass and heaped dead to enter a swaying skyscraper was the most natural thing in the world.

"B-But I live here."

How could that be true? How could anyone live in that structure? My apartment building was bad, but it was nothing compared to this. Behind Roosevelt, I could see the chipped and mouldy tile floor of the lobby.

"You live *here*?" I asked him.

He nodded and again turned toward the building. He skipped around the bodies, over the glass and disappeared inside.

I picked up a fist-sized piece of glass. It was heavy and caked with mud. I brushed the mud off to see the scratched green underneath. The edges had been worn down smooth by years of weather. That piece of glass probably lived in that building for years, decades even. I wondered if it had spent more years on the ground than in the air.

Roosevelt's face reappeared in the doorway, he was waving his hand at me to follow.

I took one last look up the side of the building and closed my eyes against the falling rain. Above me the thunder rumbled and the wind continued to howl. A shiver ran through my body as much in fear as in cold. It was either follow this lunatic in the hope that he was not a deranged killer or go home to my lonely apartment. Looking at the smashed building I knew it was more than a hunch that he didn't know anything about my numbers, I knew it for certain. The boy was nuts. But going back without at least taking a look inside seemed a waste. If nothing else, the experience would be another memory to file away. Climbing forty flights of stairs with a disturbed kid in a cape seemed like a ridiculous thing to do, but it sounded better than trudging home to a cold pot of hard potatoes.

What the hell.

I opened my eyes again to see the young man still waving at me. He was persistent; I'd give him that.

The lobby was massive. Flat, grey light entered from all sides through the huge glass walls. The ceiling tiles were missing, exposing miles of rusted pipes and ductwork. Liquid was dripping everywhere.

The most striking thing about it was its emptiness. There was nothing on the floors; they had been swept completely clean. No bodies, no garbage, not a shard of broken glass.

Roosevelt stood in the centre of the lobby. His arms were out at his sides and he was smiling. "Welcome to my home," he said.

His manner changed once he was inside the tower. He still twitched and fidgeted, but his slouch disappeared as soon as he stepped through the doors, shrugging it off as if it were a heavy coat. He was actually quite tall when he stood up straight.

His arms swung almost merrily as he skipped away from me.

His new manner was unsettling, but not as unsettling as his destination. Roosevelt was skipping toward the elevators.

He entered the open elevator car and again motioned me to follow him. Following him through open streets was one thing, following him into a dark, tiny elevator car was another.

"Listen, kid, I don't know about this."

Roosevelt emerged from the elevator, grabbed my shirtsleeve and pulled me across the tile floor by the arm. "C'mon," he said. "You'll like it, I promise."

If I didn't see his hand on my arm, I would never have known it was there. He didn't hold my arm, he cradled it like a child holding a rose. If he had any evil intentions in mind, I could easily stop him from doing anything I didn't want him to do.

I allowed him to lead me into the elevator. I might as well humour him, a couple minutes of make believe here before returning to the apartment to get those potatoes boiling again. I supposed I owed him that much for breaking his glasses.

The elevator cabin was dark. Large jagged cracks ran across the mirrored walls and the buttons were coated in grime. A boom of thunder pounded the air and the building groaned high above.

Roosevelt produced a small key from under the stretchy, purple shirt he was wearing. The key was attached to a long gold chain around his neck. He pushed the key into a slot in the panel, twisted it and pushed the button marked "PH". While most of the buttons were blackened to the point of being illegible, the PH button was clean and well worn.

Nothing happened.

I closed my eyes and massaged my temples. When I opened them again I could see Roosevelt beside me in the grey half-light grinning like an idiot. Many of his teeth were missing and the ones that were left were the colour of burnt plastic. This poor kid in his tights and his stupid cape, the Darkening must have scarred him something terrible.

I smiled back. I couldn't believe I'd ever been afraid of him.

For a few long moments, only the sound of the rain hitting the pavement outside and distant thunder could be heard.

"Are we almost there?" I asked.

Roosevelt scowled. "What d'you mean? The car isn't even moving yet."

A chain rattled above the elevator car followed by a heavy metallic clunk.

"Sometimes, it just takes a minute to get going."

The elevator jerked upwards. My legs buckled and I fell to the floor with force, putting my hands out just in time to keep my face from smacking into the floor.

Roosevelt said nothing, he just stood in the corner, that idiot-grin still on his face.

A slow moan of grinding metal engulfed the car as it wheezed into motion. I grasped the handrail and pulled myself up. Below me, the ground floor slowly dropped away through the open elevator door. "How did–"

"The doors actually do work, but I like to keep them open," he interrupted. "Bit claustrophobic."

Each floor appeared from above, loitered for awhile in front of us and creaked away as the elevator ascended. Each one, the same as the last. Stained wallpaper, punched plaster, ripped carpets and missing doors. As each floor passed by the open doors, the city could be seen through the windows falling away from us. The air rhythmically pushed and pulled on the elevator car as if the building itself were breathing.

"Hold on," Roosevelt said. "Twelve is a bit exciting." His grin was gone and he was grasping the railing with both hands. He was bracing himself.

I wrapped my arms around the railing just in time for floor twelve to appear from above. A gale roared into the car, sucking my feet out from under me and pulling me through the open doors. My body snapped out straight, and I held onto the railing with both hands. I kicked out hard, trying to pull my dangling legs back in, but the force of the wind was too strong. Roosevelt was saying something, but I couldn't hear it. Beyond the doors was empty space. No walls, no windows, just the black sky, rain and oblivion.

The wind pulled at me harder as floor thirteen descended toward my legs. I was screaming. Just as I managed to pull a leg in, my boot slipped and again my legs were whipped out through the open doors. Floor thirteen was only inches away; I was going to be crushed!

Roosevelt reached down, grabbed me by a pant leg and pulled me into the car just as the thirteenth sliced into the elevator doorway. The roar was snuffed out and everything again went quiet except for the ringing in my ears.

I scrambled to the back of the car, crouched down and grabbed the rail with one arm, feeling my legs with the other, my eyes tightly shut. I felt no pain and both of my legs were where they were supposed to be. My fingers rolled over my toes through the cracks in my boots. I counted them: Onetwothreefourfive, Onetwothreefourfive. My chest was heavy and I gulped at the air, my back was sweating and there were hot tears on my cheeks.

"Woof, it's a bad one tonight," Roosevelt said. His arm was again on my shoulder, stronger this time. He was trying to help me to my feet.

"Don't worry," he said. "Should be fine from here."

I opened my eyes and stole a look through the elevator doors. Floor thirteen and fourteen were much the same as the earlier floors. I had never been more happy to see mouldy walls, peeled wallpaper and curled carpet.

I stood up slowly as fourteen became fifteen. It wasn't until I had fully regained my feet that I realised I was shaking. Roosevelt watched me get up, but when my eyes met his, his gaze dropped to his feet.

Three more floors rolled past before I was able to speak again.

"Fucking claustrophobia?"

He shrugged. He was fidgeting with his cape again. "Twelve isn't usually *that* bad."

Up through the spine of the building we ascended. My hands stayed glued to the railing the rest of the way.

There were other 'exciting' floors as Roosevelt put it, but nothing like twelve. Once we passed nineteen, the fluorescent light in the ceiling flickered once, twice and then remained on, filling the elevator car in a hollow white light. Roosevelt beamed. "The friction," was all he said.

The milky light bulb hummed. The light that fell on my hands was unlike anything I had ever seen. The ghostly whiteness and the sharp shadows made my hands look false, like they belonged to a puppet.

"Bulb needs changing," he said.

Somehow I knew what he meant by his 'friction' comment. The elevator light worked like an old bicycle headlamp generator. A vision of cycling up a steep hill at night, the generator attached to the rim of my bike wheel making my progress ever more difficult. I was a child delivering newspapers in the early morning.

It was a memory. A real one. I could taste the dew and see the numbers on the houses. Grumpy, old man Witherspoon lived at Forty-eight. Never tipped me once, the stubborn old goat.

The memory blinked out as quickly as it came.

The elevator moved faster and smoother the closer to the top it got. 25, 30, 35, 40, the floors passed without incident. The odd fake plant or upended food cart were the only things to differentiate one floor from the next. Roosevelt and I didn't speak the rest of the way; we just stood in a kind of awkward silence.

It was around the thirtieth floor that I noticed the terrible smell in the elevator and the thirty-fifth when I realised it was me. How long had it been since I washed? I was definitely due.

The car slowed and stopped softly at the top. The room in front of me was completely black.

"Penthouse," Roosevelt said. "Lingerie, home furnishings, and–"

He disappeared through the open elevator door into the darkness.

"Wait!" I shouted grabbing at the air where he used to be.

Roosevelt didn't answer. The fluorescent light in the elevator quickly dimmed and blinked out. I was in total darkness and I didn't know where Roosevelt was. This was his home. The spider had caught his fly.

I unshouldered my backpack and fumbled madly for the zip. I opened the bag and heard the knife clatter to the floor. I dropped to my hands and knees scrambling for it.

I heard a heavy *ker-clunk* somewhere far off that was followed by Roosevelt's voice.

"–electricals!"

The room exploded in a volcanic display of swirling blues, reds and yellows. Flickering, spinning and dancing, the light moved across and through the room. And from every corner, noise. Toy trains rattled over long tables covered in track, airplanes buzzed around in circles above my head attached to string hanging from the lofty ceiling. Telephones bleeped, horns blared and kettles hissed.

Every couch, table and chair and every inch of the floor was covered in electric gizmos. Flickering screens, clattering toy robots, crying dolls. Glowing tubes of coloured light and lamps of all shapes and sizes glowed and swirled. Long strings of multicoloured lights hung down from the ceiling and wrapped marble pillars like pieces of hard candy. A wall of television sets at the far end erupted into light and sound.

Everywhere I looked, it whizzed, pulsed and popped.

I gazed at it for a few moments before I realised I was holding my breath. My arms and legs numbed and I could hear my own heartbeat and my head was aflood with image and sound. Visions of drinking beer in the back of a truck, watching a High school football game, exams in college classrooms, men in army uniforms. And faces. Glorious faces. A woman with straight, black hair dancing in a bar, smiling up at me.

"It's... amazing." I could barely hear my voice over the clattering.

I walked toward the tables full of trains in the centre of the room. Roosevelt grabbed me by the hand and raised a finger. "Give it a minute," he mouthed through the din.

As if on cue, the rattling toys and appliances settled down. The airplane's propellers stopped spinning above and they glided silently in decreasing circles. One by one, the kettles and appliances went quiet, the toy cars wheezed to a halt, the televisions were muted, the robots rested, the clocks calmed and the dolls dozed.

After a few moments, the room was still. Only the swirling and blinking lights and quietly rattling trains remained.

Roosevelt whispered into my ear. "I leave the trains on cuz I like the sound."

It was even more beautiful in the quiet. Roosevelt led me through the colossal room. Long, colourful cables of every conceivable thickness and length coiled and stretched across the dusty carpet like snakes across a jungle floor. I half expected them to turn and hiss as I stepped on them. Bright green circuit boards adorned with shiny gold bits of metal were scattered everywhere amongst the toys and appliances.

Circuit boards. The green panels I saw in his hands as he searched the streets, they're called circuit boards.

"Watch your step," Roosevelt said, pointing at a small robotic clown lying limp on the floor. The white paint on his face was chipped, exposing rusted metal beneath. Its eyes were dead and its smiling, mechanical mouth was frozen open. "That one always manages to find itself on the floor. I think it's suicidal."

Together we moved across the wilderness of cable and light toward a pair of large glass doors at the far end of the room.

Roosevelt took the handles of both doors in his hands and pushed them apart. They slid smoothly in their tracks. The hush of the room was suddenly invaded by the roaring wind.

The rooftop patio was vast. Rain pummeled my face and jacket and splashed in small puddles. Coloured light poured out through the open doors onto the roof, but none penetrated the emerald glass. From the outside, you could see nothing of the Wonderland that existed beyond.

Roosevelt rapped on the window with his knuckles. "Mirrored."

Stretched across the roof, an enormous bank of glass panels pointed skyward. Reflections of the grey clouds swept across the huge lake of glass, moving in unison with the actual sky above. It was two skies; one created by god above and one created by this strange man.

"Solar panels," he said.

Solar panels generated electricity from sunlight. I looked up at the dark clouds.

"Not today, of course. They charge the batteries on sunny days," he said pointing at the row of garden sheds lined up at the far edge. "Manchester weather doesn't allow me to do the light show every day, but I'd hoped you'd be coming by tonight. I don't get many visitors."

He'd prepared that show just for me. It must have taken him ages to store enough power to do that.

"Come on," he said.

He led me back into the warm room and whooshed the doors closed, they came together with a snap. We passed the bank of muted television sets. In one of the screens, a man walked through a desert with a baby in his hands, in another, a man and a woman were kissing and in a third, two men in black suits held out a pair of pistols. Each screen showed a different movie; all of them in sunny locations and all completely silent. Roosevelt himself moved without sound. Only my squeaky bootsteps and the distant clacking of the toy trains disturbed the silence. We were heading toward a small wooden desk and a chair with wheels on it.

On the table sat a flatscreen computer monitor and a plastic keyboard. Both of which seemed to be working.

Roosevelt stopped suddenly and looked back at me. "Do you mind if I have a look?"

"At what?" I asked.

"Your… you know," he said flicking his index finger at his bottom lip.

The numbers. He blushed despite himself. He knew what the numbers were, but he wanted to see them for himself. There was something about his boyish curiosity that felt familiar.

I nodded.

He moved to me and took my chin in his hand.

"Can you open your mouth wide so I can look all over in case there is anything else?"

I nodded and opened wide. He would not find anything, I had checked every square inch.

Coloured light blinked and floated across his face as he peered into my mouth. His eyes squinted through his glasses and his face darted this way and that as he conducted his examination. I flipped my tongue up and down allowing him a look into every crevice.

He motioned for me to flip my lips back. I complied.

"Hm," he said.

"What?"

"The numbers on your lip are perfect."

"Gee, thanks," I said.

"No, I mean they are *too* perfect. They weren't just drawn on by some greasy bloke in a tattoo parlour. The lines are capped and inked in different widths like in some kind of fancy serif font."

I let my lips drop back into place and swallowed. "Believe it or not, kid, I already figured that out."

"I doubt anyone could have been capable of inking numbers of that quality and so small on a person's lip. No hand was that steady, even in the beforetime. They don't look drawn, they look *printed*."

"Yeah, I–"

He interrupted. "But you know what's really weird?"

He sat back down at the chair staring past me.

"What?"

"It's not an *old* tattoo. My Dad had tattoos. Really good ones from the beforetime and even the ink on those had bled a little bit. There is none of that on yours. Those numbers look like they were put on yesterday."

Well that settled it; the doctor had done it. But why? Why would he do that? How could he have known I would find the website thing

Roosevelt had spoken of, and even if I did, why go to all that trouble? Surely, it would have been easier to just tell me about it.

"Are you sure there isn't another tattoo somewhere else, maybe–"

I stopped him before he could finish. "I'm sure."

"But maybe somewhere you couldn't see–"

I put my hand up to stop him speaking. I would let him look in my mouth, but that was where his examination would end.

Roosevelt sat down in the chair and tapped once on the screen. The monitor awoke and bathed his face in pink light.

"64 full stop 22 full stop 66 full stop 50" he said, pointing to where they were typed at the top.

"You see?"

The pink screen was covered in rectangles and small boxes with red x's.

"My father and I searched for a functioning website for years and years. This is the first one I've ever seen."

Roosevelt's stammer had lessened and his boyish mannerisms were now but a memory. His voice was still soft and childlike, but his fidgeting and shyness were gone. For the first time, he seemed to look *comfortable* in his teen-aged body.

"Do you know what these are?" he asked me, tapping the rectangles and red x's.

I shook my head at him.

"Broken images. The server that is hosting this site was pulling the images from somewhere else."

I hadn't a clue what he was talking about.

"It's to be expected seeing as how the world has ended I suppose," he said. "This is the important bit here."

Roosevelt pointed at a black square with a triangle on the front. Underneath the black square was a white box next to a single word. Password.

"This might be a bit... erm strange for you."

Roosevelt tapped the triangle with his finger and the black square disappeared.

In its place a movie was playing. On the movie an empty chair was filled with a man.

A man who looked like me.

The 'me' on the screen scratched his nose and stared at the camera silently.

He looked like me, but his cheeks were pockmarked and he had a large mole on his top lip. He was also completely bald. His face was fuller than mine, but his skin was pale and sickly and dark circles ringed his eyes. He was wearing a short-sleeved shirt with a collar. A pair of dark rimmed spectacles dangled from his chest pocket and his chest rose and fell as he wheezed. Perhaps the man was my brother.

"What is this?" I asked Roosevelt.

Roosevelt shook his head and shrugged. "Just watch."

My screen brother checked his watch and nodded his head as he counted the seconds. When he was finished counting, he picked up a large white piece of card and held it in front of his chest.

The card read:

My name is Seth Cohen. I am an engineer and a physicist.

He held the card up for a few seconds and flipped it over. On the other side it read:

Your name is Seth Cohen. You are an engineer and a physicist.

The screen displayed the back side of the card for the same amount of time as he had for the front side.

"Is he talking to me?"

Roosevelt shushed me and pointed back to the screen.

The screen me dropped the card and picked up another one. It read:

Watch the video in full screen very closely, Seth. Do not turn away. No matter how painful.

The words 'No matter how painful' were written in heavy red ink and underlined several times; the underlines pressed hard and drawn repeatedly.

The screen me disappeared and the video went black. Roosevelt tapped something on the monitor and the black square enlarged to fill the screen.

The square flashed brightly once, burning my eyes.

On the backs of my eyelids, the words 'open your eyes' remained. A campfire smell filled my nostrils.

"Open your eyes, Seth. Keep watching," Roosevelt said.

I opened my eyes and the screen flashed a second time, even brighter. This time I saw the words on the screen before I shut my eyes. '*Open your mind'* it said this time, burning again onto my retinas. The room swirled and my stomach turned. Panic struck me from within.

This had happened to me before.

I opened my eyes a third time. The screen strobed violently with bright white light and I felt myself falling backwards.

The shocked look on Roosevelt's face was the last thing I saw.

★ ★ ★

When I awoke, I was lying on the couch. Roosevelt stood over me, holding a glass of water.

"I'm sorry, I'm sorry!" he said, his eyes wide. "Are you alright?"

Behind his face the room twinkled in their blues, yellows and reds. I put a hand to my face and ran it across my cheek.

"Yeah, I think so."

"You scared me! You were shuddering and twitching everywhere."

"Yeah, yeah I know. It's epilepsy. I have epilepsy."

There were three stages to the tonic–clonic seizure:

1. ***Aura.*** *The epileptic feels dizzy with a sense of foreboding or even strong de ja vu.*

2. ***Tonic phase.*** *The epileptic loses consciousness and the muscles tense. If the patient is standing, he or she will fall.*

3. ***Clonic phase.*** *Muscles contract and relax rapidly, causing convulsions. The epileptic may roll or stretch as the seizure spreads throughout the body. The eyes roll back or close and the tongue is often bitten. Incontinence is common in this phase.*

I reached down to my crotch. It was dry. Small miracles.

"Don't watch that video again," he said.

I smiled at him. "Don't worry, I won't."

Subject 5C009 didn't need to be tortured. The memories came back to him on their own.

After an epileptic seizure.

"Seizures trigger neuronal activity," I said to Roosevelt.

"What?" he asked.

I stood up and walked back to one of the gadget tables and picked up a smartphone. There was a movie playing on its tiny screen. A car was ploughing through a sunny city at full speed. A man in a black sweater at the wheel. The car twisted and turned, careening through the steep city streets. I put it back down and picked up a camera. On the back, a digital screen displayed a photo of a young woman with long blond hair in shorts and sunglasses standing in front of a sign that read 'Route 66'.

Smartphone. Camera. Bicycle. Bugatti Veyron. Newspaper round. High School Football. College Classroom. The Marines. A dancing girl with straight, black hair.

"What? What is it?" he asked.

I batted a hand at Roosevelt. It was my turn to shush him.

I pushed a pile of circuit boards off a second couch and sat down. The bank of televisions loomed high above me. I closed my eyes and massaged my forehead. Flickering shapes were cast onto my closed eyes by the wall of television screens.

Roosevelt was speaking again. "Do you remember something?"

The TVs buzzed and somewhere a doll cooed.

I placed my palms over my eyes and let myself sink into the soft leather of the couch, losing myself in the hypnotic sounds around me. The toy train rattled and whistled as it clacked softly past my head. Raindrops tapped softly at the glass; the storm was easing. A mechanical toy laughed its wheezing, tinny laugh far off in the distance and a childish voice spoke in muffled words from inside a box. The coloured lights dissolved into the backs of my eyelids. They danced and swirled into images.

Before long I was dreaming. A strange child sat at a table blowing out candles from atop a large silky white cake, a pair of hands on a steering wheel, a man with curly hair standing over a large table, carving a turkey. A faceless woman in a yellow jacket held a newspaper over her head to keep the rain off.

Men. Lots of men. Shouting.

"On your feet soldier!" It was a man with a short black moustache. His eyes appeared through the blurred flesh and shiny bits of metal on his shirt snapped into focus. Heavy eyebrows and dark eyes. A sharp nose and full lips. Coffee-stained teeth, coffee-stained *breath*.

I recognised him.

The man stood over me as I sat in my office in front of a computer. On the monitor, a machine simulation spun and moved. Across the top Numbers.... numbers...

Inside my head things were happening. More faces pulled forward, clear and distinct. A man in a lab coat, a woman in a wedding dress. They were my friends. Perhaps my lovers. I could feel my mind stirring from its cold sleep. Synapses crackled. Switches were flicked. Fluorescent lights in my head blinked into life. The room, the toys–

I opened my eyes.

"I remember the password."

Roosevelt jumped up from the chair. "You do? you do?"

My brain was firing. Generating thoughts, calculating. I could feel the electricity pulsing across synapses into my head and across my body.

Henry was a child when the Darkening started. A *child*.

Lucy was my daughter.

A small face arose from the gloom in my mind. Black pigtails. Red dress, Hello Kitty backpack. I was pushing her on the swings.

Her mother and I were divorced, I only saw her on the weekends. Lucy played the flute and went to music school. I'd hated that. Her mother tried to keep her from me, but she would sneak away and we'd have movie nights together. She was beautiful.

Roosevelt placed a hand on my shoulder.

I grabbed my coat and ran for the door, hopping over the yards of twisted cable, leaving Roosevelt and his pleas for me to stop behind me.

"The password, Seth! The password!"

I stopped with my hand on the door.

His eyes were huge and he was staring right at me. It was the same expression he had when I saw him outside my front door. I was frightened at the time. I wouldn't be frightened anymore.

"jellyfish–1–9–8–8"

He smiled and I opened the door.

"Wait!," he shouted. "Don't you want to see?"

I smiled at the boy.

"I don't need to. I already know what's there."

Into the elevator and down I went. It dropped through the building much faster than it had risen up. Floor 12 was less windy, but still had a go at tossing me into the ether. The car jarred to a stop sharply at the bottom.

I ran through the streets as the memories rolled over me like water from a hot spring. The clouds were breaking and the streets were shining as streams of sunlight poured down from in between the cracks in the clouds.

I burst through the door in my apartment lobby, took the stairs three at a time and spilled into my apartment.

As I stood looking at my pitiful room and my meager possessions something hit me. The most wonderful thought in the world. It was more than just a thought; it was a realisation. A realisation so powerful and bright that I thought my chest would explode with the joy of it. I skipped around my living room with an imaginary partner, singing a forgotten song at the top of my lungs. Through the hall, past my old bedroom, I bounded in a state of delirium before collapsing on Lucy's bed in a fit of laughter. I lay there rolling this same thought in my head over and over before falling into the heaviest sleep of my life. Soon my fears and night-mares would be over. Soon the locals, the death, the destruction would be a distant memory, existing as nothing more than something to look back on with fondness, something to say 'I lived through that'. The thought was something so bewildering but so certain as to be barely thinkable.

That was the best part. It was something I *knew* it to be true. I didn't *think* it was true, I knew it. My very existence was proof of its trueness!

When I awoke the next morning the same thought pulsed from my brain sending shockwaves through the room and the universe beyond.

I know where the machine is.

Seventeen

My father was indeed a farmer. The doctor had gotten that one right as well.

We had a farm just outside of Stavely, North Dakota. Wheat and cattle. He moved out from New York in his twenties looking for some space. There was no space in New York, he'd say, especially for a New York Jew.

He hated New York City. If it wasn't the oppressive heat, it was the terrible cold; if it wasn't the cold, it was the smog, the poverty, and especially the cramped living conditions. He hated apartments.

"The only difference between a prison yard and New York City is that in a prison you march in circles, in Manhattan you march in squares". Most people in Stavely spoke about New York like it was some sort of alien wonderland. Skyscrapers hurtling toward the sky, Broadway, Times Square. Not my father. To him it was nothing but a cesspool stacked to the gills with prostitutes, disfigured homeless and 'banker assholes'.

"Only people who've never lived there think New York is great," he would always say. "New York is a nightmare. Do you know what a one bedroom apartment goes for out there? Oy".

'Oy' was the only even remotely Jewish thing he ever said. All his North Dakotan friends teased him about it. People in Stavely didn't say 'Oy', they said things like 'Jesus Christ' and 'For shit's sake'. They said 'Fuck Off' like a braying donkey.

My father said 'Oy'. He said 'Oy' just like a New York Jew.

He loved farming. A thermos of hot coffee, a denim Storm Rider and a copy of the Stavely Bulletin were all that he needed. Dark, autumn mornings were his favourite. The dew on the grass, the heavy mist blanketing a heavy crop and the puff of black smoke from a diesel engine as it sputtered to life. He loved everything about working the land; the isolation, the clacking of the machinery and the clacking livestock. He even liked shoveling manure, he could wax poetic about the *smell*.

The weather was unpredictable back then; it buried many other, softer, farmers who were used to more reliable weather conditions. Not my father. He thrived on variability, it gave him something to complain about. As an orphan growing up in New York, he didn't know what was going to happen from one day to the next. People, businesses, came and went every day. Neighbourhoods rose from the earth and collapsed back into it with the regularity and severity of a Wall Street commodities market. New Yorkers adapted, they rolled with the punches. The sky could fall overnight and a New Yorker would barely give it a passing glance; he'd step over the sky on his way to work. A little thing like drought or early frost was not going to stop my father.

He conducted my bar mitzvah in the field. Just me and him. We were the only Jews in Stavely, probably the only ones in the whole of the Midwestern United States. It certainly felt that way. He didn't want to do a Bar Mitzvah at all, he was never a practising Jew by any stretch and because my mother was a shiksa, apparently, I didn't really count as a Jew anyway. The irony being that it was my shiksa mother that made him give me a Bar Mitvah, she said it was important for us to keep in touch with our 'Jewish roots'. She was more proud of her Jewish family than her Jewish family were. I couldn't have cared less, if I was honest; frankly, the fewer of my classmates who knew I was half-Jewish, the better.

She had none of it. When you were a sixth generation North Dakotan like my mother was, you clung on to anything that made you different. Her best friend in grade school would still be three houses down on her dying day. Everyone in town called her Milly and knew everything about her. They knew her Dad had run the local stereo shop and that at her prom she was homecoming queen. They knew that her first car was a Chevy Nova and that she was the first one in her school to have her period. The desk in which she was sitting when the red plague had unexpectedly paid its first visit was still there in Mrs Samuelsson's grade six Language Arts class when I found myself there. Greg Wilson, a bully who would later act as starting linebacker for the Stavely Giants and who was at least half orangutan had forced me to sit in my mother's 'rag desk' as it was still being called twenty years later.

In North Dakota, routine and the safety it brought with it were really all a person had. If you had a functioning cerebral cortex (and believe me, most in Stavely didn't) you needed to find a 'thing' to make life livable. If you didn't have a 'thing', your time in Stavely was spent drinking, fighting and going slowly mad. You could only go up to the Red Rooster for cigarettes and beer so many times before a twelve gauge found its way into your mouth. You needed a 'thing' to give you something to talk about and even more importantly something for others to say about you behind your back.

Dick Dyck had a number of 'thing's. Collecting butterflies, beekeeping, his National Geographics. You needed a lot of 'thing's when your name was Dick Dyck. Walter Smith was into tattoos. After every harvest he would drive up to Fargo with a sketchy drawing and a hundred bucks and come back with a bloody bandage. Walter's new tattoo would get everyone talking, the removal of the bandage could've been the unveiling of a travelling Picasso judging by the crowd it drew. All of his tattoos were puns. 'A heart on his sleeve' and a rooster on his leg with a noose around its neck so he could boast of a 'cock that hangs below his knee'. The last one I saw before I left Stavely were eyes tattoed to the back of his head.

Having a Jewish family was my mother's 'thing'. Of course, no one else had gone to such extremes as marrying a Jew, but (although she'd never admit it) my mother loved being talked about. Until one of the local girls married a black man, she'd be the most talked about woman in town, and that suited her just fine indeed.

It was a very tough autumn the year of my Bar Mitzvah. We'd had three straight weeks of rain and the forecast was for snow on the weekend. Our window to put the wheat on the ground was smaller than it had ever been.

I'd been on the tractor for fourteen hours and could barely keep my eyes open. I'd eaten all the food and had drunk all the coffee. It had been sunny that day and the sun was just retreating below the horizon. Long, thin clouds strafed the sky in orange and purple. The endless prairie in front of me was going dark and soon I wouldn't be able to see much of anything.

I reached above my head, flicked a switch and blinked twice as the cab was filled with light.

The rain was responsible for the delayed harvest (which meant it was responsible for my long days on the tractor) but at least it kept the dust down. Back and forth I drove the huge red machine, relieving the standing wheat of its grain and spitting out the rest into long thin piles. Tomorrow or the next day, I would be back on this field, bundling up the hay into bales. The combine moved steadily forward hour upon hour, the monotonous drone of the reels and augers made for a perfect lullaby. I shook my head in an attempt to expunge the cobwebs and picked up my thermos again hoping some coffee had materialised. It hadn't.

You never saw my father's dusty old pickup coming, you always heard it first, the loud chugging of the busted exhaust followed by the whirring timing belt and finally the metal on metal squeaking of the brakes and the audible clunk as he threw it into Park.

Many times that day, I swore I had heard his truck's approach but it was always something else. A passing earthmover levelling the gravel road, a spray plane overhead, a squeak inside the cab, or a squeak inside my sleep deprived head.

As I rested my chin on the steering wheel, I heard the thumping sound again, but couldn't bear to look. I couldn't risk being disappointed again, I had been on the rig too long. If I looked back into the empty space where my father's truck should be once more, I'd go crazy. Instead, I kept my heavy eyes on the lines. The lines.

The thumping sound grew louder before it was joined by a whirring and a squeaking. That definitely sounded like the truck. My betraying eyes stole a quick glance at the rearview before I could stop them. In the mirror, my father's old Ford lumbered toward the tractor. Grey curls of jewfro and mirrored shades bobbed up and down behind a cracked windshield; a coffee thermos and ziploc bag of sandwiches spread across the dash.

I brought the combine to a stop and slithered out of the cab into the hot evening air.

He pulled up and flung the truck door open. I trudged toward him like a zombie, visions of my mother's mashed potatoes and my pillow in my head.

"Good job, son," my Dad said as he walked past me toward the combine.

I nodded at him and climbed into the truck.

"Hang on a sec, kid." he said and walked back. Reaching behind me into the back seat, he pulled out a cardboard box and plonked it into my lap with all the ceremony of a fisherman tossing back an unwanted dogfish to the sea.

"Here."

I stared at the box and looked back up at him, barely able to lift my head. The *gubba gubba gubba* sound of the giant, idling tractor in my ears.

"Happy Bar mitzvah. L'Chaim and shit. You're a man now, congratulations."

He patted me on the shoulder, climbed up into the cab and pushed the huge machine into motion.

The box, like everything my father touched was dirty, beat up and sealed with duct tape. I started peeling the tape back when the combine stopped and the door flung open.

"Jesus Christ, kid, your lines are crooked again!" he shook his head, snarled something I couldn't make out, slammed the door and set off.

Oh yes, he was now saying 'Jesus Christ' as well as 'Oy'. Unlike my mother, my Dad didn't like being talked about. He liked to fit in. As his paunch increased and his gait widened, he looked and sounded more Stavelean than the Staveleans did. And to be fair, if anyone had the right to take His Name in vain, it was a grizzled old farming Jew.

In the box were two playboys, two cuban cigars and a bottle of single malt scotch. Not just any playboys either, no, these were the Special Issues. The big thick ones. *Lingerie* and *College Girls.* Special issues were never released back-to-back; the old man must have waited for them. A quick look at the dates showed they were published six months apart. In fact, College Girls was almost a year old and was wrapped in foil. A year this magazine was in my father's possession and he did not have a look, it must've almost killed him.

Most people would've thought it a strange gift, but I was truly touched. It was the nicest thing the man had ever done for me and I would say one thing for him, he had impeccable taste in pornography.

Unfortunately for my father, I was no dummy. I was smart even by Jewish standards. Not just a bit clever, no, I was like freaking *Einstein* smart. Numbers were my thing even from a very early age. Mathematics. I laid claim to every scholarship my high school had to offer, even beating out the Japanese exchange student. I aced my Math, Physics and

Chemistry exams. I don't mean 'aced' colloquially as in 'I did fairly well', I mean *aced*. 100% in Math, Physics and Chemistry; the first time in the school's history. The first time in the state's history.

To finish perfect, even in a hick school like Stavely High, was unheard of back then, but that stuff just always made sense to me. I never filled in a university application; the recruiters came to me. They actually *heard about me*, gave me 'special' tests, Calculus, matrices, game theory, differential geometry and I aced those as well, or so I think. They never did give me the results, they only gave my father promises.

Fifteen years old and I had college recruiters at my door begging my father to let me go to their universities early. I was a Jewish father's dream. Not my Jewish father of course, he wanted a son who liked farming.

I didn't. I never had.

The land clearing, the rock picking, the levelling and the seeding only to have half the crop lost to hail and the other half frozen stiff? I could have understood the appeal if the work itself was interesting, but pushing a tractor across a field for fourteen hours a day, shovelling shit and pulling calves?

If you were a clever kid in the United States of America, it wouldn't be long before the military showed up as well. Their tack was somewhat less subtle than the university recruiters. They gave my father that whole spiel about how he'd be doing the *nation* a disservice by keeping his brilliant son on the farm. They went on about codebreaking like we were still at war with the Nazis or the Commies. The US was the big dick in the world in those days, what did they care about codebreaking? Like some camel fucker in Kazbleckistan was sitting down at a computer in a cave somewhere hacking into the pentagon. Please.

Like all farmers, my father hated the government and he never accepted subsidies. It meant there were nights when we only had minute steak and fried greens for supper and that all of his machinery was from the stone age, but the government would never have him in their pocket.

He only let those military boys in the door so he could give them a piece of his mind personally. If there was one thing that did not work on Frederick Cohen, it was guilt trips. Especially nationalist guilt trips. Nationalist guilt trips delivered by two pimple-faced grunts lacking the good sense to remove their shoes on his wife's living room carpet? Ha! They were lucky not be leaving with both of his feet broken off in their asses.

"He's staying right here until he graduates like everybody else and then he's going to take over this farm. If the US army don't like it, they can kiss my big, fat Jewish ass."

I believe he knew in his heart even then that I wasn't going to be a farmer, but he wasn't going to let some penis with a buzz cut and a green suit have the pleasure.

★ ★ ★

I did go to University in the end against my father's wishes. Undergraduate degrees in Math and Chemistry at Brown, Graduate degrees at MIT and Princeton. The robotics stuff we did at MIT was nominated for a Nobel Prize. I could've done anything I wanted, went anywhere. Professorships, Consulting, even bloody speaking tours; I was only 24 years old. I'm sure the farm suffered in my absence, but my father never let on. Before he died, he told me he was proud of me, but it was my mother who never forgave me for leaving. She took any words of love or encouragement for me to her grave.

Despite that, the farm was left to me, but I couldn't have managed it even if I wanted to. I sold it to old Dick Dyck for half of what it was worth and never went back to Stavely. I like to imagine that the old boys still talk about their crazy Jewish buddy in the bar, the man with biting tongue and the John Deere hat who never took a penny from Uncle Sam, but they probably didn't. Time moved on, even in Stavely. A couple Christmases would pass and it would be like we had never existed. The two graves in the small plot in Stavely cemetery would be worn down to nothing in the years to come and before long the Cohen name would be erased from Stavely forever. My mother's sister and her friends would probably leave flowers on the graves for a while, but once they had wilted and blown away, that would be it. The old farm with the lines of elm trees was always the Dyck farm as far as the locals would be concerned.

It wasn't a slight on the people of Stavely, it was just the way of things.

★ ★ ★

If selling the farm wasn't pissing on my father's ashes, then moving to England certainly was. The land of rotten weather, rotten food and rotten teeth.

But the call from a small, private, well-funded institution was too good to pass up. They offered me an obscene amount of money for four lectures a year. Four! The rest of my time could be spent doing research.

165

No proper university would have the balls to do that with a man as young as I was, but The Manchester Institute was no ordinary university.

The stuff that went on in the Institute's basements was mind-blowing. New materials, gene therapy, nanotechnology, bioprinting. The things we did in Manchester, I could not have done anywhere else.

My machine could only have been built in Manchester.

Eighteen

It was also in Manchester where I'd met my Midori.

It happened in a retro nightclub called the New Hacienda. Apparently there was some big music scene here in the 1990s that was making a comeback and the New Hacienda was where it was all happening. Nothing new was happening in those days; music, clothing styles, cars, everything had been done before and I seemed to be the only one who'd noticed.

It was at the New Hacienda where I realised I hadn't any friends. It hadn't even occurred to me until then. Like my father before me, I had become an orphan of a kind, abandoning my family and moving far away, but unlike my father, I never cared about fitting in. In fact, I enjoyed not being one of these people. These English. I had been working non-stop for years, the research and the planning had completely taken over my life. I was still a young man in the middle of this huge re-born music scene and I found myself standing in a corner of a dance club alone.

Most of the people in the club were off their faces on a new drug made from fertilizer mixed with some sort of household cleaner. In day-glo t-shirts and silver trousers, they bobbed around the dance floor looking to the sky with eyes wide open, asking the ceiling tiles for the answers to the great questions in life. Questions like: 'Where could I get a burger at this time of night?'

The retreating hairlines and bouncing bellies of the dancers suggested that they should be too old to be into that sort of thing, but Peter Pan syndrome was the "in" thing. I was one of the youngest people in the place, yet somehow I felt as if I were babysitting. How could all these people afford to spend their nights in nightclubs? The economy had tanked and unemployment was at an all time high. I remember thinking that if the impending Depression wasn't enough to bring these people back to earth, then what could? Nightclubs and fashion shows, Psychedelic drugs and reality TV. No one lived their lives anymore, they just passed the time in a haze of perpetual childhood, entirely ignorant or worse, entirely uncaring of the crumbling world around them.

Standing there in my button down and slacks amongst all the face paint and glitter, I could only have looked more foreign if I'd had a horn growing out of my head.

I had finished my rum and coke and was about to leave the club when Midori walked over. She was a tiny woman and the only other person in the club dressed as an adult. Black skirt, black stockings, she looked as out of place as I did and her pretty Japanese face was smiling up at me. She motioned for me to lean down and in my ear she shouted over the music.

"Do you want to go get a beer somewhere?"

I had never been hit on before. If she had asked me to marry her that night, I would probably have said yes.

As it went, it it was a year before we were married. She seemed fine with my long absences in the office as she was busy with her job as well. A household with two earners was fast becoming a rarity as the economy sickened but we didn't feel so much as a tiny pinch. Quite the opposite. While others barely scraped by, we had enough money to survive and then some. We had money to *invest*. Gold, Pharmaceutical companies and discount retailers, there were many things to make money off of in the bad times.

We invested heavily in Health Informatics.

When my research neared completion and it looked time to start putting it into practice, the institute didn't flinch. Traditional universities didn't like building things, they were more concerned with prizes and research grants. Nothing made universities more nervous than the words 'Expensive' and 'Dangerous'. The Institute wasn't shackled by such conventions. The machine was 'go' almost before I'd finished my pitch.

There were always rumours about a relationship between The Institute and the British military, but it wasn't until men in green suits started finding their way to my office that I believed it.

Abandoned the farm, moved to another country and working with the army. If my father had still been alive, that final betrayal would have killed him.

Only Midori could have been more disgusted with my relationship with the military than my father. She was from Hiroshima and her great grandfather had been killed by The Bomb. There was a time I thought about finding a different job, but there was nowhere else that would fund my machine.

Midori would eventually forgive me once the machine was built and the plaudits would roll in, but while I worked on it, I had to become a very good liar. I found I actually enjoyed lying, even to my wife. Especially to my wife; it made me feel like a secret agent, which after a time wasn't too far from the truth. She trusted me completely. There was never any real threat of being caught fraternising with the squaddies, Midori didn't visit even once. I thought as the years went by her curiosity would grow and that eventually I would have to tell her more, but that simply wasn't the case. I wondered about that for a time; why *hadn't* she cared about my job? Most wives were interested in what their husbands spent their days doing weren't they? Was she just happy to see the pay cheques coming in? There were nights where I didn't slither into our bed until well after one in the morning. Not a single query. She would simply roll over, give me a peck on the cheek and go back to sleep. Maybe she really did trust me implicitly. Or maybe she didn't want to know.

Little Boy. Beautiful piece of engineering that bomb; so simple. It was incredible when you thought about just how easy it was to win that war. A bit of TNT and a bullet made of uranium. All the problems in the universe had simple solutions; you just needed the will. The will and the ability to look past that neanderthal, two-thousand-year-old myth that human life was worth a damn. If there was one thing that human life was not, it was precious. There were far more of us on this rock than it could support and yet what did these pseudo-adults do? They had *more* children. Children having children. Outside of Midori and the people I worked with, there didn't seem to be any grownups around anymore. Scally families with fake jewelry and tracksuits and their fifteen kids standing in endless McDonalds queues. All with rickets and greasy, distended bodies like half-risen bread dough. Pasty bulbs of flesh poking out between the cracks of elasticated nylon.

It was the will to do terrible things that won wars. That, and a shed-load of money. Uncle Sam had always had both. No other nation on earth would've dropped Fat Man on Nagasaki after seeing what Little Boy did to Hiroshima. Who could look down on destruction like that and drop another one?

Only America.

That's what I had used to think anyway. After working for the British Special Forces for a few years, it became readily apparent that Britain would've pushed the button if she had had a button to push. The same army General who had green lighted my project had his office walls lined with photos of Hiroshima's nuclear shadows he'd bought on an online auction. Photos of the remains of people who had lived at ground zero when the bomb was dropped. Vapourised on impact, leaving nothing but a black mark on the pavement. The one with pride of place above his desk displayed the shadows of two lovers in an embrace, kissing at the moment of detonation. The black stains on the walls almost perfect silhouettes, you could even make out the hair on their heads. The remains of Midori's great-grandfather could very well have been in one of the General's photographs. When questioned about them, he told people they were there to remind us of 'the horrors of war'. To 'make sure a World War never happened again'. It was bullshit. If he had a time machine, he would have gone straight back to 1945 so he could've seen the mushroom cloud over Hiroshima in person. So he could've been the one to give the order. Hell, he would've happily been the one to open the bomb bay doors.

Nineteen

Light filtered into Lucy's bedroom through the cracks of the weatherboards and fell across my body in blue streaks. My icy breath rose toward the ceiling through the light beams in frosty puffs. I had two tatty duvets wrapped tightly around my body, but the cold still managed to find a way through.

I hadn't slept. My last night in Manchester was spent in similar manner to most nights in Manchester; awake. Only instead of being awake with terrorising thoughts of torture and hunger, it was spent listening to my mind as it revealed things about my life from many years ago.

My Dad removing his John Deere hat every evening at the dinner table, leaving his white hair flat and hat-shaped on top, puffed out and curly at the ears like the powdered wig of an English judge.

My mother with her long, grey locks, her gardener's hands and her collection of designer spectacles. DKNY, Chanel, Armani; how my parents would quarrel over the cost. My mother didn't spend a lot of money on clothes or shoes (she couldn't really) but she insisted on the best glasses money could buy.

Midori's flawless skin and her jet-black pony tail. Lucy's pigtails and eyes the colour of charcoal.

Her eyes couldn't have been more different to the eyes that I saw in the mirror in the mornings. The 'me' in the video had dark eyes like Lucy's, but the eyes that currently rolled around in my head were blue. They were blue because I'd programmed them into the machine.

Soon, I would be back with my family and all would be well. I only had to remember how to run the machine. And at the rate my mind was returning to me, it wouldn't be long.

It was strange lying in the chill of Lucy's room, listening to my mind expose my old secrets to myself. It didn't feel like I was seeing images from my old life at first; it was more like watching a program on some famous person's life on the Biography channel. I could almost hear the cheesy voiceover. "Seth Cohen was a giant in the world of physics. He had answered the question humankind had been asking for years:

'Was it possible to change ones own destiny?'

My natural instinct was to question my new memories. Each one appeared like a foreign object in my brain; a malignant tumour, or a bullet fired from a gun. My immune system fought the memories, attempted to convince my brain that the alien thoughts didn't belong. But the flow was too strong and too fast. By the time a new memory rose from the muck of my subconscious, the last memory had soaked into my blood and tissue; accepted into the fabric of my very being so fully and completely that the earlier question of whether it was real or not had itself become a memory.

Before yesterday with Roosevelt, I couldn't tell if the demented visions I was having were dreams or memory, but that was no longer the case. Last night, I could feel the division being created in my brain, like a wall of foam that slowly hardened into steel. The ability to separate reality from unreality was possible again.

And still the memories kept coming.

An argument between my father and mother about trying out for the high school football team. "Leave him alone, Fred, you know Jewish boys don't like football."

I missed her small town racism.

She was right though; football was never for me. The classrooms and the labs of the world were to be my playground.

I remembered my wedding.

Midori in her designer wedding dress, my father in his western suit and cowboy hat scratching at something on the lapel, my mother batting his hand away. She arrived to pay her respects, but said only the bare minimum in order to be polite. Until I agreed to come back to the farm, to America, we would never regain the closeness we once had. At the time, I'd laughed it off, thinking that she would have to come around eventually. The wedding was to be the last time I saw them both, cancer would take them in the coming years, their deaths separated by mere months.

My marriage didn't feel right even then. I didn't know what love was and Midori didn't either. We'd just assumed that the idea of enjoying one another's company and respecting a partner was what love was. We shared a love of learning, of science and our politics and religious leanings were in tune with each other. When we walked down the street, her shoulders were at just the right height to put my arm around. We looked good together, our parts fit together. If our relationship was a survey, all the boxes would have been ticked. At the beginning anyway.

It wasn't until our daughter was born that we knew that what we had together was not love. When our daughter was born, Midori and I instantly knew what love was and had something to compare our feelings for each other to.

Her name was Lucy.

I reached under the bed and withdrew the dictaphone. The Lucy on the dictaphone was my Lucy. The apartment the doctor forced me to live in was the very one I lived in after the divorce; my inner city bachelor pad. It was in the very room I was currently freezing in that I'd discovered Lucy had erased weeks worth of notes about the trials from the dictaphone. Notes on the machine's successes and of its 2B156's.

I squeezed the dictaphone in my hand tightly. I had been furious.

The doctor had orchestrated my whole life in the post-Darkening world. The torture, the apartment, the dictaphone, even my name. They were simply following the memory recall playbook I'd devised.

Step one: Exert physical pain on the subject until near breaking point. Chances of total recall decrease with time between subject's reconstruction and interrogation. Often, painful interrogation alone will jolt the subject's brain into action, but for subjects who have been in storage for long periods, additional methods may be necessary.

2062. I had been in storage for close to thirty years, longer than anyone else had ever been. Thirty years I lingered as nothing but liquid. Lucy's fiftieth birthday would've been two months ago. Could she have survived? Was she celebrating it in some hidden corner of the city?

Another frozen breath rose to the ceiling. It wasn't likely.

Step two: Place the subject in a familiar environment.

That would've been exceedingly difficult considering nothing in this world was familiar to me. The apartment could only look more different to it did to when I lived here if it had been burned to the ground.

Step three: Revisit the subject after seventy days. In most cases, the memories will have returned. If a subject's mind rejects his memories after seventy days, the reinstated mind will never accept them. Subject is to be neutralised.

Neutralised.

My head began to hurt. I ran my fingers through my bushy hair and squeezed my temples with my thumb and forefinger. I had never recorded my findings on epileptic seizures and their effect on memory recovery, I had only just discovered it myself.

There were so many people starving and homeless in those days. Alcoholics and drug addicts with no hope for a future. Nothing but a drain on society, a drain on themselves. I was doing those people a favour sending them through the machine, doing *society* a favour. Giving their lives some purpose.

Many of the subjects were rendered completely senseless on their trip through the machine, worse than me. Many didn't just lose their long term memories, many (especially in the early days) lost motor functions and speech. Some could do little more than babble and drool, others starved to death pondering the logic of their own hands. Out of the machine they would come, one after the other. Disfigured zombies with melted organs, elbows in the wrong places or missing completely, mouths that didn't open, eyes that didn't close. It took a long time to get the reconfiguration right.

And many tries.

Mercy killings I had told myself, ends/means.

I sat up on the bed still wrapped in layers of duvet. The light peering through the cracks of the weatherboards grew bright and frost twinkled on the walls. It wasn't cold by English standards; the room was Stavely cold. Below zero.

Gooseflesh had risen on the two pasty legs sticking out of the bottom of the duvet and tatty socks hung off my feet like a pair of full nappies.

I stood up and walked toward the window with the duvet around me. The frozen floorboards caused me to shiver through my socks.

The weatherboard over the bedroom window was frigid to the touch, but strangely dry. I grasped it with both hands and wrenched it off the window, the nails gave way with a creak and a snap.

Everything was white.

Long icicles dripped off buildings, the rubbish in the canal and the rusted cars on the streets disguised by mounds of heavy snow and the streets were virgin lanes of white. The early morning sunlight glinted off the crystallised air and smoke rose up from chimneys far away.

It was beautiful.

I half expected people to emerge from the front doors of the surrounding apartment blocks with pieces of toast hanging from their mouths, disappearing into warm cars and rushing off into their morning commutes.

I pulled my jeans up and threw on three shirts and my jacket. The cold air nipped at every exposed bit of skin.

Clothing up to this point hadn't been a concern for me at all. If there was one thing I could say about the English weather, it was that it was consistent. Muddy clothes could be washed in the sink, wet clothes could be hung up to dry. Not anymore.

The jacket took the edge off, but I would need to find a heavier one soon. Along with some more socks and a new pair of boots. They wouldn't have to last long, but they would need to be warm.

I wasn't long for this place, this world, this Manchester. I had a new goal now and a journey ahead.

The machine was close by pre-Darkening standards, a quick jaunt, but it would take some time to get there in third world conditions. And it would mean walking through the outlands. I wasn't going to be able to do it alone. I was going to need the help of my murderous new friends.

As I looked for my boots, a buzzing sound entered through the window.

Distant, irregular and whining, like a chainsaw felling trees in a forest on the edge of town. *Bwuzzzzz, bwa bwa, bwuzzzzz*

The buildings stood in heavy, silent contrast to the buzzing. A large slab of snow slid slowly off the slanted roof of an old newsagents on the other side of the canal, plopping heavily into the snowbank below with a crunch.

The buzzing loudened, echoing off the brick and stone buildings of the city centre making it difficult to pinpoint its origin. Was it coming from the city's heart or from the suburbs? As soon as I had convinced myself it was coming from the east, the buzz switched to the west. When I turned my head in that direction, it changed again. The sound swerved and bounced, playing amongst the buildings.

Three hard raps on wood behind me. Someone was at my front door.

My feet froze in place, my body as immobile and silent as one of the icicles hanging off the rooftop. I wanted to move, to escape, but my feet wouldn't budge. Outside somewhere over the buzzing, a bird chirped its morning greeting to no one.

The knocking came a second time.

Behind the door, a woman's muffled voice shouted.

"Oi, Sethie! It's me! Open the door, will ya?"

I forced a shiver to wake my numbed extremities and made my way toward my door. The bathroom and the second bedroom were dark, but there was light in the living room. One of the weatherboards had fallen off and snow spilled through onto my living room floor. I grasped the brass handle and twisted, the frozen knob burned in my hand.

"I didn't interrupt your wanking did I?" she asked. Smiling as she walked in.

I closed the door behind her and found my hand was stuck to the handle. I pulled my hand free of the knob leaving a sharp sting on my hand and a thin layer of skin on the door.

Zara was wrapped up in a heavy blue ski jacket, matching snowpants, gloves and thick, black leather Doc Martens. The hood on the jacket was cinched tight around her face. In her hands she held a woolen hat and a pair of bright pink snow pants.

"Here," she said, holding them up. "I reckoned you'd be shivering here in your keks."

I took them from her, eyeing the snowpants.

"I figured the pink ones would be your style." Her laugh only slightly muffled by her hood.

Snowpants. No grown man in Stavely would dare be caught in a pair of snowpants. But this wasn't Stavely. I put the hat on over my ears, thrust both legs into the heavy nylon snowpants, removed my jacket, cinched the shoulder straps tight and replaced my jacket as quickly as I could. The few seconds with my jacket off was all it took to get me shivering. Once everything was covered, my body warmed quickly, especially my legs. The snowpants could have been leopard print and finished in lace for all I cared.

"Come here for a sec," I said and grabbed her by the arm and pulled her toward the bedroom.

"Mate, if you think..."

"No, not that. There's something outside."

The buzzing sound was louder now. I led Zara to the window. There was no doubting from which direction the sound approached, it was coming from the centre of the city and it was getting close.

And there was more than one. As the sound amplified, it became apparent that there were at least three different buzzing things, all slightly different in pitch. *Bwuzzzz, bwuz bwuz bwuuuuzzz* Each buzz followed by a mechanical *clack-clack*.

Together we stood at the window listening as the sound flooded the streets, gaining ground.

I recognised the sound, it was one I had heard before, but couldn't zero in on it. I closed my eyes and forced my brain into identifying it. It wasn't animal, it wasn't human. In the trials, one of the subjects brought memories forward by moving chess pieces across a board in his mind's eye.

"Motorcycles," Zara said.

I opened my eyes just in time to see a yellow motorcycle flying around the apartment building next to mine. It was a Suzuki dirt bike. RM 250. There were two men on the bike: the driver a large man dressed in ski goggles and green army fatigues, the passenger was the doctor. Again, he was early.

Two more motorcycles whizzed into view, each of them sporting two men in full jungle camouflage, carrying machine guns.

Zara pulled me hard, away from the window toward the bedroom door. The dictaphone leapt from my hand and skittered under the dresser.

"Wait!" I said, pulling myself free of her grasp. She looked back at me from the bedroom doorway. Her face was serious, but unafraid. I fell to the floor and flapped around under the dresser, fumbling for the dictaphone.

"Come on!" Zara's shouted.

I snatched the dictaphone up in my hands and jumped back to my feet, stealing another glance out the window.

The doctor's bike skidded to a stop leaving a black arc in the snow in front of my building. The first soldier burst through the lobby door and the doctor followed. The old man's black hair flapped behind him and his backpack bounced as he moved, his heavy boots crunched the snow. The other two motorcycles closed quickly behind.

"They have guns, Seth. Come on!" she shouted.

Zara grabbed me again, this time by my shirt and yanked me through the bedroom doorway. My feet tried to work underneath me but they buckled and I fell to the floor a second time. Zara took the front of my shirt in both hands and hauled me back up.

She pushed me backwards out the bedroom and into the living room. Her face was stern, but cool. She wasn't rushing mindlessly, she moved with purpose. Her eyes darted around the living room and kitchen. She was assessing the situation while throttling me around my apartment like one of Lucy's old teddies.

At my front door, she released me and jerked the door open.

The sound of pounding legs and squeaking boots erupted from the staircase. They were advancing quickly. I gave a thought to my own boots, but there wasn't time.

"Is there another staircase?" she asked me.

There was on the opposite side of the hall, but most of it was destroyed and hanging off the side of the building. I shook my head.

Without hesitation, Zara pushed me back into the apartment, threw the door closed and latched the deadbolt.

"Come on," she said and pulled me across the floor back toward the bedroom, stopping at the doorway to the bathroom.

Zara released my hand and jumped up onto the lip of the bath tub, placing her other foot on the sink. She reached up and pushed a board in the ceiling away to the left. A sliver of light streamed down from the hole, casting light into the bathroom and disclosing a large attic above. In all the time I had lived in the apartment, even in the beforetime, I'd never noticed it.

Bang, bang bang. They were at my door.

Zara held both arms down through her legs, linking her fingers together with the palms up. "Step here, I'll haul you up."

The crawlspace in the ceiling was high over her head. She was strong, but not strong enough to haul a fully-grown man over her head.

A thunderous crash erupted from behind me as a great weight slammed into my front door. Somehow, the deadbolt and rusted hinges held, but they wouldn't survive too many more of those.

"Seth!"

There was no other choice. I placed my hand on her shoulder and stepped into her clasped hands. My weight had barely registered before

I found myself catapulted into thin air. The bathroom fell away and I tumbled into the crawlspace, struggling to grab onto anything and failing, instead smacking face first onto the wooden overside of my bathroom ceiling.

A second wood cracking smash as the large body buried itself into the door.

I scrambled to my knees. Light poured into the crawlspace, through a large hole in the rotten floor above.

A wooden ladder led up through the hole.

The ladder wasn't being stored in the crawlspace. It was serving its main purpose. Someone had put it there and that someone wasn't me.

"Gimme a hand!" Zara shouted.

She was still standing with her legs on the sink and bathtub, but her hands were now in the air reaching toward me.

I pointed toward the ladder. "Did you–"

The door disintegrated in an explosion of smashed wood and bouncing hinges. Heavy footsteps followed through and a second crash followed as whomever came through the door wordlessly clattered into the floor.

I reached down into my bathroom with both hands. Zara grabbed my wrists and I locked onto hers.

"Seth!"

The doctor's voice hit me like a truck. Below me, Zara looked up into my eyes and it was the first time I had ever seen fear in them. I could wriggle free from her grasp and run to the ladder. The doctor knew Zara, he'd tortured her like he'd done me. Leaving her behind would buy me some time.

From the other room, I heard the sounds of swishing fabric and clinking buckles as the human battering ram stood up and brushed himself off.

"Pull me up, Sethie."

Her voice was calm and small in temporary silence inside my apartment. She knew what I was thinking. If she was up here and I was down there, would she have helped me? Her hands were sweating, all I had to do was let her go.

Two sets of footsteps moved through my living room at walking pace. Soon they would be in my bedroom and see the slept-in bed and open window and know that I was here. Several more heavy, buckled steps pounded some way behind them.

Zara's breathing steadied and the fear in her face dissolved.

She smiled and released my wrists.

I remained holding her suspended in the air.

"Let me go," she said.

My face went hot and my stoney limbs were set as if cast in concrete. I couldn't move, I couldn't hide. Just a few more steps and the doctor would have me. My knife was in my backpack somewhere. Miles away. The tiny woman in my hands was the difference between torture and escape.

"I saw you at the window," the doctor said, his voice mere metres from the bathroom's entrance.

"Grab on, dammit!" I shouted.

Zara re-gripped my wrists and I thrust her up, pushing hard with my legs. She sprung up through the hole and we both fell into the attic together in a tangle of arms and legs.

For a moment, she lay on top of me, her hooded face close enough that our noses almost touched, her eyes locked on mine.

"You've learned nothing," she said and rolled away. She stood and moved toward the ladder. "Put that back," she directed, pointing toward the hole.

I sat back up and dropped the board back into place.

A deafening clap sounded below and the board exploded in a shower of splinters, embedding themselves into my hands, my arms, my forehead, throwing me backwards.

My ears were ringing. Time slowed to a creep. I brought my hands down from my face and looked at them. Splinters had peppered the backs of my hands and the sleeves of my jacket, but I didn't feel any pain. Behind me the shimmering beam of yellow sunlight remained, still and alien, piercing the darkness from above.

Zara was waving her arms and shouting something at me, her hooded face and snowpants giving her movements a comical quality like a children's entertainer. I could imagine her cartwheeling about the room. Her crimson face was curled up and furious which only made her look more childlike. I laughed.

A second explosion ripped through the hole, and I was blown onto my back a second time. Sparks and glowing chunks of wood fizzed and fell around me like fireflies.

I was now moving backward toward the ladder, the ringing in my ears all I could hear. The ancient wooden slats and beams of the floor above moved past my eyes. I tilted my head back to see Zara dragging me.

And then I was in the beam of light. Above me was nothing but cold, blue sky shining down through the hole in the floor of the apartment above and the roof above that. Winter's air rushed across me, raising gooseflesh on my hands and my exposed stomach revealed by Zara's dragging. When she released my hands, my jacket fell back into place. I pulled a long, thin splinter out of my hand and held it to my face. A tiny drop of blood stained the end. I was going to throw up.

With one hand, Zara grabbed me by the face, forced it up to hers and brought her other hand down, slapping me hard across the cheek.

"Snap out of it, you idiot septic!"

At once, the sound and the pain of the world returned. Soldiers were shouting from below, Zara shouting from above. We weren't caught yet.

Zara shot up the ladder into the apartment above and I followed. Once at the top, I pulled the ladder up behind me, giving one last look into the crawlspace below. The crawlspace was not tall enough, the missing ladder would only buy us a few seconds. A helmeted head appeared from my bathroom. It was the large, sunglassed soldier from the doctor's last visit.

"Your hands," Zara said.

My hands were stinging and small trickles of blood ran from many of the splinters. I touched my forehead, there were more splinters embedded there.

Zara smiled. "Maybe, we'll make a man out of you yet."

We were in the upstairs apartment where I had gathered wood only yesterday. It was the second bedroom. All the apartments in the building were identical in size and shape. This one was just like mine, only in reverse. Sunlight streamed in through the collapsed roof and open windows. I couldn't remember the last sunny day.

Zara pulled me across and over the rubble on the floor. We skipped across the broken chunks of wall and ceiling, careful not to step on any nails.

We found the front door, burst through it into the hallway and ran to the staircase and listened. It was as empty and as quiet as a church.

We entered the darkened stairwell; this time I led Zara down. I didn't have to feel my way down, I'd made this trip a hundred times. There was no squeaking anymore, even the rats had abandoned me. As we passed my floor, I chanced a quick peak down my hallway. The light from my open front door was all that I could see. No soldiers, no doctor.

I ran down the stairs as fast as my feet could move, pulling Zara behind me.

As we reached the bottom of the stairs, another thunderous bang erupted from above, splitting the darkness with an orange flash from the muzzle of the soldier's gun.

The darkness was shattered again with the *bakabakabaka* from a second soldier's machine gun. I kicked the door open at the bottom of the stairwell and pushed Zara through it into the lobby. The stairwell door slammed shut behind me in a hail of orange flashes and bullets.

We ran through the lobby and burst outside through the glass doors.

Outside, in the bright sunshine it was quiet except for the soft gubba gubba sound of the motorcycle engines. Hot breath pumped from us and the snow crunched under foot. My socks were immediately sodden in the snow. Above our heads, tattered curtains flapped out my bedroom window.

"Quick get on that one," I said pointing at the bike closest.

Zara nodded, slung a leg over, and gave the throttle a couple hard revs.

I ran over to the next bike, turned the key and pulled it out. The bike's engine spluttered to a stop.

"Come on!" Zara shouted.

I ran to the second bike and grabbed the key. The stairwell door burst open and a soldier was running through the lobby, his weapon drawn.

"SETH!"

I kicked the third bike over and ran over to Zara's bike, my feet skidding in the snow.

I hopped on the back of the bike, wrapped my arms around Zara and buried my face into her back. She twisted the accelerator and the bike roared, spinning the back tires in the snow.

The lobby doors shattered in a shower of glass.

The tire found purchase in the frozen earth and the bike lurched forward. Soldiers poured out of my apartment building, their guns raised and shaking with bursts of fire as we rocketed away from them on the Suzuki.

More bullets whizzed past. The back fender shattered into shards of yellow plastic, kicking out the tail of the bike. Zara turned the wheel to compensate, and the bike lurched hard before the tyres again bit into the ground. Zara cranked the throttle and stomped down on the gearshift lever, clicking through the gears. The bike ploughed through the street kicking up a snow stream behind us.

I chanced another look back. A soldier continued to fire, the bullets bounced off the pavement and pinwheeled in the air.

Zara turned the corner and the soldiers and the doctor disappeared behind a wall of redbrick. The last thing I saw was a soldier was picking the motorcycle I'd kicked over up off the ground and trying to kick it back into action.

It had stalled. Small miracles.

The Suzuki blazed through the snowy streets, the hydraulics of the front suspension pumped rapidly and smoothly absorbing each bump and buck of the hidden cobbles and street junk. Once we were sure the doctor and his cronies were far behind us, Zara squeezed the brakes and slid the bike to a stop.

She turned the key and again the world was silenced. Not even a bird could be heard.

We were stopped in the Northern Quarter, across from Bill's pizza. Back to where it all started.

"You can let go of me now," she said.

I hadn't realised how tightly I'd been hanging on.

I released my grip slowly and looked down at myself. Ice crystals had already started gathering on my sodden socks that poked out the bottom of my pink snowpants and my feet were burning. The backs of my hands were bleeding from the hundreds of tiny slivers buried there and my forehead felt as if it were on fire. As I ran my fingers across my hairline, I found more splinters. I grasped another large one with my thumb and forefinger and pulled it, it scraped on the way out. The sliver was the width and breadth of my pinky nail and about an inch long. Warm blood ran down my forehead.

"How did you know about the ladder?" I asked.

She laughed. "No idea it was there, mate. It was into the attic or out the window. Got lucky."

I tossed the splinter into the snow and rubbed the bloody wound where the splinter used to be. The morning was still quiet, no buzzing motorcycles yet, but there would be soon.

Zara twisted around in the seat to face me. "Where to?"

It was a good question. I couldn't go back home again and I couldn't make my way to the machine alone. And I was hurt.

"Raj's place. But we need to make a stop first."

She pulled the hood of her jacket down. Her cheeks were flushed with cold.

"Better be close, the tank's empty."

"It is."

"You know, if they've been watching you, they'll know about Raj's place."

She was right, but I had no choice. There were many problems with the next part of my journey. I had to avoid the doctor, survive the out-lands and oh yeah, save the world. Luckily, solving problems was what I did best.

"What about you? Won't they come after you?"

Zara laughed. "Even if they knew where I lived, which they don't, they'd know better than to come find me."

She kicked the Suzuki back into life and revved the engine to break point before engaging the clutch and propelling me headlong to the end of my time in Manchester, spinning the wheels madly, unafraid of who might hear.

Twenty

It was the middle of the night and again I was awake. I'd poured myself a beer and was sitting outside the front of Raj's bar with only a lit candle and my returning mind for company. A soft breeze whistled through the snowy mountains of junk around me.

I remembered the day I first met Dr Holstetter; the day I first saw his bio printer. They had experimented with printing heart valves and had gotten some good press, but it wasn't until I showed up with the might and money of the Institute and the British military behind me that really got things moving. We went from building a human kidney, to an entire human body in sixteen years. Sixteen years.

Back then, the doctor was a scientist. Young and eager not unlike myself. The idea of using the bioprinter to build a body from the ground up had never even occurred to him. When he'd first developed it, he saw it being used to create bone fragments and bits of tissue. Once we'd built a perfect human kidney, he knew the machine was out of his hands.

They hadn't been able to successfully print another person after me. I was the only one. If they had managed it, I would not be alive; they would have erased my profile long ago. Abandoning them while the world ended, robbing them the chance to save the world just to save myself from cancer? There was no forgiving that.

Before I let the machine take my body, I had thought of disclosing the final sequence to them in case something went wrong, but changed my mind at the last minute. It was ego that stopped me giving them full disclosure. I didn't want them taking credit for my machine while was gone.

But I hadn't expected to be in storage for so long. And how was I to know the world would be destroyed?

I could understand why the doctor felt the need to go overboard on my torture. I had left them with nothing.

Raj and his chef Dave were both asleep somewhere in the bowels of the bar. The little man had allowed me to stay and even helped remove the splinters from my head and hands. The bandages were his, the shoes on my feet were his and the heavy dressing gown wrapped around me was also his.

It was good to see them again. Raj's tutting and Henry's eyes, stretched into maximum openness in childish wonder as I told them of my memory recall at Roosevelt's and my motorcycle escape. Raj knew I was bringing trouble to his bar, but he let me stay anyway. The idea that I had to somehow "forgive" him and Henry for what they had done during the Darkening seemed ridiculous when compared to the hundreds of people I'd killed testing the machine.

Do you ever wonder why the death of this city doesn't bother you?

A gust of wind blew across me, displacing a bit of dressing gown over my left thigh, replacing it with a skiff of snow. I shivered, pulled the gown back over my leg and buried my hands into the warm, flannel pockets.

Above me the clouds had parted sufficiently to allow just enough moonlight through to see the destruction around me.

Across the street, a leafy tree stood in between two smashed buildings, caught off-guard by the early winter's snow. The branches were wild, crooked and heavy with icy apples. A magpie picked at one that had fallen to the ground.

European Magpie. *Pica pica.*

It was funny what the reanimated mind chose to remember and what it managed to forget. Sparrows in the brambles that lined the railroad tracks, housemartins watching me dig, scattering starlings on my bike ride. Remembering car parts, bicycle parts, gears and levers made sense; I was an engineer after all. But birds? The faces of my family, the ability to grow food and even my own name were things my mind had locked away at the expense of bird identification. I wasn't even entirely sure I would've known what a housemartin looked like in the beforetime.

The doctor and I were the same age: Thirty-seven years old.

We were both born in 1995. The rage that my new, pristine body must have raised in him, knowing that I had left them and taken the secrets of the machine with me must have been unbearable.

I ran a finger over a ragged scar on the back of my arm. It truly was a miracle I made it off that hospital bed alive.

The clouds closed again, dropping blackness on everything and throwing another gust of frigid air across my face. I took a last swig of beer, rubbed the cold out of the tip of my nose and walked back into the pub and back to my room wishing I had a cigarette to butt out.

★ ★ ★

I slept heavy and long that night and it was after midday when I awoke.

I shuffled into the bar, Raj's dressing gown over my tshirt and jeans to see Henry and Raj in their usual places. It was cold enough for my snowpants, but Henry would tease me.

"L'Chaim sleepyhead!" Henry said holding up a glass of something cloudy. Raj was wearing a woolly hat, scarf and mitts to shield from the cold, but Henry was his usual over-exposed self. Wind, rain, blizzard, typhoon, he would be there in his short sleeves and short pants grinning like the Cheshire cat on Crystal Meth. Give him a pair of combat shorts and a glass of beer and the man could live comfortably on mars.

I circled the bar, taking my usual place beside Henry.

"Shouldn't you be out madly chopping wheat?"

"Way ahead of you, mate. In the mill as we speak. A week from now and I will be a rich man."

"Well then, you can buy me one," I said.

"Way ahead of you again," he said as Raj pushed a beer in front of me.

The three of us cheersed and drank.

Henry sat back with a toasted look and outstretched arms. "Look at us, eh? It's like the bloody United Nations in here. Muslim, Christian and even Jew all drinking together."

Raj put a frustrated finger up in protest.

"Yeah yeah, you're not a Muslim," Henry said batting a hand at Raj. "I'm not Christian either. Well, not really. Just trying to make our Jewish friend here feel more welcome."

I took another pull from my glass and gave the comment some thought. "I'm not sure I'm Jewish anymore either."

"Oh, that's where you're wrong, my friend. Even if you don't believe in a Jewish God, you're still a Jew. It's not just a religion, it's a.. a uh..." Henry swirled a hand in the air with his eyes closed searching the ether for the right words. "A uh racial thing."

I took another swig of beer. I was glad I wasn't wearing the snowpants.

"I can say I am not a Jew if I want."

"Fraid not, matey. You're stuck with it. Just like I'm stuck with being the beautiful ebony heartbreaker you see before you and Raj is stuck being..." Henry swirled a hand a second time again trying to conjure the word. "You know, whatever he is."

Raj rolled his eyes, contemplating a reply before deciding wiping down another bottle was more important. He was a good landlord, Raj. It may have taken the end of the world, but the British had finally learned that the customer was always right.

"Seth is the Jewiest name there is," Henry continued. "Plus you look like a Jew. You got Jew hair and that rather impressive conk. The blue eyes threw me a bit. Must be some half Jew or maybe some kind of genetic freak." He laughed again.

He was right on both counts.

The bandage on the back of my hand itched and was red with dried blood. I scratched at it.

Raj slapped my scratching hand. "Don't scratch!" he scolded.

I owed Raj a great deal for helping me. I warned him of the doctor's likely arrival, but he'd insisted I stayed at the bar at least until my wounds had healed. I wasn't sure if he really was concerned for me or if he just wanted me to use up the curries and beers I was owed.

Zara seemed unafraid of the doctor as well, insisting on going home. "If that doctor person shows up at mine, he'll be leaving with one hole in his head more than he had when he arrived". Whether it was true fearlessness, naivety or false bravado I couldn't be sure. My memories may have returned, but my ability to read her was still sadly lacking.

Though she wasn't exactly forthcoming with an invitation for me to stay with her.

I ordered another beer for me and one for Henry.

I needed to tell them about the machine. I needed to convince them to help me find it. But how did you tell people who lived in a world without running water that it was possible to have a machine that moved people through time?

There was no way to finesse it. And even if there was, these people would only be insulted.

"What would you two say if I told you I could fix the world?"

The words hung in the air as both men carried on as if I hadn't said anything.

Raj placed two more glasses in front of us and cleared the empties away without so much as an raised eyebrow. Henry spoke without looking at me.

"I would say you were off yer nut."

I took the glass of beer and swallowed three large gulps, and smacked it back on the bar harder than I had intended. I recognised the herb Raj used in the beer and remembered that I didn't like it. Coriander.

"I told you last night my memories returned, right?"

"Yeah," Henry said, folding his arms. "The little purple freak and his computer."

The two men looked at me expectantly. Daring me to lie to them. The gravity of my next words dizzied me. I swallowed and briefly mulled them over in my head.

"The machine was built to cure disease," I began. "I was dying of cancer and the machine cured me. I just happened to move forward thirty years in the process. I was born in 1995. If this year is 2062 as you people say it is, then I am in effect, sixty-seven years old. I reckon that is older than Raj even."

"Whoo, that is old," Henry said. I wasn't sure if he was mocking Raj or me. Most likely, both.

I was not winning them over, but I continued anyway. "I started work on the machine a year before my daughter Lucy was born." I pulled the dictaphone out of my pocket and waved it at the men.

"The doctor left that dictaphone, my dictaphone, in that apartment. My apartment."

I looked at Henry. "Lucy was born in 2012."

Henry looked back, curling his lip. He took my scrawny body in, scanning it up and down causing my knee to bounce nervously. A stupid habit I'd always had and that Midori hated. I placed a hand on my knee and squeezed until it stopped bouncing.

When Henry had finished looking me up and down, he barrelled his chest out like he was readying to shout, but instead blew a raspberry and uttered a single word before turning his attention back to his beer.

"Bollocks."

The door opened and Roosevelt walked in. I'd never been so happy to see someone in all my life.

"Look, ask Roosevelt," I said, pointing at the young man.

Roosevelt said nothing, choosing instead to turn back to the door he had come in through and let himself back out.

"Wait!" I shouted and moved toward the door. Roosevelt turned toward me, giving me the old blank face he gave me before the night in the tower.

"Go on, tell them about the computer."

Roosevelt shook his head and swallowed. "I-I don't know what you're on about."

His face was that of the scared kid from my apartment. The simple garbage collector with the cracked glasses had retaken the body of the confident man who lived in the tower who stole his energy from the very sky. The man who gave me back my mind.

He leaned on the door handle and silently pushed his thick glasses back up his nose.

"Ah, leave 'im alone," Henry said.

"These men are not going to steal your computer. Do you think they could even get it working?"

He turned to the door a second time and walked through. I grabbed him by his cape and held tight. He spun around quickly, his right hand a blur in front of my face before finding its mark on my chin. I stumbled backwards and fell over a chair on my tumbling way to the floor, knocking over several chairs on the way down.

Henry laughed.

The punch felt as if it had been delivered by a lead fist. I held my arms over my face and peered in between them expecting another blow. Roosevelt stood over me, his expression unchanged.

The only reason I'd overpowered him on that day in my apartment is because he allowed me to. He made himself look weak for a purpose; to get me to follow him, to give him my password. He, like all survivors in this place, were just as skilled at using the carrot as they were in using the stick.

Roosevelt assessed the bar and its inhabitants. Henry and Raj made no attempt at movement. The young man shook his head, readjusted his glasses again and puffed air out of his mouth, while I rubbed my aching jaw. His face a picture of remorse.

After a few moments of silent contemplation, he lowered a hand to me.

I took it and he pulled me to my feet.

"Thanks kid, I needed that," I said for no reason at all. My jaw still thumped with pain.

Roosevelt shook his head and sighed through his nostrils before speaking. "I may have a computer. I may have seen something about his machine."

"You see?" I asked.

"Fuh–lipping eck," Henry said. "You've got a computer? Like, a working one?"

"Yes!" I shouted. I put my arm around Roosevelt's shoulder, and squeezed before pulling it away sharply again. I could have kissed the boy, but I doubted that would do anything to further my cause. Instead, I shoved my hands into the pockets of the dressing gown and rocked back and forth on my heels twice in a futile attempt to look aloof.

"Yes," I repeated.

"Let's hear it then," Henry said pushing a second stool in front of him for Roosevelt.

★ ★ ★

The journey to the machine would be dangerous, it would involve a long trek on foot across land that had probably been untouched for decades. Henry knew the land and the perils that it brought, but convincing a man of the Darkening that such a machine could still work in a world without electricity was a tall order. Henry and Raj were not engineers or physicists like me, I couldn't use science as my ally. They were men of the earth, men of physical deeds and gestures, men of beer and bartering. Theory and schematic would mean nothing to them; if it wasn't something they could see or taste or hold in their grizzled hands, it simply didn't exist in their world. Henry's world was a world of solid things, of bones, of seed and blood. My world, the world of time machines, the world of dreams was long gone.

I needed to keep my story simple, I needed to tell them only the things that they would need to know in order to join me in my quest. Some talk of physics and fission would be necessary, but I had to keep those things to a minimum. Focus on the whats, wheres and whys and forget the hows. Roosevelt was a technical boy, he could be seduced by the hows, but the other two men wouldn't care. The machine had survived the Darkening, my very existence was proof of that, but convincing

Raj and Henry of that fact was an entirely different prospect. If I was going to have any chance at all, they would need to lust for the old days.

I would again tell these strange men a fantastic story, a story of rebirth, a story of hope, a story of time itself. Curing diseases did not happen overnight, a person's data needed to be assessed before it could be repaired. These things took *time*. My cancer was aggressive and advanced, I knew my new body wouldn't emerge from the machine overnight, but thirty years? That was at least five times longer than my most liberal estimate.

There was more to the machine than curing diseases and moving forward through time. There was a second function, a second room capable of thrusting a person *backward*.

The story I told them would be unlike any that had been told before. A story of gears and levers, of spindles and thread, of transistors and microchips; of Manchester and its machines. If my mission was to be successful, I had to remind them of the Manchester that existed, not as a graveyard, but as a jungle gym for geniuses. A place that gifted the world its first computer, its first train line, technology itself. "What Manchester does today, the rest of the world does tomorrow". It was the motto of the Industrial Revolution.

Manchester had always a bad habit of changing the world. She hadn't done much for a very long time, but that didn't mean the city had completely forgotten how to turn the planet on its head; perhaps she just needed some reminding.

Twenty-one

Above my head, the celestial bodies glimmered brighter than they'd ever had, but none brighter than Betelgeuse. The famous red star who'd looked down on earth jealously from its perch on Orion's shoulder had decided now was the time to take from the moon the award for the Sky's brightest. In the basement of the collapsed house in Urmston, it had been Betelgeuse and not the moon that helped me find the bicycle and lit my path through the streets. The cowardly moon with its rabbit tattoo had retreated, dull and cracked to its own small patch of sky by the new bully in town, choosing the safety of a quiet corner instead of a fight. But like the rabbit, the moon was clever, it knew its time in the shadows would be short; Neil Young was wrong, it was not better to burn out than fade away. No way, burning out was for the birds. The moon knew full well that the joke was on Betelgeuse, choosing to shine at a time when no one would notice or care. No one, that is, except for one idiot physicist in a place where he didn't belong.

If there was a God, he was truly laughing.

The snow was gone, but a biting chill remained. I was lying on the roof of an abandoned house at the edge of town and beneath me slept my three companions. Dreaming of an old world; a world that reunited them with long dead family members and the comforts of an early 21st Century Britain.

My story had been good enough to enlist Roosevelt, Henry and Zara, but old Raj chose to stay with his pub, a man too important to the city to leave. The others couldn't wait to start, seduced by thoughts of hot baths, supermarket shelves and, for Henry at least, fast cars.

If there was one thing I had learned about the human species in my experiments, it was that virtue could be bought.

Betelgeuse burned small and red when Einstein developed his theory, when John Cabot first set foot on the New World and when Galileo was arrested for having the nerve to suggest the Earth was not at the Universe's centre. Betelgeuse witnessed the rise and fall of empires, oversaw the births and deaths of Kings and Queens and witnessed man's greatest discoveries and its most heinous acts. When the moors invaded Spain, Betelgeuse watched. At 9/11. It was at the Battle of Hastings, Waterloo and at the shores of Normandy. American soldiers looked up at Betelgeuse from their foxholes in the jungles of Vietnam as they sucked in Agent Orange and dodged napalm. Betelgeuse was not just a casual observer; he played his role in these earthly conflicts, directing adventurers and conquerors across the seas. He was there when the pyramids rose and when the Titanic sunk. He looked down on Newton's head as the apple made contact, and he watched silently as the blood of six million of my ancestors flooded the streets of Warsaw and down plugholes of Auschwitz.

But soon, he would be nothing more than a forgotten speck in the sky and I, with my machine could outlive the very stars.

The moon was almost at full invisibility, existing only as a sliver of silver; the unlit side of the moon backlit by surrounding starlight. Six American flags were on that moon. For almost a century, they've remained, flanked by footprints and three seized moon cars. We were good at that. Leaving our broken shit everywhere. When I next arose from the machine, perhaps I would bear witness to the earth's complete destruction. Earth's destiny was indeed to become a twin of its cold, lifeless neighbour, it was only a matter of time. If a planet and its moon were the same, how would you know which was which?

All of the world's problems are easy to solve when you accept the fact that human life is neither special nor precious, that it is in fact the opposite. A human "being" is no better than a dog or even the fleas that suck their blood. Humans are worse than dogs. A dog doesn't shit in its own food bowl.

That was the first page of my powerpoint presentation to The Institute's board. I was very fond of that little passage despite the fact that my first dog did exactly that, and worse. My father ironically named him 'Flash'. Shitting in his food bowl and chewing steel sprinkler heads like they were Milk Bones were the only two things Flash did with any level of proficiency. By the time Flash died, he hadn't a single tooth left in his head.

I was a 'radical thinker'; that's what Time magazine called me, a 'Renegade of the physics world'. What a joke. Raj was right; I was a fraud, a charlatan. Physics wasn't my true talent; it was sales. Einstein, Galileo, Hawking and Newton. They were true geniuses. While they used reason and research to construct their theories and ideas, I attacked man's problems with a sledgehammer. They thought laterally and used data and algorithms to predict the future; I threw shit against the wall to see what would stick. Most people at The Institute had no idea how far I was going with my experiments; they were more interested in the positive market-ing. They enjoyed telling other institutions they had a lecturer who was 'experimenting with bioprinting'. It looked good on a brochure, pimp-ing for students. They never truly believed I would be successful. The General was different. He wanted results and were more than happy to turn a blind eye to the darker parts of my research. But I doubt even he knew how far I was going or how fast I was getting there.

Live subjects were the only way to perfect the machine in my life-time. Why waste time on simulators, when it was easier to walk a willing person into the machine on a promise of a couple bucks and a hit of heroin? Taking live data and making adjustments on the fly was the only way to go. Tweak the tweaker.

★ ★ ★

We were up and dressed early. My waking hours on the roof were spent eliciting visions of the machine, but the dreams that invaded while I slept were of my daughter and of Midori. There was only the briefest moment in time when the three of us were all happy together under the same roof. It was Lucy who had forgiven me for my late nights in the lab and my cynical views on the human species in general. "Oh Dad," was all she'd say after I'd shout something nasty at a news item about a local murder or protests against welfare cuts on the TV. She was very pretty and a lot more like me than her mother would have liked.

When I woke, there were tears at my eyes edges, but I couldn't allow them to surface. If they started falling properly, I wasn't sure I would be able to stop them.

"You ready, Sethie?" Zara asked.

I drew the back of my hand across my eyes and cleared my throat. "Yup."

It would be a long walk today. Sixty miles, if memory served.

Even though the temperature was no more than five degrees, Henry's only additions to his ensemble was a faded, cotton hoodie and a hip-holstered 9mm pistol that slapped against his thigh as he walked. Zara had her hood up again, cinched closely to her face, an old rifle slung over her shoulder and Roosevelt was again dressed as, well, Roosevelt, with the addition of a woman's rabbit fur vest over his purple lycra. Banging against his hip was the only weapon Roosevelt carried; a shiny fencing rapier. Where he found that, one could only guess. He mentioned something about a concealed pistol, but as was readily apparent by the revealing bump in between his legs, lycra was not good for hiding things. If he was packing, it could only be under that stupid hat.

In addition to my pink snowpants, Zara had scrounged me up a new pair of boots to go with my new winter jacket. In my hands, I carried Raj's shotgun. The gun and three boxes of shells had greeted me at the front door of the house this morning with a note that read simply:

Try not to shoot yourself in the face with it. Raj.

Raj wasn't coming. It was more than just his shop that kept him from coming with us, he didn't believe in my machine. He scoffed at my suggestion of going backwards in time to save the world and he even tried to stop the others from following me, calling me a snake oil salesman with no snake oil to sell. He was right, of course, but curiosity was a powerful thing. Especially in a world where there was nothing better to do.

★ ★ ★

"This. This is why you cannot stop the Darkening," Raj said as he gave a large plastic bottle two hard shakes and plonked it on the bar. It was half full with a thick, pink liquid. The label was sun-bleached and brown at the edges. 'Smoothie' the only word I could make out.

My case for the machine was made with reason and by appealing to their base needs of comfort and family, Raj's case against was being made with an ancient tub of pink goo. I had no idea where he was going with it, but I smelled a trap.

"Open it," he said.

What role could that inert, pink liquid have played in the Darkening? It was too thick to be an acid and couldn't have been corrosive if it had remained in that bottle all this time. Was it some kind of poison?

Raj answered my questioning look. "Just open it."

I grasped the top and twisted. It was sealed tight. I twisted again, harder this time, using my shirt to get a better grip. It wouldn't budge.

"Give it here," Raj said, snatching it and popping it open with a crack in his small, but heavy meat hooks. Dried pink flakes snowed down from the lid onto his dark skin as he twisted it free.

He handed the bottle back to me and I peered into it. The pink liquid sloshed and clung to the sides.

Raj motioned me to bring it to my nose. "Get a whiff."

I looked once at Henry and Roosevelt, seeking their advice. They both shrugged without irony.

I brought the bottle up to my nose, not too close, and took a quick sniff. It smelled of fresh strawberries. The word 'smoothie' felt familiar as something pleasant. A drink.

Raj nodded at me. "Nice, innit? Have a taste."

I searched Henry's eyes a second time for a clue. His face was stone. He looked to be as dumbfounded by it as I was. If this liquid had a role to play in the Darkening, if it was a poison leeched into the ground-water, surely Henry would've heard of it. Roosevelt's face was one of wonder.

"I'm not drinking it," I said putting back down on the bar. "It'll have gone off by now."

"You say your memory is back, yeah?" Raj said, lifting a bushy white eyebrow at me in direct challenge. We were duelling, he and I.

I nodded.

"And you say that you were born in 1995, right?"

I nodded a second time. "Yes."

"Well, then, Einstein, if your memory has returned and you were an adult as you say before the Darkening, you would know about preservatives. About food technology. Before the Darkening, food and drink could be made to last, unrefrigerated, for centuries. Processing, E-numbers, chemicals that sort of thing. You say you are a scientist. So if you remember everything, why don't you remember that?"

He was right. Twinkies had a shelf life of seventy years. We could send freeze-dried food into space. It was possible that someone had indeed made a strawberry smoothie last thirty years, but it was equally plausible that Raj was to poison me. They were not just his friends that would be risking their lives; they were his customers.

All three men watched with intent as I looked the bottle over. If these people didn't trust me, it would be the outlands on my own. I had no proof other than my very existence that the machine was bona fide. I was asking an awful lot from them, I was asking them to trust me. The least I could do was return the favour.

I picked the bottle back up and took another sniff, deeper this time. It wasn't just strawberries I smelled, there was mango in there as well, or maybe peach. Saliva poured down the walls of my mouth in anticipation.

I brought it to my lips and drank.

The thick, flowery liquid coated my tongue and slammed into the back of my throat, choking me.

I dropped the bottle to the floor and hacked the liquid onto the bar through my mouth and nose. I tried to breathe, but the acrid chemical again hit me in the lungs. I fell to my knees and vomited.

Henry said something to Raj and I continued coughing, unable to speak, scraping the clinging lotion from the top of my tongue with my fingers.

"It won't kill him," Raj said to Henry as he casually appeared from behind the bar with a mop.

I retched again but there was no more to throw up. A line of drool hung from my bottom lip. I coughed again before finally able to draw breath. Raj sloshed the mop around my hands and knees, oblivious to the puking man in front of him.

After a couple more dry heaves, I was able to sit back and breathe. The liquid drained from the overturned bottle in thick glugs. It was foul, but it was not rotten and it was not poison. It was a detergent.

"Are you crazy?" I asked him when I recovered the ability to speak. "That was soap!"

He picked up the now empty bottle and placed it on the bar. "Body wash, actually. Using the nutrillium and moisturosity of the gogoba plant, New Strawberry Smoothie helps your skin become more luxuriant and boisterous."

Slowly, I stood with Henry's help, still gagging and scraping the liquid from my mouth with my fingers. I used my shirt to wipe the insides of my cheeks and nose. My shirt was so caked with mud and grease, it was hard to find a clean bit with which to wipe.

Raj stopped mopping and looked me in the eyes.

"Do you understand my lesson now?" he asked. Unless the lesson was 'Don't drink body wash', I hadn't a clue what the little man was talking about.

"If as you say, you were not present for the Darkening, except as a frozen brain and tubes of liquid skin and bone, you don't know what it was like."

Raj rinsed his mop in the bucket, plopped it on to the floor and swished it around. I waved Henry away and used Raj's robe to wipe the sick off my jeans and boots.

"That soap was made from *actual* strawberries," Raj said as he continued mopping. "It was in all their adverts at the time. New Strawberry Smoothie Body Wash made with Real Fruit. Look," he said lifting the mop to my face. "You can even see the seeds."

The mop was horrid, caked with a mixture of smoothie, half digested chicken, rice and beer. Bile rose in my throat again and I turned away. I had seen the seeds in the liquid, what I could not see was his point.

"You really are from the beforetime, it's the only way you could be this stupid. This soap was made while the Darkening was happening. *During*. My wife purchased that very bottle two weeks before my son was killed."

They were all looking at me now. Eyeing me like I was the dumbest person on earth. Henry's eyes were pleading with me, begging me to connect the dots.

And then I did.

"You are saying that people who make food into soap are not worth saving."

Raj slammed his hand down on the bar. "No!"

Raj reached up and pulled me down to his level by my collar.

"Idiot! You think I do not want my family back?"

His white moustache twisted into a scowl over his lip. It was the very face he made while shooting the woman in the photograph.

"No, I—"

Raj pushed me away and addressed the others.

"Time machine! Do you hear this man?"

He shook his head in disbelief.

If Henry and Roosevelt's doubting faces were to be believed, he was right. Roosevelt's eyes were no longer curious, they were on his clothing unable to face me, tugging at a wayward thread on his cape.

Behind the website he found, on the other side of the password screen, the plans and schematics of the machine were stored. Plans and schematics that he must have seen. He was different from the others; he had a technical mind.

I pleaded with the boy. "You've seen the machine. You've seen the video. You've a scientist's mind, you know it to be true."

Roosevelt puffed his cheeks out and released the air through exhausted lips. Speaking with human beings was not his strong suit.

"Maybe," he said.

Raj laughed.

"Time travel. I cannot believe what I am hearing. Even if it was possible, who on the other side would believe his words of the Darkening? Would you have believed it if some fool had come to you with the story of society's impending collapse?" he asked Henry. Henry moved to speak, but Raj continued. "Even if you could somehow be convinced, how would those people begin to try to stop it? Even now, most of us aren't even sure how it began."

He walked behind the bar and back onto his step. No one else said anything.

"Well? Go on then. Go get your cars, your playstations and your microwave ovens. Go get your plasma screen TVs and your V8 engines and your precious mobile phones. If those are the things you hold dear, than the Darkening has taught you nothing."

At that moment, as ever, I could not read those people. There was no excitement, no curiosity in them, not even Roosevelt's. They weren't contemplative, they weren't searching, these faces of the locals were as they always were; as serene as empty swimming pools. There was a very good chance I would be walking out of the pub alone, but there was nothing else to be said. I pulled my jacket off the hook and put it on over the bathrobe. And then I left.

Outside, it was grey and cold. The falling rain had laid waste to most of the snow and reduced what was left to brown slush. I stood outside the door looking back at the pub and at the wreckage that surrounded it. The little man was wiser than he knew. He was right not to trust me, to try to talk them out of it. The doctor hadn't come across me by chance, he was well aware of my final destination and he was patient. He was there at the machine to greet me on my first day in this world, chances were good that he would be there for my last. That coupled with the fact that my mind had yet to fill in the missing pieces of the machine's actual operation meant the journey could very well be for naught.

There were two rooms in the facility, one that housed the bioprinter and another, the one that propelled a person backward, that I still had to make sense of.

I closed my eyes tight to force the second room into focus. It was a bright room with flashing panels on the walls with a large hole in its centre, but that was all I could see. There was no guarantee the details of the second room would ever return, but I would make my way to the facility anyway. I could not live another day knowing it was there, knowing that I was not making my way toward it, psychotic doctor or no.

Minutes passed and the rain poured down harder, the water drops struck the twisted metal and piles of old plastic to create a deranged, mechanical symphony of dings and thuds. A frenetic, cacophonous ode to the dead. The door remained closed and those inhabiting the other side continued their inhabitation. I didn't expect Roosevelt to come through the door; he was a smart kid. He was a teenager, born after the Darkening. *After*. His parents were brought together in the ensuing madness. Before the Darkening, they were probably married to different people, the vows broken only by death. Would they find each other in a world that didn't end?

I didn't want to mention it inside the pub, but stopping the Darkening could mean the end of Roosevelt's existence. *Would* mean the end of his existence.

As I stood watching the door in the rain, a blurred memory floated across the backs of my eyes, a nagging twinkling.

Paradoxes. Something about paradoxes.

I had abandoned my family when I entered the machine the first time, but I hadn't any choice. The cancer started in my lungs and moved to my spine, liver and spleen. I hadn't chosen to remain in the machine for thirty-seven years; that was simply the amount of time it took for the machine to find and delete the cancer; the faulty bits of data in my body that weren't supposed to be there. To *clean my numbers*.

A frozen brain and tubes of liquid bone and skin.

I had never heard anyone describe it quite like that, but I suppose it was apt.

My desire to move through time now was a selfish one, just as it was the first time. Escape.

Lucy was gone. It wasn't just playing the odds, of the knowledge that the city's population had been reduced exponentially, I knew she was dead. There was an empty space in me that used to be filled with her life. That space was now as dark and as black as the sky above. It was supposed to have been me who was risking his life going into the machine. I had transferred the bulk of my savings to her, she should've been taken care of. But paper money had no use in a world without economy. How was I to know?

A hard cold fell through me and I was glad for the freezing rain.

I was about to make for a quiet place to spend the night when the pub door opened and Roosevelt appeared through it.

He held the door open and Henry joined him outside.

"You go now and you can't come back!" Raj shouted from inside.

Roosevelt shut the door and they both walked toward me. I wiped the gathering tears from my eyes and forced a smile.

"You're giving up Raj's place for me? What if the machine doesn't work?"

Henry smiled his massive smile through the rain despite the soaking his summer clothing was getting. "Believe me mate, if this all goes tits up he'd die before he gave up the opportunity to rub it in our faces."

"Here," he said tossing me the pink snowpants. "You'd forget your damn head if it weren't bolted on."

I searched Roosevelt's face for his true feelings on the subject. His eyes were on the ground. I thought about telling him of the consequences of going back in time, but it didn't matter now anyway.

And to be perfectly frank, I needed him the most.

Twenty-two

An independent power supply, lubrication and spare parts, that's all you needed to make a piece of machinery last for decades. My father had taught me that. My machines wouldn't be in the sterile, laboratory condition I had left them in, but they would be in much better shape than my father's Massey Ferguson.

It was easy to understand Raj's cynicism, all one had to do was look around at all the rusted things to know that metal and electronics did not do well when they weren't maintained. Would Raj have been so certain of our failure had he visited Roosevelt's wonderland? If Raj knew what I knew and truly did want us to fail in this mission, I may have gotten more acquainted with the business end of the shotgun in my hands than the stock end. Luck was on my side.

I had no idea what I was going to do when I met the doctor. He knew two things that hurt our chances for success: The exact location of the machine and that I would be making my way toward it.

I remember nothing of the days following my reconstruction. My first memory of this place was being strapped to the Doctor's hospital bed. He must have watched my reconstruction at the machine, there was no way I could've made it to Manchester on my own in that condition. Subjects were little more than zombies when they are first reconstructed.

Time travel was not a perfect science. It wasn't as it existed in science fiction movies and books where one simply typed in the year into a console and hit 88 miles per hour. No, choosing an actual day and time of destination had no part in it at all. With my machines, you rolled the dice and took your chances. The doctor, or at least one of his lackeys, must have been stationed in front of the reconstruction chamber for years. Every day coming into work, staring at the still and empty receptacle wondering if today was to be the day of my arrival. Decades they waited. Sitting patiently at a workstation while their families and friends were raped and murdered. There was something to be said about military discipline. When I finally did make an appearance, the temptation to kill me must have been fierce, especially when it was discovered I had taken the time to give myself blue eyes. Such vanity! It was no wonder the doctor took enjoyment in my torture. Had our positions had been reversed, I doubt I would have been so restrained.

The most frightening prospect of the journey ahead was the fact that I may actually need the doctor to see this to its conclusion. If I was going to be successful, the instruments would have needed to have survived the Darkening. There were many things I built into the machines to ensure their lasting presence, but even I hadn't planned for the collapse of civilisation. The doctor and his boys may have had to improvise, make sacrifices or, dare I say it, *improvements* that I would no longer be familiar with.

★ ★ ★

The road in front of us was cracked and black with frozen mud. We walked in silence, each of us leaving the others to their thoughts. This still, morning silence broken only by the sounds of our clomping boots, my swishing snowpants and Roosevelt's whistling of a tune I didn't recognise. It wasn't a tune he was whistling so much as a string of random notes piled into one another. He didn't strike me as the whistling type. Was he nervous? It had probably been years since he had spent more than an hour in the company of others.

My jacket felt heavy and thick and soon I began to sweat underneath it, despite the cold. I unbuttoned the front and could almost feel steam rise out of it into the cool winter's air. Zara's hood was again down and her jacket unzipped. Her cheeks and neck had blushed rose with cold and she moved with her usual assurance along the busted road.

Why not, I've got nothing better to do was all she said when I asked her to come. She wasn't seduced by modern conveniences a non-Darkened world would bring, the promise of adventure was all that interested her.

Ahead of us, a rickety bridge stretched over the M60 motorway. Ancient, burned out cars lined all eight lanes, stretching out to the horizon in both directions. Every inch of road was packed bumper to bumper with rusted automobiles.

Huge chunks of cable and concrete hung from the bridge, declaring it a no go. Instead, we dropped down the bank, climbed a chain link fence and weaved in between the cars across the road. Open suitcases spewed their contents into the spaces in between the cars. Thankfully, there were no bodies here, the owners of these vehicles, quite rightly, deciding that the M60 was too depressing a place to die.

On the other side of the M60, we picked up the A56 towards Bury. Twisted thatches of copper bracken obscured our view of the shops and houses on either side of the road in the outer towns. This proved to be a blessing for when the thatch parted, what you saw beyond was death. Bodies out there outnumbered the ones in the city centre by at least four to one. When the bracken resumed its place and the road was again all that we could see, I was thankful.

If the doctor hadn't been there on my first day to shuffle me into Manchester town centre, these outer townships would have been my final resting place. Who would be on the other end this time to save me? Would the me from the video, the beforetime me, the cancerous me; recognise his own face and body as it travelled back through time to him?

★ ★ ★

Bums and tramps my subjects were, well most of them anyway. Trading their lives for a couple hundred bucks. Memory loss was always a consequence, despite the fact that subject's old brain was transferred in tact. I was now like my subjects, the only part of me that was original was the grey lump of sludge in my skull. Everything else was aftermarket. I was like a scally's Ford Mondeo; all alloys and bondo with an engine made from old hammers.

Most of my subjects, especially the early ones, never retrieved their memories. Torture was the only thing that worked and even then, the results were spotty. There was no scientific reason for the memory loss, other than the fact I was transferring a human brain from one body to another.

Before I got the mixture right, I'd made many a midnight dropoff at A&E, the subjects shivering and covered in their own piss and blood. The dropoffs were for my own conscience, I knew damn well they would never recover, I may as well have dumped them in one of these fields. Microchips and maths were my thing, Flesh and blood was a doctor's specialty.

5C009 was a fluke. He seized whilst being reconstructed, just as the last few layers of skin were being formed on the top of his head. The twitching had thrown the program off and the top of his skull was left empty, but he was the only one to leave the machine with his memories intact. It was 5C009 who provided the link between epilepsy and memory recall. It was possible for *me* to make it through. Better than possible!

Entering the machine in the beforetime was risky, doing it now almost forty years later in a deadened world was suicidal. And I didn't have cancer this time to force my hand, I had only the end of the world. But I had to go back in. I owed it to the subjects, I owed it to 5C009 to go back. I couldn't allow their deaths to be in vain.

My legs were tiring, but I trudged on. My three companions looked as though they were on a leisurely stroll through a flowery park. Henry was smiling.

The late afternoon sun threatened to poke through the clouds and if I hadn't known better, I would've said I too was enjoying myself. There were to be parts of this journey where there would be no houses, no death and no destruction. Just lush, rolling, English fields of green. The thought of crystal ponds and crisscrossing stone fences that we would see that afternoon brought a smile to my face as well.

There were four pizzas in my backpack, split into pieces and stacked tightly in sealed plastic containers. The WD40 had finally made its way to Bill, he could hardly disguise his delight.

I pulled a container out, popped it open and began munching. I didn't offer any to my companions; they had their own food stashed in their packs. Two artichoke and two ham and tomato. Bill said this would be the last day for fresh veg on pizzas, it would be dried and pickled toppings from now until Spring.

It had been good to see him again. A beforetimer had no business holding a grudge, Raj was right, I hadn't lived through the Darkening, I had no idea what it had been like. At least Bill had the Darkening as an excuse for committing murder, I didn't even have that.

I didn't tell Bill I was leaving this place and he didn't ask, but he knew something was up and not just because I'd ordered twice as many pizzas as I'd ever had. He didn't even ask me about the two days of gardening I still owed him. Something I did or said had told him all he needed to know.

"We'll see," Bill said when I told him I'd see him later.

We were walking the long way to the machine; the scenic route. There was a more direct route, straight up the motorway, but that would be the route most likely travelled by the doctor.

I knew the roads, I'd travelled them many times before. Even in their current overgrown state, I recognised them. If we carried on as we were, by this afternoon we'd come across a number of old chocolate box B&Bs with Dickensian names like *Dumblebey Inn* or the *The Wayfarers Rest*. It was in one of these places that I had proposed to Midori. Crystal bowls, stained windows, Tudor beams and antique mahogany furniture. Perfectly primped out-of-season carnations bursting from vases and hanging baskets. A huge grandfather clock in a hidden corner, chiming on the hour. Lace curtains, lace bedspreads, bloody lace doilies on every flat surface. It could only have been more English if there was a bulldog in a top hat lying on the front step. Midori loved it.

Would she have taken me back had I asked her? Not likely. I was awful to her in the later years; Lucy largely grew up without a father. I didn't tell either of them of my impending departure, they didn't even know about my cancer!

I wondered who had first broken the news to them. Had the doctor done it personally?

I am staying with Jo at her parents place until things cool down...

The words hung thick in my ears. I could feel the tears burning up again, and one trickled down my cheek before I could stop it.

We moved north, the Yorkshire Dales our destination.

Town after depressing town we passed, each one more devastated and empty than the one before. It wasn't until we were free of Greater Manchester and into the countryside proper that anyone felt like speaking.

"How long til we get there, do you reckon?" Henry asked.

I wasn't sure, but I was careful not to underestimate. It would be better to pad the time out and have them happily surprised at an early arrival than be upset with me for it taking longer than it should. "If I remember correctly, we're about half way. Must be thirty miles or so from here."

"What is it we're looking for exactly?"

The facility was underground. Deep underground. There were two elevators, one small one for me, the doctor and a handful of military personnel and a larger freight elevator. The freight elevator came in handy when one didn't feel the need to share a small space with a drooling, crying, poorly reconstructed pseudo-human. Often, shivering and screaming in pain or worse. There were many nights where I would scoop what was left out of the freight elevator with a shovel. Speech was the minimum specification a subject would need to exhibit in order to win a ride to the hospital. Anything less than that and it was a trip to the incinerator.

"A mine," I said. "An old coal mine, I think it was. Should be a big, tall brick tower with an iron wheel on top of it."

"What's the wheel for?" Roosevelt asked. Again, with the technical questions, there was an engineer in him somewhere.

"Not entirely sure, extracting coal wagons I suspect. We didn't use it."

Farmhouses and cottages dotted the landscape and were in remarkably good nick. The further away we walked from Manchester, the more manicured the fields and hedgerows became.

It wasn't long before we saw other people. Farmers swinging scythes from side to side, rhythmically and in unison, sprays of wet grass flinging into the air with each swipe before coming to rest on the ground. Chopping crop in the wet, how many times had I had to do that? Half-frozen, emerald forms chopping away, refusing to let a little thing like snow stop them from feeding their families. I could almost hear the rattling of my father's old Ford coming up from behind.

The metronomic movement of the farmers reminded me of the nodding pumpjacks in the wheatfields back home. The look on my father's face when the oil landmen came knocking to convince us to postpone growing barley on a quarter acre so they could drill. 'Hell yes!' he'd say. He wasn't exactly a cheerleader for the oil industry, but he was happy to accept the extra cash. Anything to keep us from approaching the government with our hands out. We ate well in the oil years, despite the fact they never found a drop.

"There's a town up ahead," Henry said.

"So what?" I asked. We had passed plenty of old, empty towns. What made this one any different?

"I mean a proper town. With people. You may want to sling your gun around your shoulder. We don't want to provoke 'em."

Raj's shotgun had been in my hands the entire time, pointed straight ahead. It could only have looked more aggressive if I'd tied a red bandanna around my head. Despite being the only American in the group, I was the least accustomed to holding a weapon. How times had changed.

A number of small cottages butted up to the road as we entered the village. Stone walls with thatched roofs. They'd been repointed roughly and the doorjambs and window frames were freshly painted black. We moved further into the town and before long, the cottages gave way to shops and empty, wooden market stalls. We rounded a corner and the town square opened up in front of us. My friends stopped dead and Zara pulled me back by the arm with a sharp tug. Henry stood, staring, assessing the situation, his eyes on the far end of the square.

"What is it?" I whispered.

White stone shops lined the square on all four sides with signs hanging from chains or bits of old rope. Single words adorned each sign, the letters hand-painted in black on a background of white: "Bakery", "Fishmonger", "Butcher".

The roads here, as everywhere, were in pieces, but they were distinctly clean. There was no rubbish, no rusted chunks of metal or even a single piece of greenery poking up through the cobbles. The buildings, although slanted and wonky looked as though they had been put up yesterday. Many were empty and boarded up, but even those ones had sound roofs and freshly painted walls.

Zara pointed toward the place Henry was looking at the far end of the square past a large statue of someone regal I didn't recognise. Unlike the statue of Queen Victoria in Manchester, this one's head had been reattached. At the end of Zara's finger, stood another white building with a swinging sign. I squinted and could just make out the black letters: 'Pub'. Under the sign sat a half a dozen people at tables and chairs, drinking.

"Let's go," Henry said taking a step toward the square.

I grabbed his arm. "Are you sure?"

"We need to find beds for the night, yeah? We're not getting to this mine place before nightfall are we?"

He was right. We had been walking all day, but were still a fair distance away. We could have made it before dark at a push, but then what? Did we want to run into the doctor after a long day's walk? I could already feel my legs tightening up and the thought of a bed and a beer too tempting to ignore. One last drink.

"Besides, they've already seen us."

Henry was referring to the men sitting in front of the pub. They didn't appear to have noticed our approach, they seemed more concerned with their beer and conversation. But this was Henry's world, if he said they'd seen us, then they probably had.

Now that we faced the danger Henry had prophesied, I felt guilty about bringing them to this place. If I had really cared about them, I would've laid low for a couple years, walked down to Birmingham or something until the doctor got bored of waiting, or died. Walking straight to the mine was making it easy for the old man, all he had to do was bunk out and wait.

"Will these people be alright?" Roosevelt asked.

Henry smiled at him and grabbed him by the shoulder. "We're paying customers, kid. They won't be rolling out a red carpet, but they're businessmen just like everyone else."

Paying customers. The thought hadn't even occurred to me. What were we going to pay with? Henry read my thoughts and raised a finger. "Don't worry about it."

Roosevelt pulled his hat down over his eyes and pulled his cape tight around him, hiding himself under it. Henry and Zara walked ahead and we followed.

The chatting men outside the pub hardly gave us a glance as we approached. Henry nodded at them as we passed and received no reply. They were all in dirty jeans and collared shirts. Their rolled up sleeves exposed dark, deeply tanned arms to match their dark, cracked faces. Dirt and crud had found its way into every crevice; the crick of their elbows, behind their ears and at the corners of their eyes. I knew that look, they looked like my father. I forced a friendly smile and thought about putting the shotgun in my backpack to appear as unthreatening as possible, but it was too late. I tried holding the weapon over my shoulder as casually as I could, swinging it stupidly like it was a handbag. My efforts were unnecessary. As we passed them and made our way into the pub we were ignored.

The pub was warm with orange gas lights and a burning coal fire. Ornately carved oak chairs and tables sat neatly, in front of a large oak bar. The pub must have been four or five hundred years old and it couldn't have looked much different then as it did when it had first started trading.

The pub landlord stood behind the bar wiping it down just like Raj did, wearing the same cracked face as the farmers. He was tall and thin and his scraggly straw-coloured hair and moustache made for an odd contrast to his deep, copper skin. He looked a younger, taller, less indian version of Raj except for the ashen eyes buried in a mass of heavily freckled forehead and cheek.

Henry dropped two gold rings onto the bar. They were of fairly low quality, even I could see that much. One was thin and bent and the second was missing whatever stone it was that had originally adorned it.

"Rooms, beers and breakfast. That alright?"

The landlord nodded, scooped the rings into his pocket and started pouring the pints. He pumped the wooden tap up and down, filling the heavy earthen mugs with a dark, black, frothy liquid.

The landlord didn't say much, which was hardly surprising. He certainly didn't look threatened by us, not even of big old Henry. Perhaps the rifles strapped to every wall and the knives and pistols dangling from every other farmer's belt had something to do with that.

"You from the city?" he asked.

Henry replied. "Yes, we—"

"Jesus lad, what have you come as?" the landlord said, looking up from his pouring to Roosevelt. This brought laughter from a couple of farmers at the bar and from Henry.

Roosevelt looked at the floor like he wanted it to swallow him up.

Henry scooped the four pints up and gave me a wink as he walked past me to the table.

★ ★ ★

The chat that evening was nervy. Henry was his normal, jovial self, but Roosevelt and Zara were more subdued.

"You guys worried about tomorrow?" I asked.

Zara shook her head. "No way. I'm not the one who's got to jump in that machine. This time tomorrow night, I'll be back at my house with a pantry full of vodka and pies."

Zara took a swig of beer and placed the glass back on the table. "That is, if you haven't saved the world and all. Obviously."

That brought a chuckle from Henry. They still had doubts about the machine. Did they really believe I was lying after all this?

"It's not that we don't doubt your ability, mate, it's just that... well, we'd be stupid not to have other plans in case your thingabob goes tits up."

Goes tits up. If the machine goes tits up, I would die. It was a bit on the callous side, even for a local, but I took his point.

Roosevelt said nothing. I felt a closeness to Roosevelt at that moment, moreso than anyone else. We were brothers, he and I. We were technical people, better with circuits and maths than with human beings. He had let his curiosity for the machine cloud his judgement though, had he truly not seen the danger in my going back in time? I supposed there was a chance his parents could find each other without the Darkening to bring them together, but the odds of it happening were astronomical.

If the machine didn't work, I could end up one of the many twitching lepers being shoveled out of the freight elevator, and if it did, Roosevelt would never be born.

If he'd asked me just then to call the whole thing off and stay with him, I would have.

Probably.

Henry let out a loud belch, the sound moved through the pub like gunfire. The other patrons of the pub tutted and glared at our table in disgust. Henry blushed as much as an enormous black man could before releasing his twittering laugh.

He leaned over and punched Roosevelt in the arm. "Cheer up, eh? It's like a morgue at this table."

Roosevelt looked over his still cracked glasses at Henry. "No thanks to you, big mouth."

"Whoa, look out!" Henry said. "Rosy here is growing some balls, now. Lemme have a little lookie at these big balls." He reached toward Roosevelt's lycra'd crotch, Roosevelt slapped his hand away. Henry laughed again and raised his glass.

"Here's to—"

"Never mind that," Zara interrupted. "Let's get pissed," she said and emptied her glass in one.

Henry shrugged and smiled. "Yes, ma'am."

I obliged and drank. The chocolate-coloured beer was thick and heady with a bitter aftertaste, not unlike Guinness. It was a proper pint and without a hint of coriander.

Henry lowered the mug from his lips. "Oh mate, we can't tell Raj about this stuff."

Raj's beer was nice when you considered the fact that the world had ended, but the beer in my hand was better than good. The beer in that lonely pub in the middle of nowhere could've been poured from a tap in the beforetime.

I would enjoy myself that night but I needed to keep my head straight about the following day. My memories were still coming back and my head was becoming more clear with each passing minute. I had a detailed picture of the mine in my head, but only as it existed in the beforetime. The tower was so tall that it could be seen from many miles away if it was still standing. At the bottom of the mine there was a hallway, covered in dials, lights and buttons. So much circuitry and mechanics. So many stupid things that could go wrong.

Henry punched me in the arm. "Don't you start bloody moping now!" and motioned me to finish my beer as he held a hand up to the landlord for another round. I did as I was told.

Long into the night we drank, exchanging loose and happy talk, leaving the anxiety of the next day's events float above us in the ether. I briefly thought we should come up with some sort of plan, but changed my mind. I didn't want to think about the next day and neither did anyone else. Pubs were for forgetting the terrible world outside, even in the beforetime, especially in the beforetime. Whenever someone broached the subject of the mine, someone else would interrupt with a joke or a motion to drink up. Henry liked to change the subject by punching. A playful shot in the arm from his meaty fist would shut anyone up.

★ ★ ★

At closing time, we all retreated up squeaky steps to our rooms. Drunk.

Heavy curtains hung from a rusted rail and an even heavier quilt lay atop the bowed bed. Hand-built side tables and a dressing table surrounded the bed, coated in a fine layer of dust. The furniture was square and unfancy and there was a distinct absence of doilies. Even the quilt was plain, each sewed square a simple blue or black with no pattern, frill or artistry. It was utilitarian; a room decorated by proper men *for* proper men. I liked it.

I sat on the bed and began untying my boots when there was a knock at the door. It was Zara. She held a dusty green bottle and two glasses.

"Care for a nightcap, Sethie?"

She let herself in. "The barman says this is homebrew wine. Said it will 'blow our 'eads off'. Sounds pretty good to me." Wine glasses. The glasses back in Zara's cupboards with stems were not for vodka at all, they were for wine. No wonder she thought I was insane when I had filled them with vodka. The strange things the mind chooses to forget as it is transferred from one body to the next. I wondered what my brain would lose next time.

She placed the bottle on the dressing table, pulled out the wooden stopper and had a sniff.

"Oh ho ho, this is some good stuff."

I closed the door while she poured out two glasses of the wine and handed one to me. The liquid was a deep violet, bordering on black.

"They're not going to drink themselves!" She tipped it back and drained it in one. When her face returned level, she was pinching her nose and squeezing her eyes shut tight. After a moment she shook her head. "Wow!"

The liquid in my glass looked as if it should be sizzling. I brought it up to my nose. It smelled of paint thinner.

"Bottoms up!" Zara said.

The wine tingled as it touched my tongue and scorched the back of my throat. I swallowed the liquid and fire was in my nostrils and behind my eyes.

She was laughing.

She took my empty glass from me and placed them both on the dresser. As I wiped the tears from my eyes for the third time that day, she pushed my hands away, grabbed me by the face and kissed me hard on the mouth. Her lips were strong and full. Her breasts pushed into me causing a tickly heat to jump through my chest.

She pulled her face away from mine with force and looked me in the eyes, biting her bottom lip playfully.

"Let's go out with a bang then, eh Sethie?"

Twenty-three

When I woke the next morning, Zara stood at the foot of the bed towel drying her hair in her underwear. Her black bra and panties were fraying and patched, but managed to hold her curvy bits in place, her skin pink from having been scrubbed. Before me stood the answer to the question I had asked myself on our first meeting. The freckles did go all the way down.

I had only made love to two women before last night, Midori and a girl from high school. The high school session was an awkward bit of sex with an awkward mormon girl named Tammy who was only into it because screwing a Jewish boy would piss her parents off. She wanted to do 'one bad thing' before she got married and sleeping with a half-Jew was it. I suppose I should've been offended, but hey, I was sixteen and screwing a pretty blonde. She could have been Eva Braun herself for all I cared. The sex was stop/start as she battled several inner crises and finally finished with her in a flood of guilt-ridden tears. I couldn't even remember if I came or not.

Midori's lovemaking was a scheduled affair. Even before we had Lucy, sex only took place in the mornings and consisted of the same two positions every time. It would start with her on top, and then we would flip over and continue until we each politely orgasmed. We'd then spend the rest of the morning sitting in bed reading the morning papers.

Zara abducted the sex from me. I suppose it shouldn't have surprised me that she would like it rough, but still. Sex with her was like wrestling a wolverine. She'd thrown my body about the room like it was borrowed, slapping me in the face and pulling my hair whilst playfully forbidding me to do the same. But it had awoken something primeval in me and her accompanying smirk was all too much for me to bear.

I had grabbed her by the wrists, pinned her down and drove myself into her. She moaned and wiggled her arms free only to carve crimson trenches in my back with her fingernails. I stifled a scream before she rolled me off the bed and onto the floor. The rest was a rather painful blur of sweat and skin. A beautiful, painful blur.

Her breasts quaked comically with the violent movements of her pistoning arm, working the towel over her head over-roughly, as women do. It could have been Midori's head under that towel, they were both about the same height and build, the only thing missing was the legion of creams, sprays and lotions on the dresser.

She stopped scrubbing her head and poked her head out from under the towel, strands of black hair plastered to her face.

"They've got a working shower here, Sethie. You could do with one."

My fingernails were black with dirt and I smelled terrible, but besides that I didn't think I looked too bad.

"Didn't seem to bother you last night."

She smiled. "That's because I was half pissed and well up for it. I would have shagged that skinny little weirdo with the hat if he'd asked me nicely."

I sat up in the bed and flopped my feet onto the floor. The movement made my room spin. The walking, the drinking and the rough sex had made me feel as if I'd lost a fight. My body may have been only a few months old, but just then I felt all of my thirty seven years. It was hardly the condition in which I wanted to be in to face the doctor, but one way or the other, the hangover would only be temporary.

By this time tomorrow, I would be either dead or in the machine.

I stretched and rubbed my eyes before coaxing my legs into standing.

Zara had stopped drying her hair and was holding her face up to a mirror attached to the wall and squeezing a pimple. She wiped the spot and turned toward me to grab her shirt on the bed and in an instant, the warm, fizzy morning-after trance I had been in drained from me as if being sucked out through the floor through a pneumatic tube.

The scars were missing from her arm.

I turned away from her and looked through the door into the hallway. Had she seen me looking?

Down the hall was only emptiness, half open doors, peeling wallpaper and warped floorboards. Behind me, Zara opened a window and the room was filled with the sounds of wind, rustling trees and quiet murmerings of farmers who'd decided to take their breakfasts outside.

The scars were definitely not there. It wasn't as if I had looked at the wrong arm; when she picked up her shirt, both forearms were exposed and both were as unblemished as the day she was born. Had they been there last night? It was impossible to know for sure, I was too fucked up on sex and moonshine.

"Come on, Sethie, chop chop," she said clapping her hands.

I stood up without a word and walked down the hall in my pants in search of the shower and some thinking time.

★ ★ ★

The bathroom was as expected. Chipped and broken white tiles, replaced here and there with yellow ones and red ones. The toilet and the bathtub were scratched and black with grime, but looked in working order.

The pipes groaned and shook as I twisted the shower knobs and the water they delivered was brown and freezing cold. I held my hand under the water hoping it would heat up, clear up, or both.

I needed to think rationally about the missing scars. Zara could not have known about my torture before I told her about it. One look at the deep red marks on my arms put any thoughts of hers healing out of the question. Mine looked exactly as they did on the day we first met.

She could have used makeup to conceal them. But no, there would still be bumps... There were freckles where the scars should have been.

The water trickling through my fingers was not clearing; if anything, it was colder and browner than before. I pulled down my shorts and looked at the scars on my legs and ankles.

I had never resorted to cutting in the torture sessions. The doctor had gone further than I had. Torture was used only to jog people's memories. Whatever the doctor's beef had been with Zara, it couldn't have been to jog her memory. I was the only one to come through the machine.

There was only one explanation for the missing scars; she had never had any.

I stepped into the bathtub and hopped under the old shower head for as long as it took to rub the gritty hunk of soap over my body rinse it off.

I grabbed a towel folded on a shelf and patted my body down, giving my face one last look in the mirror. My hair was thick and matted, My sunken cheeks visible through my long beard and my eyes were wide and red with age and worry. I looked exactly like a man who'd discovered his lover was his enemy.

No idea the ladder was there, mate. It was into the attic or out the window. Got lucky.

I replayed the escape in my head. The soldiers were shooting at us, they would have killed us. If Zara was with the doctor, then why—

The bullets had bounced. They *bounced*.

I pulled my lip down and looked at the purple numbers printed there by my machine. The doctor had never found the tattoo. The machine was operational, the server that held my plans was operational. Had he found the tattoo and unlocked my files as Roosevelt had done, I would be dead.

He needed me to operate the machine. *They* needed me.

I looked down the empty hallway again, the door to my room was open, but the room was empty.

I rushed into the bedroom and threw on my jeans, t-shirt, snowpants and jacket and descended the stairs into the loud and boisterous pub. Farmers and townspeople were happily munching away before their day's work, as were my friends.

Henry was stuffing food into his mouth as fast as he could while Roosevelt and Zara sipped from mugs.

I stood at the bottom of the steps, watching the three of them chatting, their conversation light and unworried. Steam rose from plates and mugs and gathered at the ceiling making the grey light seeping in through the windows look ever greyer.

Zara and the boys sat at the far end of the bustling pub; in between me and the table sat five staggered tables, the bar and the door. Did I still need them? Did I still want them?

The door swung open and clanked against the wall and in walked a small, meat cube of a man with a string of pheasants over his shoulder. Ignoring the now open door, he stomped straight to the bar.

A frigid air invaded the room through the open door and across the tables and floorboards; its cold hand scraped at my cheeks, beckoning me outside. The mine was not far; I could make it by noon if I hurried.

I would be doing them a favour.

A large, ginger haired woman in a heavy fleece, holding a tray slammed the door shut.

No, there was nothing for it. I had come this far with them, I would go the distance with them, scars or no scars.

As if hearing my decision, Zara looked up and invited me to sit down. I forced a smile as I sat down beside her behind a steaming plate of eggs on toast.

"You look a whole lot better," she said.

She wore two shirts today, both of them long sleeved.

Zara could have killed me in my sleep had she wanted to, she could have killed me on our first meeting.

"Thanks," I said.

But killing me was not her job. She fed me when I was starved, taught me to survive when I was doing a poor job of it myself and even helped me to escape from danger on the doctor's motorcycle. It was textbook Good Cop/Bad Cop. Her job was to protect me; to make sure I made it into the machine.

I picked up a piece of toast, dunked it into an egg yolk and shoved it into my mouth, letting the salty, yellow goo warm my insides.

I smiled through a huge gulp of monstrous tea, more assured of reaching the mine than I ever had. What happened once I got to there was a different story, but for now and for the first time since I woke up on the doctor's table, I was safe. I was free from harm.

"H-how long do you reckon it will take us to get to the mine?" Roosevelt sat with his mug in both hands. He was again dressed in his lycra, cape and hat despite the barman's comments the evening prior. Good on him.

Twenty-four

We set off into the English countryside and it wasn't long before we arrived at Skipton village. From there, the mine was only a ten minute drive, which meant it was an hour's walk. Skipton used to be a beautiful village, full of friendly Stavely-like people who kept their small town xenophobia hidden behind smiling faces in the hope of a tourism buck or two. The kind that would have happily pointed out the quickest way to the mine in the beforetime. But this was not the beforetime; this was A.D. After Darkening and as such, I was happy to see it completely deserted.

It was raining hard when we entered the village, the falling drops popped and pinged as they slapped against our jackets and guns. It sounded like a camping holiday, as if the drops were falling on tents and pots and pans left out in a storm. We trudged along the sodden ground, in high spirits despite the rain, none higher than mine. Henry looked miserably under-dressed for the weather, but he didn't complain. "The less you wear, the faster it dries," he said.

Zara walked with her eyes on the horizon for the rest of the journey, her face in a strange, still place that was out of character and that I couldn't decipher. I felt the need to say something, but couldn't bring any words to my lips. What could I say? "Last night was great, I need to thank the doctor when I see him?" Making love to me didn't make sense. I had already set off on the journey and was intent on reaching the mine and entering the machine. If anything, sleeping with me give me a reason to stay in the broken city. What if I had fallen in love with her? Maybe it was like she said, sex for sex sake, satisfying the most base of human urges. But risking the whole shebang for a roll in the hay seemed foolish; falling in love with her could not have been part of the doctor's plan.

The tall tower of the Greenfields Colliery showed itself to us just before noon. The enormous iron wheel at the top of the stack seemed to rise out of the ground, pulling us forward. It looked exactly as I remembered it, thirty tumultuous years had gone by and it hadn't seemed to have moved even a quarter turn. Adrenalin pulsed through me at the first sight, but I settled myself down quickly. The tower being intact was only Step One.

The feeling of elation brought on the sight of the tower quickly changed to one of dread as I spotted the fresh tyre tracks carved deep in the mud leading directly to the tower. I needed no further reminder that my time of safety was over.

Henry glanced at the tracks, but said nothing, choosing instead to crunch his way through an apple like he hadn't a care in the world.

"Hold on a sec," I said. "What's going on?"

Henry looked me in the face, took another bite of his apple and shrugged.

"What d'you mean?" he said with his mouth full.

"The tracks," I said. "You've seen them."

"Yes, well, so did you," he replied, spitting bits of apple.

Henry took two more massive bites, tossed the apple core into the grass at the side of the road and wiped his hands looking at me as if expecting me to say something.

"Well?" he asked.

Henry folded his arms and swallowed.

"I don't know what you want me to say."

"I want you to say, 'Yes Henry, I see the tracks. Yes Henry, I saw the tents, Yes Henry, I noticed the barman giving us all a night's accommodation and drinks for a couple worthless rings'. That's what I want you to say."

Henry unfolded his arms, approached me, dropped a hand on my shoulder like an anvil.

"You are one idiot Jew, you know that?"

He squeezed my shoulder where clavicle met humerus, threatening to separate the two permanently. I winced and pulled away, finding freedom from his steel grip only because he allowed it.

His smile broke across his face and Henry laughed at me. Again.

"Mate, if you truly did not realise your doctor friend was paving the way for us until just now, then you really did need us out here."

I had figured out the doctor was paving the way, thank you very much. Perhaps I hadn't noticed any tents, or saw anything strange in the transaction with the bartender, but I had noticed something that led me to the same conclusion. Zara was digging through her pack with one hand holding some sort of pastry with the other, unable to look me in the face. Her jacket was zipped up tight and her hood cinched, her arms, free of scars buried in three layers of clothing. Movie makeup would have been needed to create the convincing scars on her arms; latex. How they managed to create latex in a Darkened world was beyond my comprehension, but I suppose it wasn't out of the question if they could keep a motorcycle running.

Zara placed the pastry back into her bag, shouldered the pack and began walking in front of us, in a hurry to see her job finished.

We followed.

It was strange that Zara would forget to apply the makeup to her arm, she wasn't the forgetting type; forgetting was my M.O.

How would things play out at the mine when we arrived? The doctor would certainly be there. Would he congratulate me on my successful arrival or shoot us dead on the spot? All he needed to save the world was my brain, the body merely acted as vessel. He wanted me in the machine, that much was clear, but it was easier to carry a bleeding body into it, than convince a rational human being to enter it willingly. Especially a second time.

And Zara. At worst, she was a threat, at best, a distraction.

She walked ahead toward the enormous building on the horizon. Raj's shotgun was in my hands, all I had to do was pull the trigger. It was the same choice now as in the apartment.

Let me go, Sethie

The boys walked on either side of me. I thought about telling them about Zara's missing scars, but to what end? We were close enough to the mine now for gunshots to be heard; killing her would alert the doctor to our approach, but he was surely aware of it anyway.

I squeezed the trigger of the shotgun with a feather's weight, testing my own mettle. Adrenalin pumped through my chest and sweat gathered at my forehead.

Zara marched ahead with purpose, driving her feet into the muck. There was nothing womanly in the way she moved now, she didn't have to pretend we were friends or sweethearts anymore, her mission was mere minutes away from being accomplished. The prey was walking into her trap and it was too late to turn back.

I stopped walking and stood staring at the disappearing Zara in front of me. I closed my eyes and slowly took air into my lungs through my nose, the morning's scent sweet with cut grass and fresh bread.

When I opened them again the three of them were watching me. At the end of the barrel of my gun was Zara.

"What's up, mate?" Henry asked.

Zara's eyes were soft and unworried. She either knew I couldn't pull the trigger, or that I could and didn't care.

I shouldered the shotgun, caught up with Zara, took her face in my hands and kissed her on the mouth. Her lips were soft and welcoming. She placed her arms around my waist and squeezed back, kissing me hard.

When I opened my eyes this time, she was smiling wickedly.

"Job's not over yet, Sethie."

"I know," I said. "I just wasn't sure I'd get another chance to do that."

One way or another she would be present at my death, of that I was certain. Whether it was holding my hand or putting in the knife, I didn't know, but there was no point in denying it. And, if I was honest, I couldn't think of anyone I'd rather have with me.

★ ★ ★

The rain had stopped by the time we reached the entrance to the colliery. Three redbrick buildings stood on the site: A small gatehouse at the entrance, a slightly larger building behind that and the towering building with the iron wheel at the far end of the lot. They looked good. A cloth mannequin hung limply from the smashed window in the gatehouse.

The second building housed an old mining museum. Inside, it used to be filled with ancient mining implements and excavated chunks of coal. Leprous, animatronic dummies played tour guides, pointing at old photos of the mine and telling old stories of mining deaths and buried roman hoards. I didn't have to go inside to know the coal pieces would be missing.

The buildings were long disused even before I had started work on the machine, Thatcher had made sure of that. The voices of the dummies were bubbling and sickly, their plastic faces chipped and soulless even in my time. I had no idea what decades of further disuse would do to a mannequin and I had no interest in finding out. My gaze was firmly fixed on the large redbrick building that loomed large over the site.

The engine room.

A large metal staircase led to a door halfway up the three storey building. The motorcycle tracks (now flanked by heavy bootprints) led to the bottom of the stairs and to four men. Two of them were dressed in fatigues and carried mismatched guns. They looked like the men who chased Zara and I from the apartment, but who could be sure with soldiers? I doubted very much those guns would be loaded with rubber bullets this time. Beside the soldiers stood the doctor in his lab coat and one General Arthur Hardacre. Or as we knew him back then, simply, "The General".

The doctor smiled, his pencil-thin lips spread wide across his pale face. He took a single step toward us before his neck exploded.

The crack of a rifle ripped through the air and echoed off the buildings.

The doctor clasped his neck with both hands, sending his spectacles tumbling into the mud. Blood sprayed through his fingers and onto his white coat. He collapsed to his knees, his top half a flood of red. He reached out with a hand and tried to speak, but could manage only a gurgle before following his spectacles into the muck.

Beside me, Zara stood with her rifle at her shoulder, smoke rising from the barrel. She flipped the bolt handle up and forward before clicking it back and down, transferring a second bullet from the magazine into the chamber. The gun cracked a second time and bucked in her hands and another splash of red erupted from the doctor's twisted, motionless body.

The boys dived behind a large tractor wheel while I stood trying in vain to process what had just happened. My arms and legs cemented in place, Raj's shotgun had dropped to my feet and began sinking into the mud.

The soldiers fumbled for their weapons, one slipped and fell trying to bring his gun up too quickly.

Zara cocked a third bullet into the chamber and aimed the weapon at the General. The soldiers gathered themselves and raised their own rifles to us, but the General calmly waved his hand at them before they had a chance to fire.

For a few quiet moments, we searched the faces of our enemies while the last remnants of Zara's rifle blast dissipated into the morning air. The birds that had leapt from their branches now mere specks on the horizon.

One thing was clear, I knew nothing of the woman standing next to me.

"Pick up your gun, Sethie," Zara said.

I reached down and plucked the shotgun from the ground, flicking the bits of mud off the stock. Some had found its way into the barrel itself, but I thought better of digging it out. I held the gun at hip height and aimed it at the General.

"I see your little trip through the machine hasn't improved your respect of weapons, Lieutenant," the General said, putting great emphasis on Lieutenant. "More likely to explode than do any damage to me in that condition."

The General was a nazi when it came to weapon maintenance. *The person you shoot should die of lead poisoning, not e. coli.*

My sidearm was never cleaned or loaded, probably because I'd had no intention of using it, but it was just as likely to be out of spite. I was a Major when I went into the machine. He'd only busted me two ranks for going AWOL for almost forty years. Too lenient.

The General drew his hat up from his head, ran a hand over the top of his white hair before setting his hat back down.

He waved his hand at his men a second time. They exchanged a quick glance and slowly began lowering their guns. The General took two steps toward Zara and me.

I chanced a second glance at my companions. Like Zara, their arms were outstretched over the tractor tyre, weapons in hand. Roosevelt did indeed have a pistol and it wasn't a small one; it was a .357 Magnum. The gun looked awkward in his small hands, but it didn't shake, not like my shotgun was doing at that very moment. I didn't know where he had been hiding the gun, but it certainly wouldn't have fit under his hat.

The General moved casually forward toward us, as if the doctor's dying body wasn't cooling in front of him. His face was much different now from the one I remembered. It used to be soft, heavy-set and gin-blossomed. Like many in the military of those days, he was a man of action as long as it was others who did the acting.

The man who walked toward me was no longer the paunchy pencil pusher who hurled grenades from a command centre half a world away. The man who advanced on us was beat-up and as thin as paper. He was worn out like one of my old batteries; Rusted and foaming and curling at the edges. His face was as pale and sickly as the doctor's. As the doctor's *used* to be.

Like me, the General had been a pretend soldier. He was an academic and a diplomat. In the old days, we were quite similar, he and I. Big ideas and few battle scars. Unlike me, however, killing was never something that he personally had the stomach for. He was more than happy to leave that sort of thing to the pleb soldiers from the slums of Wigan, Moss Side and Middlesbrough. If Hardacre was at the head of your chain of command, then your future was not in a cushy office in Catterick or at GCHQ. If you reported to Hardacre, your place was in the sand.

There wasn't a day that had gone by that I didn't thank God he was not my direct report.

The General of old would've jumped at the sight of a man killed before him, even if that man had been the doctor.

Looking at him now, the dead eyes, the blithe response to the death of a man he'd known for half of his life; it was not the man I once knew. Before me was a man who had seen action first hand; a cold man without a care in the world. A local.

"Not so close, General," I said, lifting the shotgun to shoulder level.

He ignored me and continued walking. Zara kept her rifle trained on his forehead.

"I'm here to make sure you complete your mission. As misguided as it is."

He stepped over the doctor's body and was now only a few short metres away. I took a step back and stumbled. "I mean it General, I will shoot you."

The General stopped. "You will shoot me, will you?" he said, his lip pulled back from his rotting teeth. His clenched fist betrayed the rage he was struggling to keep at bay.

The strap of the gun clicked against the stock in my vibrating hand. Sweat ran from my forehead into my eye and I blinked it out. I hadn't a plan, but if I had, Zara shooting the doctor wouldn't have been a part of it. Seeing Zara's scarless arm, the realisation that she was with them and that the doctor, Zara, the General, they all wanted me; no, *needed* me to enter the machine had given me hope of making it. But, when human beings were part of the equation, nothing was predictable. Especially human beings like these who had been abandoned by the one man who could have saved them. I was naive.

Another couple steps and the General would be on top of me.

"I couldn't have known about the Darkening. How could I have known?" I said to Zara and the boys as much as to the General.

His face relaxed a little, disclosing a glimpse of the soft man who used to own that body.

"That, lieutenant is the only reason you are still breathing."

I took a further step back and grasped the gun with sweating hands, trying and failing to stem the shaking. Zara's rifle was still aimed at the General. Roosevelt and Henry still had their weapons trained on the guards, but they were looking at me. Looking *to* me. Did I actually need the General? Roosevelt probably knew more about the machine than he did. I could blow the man's head off and I would have lost nothing.

The General walked with a limp and his shoes squelched the mud, heavy and relentless as a heartbeat. Ba-bump, ba-bump, ba-bump. It wasn't a limp due to injury, it was a limp that he'd had for a long time, one that he'd become comfortable with. He didn't overcompensate or wince with the pain as he stepped through the mud. It was the limp of an old man.

His eyes straddled the gun barrel as he approached. The gun was heavy and my arms were aching, pleading with me to fire. He wasn't begging for his life, he wasn't even asking for it politely. The General really didn't care if I pulled the trigger. I took a further step back, the gun rattled in my shaking hands.

He carried on walking toward us. He knew I wasn't capable of shooting him, but how could he be so sure about Zara? Were they still on the same side? Was shooting the doctor a part of the plan? If I shot the General, would Zara turn her weapon on me? If similar questions were going through the General's head, he wasn't letting it show. Zara could have been pointing a feather duster at him for all the attention he gave her.

I needed time to give it some thought, but mine was running out. It would be seconds before the General reached us, there was nothing for me to do but let the scene play out.

My bluff had been called and everyone knew it. I lowered the shotgun.

When he was a handshake away from me, he held out his hand. It was crawling with purple veins and peppered with liver spots.

"It is nice to see you all the same, soldier."

Zara stood razor straight with the rifle still drawn, the barrel mere inches from his head.

I grasped his hand and shook it. Hardacre was never a saluter; he was a hand-shaker. In the old days, his grip was falsely overfirm to the point of bone crushing. It was one of the 'power tools' he had acquired from his Oxbridge business school education. A Hardacre handshake held you hostage; it made you question whether your hand would still be attached when he finally decided to release it. The hand in mine at that moment was not the hand of a army General, it was the welcoming hand of a starving pensioner.

Up close, he looked an even bigger shadow of his former self. The skin on his face was loose and wrinkled with globs of anaemic flesh flowing down his face like candle wax. His once sharp sapphire eyes were clouding to match his grey hair. He was impossibly old.

"You look terrible, General."

"You don't look so good yourself. What do you call that?" he said, pointing at my scraggly beard.

The General took his hand back and performed the hat–lift/hair–straighten thing again. "Are we finished messing about like children? Can we save the world now, please?"

Zara raised her head from the gun sight.

"What do you think?"

Lady, I hadn't the first clue.

I was shaking the hand of a man who despised me, the woman who wasn't supposed to be on my side and just put two bullets into the man who had made the last six months of my life spent in worry and pain and I was minutes away from having my body ground to dust on the off chance I could save the world.

"I guess we follow him," I said.

The General led the four of us toward the engine room stairs. Roosevelt and Henry kept their guns on the soldiers as we approached the engine room.

The General stepped over the doctor's body a second time without looking down at it. Blood oozed from him, soaking his lab coat red except for an inch of white at the bottom hem. The face of my torturer buried in the mud and for that I was glad, never again would I hear his voice in my ear or feel his hands on my body.

When we reached the bottom of the stairs, the General motioned for his soldiers to lead us to the door at the top.

"No. The soldiers stay here," I said.

He spun toward me on his heel. "But that will leave me defenceless."

"If they go up those stairs, then I don't."

The General pondered this for a moment. His soldiers looked to him for an answer.

"If mine stay down here, then so do yours," he said.

The first soldier threw his arms up in a huff. "But I want to see it!"

The General only needed to put an eyeball on the soldier to make him zip his lip.

A small army could be waiting for us inside. *Would* be waiting. There was only two outcomes possible; either I was getting into the machine or I wasn't. Bringing Henry and Roosevelt in would only put their lives at unnecessary risk. For once, I would do the honorable thing.

"I need Zara. I can't set it off on my own," I said. "I need someone I can trust."

I looked at Zara as I spoke the word 'trust' searching her face for a guilty disclosure. A twitch, a sideways look, a trembling lip. But I should have known better, she did none of those things, she simply smiled, and drew soft lines down the back of my hand with her fingers like a prospective girlfriend on a first date. Like she was thanking me for the compliment.

The General nodded and began climbing the stairs.

Roosevelt bunched his face up into a pout to match the one of the gobby soldier. My original intention had for him to accompany me into the engine room, he had a technical mind and had seen the plans. He no doubt spent a week with that password poring over the schematic on his computer. He was the only other person in the world that knew how the machine worked.

I put my hand on his shoulder.

"When I go back, I'll find you and show you how it works. I'll look you up on the internet, show it to you on your sixteenth birthday."

I expected him to argue with me, but he didn't. He simply nodded agreement and shifted position from one foot to the other. In a few moments, he could be erased from existence and yet he didn't protest. He faced oblivion so easily. Too easily. If it was faith in his parents' ability to find each other in a world without the Darkening, then he was a fool. The odds of it happening were almost as infinite as time itself.

Roosevelt turned his attention back to the soldier without a word. I didn't bother asking him for his real name.

Henry opened his arms and beamed, folding me into his giant body, stopping just short of snapping my spine in two.

"If it does go tits up in there, there's always a place for you in the back of Raj's," he said. "He needs a good dishwasher."

When he released me, he was smiling widely with streaks of water running down both cheeks. He hadn't known me for very long, but he loved me. How a man who had lived through the terrors of the Darkening —who had lost everything– could still manage to love another person, especially one like me, only god knew.

Henry's smile disappeared and his face turned serious again as he faced the soldiers.

An unseen crow squawked from somewhere far away, from a tall branch in a free place and in that moment I wanted to run. Run back to town, and through it. Run down the freeways past Zara's house, past the shit chippies, the football ground, across the rotting freeways and over the mountains of green glass of Beetham tower and past the markets and Bill's pizza to my apartment; to my bicycle. Ride down the railroad tracks to the coast, to the Liverpool docks. To find a ship and sail back to America, back to Stavely, to see the graves of my parents, to see a sunny harvest and Dick Dyck's latest tattoo.

But there wouldn't be any ships. and it would not be long before the draw of the machine again consumed me. We were connected now, me and *it*. My mother and father were no longer a New York Jew and a small town hick, my father and mother were made of steel and copper. They were a robot without emotion or a soul, if there was such a thing. I, like my creator was an empty shell. A discarded pistachio shell, sunbleached and brittle, its insides consumed and sucked clean. Like father, like son.

No man with a conscience would willfully walk into a machine a second time that liquidised his skin and bone, a machine that sliced open his skull and froze his brain. It's not so much about taking a leap of faith as it is having nothing to lose.

Do you ever wonder why the death of this city doesn't bother you? the doctor had asked.

He wasn't referring to the soulless man who arose from the machine, he was talking about the empty man who went in.

5C009 was a fluke

If there was ever a man with a spirit, an essence, a man with a wife and daughter who loved him, that man was truly dead. The King is dead. Long live the King.

I nodded at the General. "Let's go."

Zara and I followed the General, rising high above the four men. The last thing I heard of that world was Henry barking something at the soldiers.

The iron door slammed behind us and I quickly remembered why it was called the Engine Room. An enormous mass of metal crank shafts and gears built to haul coal up from the depths filled every inch of the vast space. Cylinders six feet high and twenty foot across, pipes, enormous flywheels all rusted and cracked, rose up far above our heads.

The engine room was in virtually the same condition as it was when I had first entered and I took some comfort in that. I would never again set eyes on the terrible world on the other side of the door. The dying flesh, the cracked bones, the crushed brick and twisted metal would soon itself be just a memory. Soon, I would be blinking my new eyes on another world, a world of ease and luxury. A world with my Lucy. I allowed myself to get a bit excited. It was worth dying for.

An ancient control room stood high over the engine, a headless museum mannequin sat slumped over the controls, its arms hanging loose from wiry threads. I had never heard the engine running, but I could imagine the roar it would've made back in the coal mining days. The sound must have shaken the operator's ears off his head. And to think, the man who sat at those controls was the lucky one. He was the senior man. Deafness was better than Black Lung, I supposed.

We walked alongside the mass of pipes and dials until we reached the north wall. As we rounded the corner, the engine opened up in the middle into a vast 'U' shape.

"This all coming back to you now?" the General asked.

It was indeed coming back. The mine had made perfect sense. We needed a deep hole, one to make it possible to reach terminal velocity, to push a human being past terminal velocity, to speeds that no other human had ever reached.

The abandoned mine was the perfect place for our experiments. The perfect place to do unseen things.

I walked toward the bottom of the 'U' where the two engines met in the middle. Behind this wall of pipework and gauges was an elevator that would take us down to the machine. I pulled on a lever and the control panel opened with a small whoosh. The LED screen lit up with one word, "Passcode."

How many times had I punched in that series of characters? Thousands.

Capital J, small t, four, nine, zero, capital Y, small x, twenty-six, small h.

Another false panel moved, revealing two pieces of glass, one horizontal and one vertical. The panels were not installed when I built the place, they were new additions.

"Excuse me, if you will," the General said before placing four fingers of his right hand on the horizontal panel and looking into the vertical panel. Fingerprints and retina scan.

Two large clunks sounded from deep within the machine followed by the squeaking of an old elevator as it rose to the surface. It was a good thing I didn't shoot him.

"There is another person with eyeballs and fingers to open this door," the General said. "Unfortunately, your friend here shot him in the neck."

My 'friend', he said referring to the woman at my side. If only.

The rising elevator wheezed to a stop. Two doors adorned with false piping pushed outward, toward us and split open with a whoosh. Yellow, flickering fluorescents cast dull light on the steel walls of the open elevator. The freight elevator beside it remained hidden.

"What about the freight elevator?"

"Out of service," the General said.

The steel elevator walls were scratched and dull with small rust spots making themselves known here and there. In that tiny space three months ago, the doctor, the General and a quivering, slobbering, hairless, half-Jewish man with no memory had made the journey up to the broken world of 2062 together. I was probably slung over the back of the doctor's motorcycle on the way to the detention centre like a trophy deer, arms and legs flapping in the wind.

The elevator was far from pristine, but it looked better than Roosevelt's elevator. Hopefully there was no Floor Twelve this time.

Roosevelt had gotten the elevator working in a building with no windows in a city without electricity. He was too intelligent to face his impending erasure from existence with such serenity. He had actually smiled at me at the bottom of the steps. It was a tiny smile, but a smile nonetheless. Perhaps he was like me, preferring death to a life in the wilderness.

We stepped into the elevator and the General pushed a small black button, the only button on the panel. The doors wheezed shut leaving us in the flickering, yellow semi-dark. The elevator jerked with a loud clunk and began descending. Zara stood facing forward, her face was serious.

"You really don't remember coming back up the first time?" the General asked.

I shook my head.

"It doesn't surprise me," he said. "You did not look well. That reconstruction business was quite a thing to behold. Positively frightening. I didn't know what to expect, I had visions of a Star Trek kind of thing, I don't know, I thought you might *beam* into the reconstruction pod." He sneered with disgust at the thought. "You should've given me at least some idea of what to expect, I almost shut the bloody thing off midway through."

Reconstructing a human being from its base particles was indeed a harrowing thing to watch. *Printing* a human being from the ground up.

"Well, I guess you'll be better prepared the next time," I said.

He probably wasn't lying when he said he almost turned it off. Would the younger, softer General shut it off this time when I went back?

We didn't speak much the rest of the way down. The idea that my body could have so easily been stalled by the General's hand was a sobering one. I had a reason to do it last time, not just out of curiosity, but because I was dying. The elevator slowed and creaked to a stop and the doors opened a second time.

Did I have a good enough reason to take such a risk again?

The bright white light of the corridor flashed into the elevator car. Zara and I put hands over our eyes to shield them.

Once my eyes adjusted, I once again set eyes on my creation. Multicoloured LEDs flickered across control panels that reached floor to ceiling along both sides of the long hallway leading away from us. Spinning dials, dancing needles. Robotic arms swished forward and back along tracks in the ceiling, pushing buttons and squirting grease. Roosevelt would've loved it.

Chipped, yellow, painted lines ran along the floor marking a safe distance from the panels. You didn't want to get too close; taking a swinging robotic arm to the mush wasn't a pleasant experience.

Twenty feet in front of us, a rusted arm lay dormant on the floor, kicked into the safe zone under the shelf, a dry paintbrush still clutched in its dead, robotic gripping mechanism. That robot cost fifty thousand quid and its only function was to paint yellow lines. Health and safety.

We walked along the corridor toward the room at the end. Zara's face darted back and forth, trying to take everything in. She held her rifle tightly in both hands, on edge, looking as if she would shoot at shadows. The girl beside me was not the assured person I knew on the surface. The Zara in that corridor was nervous.

The General's feet clapped the concrete floor sharply as we moved down the corridor. His limp was pronounced, but it did not slow him.

There was a break in the control panels and a window that looked out onto a side room. Through the fogged glass, a robotic arm on tank tracks pushed a cylinder into a slot. Endless racks stacked in rows behind the robot stretched beyond for miles, hints of glowing green light and moving parts dotted everywhere.

I answered Zara's questioning glance with a smile. "Uranium."

"Is it safe?" she asked. It was a question she would have never asked on the surface. Up there, the primitive world of bones, broken power lines and nettle tea was hers; down there amongst the robots and radiation was mine.

"This reactor powered most of the North West. Nuclear power wasn't all that popular so it was better to keep it out of sight. We had enough protests by environmental nuts about the nuclear power plants above ground, lord knows what they would've done had they known we were building them secretly."

"You built this without anyone knowing?"

"The trucks came at night underground. A tunnel fifty miles away trucked the materials underground. After it was built, the tunnel was sealed, no one was the wiser."

The General ignored me.

"The irony being that nuclear was safer and better for the atmosphere than the coal burning plants that were responsible for most of the country's power. But you can't talk to people, you know what they're like."

Zara gave me a questioning look.

"They had no problem driving cars that ran on gasoline and flying in planes. Things that were *actually* killing the planet, but for some reason, nuclear was the real bad guy in their eyes. Fulfilled our thirst for power, closed the coal burning plants and kept the greenies happy. It just so happened to be capable of powering a time machine as well. Three birds, one stone, right General?"

He didn't look back, his shoulders bounced as he hobbled down the hall with increased haste. clip-clop, clip-clop, clip-clop.

"If this thing is still working, then why doesn't the city have any power?" Zara asked.

"That is a question for our General friend here."

Again, the General ignored us.

Zara grabbed his arm and spun him around. The General's face was blank.

"Why doesn't the city have any power?"

The General surveyed the corridor with an impatient look. "We shut the city down."

Zara eyed him with astonishment, processing his words.

"We tried turning it back on afterward, when things got really bad, but by then too much damage had come to the city. Too dangerous."

He snatched his arm from her and continued walking. I followed him and met Zara's shocked expression with a shrug. There was a battle going on between the two of them, one that could very well be for my benefit.

The closer we got to my machine, the lighter I felt. Death was coming, I should've been frightened. But I wasn't. The hallways, the electronics, the machines; this was my playground. The doctor was dead, I would never again be cold or alone or worry about my next meal. Even if I never again exited the machine, earthly things would never again burden me. There would be no dead bodies, no broken glass, no leaking apartments, and above all, no fear. I could happily live in that bowels of that mine for all time. I felt like skipping down the hallway.

The room at the end of the hall was approaching. White light poured out from the door into the corridor. The room beyond was nothing but a humming void. The imaginatively named 'Room A' and 'Room B' had been speculated upon and whispered about in the media and the wider intelligence community for years, but only a handful of people had ever seen them.

At the foot of the door, another robot lied twisted and smashed on the floor.

"What happened to that one, General?"

"It didn't do anything important," he replied.

"Rat killer, wasn't it? I'll just tuck my trouser legs into my socks, then shall I?"

The white light on the other side of the door brightened as we passed through an arched entranceway into the enormous circular room. The domed roof reached high to the heavens and long fluorescent tubes hung down vertically from thin wires. On the far end of the room a heavy steel door stood ajar giving just a peek of the Room B, but not enough to see what was inside. The dropshaft.

As we continued toward the two rooms, a tiny memory flitted across the back of my brain, like a butterfly fighting against a breeze. A panicked flicker that set down on the spongy folds of my parietal lobe and soaked into the Hippocampus.

The dropshaft didn't work. It never had.

"What's through that second door?" Zara asked from somewhere far away.

Sending matter beyond the speed of light was forbidden by Einstein's theory. Every high school physics student knew that, it was one of the first things we were ever taught.

But we didn't need to send matter, we only needed to send *data*.

The General's metronomic clipping and clopping continued on ahead. I felt sick, like I was watching the entire scene from above, watching some other poor bugger marching to his death on TV.

My cheeks were hot and a bead of sweat ran down my forehead. I brushed it out of my eyebrow.

"Seth? What's the matter?" Again Zara's voice, distant and echoing as if coming from the entrance to a long tunnel.

When a human being was reduced to bits of information, you simply needed to send ones and zeroes past the speed of light. It seemed simple when compared to the creation of a human being.

We got closer to accomplishing it than anyone else, using four-way mixing techniques to push data past the speed of light, but the pulse was not stable enough to control and was only capable of sending quantum data. Sending binary bits was a whole different matter. Einstein's reputation remained intact.

Roosevelt's knowing smile flashed against my subconscious. He knew I wasn't going backwards. He'd seen the schematics. His existence was never in danger.

The world could not be saved.

"I'm fine," I said, forcing a smile.

I knew there was no going back when I entered the machine the first time.

The biggest disappointment was not the fact that the dropshaft didn't work; the biggest disappointment was that it would never work. We continued with our experiments, but I knew they would fail. If we someone had ever managed to send data back from the future, we would have started receiving it the moment we turned the machine on. God, I had actually expected to start receiving data from people in the future as soon as we turned it on.

The General continued to lead us toward the two rooms.

The laser wasn't even in Room B anymore, it was packed away somewhere in a box. The dropshaft would become little more than a particle accelerator; a toy for lab rats.

There was no remorse on my face at Roosevelt's place; the me from the video. My face was pallid and my eyes were sunken and dark, but it was not the face of a guilty man. The me on the screen checked his watch with disinterest; with boredom! He hadn't the look of a man grieving for the impending loss of a family, of a daughter who loved him, The video me had the face of a man waiting for a bus that was running late.

I was indeed dying of cancer, but was that reason enough to abandon them?

Forward. I was going forward. So my life was to be in Roosevelt's hands after all. Who knew how far forward I would go this time, it was hardly an exact science. Without the cancer, there would be no need to clean my numbers; it should be a significantly shorter trip. I could only hope the General would be dead by the time I returned.

But what of Zara?

She had killed the doctor so perhaps there could have been a chance of her helping me, but now that the world could not be saved…Would she believe I didn't know, would she care? The instant I entered the machine, she would know I hadn't gone backward. They wouldn't wait for me this time, no, the machine was to be my grave. My existence erased with the tap of a delete key.

I inhaled deeply and wiped more sweat from my forehead, flicking the salty water to the floor in drops out of sight of Zara and the General. And moved on.

White paint chipped off the ceiling and copper water cut jagged streams down the walls in small clusters like scars; not even the infamous 'Room A' and 'Room B' were impervious to the Darkening.

Along one side of Room A was more lights, dials and monitors and on the other; the tall, glass structure of the reconstruction chamber.

I approached the chamber and ran a finger down the inside of the glass wall. I caressed the two robotic arms, hanging limp. Black nylon cables snaked over the arms, ending in two titanium nozzles. The smell of oil and disinfectant.

Inside the chamber was where I was born. Through these cables, the building medium flowed, slowly building up my muscles, my organs, my bones. Injected keratin. I brought the back of my hand to my face. When I first arrived, there would've been no hair or fingernails, they grew as I lay strapped to the doctor's slab. The robotic arms were in very good shape, in much better shape than my birth mother and father. Mortal flesh.

The chamber was spotless. I searched the cracks and the seams for genetic material, but there was none. I could fake a malfunction, tell them the machines no longer worked, but it would only delay the inevitable.

The care and attention that was obviously accorded to the chamber and the nuclear core was promising despite the General's indifferent comments regarding the other 'useless' robots lying motionless on the floor. The trail my hand left across the thick layer of dust on the top of the magnetic resonance imaging machine, however, suggested a lack of diligence toward what they probably deemed 'preliminary' or 'support' machinery. To him, the chamber and dropshaft in Room B were the things that mattered most. What he didn't realise was that the MRI was the most important piece of machinery. If the MRI was at all damaged, I wouldn't be going anywhere. And neither would anyone else.

Despite the fact that I was more than likely to die upon entering the machine, the desire to do so was intense, certainly preferable to a life of scrounging in the cold. At least I would die in the name of science, in a warm place, a victim of my own genius. That was more than I could say about the poor bastards stacked in broken piles around the base of Beetham Tower.

There was no doubting it; I *wanted* the machine to work. If they pulled the plug while I inside, then so be it.

"How long was I on the table before you decided to start torturing me?" I asked the General.

His eyes were on the ceiling and his fingers scraped across his stubble in thought. Parched and grating like a plank of wood being dragged over broomcorn, cut short.

"Oh, I suppose it must have been a couple months, really," he said. "After the first few weeks, we weren't sure you'd ever snap out of it. I'd given up hope months before you arrived. 'Twas the doctor that kept you alive. *Just one more day, one more week* he said."

The doctor waited longer than I would have. The newly reconstructed subject was incapable of speech, of cleaning itself, of using a toilet. The doctor must have changed countless urine bags and shitty bed spreads. One thing could be said for him, he was a patient man. The General didn't exactly seem to be in mourning.

As I brushed the MRI dust off my hand onto my already filthy snow-pants, the door to Room B burst open and soldiers poured into the room, pounding the concrete floor with black boots.

Like the men outside, they were dressed in old jeans and random bits of camouflage carrying a random selection of guns. Into the room they clomped, two by two, surrounding us and holding their guns to their chests. Zara took two steps back toward the hallway flitting her eyes to the men, to the General. She looked afraid, but she didn't run.

A large soldier broke from the mob and ran at her, pulling the rifle from her hands and pushing her into another soldier who held her arms. She didn't flinch or move to escape. He grabbed her around the waist and a second soldier took her by wrists.

Two more soldiers stepped toward me and brought their rifles up to eye level, training them at my head. There were at least thirty soldiers in the room; it was the most people I had seen in one place in as long as I could remember.

The General nodded at the big soldier holding Zara. The three downward chevrons marked onto his shirt sleeve with felt pen suggested a sergeant's rank. In addition to the stripes, the man holding Zara wore a helmet and a flak jacket. Precious things, those.

"So much for trust," I said to the General once the soldiers found their places.

"You have some nerve to talk to me about trust. My trust in you built this place. And how do you repay that trust? By pissing off without telling a soul."

"You know why I did it," I tested.

He scoffed. "Yes, I do. We all do," he said addressing his audience. "Cancer, apparently. No way to be sure, of course. You weren't exactly forthcoming with your diagnosis nor were you with the operation of the machine itself."

He knew more about the machine than he was letting on. I had shown him the plans in the early stages and even offered to bring him in on the experiments. But he did not want to get his hands dirty. If my late night exercises were ever exposed to the media, he wanted to be able to say 'Sorry, your honour, I had no idea our scientists were going that far.' CYA was the order of the day for a career soldier, Cover Your Ass.

He knew plenty about the machine. He had his little spies and the entire place was rigged with CCTV. He did not know enough, though. If he knew *enough*, if he knew how to make the thing work, or that the dropshaft was useless, I would've been killed the minute I made an appearance in this world. The one thing you could not duplicate in a city bereft of human beings was the trials. To get the reconstruction correct, you needed data, lots of data in order to make tweaks. Pele was not born a genius footballer, he was drilled into one. Theory was an important starting point, but to get good at anything, you needed *practice*.

"My cancer was terminal. I wouldn't have been any good to you dead, General."

He bristled, allowing the rage inside him to bubble into his face. His eyes bulged from their sockets, his thin lips twisted and his ears went pink. He clenched both gloved fists and moved toward me. His movement was quick, too quick for a man of his age. He grabbed my throat and pulled my face toward his, squeezing my airway closed.

Gasping, I dropped the shotgun and grabbed his wrist with both hands, but it wouldn't move. His arm was like iron.

His breath was on my face, hot and rotten. "Would you like to know what happened to your daughter?"

I tried to pull away from him, but he held me fast.

"She was raped. Repeatedly."

I struggled in his grasp but it only tightened. I choked and coughed, but couldn't take in air. A heat was on my face and my legs went weak. Panic pulsed through me and I shook myself violently trying to escape. He was saying something else, but I couldn't hear. I was going to pass out.

My knees buckled, and the General released his grip, allowing me to drop to the floor.

I gasped for air, taking it in in big gulps and coughing it back out. He kicked my gun away, it clattered across the floor before coming to rest at the feet of one of his soldiers. He stood over me, bending down close.

"There were witnesses. Gangs of men took turns with her one after the other. Piling on and violating her in every conceivable way."

He bent down further and grabbed me by the shirt. I couldn't listen to anymore. I put my hands over my ears, but he pulled them away.

"We couldn't get to her until after the riots had finished. By then, there were only pieces."

I screamed and lunged forward at him. He stepped back, parried my fist and brought his own into my chin. My teeth crunched together and lightning flashed behind my eyelids. I felt my legs go and the cold slap of tiled floor in my knees and wrists. When I opened my eyes again, I was looking up at him from the floor.

His lips curled back into a sickening grin over black teeth.

"You had a go, didn't you, Pete?" he said looking over his shoulder at one of the soldiers.

The soldier dragged his tongue across his teeth and thrust his pelvis forward, making a spanking motion with the hand holding a pistol. "Too fucking right, I did."

That sent the lot of them laughing again. All except Zara. She stood with her arms held behind her, looking at me on the ground. Pitying me.

The General moved toward me, holding a hand out to pick me up. "Come on then, up you get. Let's get you in this bloody thing."

As he reached down, his coat flapped open to reveal a glint of something shiny hanging from his armpit. I reached up toward his hand, but as reached, I thrust myself up toward him, plunging my hand into his jacket toward the shiny bit, my fingers wrapping around it tightly. A pistol.

His smile disappeared and he grabbed for my arm, but it was too late. He gasped as I pulled the pistol from its holster and squeezed the trigger, disintegrating his knee.

The old man collapsed, but he didn't cry out. Two shots were fired at me from the soldiers. One bullet whizzed past my head and the other buried itself into my left thigh sending searing pain up my spine.

I screamed in agony and raised the weapon to the General's head. We were both going to die today.

"Stop! Don't kill him!" It was the General's voice. He was wincing in pain and clutching his knee. Blood soaked his pant leg and poured out onto the concrete floor.

The gun shook in my hand. A hot wetness burned across my leg threatening to boil. Visions of men ravaging Lucy played in my mind. I wanted to kill this man, to see his face explode in front of my eyes.

The man holding Zara and two others quickly removed their shirts and began tearing them into strips.

The other soldiers stood firm with their weapons drawn. Tight buzzcuts and angry, greasy faces stared down at me; some through visors, others through dark sunglasses. Their fingers danced on their triggers, begging me to give them a reason to shoot.

The General laughed and spit a wad of blood onto the floor. "God, I must be getting old. Letting a little prick like you get to me."

Zara wore an expression of worry on her face that didn't suit her. The soldiers were paying her no notice. I nodded toward the entrance, signaling her to run. Testing her. She shook her head and stood firm. She would see her duty out until the end.

My thigh throbbed sickly, warm blood seeped from under my hand.

The two soldiers carried the ripped pieces of cloth to the General, ignoring the weapon I was pointing at him. Their hands moved quickly, wrapping his knee and twisting a small flashlight into the cloth to fashion a makeshift tourniquet. I wasn't a doctor, but even I could see it was only delaying the inevitable. The General and I were going to die, there was no two ways about it. There were no hospitals in this world, no anaesthetic, no antibiotics.

The General and I shared a dizzy, bleeding moment with each other. We knew we were both done for and the room itself seemed to brightened with the knowledge. The thin fluorescents pulsed and began to swing in time, slow at first but gathering pace. The floor tilted, the MRI machine rolled across the floor and the door to the reconstruction chamber creaked open to reveal a small form inside. A tiny form, pink and naked from the waist up with eyes and hair of charcoal. Her arms missing and her face, shoulders and torso melting like ice cream, spilling over a plaid skirt. Her legs sturdy, perfectly formed and stockinged, the melting skin dripping off her skirt onto her black patent fairy shoes. I turn away.

The floor glowed bright white swallowing my hands. The soldiers with their guns, stood straight as maypoles, their too red lips and eyes twisted into frightening totems. One of them—the man who ravaged my daughter—chewed a toothpick. A toothpick in Manchester. Of all the things to save.

The sergeant hauled the General to his feet. The green tourniquet had already gone a deep rust colour as it struggled to stop the bleeding. There were great vats of blood behind these walls, but only the machine was capable of pumping it into the correct places and in the correct amounts. The General winced as he was raised to his feet, but again he was silent. The sergeant held a finger up at me and the second soldier walked toward me holding out the strips of cloth. He walked directly in front of the gun barrel, blocking my view of the General and everything snapped back into focus. The lights steadied, the chamber emptied, the soldiers again mere men.

I thrust the barrel up to my own throat. "Don't move!"

The second soldier looked back to the sergeant for advice. He was busying himself with the act of keeping the General upright. The other soldiers stood straight and unmoving, some with their weapons trained on me, some with their guns held closely to their chests.

"Seth," the General said, his voice hoarse and breathy. "Let him tend to your wound."

I shuffled backward to the MRI machine on my backside. I moved to quickly, causing something deep inside my thigh to rip. I screamed and squeezed my wound to stem the pain, but it only hurt more.

I reached up and grabbed the lip of the machine and attempted to pull myself up onto it with one hand, the other still holding the gun at my throat. Without a hand on my thigh, the bleeding continued unabated. Pain was everywhere and the sudden movement made my head spin. I leaned over and puked onto the floor. Again and again I retched until my stomach was empty and the bile and floating chunks of undigested breakfast seeped into my pant leg. With the gun still at my throat, I nodded to the soldier holding the cloth.

"Do whatever you want with me."

He moved quickly and held me by the shoulders, while another walked through the puke pile to pick up my feet. Together, they carried me to the edge of the MRI, out of range of the spreading pool of sick and began their work with my thigh. I was too weak to resist. I had a small inkling of the weight of the gun in my hand, but I couldn't be sure where it was now pointing. Or if the weight I felt was merely residual and the gun had already been taken away.

Camouflaged arms moved around my body like cruise missiles. Their field dressing skills were well honed, their movements clinical and targeted. They moved together and without words, balling two pieces of cloth and burying it onto the wound. I screamed again and dry heaved.

"Hold this here," said one of the soldiers directing me to the tourniquet he had twisted on my leg. The flashlight was tightly sprung and I had to concentrate on my hand in order to stop it from coming loose.

The General was hanging off the sergeant, unable to put any weight down. His face was without colour and his hat sat crooked on his head. "Now pick him up," he said.

The two men grabbed me under my armpits and lifted. I felt something hard jar into my throat as I was chucked to my feet. In my hand was gripped the General's gun and the barrel was still aimed at my jugular. The soldiers made no attempt at the weapon.

Zara stood alone now by the control panel. And yet, she still did not run. She stood watching me, perhaps looking for a sign, a signal of some kind as to what I was going to do next.

"Go and help him to the panel, will you?" the General said to Zara and swallowed hard. "Please."

She obeyed and moved quickly, taking the soldier's place on my bad leg side.

"I've got him," she said.

He released me into Zara's arms and the two men took their places with the other soldiers.

Zara's held me steady, taking most of my weight, her arm at my back this time instead of a blade.

Ordinary or Nettle?

I tested my good leg and found I could put weight on it. Even so, there was no way I could walk to the control panel with one hand on the tourniquet and the other on the gun. There was no point in holding the gun to my throat anyway. While the General was still alive, I was not to be harmed. The soldiers eyed my movement toward the panel, many with twisted faces and clenched fists. Almost willing the General to die so they could finally exact their revenge. I needed to move quickly.

I placed the gun into my waistband and put my arm around Zara's neck. She stepped forward but I resisted.

"Let me help you," she said.

"One minute," I said. "I have to adjust my leg" and shifted my body so my arm was on her arm and my mouth at her ear. She moved with me, positioning herself into the necessary places to keep me from falling.

I squeezed her elbow, at the point of the missing scars and whispered. "Are you with me?"

She looked behind me at the soldiers, at the dying General before meeting my eyes.

And nodded her head three times.

The movement was slight, barely registering, but deliberate. She was lying, but it didn't matter. She needed to know that I had discovered her deception. I readjusted myself to face the soldiers and hopped on my good leg. Together, we limped past the General toward the control panel. His head bobbed up and down as he fought to stay conscious.

"We should send him," I said to the sergeant holding the General up.

The sergeant moved to speak but the General stopped him. "No... You."

I addressed the sergeant again. "If he doesn't go, he will die."

The sergeant said nothing. He looked once at the men and again at the General. The General's head fell into his chest and his mouth hung open as he wheezed. His lungs were shutting down.

"Look at him, soldier! He hasn't much time," I pleaded. The sergeant moved to speak a second time and again stopped himself.

"If he goes back, he can convince *himself* of the Darkening. Only the General has the power to stop it. No one will believe me."

The lie was a risky one, but there was nothing else to say.

The sergeant shifted from one foot to the other, struggling to decide. The General's head fell into his chest again where it remained. When the sergeant again raised his face, I knew his answer before he spoke. They really didn't know the dropshaft was useless.

"Ok."

"Move him into the MRI. We need to get an image."

"But sarge—" It was the man who had raped my Lucy.

"Zip it, grunt."

The second soldier zipped it.

The sergeant dragged the General's lifeless body toward the MRI as Zara helped me to the control panel.

The small computer and its database were all that was needed to go forward in time. Everything outside of Room A; the antiquated mass of panels, lights and dials down the hall and in the hordes of hidden rooms attached to it were all there to manage the reactor. A reactor that at one time powered an entire city but whose sole function now was to run the machines.

Room A was built by a genius; the other rooms built by committee.

I touched the screen and it flickered into life. Four familiar icons greeted me, "Data" "Dropshaft", "Reconstruction" and "MRI". I touched the MRI icon and a menu popped open.

Status: idle

"Better than an error, I suppose."

"What do you mean?" Zara asked.

I waved a hand at her before tapping the status bar. A new menu appeared and I ran a finger down the screen, scrolling through the menu to "Open" and tapped again. The menu screen swished to the right and the MRI behind me groaned and blue light flickered from the hole in one end, illuminating the inside. The sergeant picked the General up in his arms and placed him gently on the receiving tray.

"His clothes," I said.

Without a word, the sergeant unbuttoned the General's jacket and shirt. Two other soldiers stepped forward and the three of them relieved the General of his uniform and shoes, moving with soundless, mechanical discipline. A fourth soldier stepped forward to produce a long knife. He cut the General's trousers above and below the knee, leaving the tourniquet in place.

It wasn't until the General was fully stripped that the soldiers allowed themselves to be anxious. One soldier gasped and many others nervously whispered, pointing at the weak old man lying before them in his torn white vest and greying boxer shorts.

There lie General Hardacre. The man who commanded the last army in a destroyed world. Struck down by a single bullet and lying dead on a metal tray, a withered collection of skin, bone, blood and balls; the same as the most lowly of infantry grunts.

Death comes to us all. Most of us anyway.

I tapped the screen again and the General's body moved slowly into position inside the MRI. The magnets in the machine whirred noisily and before long, the monitor was aglow with the General's cooling body parts. In seconds, his brain, gut, muscles and eyeballs appeared. His frailness even more apparent when projected digitally. Soon, the data collected would be rattled off and stored in the database, ready for reconstruction on the other side. Litres, millimetres, X, Y coordinates and atomic weights. Ones and Zeroes. Retinas and fingerprints. Even something as supposedly precious as a human being reduced to numbers.

And I was excellent with numbers; the very best.

The EKG registered a weak heartbeat.

"He's still alive," I said and turned back toward the men. They were transfixed on the MRI monitor.

While the General was assessed, I swished the screen back to the right and punched 'dropshaft' with my finger.

The lights of Room B flickered on and the steel door opened. I felt Zara shift underneath me to get a better look into the room.

The soldiers could see who was in charge now; who had always been in charge. We had both taken a bullet and yet, here I was standing erect, lucid and there he was, old, decrepit and undeniably mortal. The pain in my leg was fierce and throbbing, but soon it would be gone. Everything would be gone.

The screen blinked green and the machine beeped. The whirring sound of the MRI faded and the General's body emerged once more.

The sergeant turned to face me. "Now what?"

I looked the sergeant dead in the eyes. For the first time in my life, I feared neither man nor death.

"Now," I said. "He is dropped."

The lights in the dropshaft burned brightly. "Take him in there."

The sergeant picked the General up again, exerting the same tender care as he had used placing him on the tray. The men parted to let him and his lifeless cargo pass into Room B. The soldiers followed the sergeant in, curiosity causing them to forget themselves.

Only two soldiers remained in Room A with Zara and me. It was far fewer than I could have possibly hoped for. Luck was again my bedfellow.

"Don't you want to have a look?" I asked them.

The smaller soldier spoke through a sneer. "No, mate. we're more interested in what happens in *this* room." His face remained fixed on mine, the finger of his right hand twitched on the trigger of an assault rifle.

"Yeah," said the second soldier, the man who claimed to have raped my Lucy, Raj's double-barreled shotgun in his hands. Why couldn't he have gone in the other room?

"Suit yourselves."

I tapped the screen again and a second monitor above my head displayed the grey-black image of Room B. On the monitor, I could see the sergeant holding the General at the edge of the dropshaft. The unending blackness of the shaft stretched wide and low beyond the limits of the camera's point of view.

The other soldiers gathered around the edge to watch. With the General incapacitated, much of their discipline had fallen lax.

The sergeant looked up from the General and into the camera. "The General's not breathing."

I spoke into the microphone. "It doesn't matter. We have time."

The lies were becoming easier to tell. The longer I remained flesh and in Room A, the more kinship I felt with my former self. We were brothers, he and I. We were more than brothers, we shared more than the most identical of twins. A used brain, the only not brand new; a brain I would pass on to the next man. He was dead now, my brother, but I would never mourn. Just like my future brother will never mourn me. Brothers across time.

Zara was still holding me up. I tried to catch her eye without the soldiers behind us noticing, but she, like the two men was fixated on the monitor. I allowed my body to go limp and fell forward toward the panel. Zara snapped out of her trance, and wrapped both arms tightly around me to keep me from falling. She looked up at me and saw me looking at her. I moved my eyes toward the gun in my waistband. It was time for her to make her choice.

She was one of them; there was no denying that. Whether she had chosen their side willingly or was coerced or bribed was moot. She was in cahoots with the General, her mission the same as everyone else's: Get the septic half jew into the machine. But in that time we had grown close, she and I, we had shared things, our words, our bodies. Had she left the fake scars off her arm on purpose as some sort of signal? Was shooting the doctor part of the plan from the beginning? Only she knew.

She was with them or she was with me, she could not be both. She needed to understand.

Her hand moved down my stomach toward my waist and she wrapped her fingers around the handle of the gun.

"Your bandage," she whispered. I had released my tourniquet and the blood was again flowing.

I shook my head. Just keep hold of that gun, girl, we'll worry about my leg later.

"You alright, mate?" the short, sneery one asked me.

"I'm fine."

"You better be. Anything goes wrong with the General and you're dead. I don't give a shit if we're stuck in the Darkening forever. I like it!"

The rapist giggled at him. "Me too!"

Through the monitor, the sergeant spoke. "What do we do now?"

My thigh was burning now and my head felt weightless and foreign. Speaking was becoming more difficult.

"Throw him in," I said.

My voice cracked as I spoke. I swallowed and forced my tongue to the top of my mouth in an attempt to force my salivary glands into action. No response, my mouth was dried up and dead.

"Toss him as close to the centre of the hole as you can."

The sergeant looked into the hole and back up to the camera. "He won't survive the drop!"

I closed my eyes in frustration and choked back my anger. I took a deep, rattling breath and arranged my thoughts into a row before speaking. Words were at a premium, I couldn't afford to waste them.

"Sergeant, the man is dying. If you toss him in now, he'll come out the other side in better shape than he has ever been." My throat clicked as I again lied. "Trust me!"

The sergeant addressed another soldier and he grabbed the General's legs, while the sergeant himself held his shoulders and moved the General into a throwing position.

Over the gaping abyss, they swung the old man, his head swished back and forth and his arms dangled limply. Once, twice, his skin around his middle flapped as his body pendulumed under the light.

On the third swing, they let him go.

The General flew from their grasp sideways before gravity took its righteous hold and dragged him down, down toward the bottom of the mine and the end of the world. If the top of the dropshaft was a dartboard, they'd have hit the bullseye with the General's body. Their aim was perfect.

As the General fell, I stole a peek over my shoulder. The two soldiers stared at their plummeting leader on the monitor with widened eyes.

Zara wasn't watching the monitor, her eyes were on me. Her face cool, her hand still on the gun. I nodded toward the two soldiers.

"Holy fuck!"

It was Sneery. In the monitor, the General's body bounced off the side wall as he tumbled. The last thing on the screen before the darkness swallowed him forever was his broken body spinning awkwardly. His neck bent backwards in half and an arm windmilling free and counter to the rest of his body.

Zara pulled the gun from my waistband, turned and fired four shots in quick succession. I grabbed the panel with both hands and stomped down on my bad leg to keep from falling. Pain surged through my entire body. I screamed.

Zara turned again, this time toward Room B and began firing into it. On the monitor above, the sergeant's head exploded as he fell backward, taking a number of the other men into the hole with him, their faces frozen in fear, their hands grasping at nothing.

And falling.

The remaining soldiers scrambled for their weapons.

I touched the panel again, swished it to the right back to the main menu and then too far. "Fuck!"

"Do something!" Zara screamed. "They're coming!".

The soldiers had gathered themselves and were now moving quickly out of the cameras range toward the door.

I swished the menus back and forth, my throat coated in sick and my brain swimming.

Zara squeezed five more shots into the room. The soldiers shouted out. They shouted to the hole, to the sky and to each other. My leg was in agony. My vision blurred and I was falling. It was no good. I was blacking out.

"Seth!"

I felt two arms under my armpits hoisting me again to my feet followed by the clatter of the pistol as it fell to the floor.

"Seth!"

The monitor was in front of me. The dropshaft menu was open. Guns were now firing from within the room and room was filled with ra–ta–ta–tats.

My fingers slid down the length of the monitor, leaving greasy little slug trails on the thick glass.

Time fell away sideways and stopped; the clock liquid and dribbling like flesh, growing slow before ceasing to tick altogether. My hands occupied nothing but space and held inside them even less. Away from me Zara rose toward the thin tubes of light and white nothingness above as cloth, glass and the very air were pierced by rocket propelled balls of steel.

The slide of Zara's pistol chinked backward along the barrel smooth and steady, belching puffs of fire and ejecting fizzing shells, gold and twinkly.

Ka-chunk, ka-chunk, ka-chunk.

I was tumbling, spinning, twisting toward hell, but instead finding and smacking into the hard, hard ground.

Twenty-five

Down the busy street, I walked. It was early evening and the sun was finding its way to the horizon. The evening was warm enough for shorts, had shorts been something I would wear. The air was heavy and close, but a northern breeze was just cool enough to keep the sweat at bay.

Chester road was a chaotic stew of honking horns and flashing reds and ambers as cars darted across lanes and into makeshift parking lots, open only on match days. Filthy men in neon vests waved cars onto lawns and into car dealerships for ten pounds a pop.

It was derby day and United's oldest rivals, Liverpool were in town.

Across the street, Henry and Trev kicked around a football, Henry's doughy frame woggled as he moved this way and that around invisible defenders. The football at his feet frayed, black with grime and half flat.

"Possession surrendered by Gerrard. Scholes takes it from his own byline, down the other end of the pitch, past one, past two across the eighteen yard box and–"

Trev kicked both of Henry's legs out pushing him to the pavement "Taken out by Vincent Kompany!"

Henry squealed and rolled on the floor, clutching his shin and kicking. "Stonewall penalty, ref! Fucking blatant!"

Other boys mingled in packs of two or three outside the front door of a large brick building. Trading cards, throwing dice and punching each other with boxing gloves. Above them, a sign, tatty and peeling read *Salford Lads Club*, the original 'r' was missing and replaced by one in pink spray paint. Once burned out and derelict, an unknown philanthropist with suspected ties to the Middle East had breathed life into the ancient boys home. A cynic would say they did it to curry favour with the city for in return for a development contract or a share in one of its football clubs, but no one cared. It took kids off the street, even if it was only temporary.

Skipping beside me, holding my hand and swinging an old teddy was my little Lucy, her eyes on the boys. "Who are they, daddy?"

"Bad boys," I replied and pinched her nose making her to giggle.

She was staying with me for a full week while Midori and her new husband, *a male nurse* were away on some sort of package holiday to some pointless, tourist hellhole like Majorca or Sharm el sheikh. Two weeks of sweltering bus tours, food with too much mayonnaise and endless gangs of fat Germans barking at each other over reserved deck chairs. Good luck to them.

I was taking Lucy to a film and a McDonalds, neither of which were approved by her mother. Some vacuous Japanese anime thing followed by a Big Mac and an orange pop. Spoiling little girls was the privilege of the delinquent father. Lucy wouldn't tell.

Ahead of us, the football people marched to the ground. Grown men clad in the same clothing as their children and singing *Build a bonfire, build a bonfire.* Enormous flags of red, white and black flapped and touts broadcast their overpriced tickets, unafraid of the yellow-jacketed police-men on horseback. The air sodden with smells of cheap lager and burnt onions.

At the intersection a cyclist with a round belly and calves like carved stone whizzed past, a blur of yellow and red and white, shouting profanities.

Europe's largest supermarket towered above us, a bright white glass block, filled to the sky with billions of coloured boxes and bottles. Those superstores were the new cathedrals, ready meals, discount booze and lad mags the new religion.

An old VW beetle buzzed past the pub with bright right red Liverpool scarves waving from its windows. Drunken louts hanging out the back of a ropey pub flick V's and shout "wanker!" at them giving my daughter another delightful English word that would need explaining later. I would let her mother field that one.

An S class Mercedes is stopped at the light in front of us. Behind the reflection of Lucy and me, sat a young Raj with his wife and two small children, laughing with the windows rolled up. Cocooned against the outside world like Lucy and I would've been if my own SL wasn't in the shop getting re-sprayed.

Raj looked at me from behind the steering wheel and motioned

The green man waved us forward and we stepped past Raj's car toward our final destination, a forty screen multiplex to watch some vacuous 3D Japanese cartoon that Lucy was in love with. A double feature.

It was heaven.

★ ★ ★

I awoke to Zara slapping my cheek, a fluorescent corona radiated from her falling black hair, her face cloaked in shadow.

The ceiling regained its focus and I grabbed her slapping hand. "I'm ok." I could feel her legs, her breasts, her warmth at my back, but little else. She was holding me in her lap. The warmth and the heavy smell of her sweat was on me. I couldn't move, I didn't want to move. The room was silent, I couldn't even hear the sounds of my own breathing.

"Can they get through that door, Sethie?" she asked, the words echoing in my empty head.

The door.

I wasn't dead, I had managed to shut the door before they could get out. All but two.

I jerked my head to the side to look past Zara. Behind her, Sneery and the man who claimed to have raped my daughter were stretched out at bent angles on the ground with open eyes and open mouths in an expanding pool of blood. I felt neither remorseful nor gratified at the sight of those two dead people. All I felt was relief. Relief I wasn't one of them.

The monitor was high above my head, the screen turned to the side.

Zara brushed her hair behind her ears and the light caught again on her face. It was the same, unflappable old Zara. She didn't seem fazed by the gunfight or by the two men spilling the contents of their heads onto the floor a few feet away. Her mind was still on the task at hand.

"The steel is a three feet thick," I said.

On the other side of the door gunfire popped rhythmically, but soft.

The popping ceased for a few moments, re-started and broke off again. The monitor displayed only smoke and dark shapes.

"What do we do now? What do we do about them?"

I said nothing. We didn't have to do anything, they were beaten. I twisted around to face her.

"Why are you smiling?" she asked.

I suppose I was smiling, I had good reason to. "Because," I started, "I think we may have just defeated the entire British Army."

I looked toward the steel door. It stood solid and unmoving. "The United Kingdom is now officially free. My wife would've enjoyed that."

"Your wife?"

I thought about that for a moment before correcting myself. "Ex-wife."

Zara's face changed. "Don't you need to get in there? You know, to go back in time?"

I shook my head again.

My legs were numb and keeping awake was becoming a chore. My throat clicked with each breath. The lights in the ceiling were moving away from me.

"But you must. We have weapons. We can finish them off." She pointed at the monitor behind me. "Half of them are dead already. We could wait—"

I didn't look. Instead, I placed a hand on my leg. It was hot and the blood was wet. My thigh tingled with pins and needles. Below my knee I felt nothing.

"You have to go back, you have to stop the Darkening."

"I can't go back," I started. I turned my hand over and looked at one of the scars left by the doctor. "No one can."

"But that room—"

"Never worked. A product of ego, bad science and too much money."

She stood up without speaking and let my body slither onto the cold floor. She paced the room, thinking thinking. She wasn't used to being surprised.

The popping started again behind the door. On the monitor, the soldiers were really going for it. Their machineguns rattled and the shotguns pumped. In seconds, the room was again clouded in fire and dust.

If they weren't careful, they'd use up all their bullets. If they were smart, they'd save a couple. Starvation was not a nice way to die.

Zara looked again toward the door and then to the pistol on the floor.

"I didn't take the key with me when I entered the machine, Zara, the key never existed."

It was her turn to wonder about the person with which she had shared a bed. She had made the decision to side with me. Why she betrayed the

General was a question that would never be answered. Her scars were fake, but that didn't mean she liked the man.

When did she decide to help me against the General? Was it our night at the Inn or the day on the motorcycles? Perhaps she made the decision as she held me up to the panel, her hand on the General's gun. I would never know for sure.

"Immortality or Death," I said.

She turned back toward me, her hands on her hips. "What the fuck is that supposed to mean?"

"It's a joke."

"You lied to me. You lied to us! We could have died for nothing!"

I could have reminded her that it was she who had lied first, who plotted to betray my trust to the General, but what was the point? She had to live in this place, this terrible city forever. I had stolen all hope from her, from everyone I had ever had known. Hope still remained for me; Manchester after the Darkening was a mere blip on my plotline, a footnote. All that trouble, all the acting to jog my memory and to bring me to the machine. For nothing.

I could understand why she felt betrayed. She had risked everything to get me here. Her house, her survival items, her very life had all been put on the line in the hopes of fulfilling a false promise.

I didn't care. I wasn't the one who put that idea in her head.

My heartbeat was in my ears and everywhere was dull and throbbing.

"You're going to have to help me. I can't stand."

"What's the point?"

She turned away from me a second time and faced the door. The popping sound had ceased again. The soldiers on the monitor were sitting down, talking to each other through dissipating smoke. Rationalising, planning. A few were holding bleeding wounds, many others stone dead. It wouldn't be long before the living ones realised the camera was still trained on them. Soon they would be begging for their lives through the silent black and white screen. Some of the men could be Zara's friends. Her lovers. Perhaps the sight of dying men pleading for their lives would be enough for her to switch sides again.

"You need to start it up for me," I said, my voice little more than a hollow wheeze. "The MRI."

There was a battle going on in her head. Putting one's life into the care of a soulless collection of steel and glass was a difficult decision for most people; especially one like Zara who had carved out a bit of a life from the wreckage. What's the point of surviving the end of the world, if you couldn't enjoy it?

In the corridor a robot whizzed down a track. Unconcerned by the silly actions of the humans in Rooms A and B, it continued; carrying out its chores as it had done every day for years and as it would for many years to come.

I had done all I could. The rest was up to her. I coughed hard and blood specked my torn shirt. My throat burned, aching for water.

Zara put a hand up to her forehead and looked around the room a second time. She scoured the chipped ceiling for answers. After a while her eyes were back on me, the momentary lapse in her resolve disappeared from her face.

"Right, what do I do?"

I smiled. She was at the controls and at least for the moment, she was with me. She knew what would happen if she let the soldiers out or if she let the ones outside live. I didn't know what her plan was and I didn't ask. What she did after I was gone was for her to know.

And for me to find out.

The screen opened up in front of her and she awaited my instructions.

Through the haze of half-death I instructed. Run tests on the software, on the robots. Test the reconstruction chamber. Some systems were down, some were on their way out but in the General's words, 'nothing important.' The robots had maintained the reactor and the machinery. The replacement boards and parts were still full and the refrigeration systems were fully operational and full of building media. For the most part we had a working bioprinter.

Roosevelt would have to do some fiddling to get things back up to 100%, but I imagined that would be something he would do with relish. At least I hoped so.

Zara pulled up the database and verified the precious data from my first trip was intact. Clean data was the key when it came to the machine. Any disease I had picked up in my brief time with the darkened city and its people would be wiped clean in my next iteration. If the machine survived long enough for a second printing, I would emerge from it to a new future as crisp and shining as a German coupe rolling off the factory line.

It was a big if.

An "if" that depended on a woman betrayed and a half-blind screwball with a fetish for toys and lycra.

The whirring of the MRI began again and my eyes fell shut.

★ ★ ★

And so it goes.

I wake up to see Zara shouting at me, but I can't hear her over the rumble of the MRI machine. Tears run down her cheeks and drop onto my face like Manchester rain. I am on the tray, the wheels of the conveyor spin underneath me, but there is a pressure on both shoulders. She is holding me back.

I reach up and again push the hair falling in front of her face behind her ear and leave my hand on her cheek. She smiles at me and leans into my hand. I am leaving the closest thing I have to family a second time.

No one has been through the machine twice.

I let my hand drop and reach into my pocket for the dictaphone. It is there, just as it always is. I hold it out to her in my leaden hand. I want nothing more than to blink this world out forever.

I did not have a heart like Henry, I have not been cured by the Darkening like he has.

I am still every bit the greedy beforetimer I've always been with avarice and violence at my core. Cancer could be detected and cleaned by the machine, but there is no cure for what I am. Not even the Darkening could have changed me, I was a murderer long before it had started. Cowardice and cruelty are too ingrained in my blood and bowel. Even as my compatriots embraced me, my friends, people who risked their lives to help me, I could only think of what lie ahead.

Anxious and excited to see what was on the other side and happy to be rid of the place.

I don't belong here in Henry's world. I have no right to walk the same ground as these people; I have no right to breathe the same air.

Soon I will be in the machine and the false panel will slide away to reveal the blades and the drills. The coring mechanisms would chop through me and the saws would soon be cutting through my skull to take my brain away for cold storage.

Zara's lips are on me, soft and warm for a long time. I kiss her back. She withdraws and fades backward into the whiteness as my battered body rolls into the machine. Past my feet, I see her one last time as she turns away.

There wasn't time for anaesthesia on this trip, no, this time I will feel the blades tear into my flesh and grind my bones to powder and I will deserve it.

With straining effort, I turn my hand over to see the lonely dictaphone still there just as it always has been.

And my world collapses into one of darkness and noise.

Acknowledgements

Thanks to Craig Pay, Guy Garrud, Andrew Hutchison, Hakim Cassimally, Kate Feld, Kate Fawl, Eric Steele, Chris Bissette, Shirley Kernan, Paul Graham Raven and the rest of the Manchester Speculative Writing Group for their support and advice, but in particular to Benjamin Judge and David Hartley for their tireless patience and willingness to read and edit an endless stream of drafts and rewrites. Gluttons for punishment all.

Thanks to Jenn Ashworth for helping me believe the book is something people might want to read, to Tom Fletcher for all his advice and to Russ Litten and Hugh Howey for convincing me "self" and "publishing" aren't dirty words when used together.

Thanks also to Ian Rogers and Steve Larder for their brilliant artistry on the cover and promotional material and to the members of The Cusp for use of their song "Blot on the Escutcheon" in the book trailer.

But above all, thanks to my Mancunian wife, Kate, for spending many evenings sans husband while I was out writing, for putting up with me when I was around and for not reading the book until it was finished. If it weren't for her, the Darkening would have taken place in Medicine Hat.

Made in the USA
Charleston, SC
02 July 2013